3.50

DEAD IN THE WATER

An Anthology of Canadian Crime Fiction

Edited by
Violette Malan
and Therese Greenwood
Foreword by Linwood Barclay

RendezVous Crime

Cover art: Trudy Agyeman

LE CONSEIL DES ARTS DU CANADA DEPUIS 1957 | THE CANADA COUNCIL FOR THE ARTS SINCE 1957

We acknowledge the support of the Canada Council for the Arts for our publishing program.

RendezVous Press
Toronto, Ontario, Canada
www.rendezvouspress.com

Printed in Canada.

10 09 08 07 06   5 4 3 2

1st printing April 2006
2nd printing May 2006

Library and Archives Canada Cataloguing in Publication

    Dead in the water : an anthology of Canadian mystery fiction / Therese Greenwood, Violette Malan, editors.

ISBN 1-894917-37-5

    1. Detective and mystery stories, Canadian (English)   2. Canadian fiction (English)--21st century.   I. Greenwood, Therese   II. Malan, Violette Anastasia, date-

PS8323.D4D43 2006   C813'.08720806   C2006-900096-4

For Steve and Paul

Table of Contents

FOREWORD

by Linwood Barclay

They don't call them bodies of water for nothing.
Ask *The Lady in the Lake*. Well, okay, that would be difficult.
The title character in Raymond Chandler's classic mystery
ended up the way a lot of characters in crime fiction do when
they get too close to the water.

They end up dead.

Water.

It's dark, it's foreboding, it's cold, it's mysterious. It hides its
secrets well. Go down a few feet, and it's as dark as night in the
middle of the day, and as cold as a killer's heart.

Water scares us on some primal level. Stumble upon a dead
guy in an alley, well, that's unsettling, no doubt about it. But
see just a hand sticking out above the surface of the water,
that's something altogether different.

If you've seen *Deliverance*, you know what I'm talking
about.

I mean, for most of us taking a dip at the cottage, all we
need to freak out is have our feet touch some weeds. Coming
into contact with a bloated corpse strikes fear into our hearts
like nothing else.

Water.

It's where the bad guys toss their guns. It's where the mob

dumps your body, after first fitting you for a pair of concrete galoshes. It's where Norman Bates dumps Marion Crane's car, with her body in the trunk. Okay, that was more a swamp than a lake, but you get the drift.

Water. In Canada, we have a lot of it. It's part of who we are. It figures in our history, our commerce, our art, our literature.

I spent my teen years living by water, in the Kawartha Lakes region of Ontario, running a cottage resort and trailer park after my father died when I was sixteen. Looking back decades later, as a writer of mysteries, I can't help but feel cheated that a body never washed ashore.

Not that I didn't give it my best shot at the time. There was that day when my friend George was snorkeling alone offshore as I headed out in my 12-foot aluminum Starcraft. I cranked the throttle on my 9.5-horsepower Johnson outboard, and as the bow rose and temporarily obscured the view ahead, George surfaced.

He shouted, but the outboard drowned out his cries of panic. He dived. He told me later that he felt the thrust from the propeller as the outboard travelled over his back.

I'm not sorry George survived. I don't need my own personal body story that badly. But had things gone horribly wrong, would it have been written off as an accident? Or would the police have had questions? About the fact that George and I had been dating the same girl? Was it possible that I wanted him out of the picture?

Water. The perfect place to make a murder look like an innocent mishap. You take someone for a boat ride, you get far enough out to sea, you knock him overboard.

"He must have fallen when I wasn't looking," you tell the authorities.

And how will they ever prove you're lying?

In this collection you'll find that water serves many purposes for a writer of dark short stories. Water is the avenue of escape. Water hides secrets. Sometimes, water makes the perfect backdrop for nefarious deeds. Often, water is the weapon of choice, because water, as beautiful as it is, as vital as it is to our survival, can take life away as easily as it can sustain it.

So dive in to these eighteen stories, and be ready to hold your breath.

Maybe you're hesitating, the way you do sometimes, standing at the edge of a cold pool.

Not to worry. Come on in. The water's fine.

Would I lie?

DEAD IN THE WATER

Dennis Richard Murphy

It was me killed The Painter.

I missed his first trip to The Park. While Matty Mattoonen and Laurence Dalton were guiding him out of Mowat, I was paddling Miss Katie Mattoonen toward the creek that runs from Canoe into Bonita Lake. Laurence Dalton got me a couple of beers without telling Matty, who was pretty nervous about his two girls and was always on about how he wanted "the best for them". I didn't think Jaako Koskinen qualified as the best of anything, but he'd married the older sister Doris.

Back in 1900, upwards of seven hundred people lived in Mowat around Gilmour's sawmill. The spur line ran up a mile to the north end of Potter's Creek and Canoe Lake Station. We'd skip school on those warm days, when the thaw had set in, and hitch rides on the lumber cars hauled up to join the main train. We'd hang around the Station until old Mrs. Ratan shooed us out, then we'd walk back to town, trying to balance on the hot steel rails, tossing rocks into the creek, and arguing about whether the pile in the path was scat from a marten or shit from a wolverine.

The Park was where I was from, more than a dirty old logging town like Mowat. The Park and me was both born in 1893, so I grew up feeling like it was my brother. My parents were dead from a bush accident, so The Park was family, and, after the other kids left for schools in Scotia Landing or Dorset, even a teacher. I just stayed in Mowat, and nobody ever bothered me about it. Visitors—we called them visitors—who came up from Toronto and the States called it Algonquin, but we just called it The Park. It was my home.

I was about seven when the mill shut down and the Gilmours left. When I was seventeen and courting Katie Mattoonen, all that was left of Mowat was thirty dead acres where they'd dumped wood chips, sawdust, pine bark and bad logs into Canoe Lake. I'll bet the ground still springs back when you walk on it. They sold off the rest of the buildings, and even the steel rails until nothing was left but the logger's boarding house overlooking the chip yard. The Irishman put up a sign on it said "Mowat Lodge".

I got two box lunches from the Lodge kitchen and a loan of the new Chestnut. I loved that canoe. She was deep shady forest green canvas on the outside with a high gloss cedar inside that shone like a summer sunrise. The seats were caned, and she sat sweet in the water, sixteen feet long with a tumblehome that made her look as slick as a speckled when you saw her side on. The Irishman said she was mine when I could afford it. I can still remember the feeling when I pushed her off from the dock, loaded with Katie and lunch and beers, like I was launching my whole life. The soft edge of the breeze, that smell of sow bugs and dead trees, new leaves and still frozen mud, the green blush of the maple buds and the black spikes of the evergreens on the western hills made you feel like you were inside some big church.

We paddled down past Wopomeo Island, past where they later found his body, and into Bonita Creek. For the daughter of the best guide in the southwest end of The Park, Katie wasn't too handy with a paddle, but I could handle it all right. As long as we were in the breeze on Canoe Lake, things were fine, but soon as we slipped into the shelter of the creek, the wind dropped and the flies came up. Visitors call them Black Flies, but we just call them flies. The damned things bite me, but they don't raise welts like on most people. Matty said it's because I got so much fly poison in me already I'm immune, like him.

Katie sure wasn't immune. It wasn't like she didn't know about flies, but she started screaming when the first one bit her, right where her black hair met the back of her white neck, and she never stopped until I got us back where the breeze came up again. Her face looked like a red pumpkin, fat with fly bites, and she was so upset at what she thought she looked like, she couldn't even talk. At sunset I sat out on the end of the dock, ate both lunches, drank both beers and thought about how pretty she looked, even all puffed up.

At the Albion Hotel, Matty told everyone The Painter said he'd lost all but two of fourteen dozen rolls of Kodak camera film when he tipped right in the middle of the damned lake because the flies got to him. He must have told everyone down south the same tall tale, because it still gets told. Fourteen rolls maybe. Fourteen dozen? That would have been over two thousand pictures. Laurence Dalton did the math. No one believed it then, and you'd think over time such fibs would get old and turn into lies and get forgotten. But the opposite seems to be true. Lies get truer with age. People believe what they want to, and that makes it true.

I first met The Painter the next summer in 1913, when he just showed up one day with a pal. Matty and Laurence Dalton were guiding a group of teachers up toward Burnt Island, but The Painter wanted to get sketching right away, so the Irishman gave me the Chestnut and said I'd show them around. Two artists from Toronto, he told me, but later I heard one of them say he made over eleven dollars a week. I knew grown men—hard workers too—in Huntsville and Dorset who didn't make that much in a month, sometimes in a winter. I thought real artists lived in attics and never had no money at all.

The Painter seemed nice enough, a tall, kinda shy, good-looking fella. Twice my age at the time. Talked more than he needed to, but he had a twinkle in his eye and a pretty good handshake. But he sure couldn't work a canoe, even though he'd convinced his pals he knew what he was doing. This one kept asking him questions about paddling and about The Park, and he'd answer right off as if he knew, which he didn't.

With me in the Chestnut and them in the red canoe, we worked our way around the lake every day for four days. The Painter kept slapping and swearing at the flies and telling me to take them here and there and asking me where could they find an old bent tree or a broke down beaver dam to draw. He seemed more interested in the ugly stuff than the beautiful places that's everywhere around. I figured that's what experienced artists do, but when his pal said they'd bought their first paint kits just the year before, I didn't know what to think. So I just kept quiet. Anyways, they talked as if I wasn't there and seemed to think I didn't see how pretty everything was, being from Mowat and all. That bothered me, I remember, but I just paddled and watched for deadheads, them logs that point up from the lake bottom and hide just under the surface. They're quiet and invisible, but they'll rip through a canoe faster than a buck knife through a doe.

In the end, it didn't matter whether they took photos, drew pictures or just gawked at the scenery, because they flipped her again. The Painter was in the stern of their canoe, and I was sitting off to port, so if they missed the dock they'd nudge me and slow down. It's a trick Laurence Dalton taught me. The Painter was changing paddle sides so much and yelling at his buddy that they rocked the same side together, and that put them both in the water. I went after the friend who couldn't swim, and the Irishman threw a line to The Painter. Four days of sketches sank clear to the bottom, but it wasn't worth getting hurt diving with all that mill trash under the dock. Matty's cousin's youngest boy from Trout Creek drownded when he got his shirt caught diving under there.

After supper, I sat The Painter down on the Lodge dock with his butt over near the edge and I showed him the J-stroke, where you draw the paddle back till you get to the end then tack on a little inside curve to straighten yourself out. Keeps you pointed where you're going, even if you're alone. No thrashing around. No changing sides. Quiet. Once he figured it out, he slapped his thigh hard and howled like a hound and hugged me until it hurt. I heard he filled up some kind of a tank with water at his work and showed everyone the J-stroke, like someone who'd discovered a new thing and had to tell everybody about it. Like when Laurence Dalton's mother found Jesus over in Kearney. He was always a better talker than a paddler or a woodsman or a fisherman or whatever he wished he was—maybe than an artist for all I know. But he never came up in the winter when the place is so damned pretty and clean and sweet you'd crack your lips when you smiled just from breathing it in your nose.

The next summer he came back, full of selling a painting for $250. I felt a sort of discomfort now that this picture was somewhere where people who'd never been to The Park could see it. His Park didn't look like The Park, leastwise not like my

Park. Like he'd told another lie to a lot of people who didn't know any better.

Matty Mattoonen and Laurence Dalton weren't too pleased that The Painter asked for me again, but from then on it was always me he hired. He'd usually bring a pal, some close shaved fella he'd filled full of tales about a northern paradise that the folks who lived there couldn't see. I actually heard him say that to a fella called Andy who was all full of the scenery over near the top end of Georgian Bay, where he said the white quartz grew right out of the ground. We had white quartz in The Park too, but we didn't go telling visitors where to find it.

We got to know each other a little better, but I can't say I got to like him any more. I finally got him to portage away from the crowds, and we'd paddle up Little Joe to Tepee and Littledoe to camp at Blackbear. I did all the work, from setting up the tent to cooking the meals and tying the food up so the bears couldn't get at it. He'd just stare off into the distance, thinking about paintings, I guess. Sometimes he'd bring a little mandolin with him and sing songs after supper, when I'd finished the dishes and built the fire back up. His voice was nice, I'll give him that, but some nights he'd drink more than a man ought to, and that'd bring out a black temper. I seen him toss his whole paint kit into the bushes, then stomp off into the dark. In the morning, he'd fish everything out of the forest and spend the whole day trying to fix the wood case where he'd broke it. He seemed to like fishing more than painting, which was fine with me, except he wasn't much good at that either. I showed him lures and lines and flies and talked about trout, especially the Lakers with their sharp cut vee tails and how they liked it deep down in the cold water. Every time I caught a mess of fish, he'd arrange them on a pan or on the grass or even hang them from a damned tent pole and take pictures of them. Maybe he told his pals he caught them. Don't matter. They were just fish.

I'd clean them and cook them. For a man who said he liked the bush, he had an odd attitude about wildlife. Where'd he think food came from anyway? He got all upset when I snared a beaver, and he wouldn't look when I butchered him or even eat any when I cooked him up. Fatty things, but food when you're hungry, and the weather's getting colder. Make a dog's coat shine.

I spent that winter reading up to be a Ranger, all about fire sighting and fighting, about how wildfires flare up with just the right amount of heat and grass and no one around and bang— you had a natural fire that could level an acre a minute. Park Ranger was the only real job besides guiding for me. Guiding didn't pay regular, and the Irishman's wife told me I didn't have the temperament to wait on tables. If that meant I didn't like doing it, she'd have been right. She didn't like me much.

The news in the papers and on the radio that year was mostly about the Great War, which seemed awful far away from The Park, except there were men up at Sim's Pit guarding the trains, so I guess it wasn't that far away. Katie Mattoonen asked me if I was gonna sign up in a manner that made me think real hard about it. With her to come home to, you'd make damned sure you lived through it. She told me Russell and Laurence Dalton had signed up, and her sister Doris' husband Jaako. She said it like they were already heroes, without a mention that there was no work for them at home anyway. I told her I'd think about it, but I thought more about her than the war.

The Painter came back in 1915 after the flies had gone, which showed he was learning something. He'd sold another painting to the government in Ottawa. Sold another piece of The Park. He'd quit his paying job, and some eye doctor was giving him money just to paint, which I thought kinda strange. Not a lot of money. He was always broke, bumming drinks from the Irishman and cash from everyone he met. Now he wanted to see The Park from higher up, said the view from the lake level didn't inspire him any more. I took some offense to that. When he'd tried painting over at his eye doctor's place on Georgian Bay, he came running back to The Park pretty quick, didn't he? We'd hike up to where the trees crowned, and on the way he'd sketch and paint some views and hang the papers on trees to dry them off. Then we'd collect them on our way back to the canoe. Sometimes animals would bother them. One time, coming down a steep trail above Blackbear, we found one picture with a pile of bear shit right on top of it. I thought he'd have one of his artistic fits, but he just laughed and said the bear was probably the smartest critic he'd come across.

I didn't pass the Ranger tests. They said I knew The Park backwards all right and how to survive year round, but I didn't do so good on the distance math, and I couldn't spell worth a damn. Matty said that was bullshit, that he knew Rangers who could add things and write good but couldn't find their way to the Albion Hotel, but that didn't change anything. That's what made me sign up. When I told The Painter, he said he wanted to sign up too, but they wouldn't take him. Once he told me it was because he'd had bad lungs as a youngster. Another time he told me he'd hurt his toe in a football match and they wouldn't take him because of his feet. I said his feet seemed fine to me—we hiked twenty miles on a good day—and he agreed, swearing a little and wishing he could go to war. I found out that was a stupid wish.

There was quite a party at the Lodge the night before I left. It was late August and cool, my favourite time of year in The

Park. There were no bugs, the days were warm, and the Lake Trout would soon come back up from deep water. In a couple of weeks, the leaves would begin to bleed colours even them Kodachrome postcards can't show right. The Painter's success, or his talking about it, had brought a bunch more artist types up to Mowat, as well as more visitors than the place had ever seen, so the wingding was a big one. They'd hired up a band from Huntsville, and The Painter and the Irishman tried to get me to dance, but I wasn't having any, because I didn't know how. I just sat there beside Katie, touching hands when Matty wasn't looking, enjoying attention like I'd never had before and half glad I was leaving Mowat the next day. Boy, she looked like something that night, I'll tell you.

When the bonfire burned down, most folks went to bed. We were all pretty drunk. The Painter pulled out his mandolin and played a song or two about being lonely and away from home and not being cared for. I was falling asleep when The Painter and Katie took a walk beyond the campfire, into the dark. I never really thought about that until I was on the train to Toronto the next day. That's when I felt most lonely of all. That's when I felt the most hurt heart I could ever remember, then or since.

I never talked much about the Great War then, and I don't now. I ended up in the goddamned mud with the Canadian Corps on Easter Monday, 1917. Four days later we took Vimy Ridge, one hundred and twenty yards high, about the same as that granite ridge just west of where Mowat used to be. I got shot in the right thigh and fell face down in a muck bog that went on to the horizon. I was dreaming I was a pure white otter diving down deep in the cool clean water of a two loon lake when somebody flipped me onto my back. Saved my life. I would have drownded right there.

I came home in July with a silver medal, a pension, a limp and an Army issue cane. At first not much seemed changed. The fat deer flies swarmed around my head just out of range like always. The hot purple and burnt cloud sunset shadows on the lakes were the same ones I'd been thinking about all the time I was away. Maybe they were even more beautiful for that. The Lodge was bigger and packed with more visitors than ever. The chip yard was growing in fast with weedy poplars and runt balsams. From the dock I saw The Painter zigzagging his way up Canoe Lake like an amateur, but it wasn't until he got close that I saw he had my Chestnut, except he'd painted her grey. He shouted my name and put his arms around me like a bear and hugged me and banged on my back like I was a relative or something. He talked about all the paintings he had done and sold, how all his pals were coming up, how The Park had been discovered. All I could smell was his shirt and his sweat, and all I could feel was my head getting hotter and hotter, till my collar was soaking and my neck burned like a fuse in the cold afternoon wind. He didn't even ask me where I'd been.

Things weren't at all the same, I saw. Matty said The Painter had made some money guiding Lodge guests around Canoe in the Chestnut. He'd passed his Park Ranger easy, said the Irishman, and had been fire spotting over on the east end side all Spring. They all seemed prouder of him than me. And I was from here. And I'd come home from away. It was like he'd taken over my park while I was gone. Never mind he couldn't paddle or find his own way to Blackbear. Never mind he couldn't catch a fish or trap a meal. Never mind he didn't go overseas. The Irishman's wife watched me real close when she said Katie Mattoonen had married Russell Dalton the minute he'd come back all gassed up from France. Laurence

Dalton hadn't come back at all, and I wished I hadn't either.

I know it don't make no sense at all when you sit back and study it. It all blew up without warning. Like white wildfire. It just blazed up when I was being hugged on that dock. Nobody saw it coming, leastwise me. He had my canoe. He'd walked out of that campfire light with my girl. He was guiding. He'd made Ranger. He'd taken my friends and my family and my town. And with his goddamned paintings, he'd stole my Park and sold it away for money. With his fucking paint brushes and smelly little tubes of paint and his foul temper and his dull drawings and his dirty goddamned gobs of colour, he'd taken my Park and made it something ugly and lonely and thick and threatening and dangerous. He'd stomped right into my church, and he'd stepped on my heart and he'd upset my soul and he didn't even see it and he didn't even give a sweet goddamn. While we stood there on that dock, him smelling like fire and hugging me and welcoming me home and waving over my head saying, "look who's here with his little silver medal," I knew I'd kill the bastard. And when the Irishman told me at supper the Ranger had seen a whopper of a Laker up by the Joe Lake portage, I knew just how to do it.

I never thought twice after that. If I told The Painter where and how he could catch the biggest Laker around, he'd believe me without even thinking about why I'd bother to tell him. He'd only think about himself, local hero, big time artist with a way in the woods and the champeen taker of the biggest trout on the lake. I told him the biggest fish on the lake was in that little inlet that runs west off the northern tip of Wapomeo Island, and that dew worms fished deep would do it in the early afternoon. Weight the line two feet from the hook, I told him, then let it out until it hits bottom, then reel it in just an inch or so. Then leave it. Quiet. His eyes opened wide when I told him, like a little kid's at the first tug from a sunfish.

In the morning, I watched from the point while he and the Ranger fished the Joe Lake portage and caught nothing. I watched him paddle my Chestnut back to the dock, go into the Lodge and come out hiding a tin of worms, looking back over his shoulder like the thief he was. I knew then I had him, like you know when you've clean lip-hooked a fine fighting fish. You just feel it. You're no longer equals. I watched him paddle down to the inlet and disappear west behind the pink granite ridge.

When I glided in, he was near the south shore shallows across from the point, not at all where I'd told him to fish. He was using copper line, which I'd taught him to use deep because Lake Trout'll bite through hair and silk, but he'd missed a cast badly and had wrapped it all around his ankle. I felt acid flush fast into my gut, and a carbon taste on the back of my tongue like the stink of a short circuit. I hit him hard with my paddle, right in the head, right over his left eye. Blood shot out his ear when he fell face down into the water. He'd been so intent on unravelling the line, he hadn't heard me; a J-stroke makes no noise if you know what you're doing. I sat in the summer sun with my paddle dripping water and blood and I watched him, unconscious, suck in the reedy black water and drown. I don't think he even saw me, but I hope he did.

I jumped into the shallows and pulled the Chestnut into shore. He had some bread and bacon in a canvas bag, which I stuffed in the crevice of the bow. I made sure the little portage paddle was fixed to the forward seat, and I lashed the other two paddles to make it look like he'd carried in from somewhere else. I threw his small axe high into the deep water of the inlet, and I still remember how the sun caught it like the glint off a white quartz outcrop. When I tipped his canoe over, I could see some green where the rocks had scraped off the grey paint. I towed his body and the canoe out into the lake and then let both float free, both face down. I threw his gear into the water and watched as the cork rod handles fought to float, then gave up and sank in the deep channel. Then I paddled back to Mowat for supper.

Oh, I followed the news. I have for years now. I heard how the fishing line around his ankle was a big mystery. Some fool said he'd probably caught the big trout and wrapped the line around his ankle to hold it. Another thought he'd sprained his ankle on a portage and wrapped fishing line around it for support. His city friends all said he couldn't have drowned himself, because he was such a damned good paddler. Others said he might have been killed because of a woman, even though he was forty, and no one had ever known him to say more than three words to one, except maybe Katie Mattoonen in the dark. Some even said he'd committed suicide because his paintings weren't selling. No one seemed to remember that he'd only been painting for six goddamned years. Christ, by then I'd been paddling for twenty.

His lies bothered me then, but now I'm old and I don't give a shit any more. I got the Chestnut back when it was found, and after a while I painted her green again. I lived in The Park on my Army money until I got hurt up on Sunbeam and was found by a long-haired kid and his girlfriend. She hardly had anything on. The Lodge burned down, got rebuilt and burned again. I outlived them all, lived long enough to see another batch of local boys go to another goddamned war and not come back the same. Or at all.

Bullshit wins the day is all I've learned from it. Everyone still thinks he was a fine paddler and woodsman and artist, even though it was only him told people that's what he was. There's a pile of granite rocks to his memory on the point where I watched him paddle past. And forty years after they found him dead, they named a lake after the bastard—changed it from Blackbear. They never named no lake for Matty Mattoonen. Or Laurence Dalton who got killed. No one remembers them.

If I hadn't killed The Painter, he'd be forgotten too.

Dennis Richard Murphy *is a factual filmmaker whose work appears in* Ellery Queen *and* Storyteller. *His "Dead in the Water" won the Bloody Words Bony Pete Award,* Storyteller *magazine's Best Canadian Short Story contest and was nominated for the Crime Writers of Canada Arthur Ellis Award.*

VOICES FROM THE DEEP

Barbara Fradkin

The first summer day of 1877 dawned an idyllic cerulean blue, with only the airiest puffs of pewter cloud to warn of the storm rolling in from the west. When Dr. David Browne finished his rounds at the Protestant Hospital, he steered his carriage onto Wurtenberg Street to take the longer route home, so that he could enjoy the view of the Rideau River from the bluff.

The tiny skiff was just drifting under the Cummings Bridge when unexpectedly the wind picked up. David watched with some consternation as the skiff blew downstream. Two young ladies alone in a boat was unusual enough, but in this case the one in the bow perched as rigid and unmoving as a statue. Her head was bowed and her gaze fixed upon the water below. No discourse passed between the two. Indeed the woman at the front, darker in both complexion and dress, seemed oblivious to her fairer companion, who was straining at the oars to turn the boat about.

From his viewpoint, David did not recognize either woman and wondered if they were new to Ottawa and perhaps unfamiliar with the changeable currents in the Rideau River. Normally sluggish at this juncture, it was roused to a frenzy by the wind and the heavy spring rains.

The young woman at the oars had turned the boat and was tugging valiantly, but could barely keep the boat straight, let alone make any headway against the wind. Strands of flaxen hair escaped her bonnet and whipped across her eyes, obscuring her vision. David glanced down Rideau Street in hopes of enlisting some aid, but the road and bridge were deserted. Urging Lady to the roadside, he vaulted from the carriage and scrambled down the steep embankment.

By the time he reached the water's edge, the small boat had caught an eddy and was swinging in an arc away from shore. The oarswoman spotted him, and the panic in her wide eyes subsided. She fought with the oars to aim the boat toward him. David waded out to his thighs, barely noticing the chilly water that rushed in over his tall boots. All the while, the woman at the bow remained as still as marble.

"Can you toss me the painter?" he shouted over the wind.

The motionless woman did not even acknowledge his presence. Her companion at the oars shook her head as if to convey the futility of David's request and continued to pull at the oars. A sudden chill descended as black clouds swept across the sun. David edged out further, groping for a foothold on the muddy riverbed. The waves lifted his new frock coat and swirled around his waist.

Wind ripped across the water, and the boat bucked in the choppy waves as the woman wrestled it toward shore. When the bow was a mere ten feet away, she gave one final yank on the oars, dived for the rope in the bottom of the boat and tossed it towards him. A perfectly centred toss that landed the frayed end neatly in his outstretched hand. Stumbling backward on the slippery rocks, he pulled the boat up onto the grass and turned to help the women disembark.

The rower was already leaping out, her nimble feet flying

over the marsh to dry land. She was flushed with exertion, but a sparkle of triumph had replaced the panic in her eyes. She seized her companion's hands.

"There, Charlotte! Safe and sound. Come, let's get out of the boat."

Abruptly, the statue suddenly came to life. She wrenched her hands free and let loose a wail that rose above the wind and waves, sending a jolt through David's core. Upon closer scrutiny, he noted the wide-eyed incomprehension of her stare and the thick bandages that wrapped her hands. He bent over them, detecting a whiff of suppuration.

"This woman is ill!" he exclaimed.

The flaxen-haired woman turned to him, undaunted. "Out to take the air, sir. I'm Melody Adamson. Mrs. Kent and I are forever in your debt for that heroic rescue, accomplished at some peril to yourself and your attire." Mischief twinkled in her eyes, disarming his anger instantly.

"I'm Dr. Browne," he replied sternly, more to stifle any impropriety on his part than on hers. "I was grateful to be of service, Miss Adamson, but I remain concerned about your companion."

Miss Adamson had taken Charlotte's hands again, and now David could see that only the strength of her grip prevented the other woman from tearing free. She was uttering short grunts, and anger contorted her thin features. Had the fever touched her brain?

"She should be under a doctor's care," he persisted.

"We have been in Ottawa but a week and are not yet settled. But I believe Mr. Kent has arranged a consultation with Dr. Petley on Metcalfe Street, who was recommended by her father in Kingston." She hesitated, concern darkening her impish features. "Is he a wise choice, Dr. Browne?"

David's pulse quickened, as much from excitement as relief. Although he had doubts about Petley's therapeutic acumen beyond the liberal dispensation of port and Godfrey's Cordial, at least the choice ensured he would see her again. He nodded. "Dr. Petley is a most experienced physician. And coincidentally, my senior associate."

The first drops of rain splattered the shore, and Miss Adamson moved to draw Charlotte out of the boat. The woman resisted, twisting her head stubbornly toward the river.

"She would spend all day on the river if she could," Miss Adamson said, casting an anxious glance at the sky. "In Kingston, she and Mr. Kent had a home on the lakeshore, and she spent many hours on the veranda, looking out over the water. This move has been extremely distressing for her. A mistake, I fear."

David helped her coax Charlotte to land. "Please allow me to offer you both a ride back to your home. I'll send someone for the boat when the storm has passed."

Miss Adamson gave him a grateful smile as she brushed grass and leaves from Charlotte's skirts. "We've already taken sufficient advantage of your generosity, Dr. Browne. Mrs. Kent's husband will be along shortly to fetch us, for he was to join our picnic beneath that willow—" She pointed to a large willow that draped its languid boughs over the water's edge about a hundred yards upstream.

She did not elaborate further, for in that instant, her gaze fixed on an object in the distance, moving rapidly toward them in a plume of dust. Her smile faded.

"That will be Mr. Kent," she murmured. "Do not mention our brush with danger. He is overly protective of her and does not approve of our excursions on the river, no matter how much she longs for them. I am charged with making her better, and he does not always look kindly on my efforts. He would lock her in her room all day to keep her safe if he had his way."

Beneath her bonnet, her eyes shone darkly blue with purpose and intelligence. Silently, they asked his complicity, and without hesitation, he nodded. "But in future, be careful of river currents, which are much more capricious than a lake. And..." he added as the husband's carriage clattered to a stop beside David's, "please ensure that Mr. Kent brings her to Dr. Petley today if possible. I fear her wounds may be turning septic."

A burly young man jumped from the carriage and plunged down the slope toward the shore. His waistcoat strained against his heaving chest, and his striped tie flapped in the wind. Beneath a tangle of black eyebrows, his eyes scanned his wife anxiously. Charlotte made no sign that she noticed him, but the resistance seemed to seep out of her. Miss Adamson led her up the path to intercept him.

"Any trouble?" the husband demanded. "Any...?"

"Not at all," David heard Miss Adamson reply. "She seemed quite content. I believe I even saw her smile."

He crushed Charlotte to his side protectively as the threesome clambered back up to the road. Neither Charlotte nor her husband gave David so much as a backward glance, but once they'd reached the carriage and the husband was lifting Charlotte aboard, Melody Adamson turned to look back at him. At a distance, he couldn't be sure, but he thought she mouthed a silent thank you.

*　　*　　*

That defiant glance, the flounce in her step, stayed with David throughout the day and on into his restless sleep. Who was she? It seemed she was of the working classes, yet her dress was refined, her speech educated, and her eyes sharp with intelligence. David was twenty-eight years old and had been in practice in Ottawa for well over a year. Dr. Petley and his own brother Liam reminded him continually that it was time for a respectable professional man to settle down. Yet none of the young society ladies whom Dr. Petley presented for his approval possessed a tenth of Miss Adamson's wit and beauty. Furthermore, his own humble origins as the son of a penniless Irish candlemaker hardly exalted him beyond her reach.

Surely it had been Providence that had placed him on the bridge that day. And Providence again that he was alone in the surgery three days later, when a carriage arrived with a great clatter outside his surgery door. Glancing out, he recognized Mr. Kent driving a rather shabby Victoria, in the back of which two figures were huddled. The distraught man leaped down from the carriage before the wheels had even fully stopped, and he charged into the waiting room like a bull taking aim.

"Petley! Where's Petley!"

David hurried forward to calm him. "Dr. Petley is out on a house call, sir, but I'm his associate, Dr. Browne. Perhaps I can help?"

"In the carriage. My wife! Damn it, she's bad!"

Outside, David found Charlotte languishing in Miss Adamson's arms, shivering beneath several layers of horsehair blankets. Her eyes were glassy, her cheeks afire, and decay hung about her like a shroud. David scooped her up and carried her inside without a word. This was no time for admonitions or questions. Laying her down on the examining table, he snapped orders to Miss Adamson to fill a pan with cold water and fetch clean towels from the cabinet. He sent the frantic husband for ice from the cellar while he removed the patient's outer clothing and carefully unwrapped the dressings from her arms and hands. As the purple, suppurating sores were exposed, he almost gagged, more from outrage at the neglect than from the stench.

"What caused this!" he snapped when the husband returned.

The husband staggered backwards from the sight and sank into a chair, his head in his hands. "She does it to herself! She won't let them heal. Every time the sores scab over, she picks them raw again. And cuts new ones, as if to speed up the process. I don't know what to do any more!"

David examined the skin carefully. Amid the inflamed flesh, he discerned the purple scars of old lesions. His anger softened. "How long has she been like this?"

The young man merely shook his head, as if his wife's behaviour were beyond him, and it was Miss Adamson who spoke. "Almost a year now."

The poor woman was clearly insane, but more crucially, without immediate medical help, she would not live to have her sanity restored. Deferring further questions, he instructed Miss Adamson to bathe the patient with ice cold compresses while he gathered the supplies needed to dress the wounds. Over the next hour they bent over the young woman, who lay limp, flushed, and beyond the reach of pain. David lanced and drained the sores, bathed them in carbolic acid and left them open to the air. Afterwards he instructed Miss Adamson to continue the cold bath while he gestured towards his office door.

"Mr. Kent, may we have a private word?"

Kent wobbled through the door and collapsed into the leather chair David offered. His hand shook as he drew it across his brow. David poured him a generous shot of Petley's cognac.

"Your wife is gravely ill, sir," he began.

Kent tossed back the cognac at a gulp and splashed a second measure into the glass. "I do the best I can. I can't be at her side every moment! I am new at my firm and must establish myself. Her doctor in Kingston thought a change of scene, away from the memories, would be beneficial, so I arranged a transfer from my firm in Kingston. I've bought her the finest new home in Sandy Hill, I've hired as her companion a young lady who's been her friend since childhood, and I've followed all the doctor's orders to the letter."

"Have you taken her to a specialist?"

"What kind?"

"An alienist."

Kent froze at the word. All colour drained from his face. "Absolutely not! It's a simple female thing, the doctor says, brought on by our..." The man's voice snagged and he gulped at his cognac. "She's had a terrible shock, and she's a girl of nervous temperament. With time, and with Miss Adamson's attentions, the doctor says she'll soon recover."

"Besides these wounds," David persisted cautiously, "how does this nervous temperament express itself? With tempers? Lethargy? Poor sleep or appetite?" When Kent continued to nod his agreement, David ventured deeper. "Imagining voices or visions?"

Kent shot to his feet, swinging his massive head back and forth. "Ridiculous! She needs protection and rest! She's ill, not a lunatic!" He stormed out of the office. "Miss Adamson, please dress my wife so that we may take her home."

David hastened after him. "But the wounds, the fever—"

"I will send for Petley the minute we return home. He's an old friend of her father's and has known her for years. I'm sure he'll know better than you how to treat her!"

*　　*　　*

"Ah, yes," Dr. Petley exclaimed to David upon his return an hour later. "Charles Kent. Not wise to mention lunacy in the same breath as his wife."

"I didn't mention it, he did. But I believe it's an apt diagnosis."

Petley picked up Kent's discarded glass, sniffed it and poured himself a generous measure of cognac. After an appreciative sip, he waved the glass in dismissal. "She's a woman, David. If we locked up all the women who have attacks of insanity, we'd be locking up half the weaker sex. As some day you'll no doubt discover, the slightest upset, at times not even discernible to the male eye, can unbalance their minds. But in this instance, the cause is clear enough. She lost an infant, and her empty uterus has unbalanced her mind."

David felt a stab of pity. His own mother had lost four of her seven children to illness and accident before their second year, and he knew how each loss wore down her spirit. Yet she had soldiered on, destitute and starving, and had never relinquished her grip on her mind. "But that was a year ago, and women lose babies in childbirth all the time."

"And some of them lose their sanity as well. But in this case, the circumstances were particularly distressing. When the baby dies through some misstep, the loss is doubly painful for being avoidable."

David frowned. "Avoidable?"

Petley paused. Twirled his amber glass. "There was a mishap in their boat, and I understand the baby accidentally fell overboard."

Into the water, David thought. That's what Charlotte was searching for in the water that day on the river. What she looks for every time she is out on the water. The baby she lost. Which is surely a further sign of an unsound mind.

Petley was sprawled comfortably in his leather chair, sipping his second cognac and waxing expansive. Prudently, David kept his doubts to himself. "What course of treatment have you prescribed?" he asked instead.

"She came as a referral from Dr. Harry Elkins, a damn fine physician. Charlotte's father and I were at school with him in Toronto. Elkins has already done extensive generalized bleeding, so I have confined myself to cupping at the neck and leeches at the temples. These are more localized, and will relieve the inflammation of the brain without weakening her further. Purgatives to cleanse the digestion, of course, and bed rest."

"She is injuring herself. Tearing at her flesh."

"Because she needs restraints, which her companion is loathe to employ. I have admonished the girl to persevere on that course, and to ensure absolute bed rest. Mrs. Kent must be kept from anything that may excite her emotions. I have also prescribed a regimen of opium and port wine, which will calm her and induce much needed sleep. If Miss Adamson would follow my instructions—with which Mr. Kent heartily concurs, I might add—Mrs. Kent should be restored to health by Christmas."

Remembering the triumph in her eyes after their adventure, David suspected Miss Adamson had her own opinions of what would restore her friend's health. It was not his affair, he chastised himself, and the patient not his to treat, but that didn't dampen his hope of seeing them both again. Over the next fortnight, he found himself taking the river road between the hospital and his house every morning, and scanning the river for signs of them.

To no avail, until Miss Adamson herself appeared, quite

without his intervention, two weeks later.

He had just left his carriage in the livery stable down the street from his surgery and was picking a path through the mud on Metcalfe Street when he spotted a woman mounting the steps to his office. In contrast to her gaily coloured boating frock, she was wearing a severe grey dress, which still contrived to cling to her slender body in alluring curves. She held its skirts clear of the mud with one hand and waved as he approached.

At the sight of her, intelligent discourse deserted him. "I'm sorry, Miss Adamson. Dr. Petley is not here this morning."

"Which is precisely why I am," she replied. "It is you I wish to consult."

Surprise stopped him on the doorstep. "Ah. Well...since Mr. Kent has engaged the services of Dr. Petley, it would be unwise for me...as a fellow professional..."

Before he could extricate himself from his babbling, she laid a quick hand on his arm. "As a friend then. Shall we take a stroll?"

Without awaiting a response, she slipped her small gloved hand through his arm and guided him down the steps. A fresh rain had washed the air, and the fragrance of lilacs mingled with the stench of manure. As they set off along the sidewalk, he cast about for a way to begin.

"How is Mrs. Kent?"

Miss Adamson tilted her head to fix him with keen blue eyes. To his dismay, the twinkle had quite died, and dark circles had formed beneath. "Perhaps you can tell me. Her body at least appears to be mending. Dr. Petley visited this morning and pronounced the wounds to be healing well."

"No new ones?"

"Dr. Petley has me tie her hands to the bedposts every

night. She sets up an awful keening, like an animal in a trap." She lowered her eyes. "It breaks my heart."

The tremor in her voice made him ache, but he could find no glib words to comfort her. "You've known her a long time?"

She nodded. "We grew up on the same street, and as girls we were inseparable. That's why I agreed to come here in Mr. Kent's employ. Charlotte is a dear, generous soul, but she has a delicate disposition, and there was always the concern..." She checked herself. "What is the matter with her?"

"What do her doctors say?"

"I'm asking you."

Her boldness startled, yet captivated him. A cart raced by, splattering mud and providing a brief distraction during which to collect himself. Steering her to drier footing, he summoned his most professional tone. "So little is known about diseases of the mind, but she appears to be suffering from melancholia. I understand she lost a child?"

Miss Adamson's step faltered. "A newborn, yes."

"In these cases, it is often best to encourage another child as soon as the mother's health permits."

"Yes, but in this case..." She resumed walking, but more slowly, as if reluctant. "There is some doubt as to the circumstances of the infant's death. Charlotte was alone on the lake with the child, and..."

She trailed off, leaving the appalling implication unvoiced. David waited until she found her voice again. "In her situation, it seemed unwise to consider further children. She suffers these attacks, during which she imagines everyone against her. She sits alone for hours, conversing with the empty air, and when she speaks, her words bear no relation to one another. Dr. Petley, in fact, has proposed a..." She drew in her breath and he felt her stiffen, "...a surgery that he says enjoys some success with female insanity. It sounds awful."

David concealed his frustration. Had the old fool not read a single medical journal in the last twenty years? Leeches, purgatives, restraints! He demurred cautiously. "The lunatic asylum in Toronto has made admirable progress in the treatment of the insane, using far more conservative and humane methods."

She looked up in dismay. "Oh, Mr. Kent would never agree to it. Nor would her father. Not after what happened to Charlotte's mother."

"What of her mother?" he asked in surprise.

She faced straight ahead, tightening her grip on his arm as if to fortify herself. "Her mother died there. The family rarely speaks of it, but her condition was much like Charlotte's. Just after Charlotte's birth, she became unbalanced and set fire to the house. On Dr. Elkins' advice, Charlotte's father sent her away to the asylum, where apparently the conditions were appalling. The poor lunatics were crowded into quarters meant to house half their number. They slept in their own filth without adequate food or ventilation. The attendants were ill-trained, dishonest thugs, and sanitation was so poor that waste leaked into the water supply. She died of cholera two years later."

At McGill medical school, David had learned of the history of corruption, mismanagement and abuse at Ontario's lunatic asylum, but had been very impressed by the physician who had turned things around. People's faith was a lot harder to restore. "It's no longer like that. The superintendent is a humane and experienced alienist. From all you've said, Charlotte's case appears much more complicated than simply the loss of her child. I believe she suffers from incurable hereditary dementia. At the asylum, they have trained attendants and a healthy daily regime of work, exercise and good hygiene, which can offer her a more peaceful and contented life than she could have at home, with you forced to tie her up at night, stupify her with sedatives and oversee every move she makes."

Miss Adamson raised her eyes to his, and he saw them slowly pool with tears. He pressed his hand over hers, longing to hold her close and give her hope.

"But to take her from all of us who love her," she said. "To lock her away. How can we?"

He thought of the young woman he had first seen in the bow of the boat. As still and frozen as a statue. "Is she not already locked away, inside her mind?"

*   *   *

David regretted the bluntness of his words the moment he saw the stricken look in Miss Adamson's eyes, but she took her leave before he could make amends. He longed for a chance meeting or news from Dr. Petley. By week's end, he could stand it no longer. When Dr. Petley returned from his weekly house call, David ventured a casual enquiry.

Petley arched his brow and cast him a knowing look. "Miss Adamson asked me today about the accommodations in the lunatic asylum."

David masked his excitement. "What did you tell her?"

"That for a woman of means, there is no substitute for the affection and comfort of those who love her." He sighed. "However, I fear the strain of caring for a lunatic is exacting a toll on Miss Adamson's own spirits. She is looking poorly, and has some bruises which she declines to explain." He shook his head as he headed to his surgery. "Appalling business all around, this disease."

*   *   *

David lay awake much of the night, thinking about the bruises and imagining all manner of catastrophes. Who truly knew the limits of the deranged mind? He resolved to get an early start to his day so that he could check on Miss Adamson himself that afternoon. Sunrise found him already on the road, plodding up Stewart Street on his way to hospital rounds. Up ahead, the river glistened through tendrils of mist, and an amber halo hung over the far shore. It was a balm to soothe the most troubled spirit, yet David felt no peace.

Out of habit, his gaze scoured the river, knowing it was far too early for them to be out, yet hopeful nonetheless. To his left below Wurtenberg Street, he could see the dark smudge of the Cummings Bridge, and to his right the vacant swathe of marshland that swept along the shore. Suddenly, far in the distance beyond the marsh, he discerned a pinpoint of red, drifting in and out of the mist. As insubstantial as a ghost.

Surely not her boat. The distance was too far from the city, the hour too early to be about. One of the local fisherman, no doubt, making the best of the dawn.

David hesitated at the crossroads of Wurtenberg Street, his gaze still fixed on the distant boat. Now he could distinguish the movement of oars and the silhouette of two figures. One at the oars, the other bent over the bow. Still gripped with disbelief, he steered Lady towards it and slapped the reins along her back. She shook her head in surprise but broke into a reluctant trot. When the road dwindled to a rutted track, he stopped to stare again. Incredibly, the little red skiff was rowing away, making good progress against the current in the still morning air.

Where were they going? There was nothing beyond but farmland and brush, but David had heard tales of a chain of treacherous rapids and waterfalls somewhere upriver. Fear chilled him. Jumping from the carriage, he removed Lady's harness and clambered onto her bare back. She shook her head again, this time no doubt to express her bewilderment, but set off at a pace along the dirt path.

As she galloped, David caught glimpses of the boat floating in and out of the fog. He could now make out Miss Adamson's gaily coloured plaid frock, and the saucy set of her bonnet. In the bow, a grey shadow was bent far over the water. As the mist shifted, clarity emerged for an instant, and he saw Mrs. Kent straining against the bow, her arm attached to something long and thin. A stick?

He urged Lady on, his hands entwined in her mane and his knees pressed around her girth. The soft marsh grass muffled her hooves as she thudded closer to the bank. A stand of willow trees loomed ahead, their wide branches draping the misty shore. The red boat disappeared, and in the eerie stillness David felt a surge of panic. Where were they?

Suddenly from up ahead, a splash and a wail, cut short as abruptly as it had begun. David kicked Lady's ribs and charged full tilt toward the trees. His eyes raked the brush. Nothing. He stopped to listen again. Heard a stifled sob and the creak of a single oar. Then the boat drifted into sight beyond the trees, its lone occupant bent motionless over the oars. There was no sound but the heaving of her breath.

Relief laced his panic. "Melody!" he screamed, leaping from the horse.

Her head jerked up, her eyes widened, and for an instant sheer panic raced across her features. "Dr. Browne," was all she said. Whether an entreaty or an expression of dismay, he couldn't tell.

He sprinted to the water's edge. "What happened! Where is Mrs. Kent?"

She lifted the oars slowly and began to row ashore. Behind her, the river was empty save for the small ripples she left in her wake. When the bow touched shore, she stood up, wavered and collapsed into his arms. He carried her up onto the grass. Gripped her shoulders.

"Where's Mrs. Kent!"

She shook her head. Flicked a hand toward the river.

He dashed to the boat and shoved off. He searched an eternity, first from the boat and then in the water, diving again and again into the murky depths, until he knew there was no more hope.

When he pulled the boat back on shore, he noticed a rope at the bow. One end was secured to the seat, the other curled loose like a knot untied. He picked it up. Miss Adamson was sitting up now, her arms wrapped around her and her chin resting on her knees. She met his questioning gaze with dry, haunted eyes.

"She said she could hear the baby calling to her. It seemed the kindest thing to do."

Barbara Fradkin *is a child psychologist fascinated by why we turn out bad. Her dark stories haunt numerous publications, and her detective novels feature the quixotic Ottawa Police Inspector Michael Green. She is a two-time prizewinner in* Storyteller's *Great Canadian Short Story Contest and a four-time nominee for the Arthur Ellis Award, which she won in 2005 for her novel* Fifth Son.

THE WILL OF GOD

H. Mel Malton

July, 1941

The Island Ferry has just finished docking on the mainland, after its last trip of the night. Halfway across the river, a waterlogged and rapidly sinking object is gently rammed by the hull of a small outboard. The boater gives a satisfied grunt, cuts the engine, and moments later, has secured the object to a tow-rope. The little boat then heads towards the city shipyard.

June, almost eighteen years later

Martha's aunt and uncle sure were scared of her moving off-island to go live in the city.

"You'd be taking your life in your hands, I swear, girl," Uncle God said, whenever she brought the subject up. "You don't know that city like I do. Why d'you think your mama brought you here in the first place?" Martha didn't know the answer to that question. Emma, her mother, had left her with Uncle God and Aunt Hannah when Martha was just a baby, and she'd never given her daughter the chance to ask why, because she'd headed right back to the city again and gotten herself killed right after.

"Life ain't good there," Aunt Hannah said. "There's no work for you there, dear, and we'd miss you something awful if you left."

"But there is work for me there," Martha said. "That's what I'm trying to tell you. I applied for a waitressing job downtown. They want me to start on Monday."

Uncle God looked like thunder.

"When in tarnation did you get away to do that?" he said. "You took the ferry and all without asking leave? Why, you could have been raped and murdered right on that boat and tossed into the water, and we wouldn'ta never known what happened to you." You could see the thought of it was making him real upset. His fists were clenched up like potatoes, and his face had gone redder than the barn roof. Aunt Hannah was looking steamed, too.

"You're an ungrateful little miss, Martha, that's what you are," she said. "Sneaking away like that."

"But I didn't sneak…"

"Maybe we ain't given her enough to do around here, Godfrey," Aunt Hannah went on, her eyes going mean like they got when it was time to kill a chicken. "Land knows she's got the poultry to look after and the herd to help milk in the morning, and the baking to do, but maybe she needs to start going into the fields in the afternoons instead of helping me in the house."

"I thought of that before, Han, but you wanted to keep her away from the Horton boy, remember?" Martha blushed to hear Uncle God mention Eldon Horton, who was helping with the planting that spring. He was the eldest son from the next farm over, and he'd been eyeing her for years. Martha knew her aunt and uncle and Eldon's parents had talked some about it, but they'd never asked her for her opinion. It would have saved everybody a lot of pussyfooting around if they had. Martha wouldn't give Eldon Horton the time of day, even if he was the last boy on earth. He was a bully. She'd stayed away from him since kindergarten, and she wasn't about to start messing around on the sly with him now, no matter what her aunt thought about it.

"I'm almost eighteen," Martha said, trying to get back into the conversation, which had somehow moved her into a kind of third-person role, as if she wasn't there. "My life is my own now, you know."

"And you want to take your life into your hands and go work in the city, full of murderers and crazy people?" Aunt Hannah had turned on the waterworks, and her hands were trembling. "You're going to leave me to manage the chickens and the cows all on my own? I'm not getting any younger, you know."

"There, there, Han. She don't mean it. Not really. She'd never leave us—she knows how much she means to us," Uncle God said, patting his wife's shoulder awkwardly. He always got embarrassed if people cried. "You listen, Martha," he said, his hand still on Aunt Hanna's shoulder in a protective way, as if he thought Martha was going to step in and start smacking.

"You know your aunt's heart isn't strong. You going away right now would pretty near kill her, and then you'd have that on your conscience, leastways until you got murdered in that dang city like your mother did. We took you in when you were a baby and treated you like our own. The least you could do is stick around long enough to help out when your aunt needs you."

Privately, Martha wasn't too sure she'd ever seen evidence of Aunt Hannah's weak heart. She wasn't more than fifty, and she could toss a bag of chicken feed around like it was a feather pillow.

"Couldn't Eldon Horton help out more, when I'm gone?" Martha said. Aunt Hannah burst into a fit of weeping, burying her head in Uncle God's overall-clad stomach.

"She don't want Eldon Horton," Uncle God said. "She wants you. Now, you write to them restaurant people and tell them you can't come. Maybe next year, Martha. But not now."

*　　*　　*

Later that night, Martha re-read the letter from the people who ran the Rainbow Diner.

> *Dear Miss Wallace,*
> *We are willing to take a chance on you, even though you say you cannot come for an interview. We both liked your letter very much, and you sound like a good girl. Also, if you grew up on a farm, we know you are more than strong enough for the work here! Regarding accommodation; there is a room over the bakery next door to us that is available. Mrs. Hunt, the landlady, has reserved it for you. We will advance you your first week's wages, if you wish. We both look forward very much to meeting you—first thing on Monday morning.*
> *Sincerely,*
> *Abe and Reena Silver*

It wasn't as if Martha didn't appreciate everything her aunt and uncle had done for her—she did. It was just that she had never, in all her life, been to the mainland. Not even on field trips, when everybody else from the Island school had gone. There was always a good reason. Her aunt had fallen sick, and somebody had had to see to the stock, or Uncle God had had to be away, and Aunt Hannah was terrified of being alone, and once, Martha had gotten sick herself—stomach flu that hit her right after lunch. That was the most disappointing one—it had been the graduation hop that night at the Harbour pavilion on the mainland. She'd cried buckets, but it was no good. She'd been too sick to stand up, and her aunt had been worried enough that they had almost called the doctor, but Uncle God said to wait until morning, and she was fine by then.

She'd seen the advertisement for the waitressing job in the city *Chronicle*. Her aunt and uncle never took the papers, but Martha had started visiting the village library on Sundays, after church. It was a fluke thing—the library wasn't normally open on Sundays, but she'd walked past it once, and it had been. The librarian, Miss Fletcher, had been very pleasant to her, and after hearing how Martha didn't get a lot of time to herself, had arranged a kind of private, Sunday afternoon reading club. It was Miss Fletcher who had pointed out the advertisement.

"You might write to them," Miss Fletcher had said. "It sounds like the perfect summer job for you, to save for college."

"What makes you think my aunt and uncle will let me go to college?" Martha had applied to various places, just because everybody else did, though she had no hope of paying for it. To her surprise, she'd been accepted by a small one in the north of the city. They had even offered her a modest scholarship.

"They have to let you go," Miss Fletcher had said. "You can't stay on that farm forever, Martha—not with your brains. You'll go crazy."

"They'll never let me leave," Martha said. "They want me to marry Eldon Horton so their farm and ours can get amalgamated."

"I've never heard such outdated claptrap in my life," Miss Fletcher had said. "You apply for that waitressing job right now, Martha. Take your life in your own hands. This is the modern world. It's 1958, for pity's sake, not the dark ages."

*   *   *

They started right after the chickens were fed, the eggs collected and washed, the herd milked and the milk weighed and processed. Martha was sitting down to a bite of toast when her aunt bustled in with a kerchief tied around her head, carrying mops and brooms and buckets and what-all.

"Stir your stumps, girl. Spring cleaning. We're taking the parlour apart," she said. And they did. They took the carpet outside, and Martha beat the dust out of it with an old-fashioned wicker beater, like a huge spoon, they scrubbed the wooden floor, washed the heavy curtains and hung them on the line, washed the windows, sponged the walls and even cleaned out the fireplace. Then they started on the kitchen.

At one point, pegging out the freshly-washed rag rugs from the hallway, Martha saw her Uncle and Eldon Horton go into the barn, Uncle God's arm around the boy's shoulders. She could just imagine the conversation.

"You bide your time," her uncle would be saying. "She'll come around." Never, Martha said to herself. Never.

Driving to church on Sunday, Uncle God caught Martha's eyes in the rearview mirror.

"We want you to come home with us in the car today," he said. "We're having company for dinner, and your aunt needs your help."

"I'd like to walk," Martha said. "I'll come right home, though."

41

"You mind your uncle, Martha," Aunt Hannah said, but Martha gave them the slip and went to the library.

"You are going to take the job, aren't you?" Miss Fletcher said.

"I have to," Martha said. "It's as if they're trying to lock me up or something. If they had a tower, I'd be in it."

"Growing your hair," Miss Fletcher said.

"Yes, although if Eldon Horton came to climb up it, I'd cut it off when he was high enough to fall and kill himself."

"When are you going?"

"I'm taking the night ferry," she said. "It's the only way, really."

"Well, you be careful. Not all your aunt and uncle's fears about the city are unfounded, you know."

"I will be. I'll take a taxi from the ferry right to the restaurant. I have a little money saved."

"Here—take this," Miss Fletcher said, and pressed a small package into her hands. Martha opened it. It was a small pocket-knife, pearl-handled, with a thin, wicked little blade.

"What's this for? Thanks—it's beautiful, but…"

"It was my mother's," Miss Fletcher said. "She gave it to me when I first moved out and went to the city. It's for protection. Like I said, not every fear about the city is unfounded. It's small enough to carry in your purse, and you might be able to surprise an attacker and give yourself time to get away."

"I could never…"

"I know. That's what I said, too. But here, let me show you." The little knife had a button on the side of it. When you pressed the button, the blade snicked out, sweet and deadly, just like that.

"It's a switchblade, as well as just an innocent little pocket knife," Miss Fletcher said. Then the librarian showed Martha some tricks that would surprise an attacker absolutely to death.

"Oh, my goodness, look at the time," Martha said, after a while. "I have to go help my aunt get supper ready. Company's coming." She rushed for the door, then stopped and turned back. "Thanks, Miss Fletcher—for everything."

"Call me Maddy," Miss Fletcher said. "I'll come and visit you on the mainland."

"I'll give you the best table," Martha said.

*   *   *

She wasn't that late, but late enough to earn a blistering reprimand from Uncle God, who was sitting in the parlour with his feet up. "You just never give a second's thought to your aunt, do you, girl?" he said. "Her in there by herself, slaving over a hot stove while you dawdle home. Get in there and make yourself useful."

"Who's coming for supper?" Martha asked, as she peeled potatoes.

"The Hortons," Aunt Hannah said. She should have known.

"Eldon, too?"

"Yes, my girl, Eldon, too. And you'll be on your best behaviour, I hope. No getting all flirty with him behind my back, now," her aunt said.

"Don't you worry," Martha said. "I won't."

Sunday dinners at home were never chatty, and having company generally cut off conversation completely. The silence was broken only by the occasional request to pass the salt or Aunt Hannah's insisting people have more to eat. "Take another helping of potatoes, Eldon dear. I know you're a growing boy." Eldon had done more than enough growing as it was, Martha thought privately. He was over six foot and built like a Massey Ferguson tractor. He ate like a pig, too. He was seated opposite her and occasionally leered at her over his dinner plate. Martha figured that his thoughts were the kind you'd expect from someone who spent most of his time in a barnyard. He made her flesh creep.

Over pie, Mrs. Horton turned to Martha. "I hear you've been thinking of leaving us, dear," she said. Martha's jaw dropped.

"I'm sure glad that you've decided to stay," she went on. "You know how much your aunt needs you. Anyway, that city is so rotten with sin, it'd eat up a young girl like you and just spit her out." On the word spit, a fragment of pastry flew from her mouth and landed on the tablecloth. Martha felt sick.

"Our Martha's not anything like her mother," Aunt Hannah said. "Why, that sister of mine just had a mind of her own, and look what that got her. Nothing but grief and trouble, and a terrible end."

"Yes, a terrible end," Mrs. Horton agreed. The men didn't say a thing, just kept on chewing. For Martha, the meal was almost unbearable. Oh, the food was fine—it always was, and there was plenty of it, but everybody at the table was watching her, like you watch a hen getting ready to lay an egg. You could just smell the tension. Maybe they were afraid she'd make a run for it right there, leap from the table and run for the door. It was clear they expected her to give in under the weight of their expectations and say yes, yes, she was staying, no she never wanted to leave, yes, she was happy to stay on the island forever. Saying that would almost be a relief, but she wouldn't do it.

*　　*　　*

44

Upstairs, under her bed, her bag was packed. The night ferry left at eleven thirty, but it was only a half-mile walk to the terminal. Aunt Hannah and Uncle God would be in bed by nine—they always were. Would they stay up to keep watch? Would Uncle God try to lock her in?

After the Hortons left, Uncle God went up to bed. Aunt Hannah and Martha were wiping the last of the dishes when her aunt suddenly made a shushing motion, pulled her towards the kitchen table and sat her down.

"I put something in Godfrey's cocoa," she whispered. "To make him sleep. You're going, ain't you?" After a long pause, Martha nodded.

"I thought as much. Well, you'll regret it. But I can't stop you if you're determined to go, I suppose."

"I'd rather have your blessing," Martha said.

"Well, you ain't gonna get it," Aunt Hannah said. "You know I need you, and I don't know how long I'll last with you gone. What with my heart and all. But if you're set on going, you'll go. Take this, now." She reached into her apron pocket and pulled out a carefully folded five dollar bill.

"That city's an evil place," she said. "I know it and you'd know it, too, if you look deep down inside of you. It killed your mother, and I'm scared it's going to kill you, too. But we brung you up right, and I know that at the first sign of trouble, you'll come on home. That's for the ferry to come back. Understand?"

"Everything will be fine, Aunt Hannah."

"Don't you be too sure. Now, you promise me you'll come right home if something goes wrong? Promise?" Her aunt's eyes were full of tears, and Martha promised.

"Now, I'm going on up. You wait awhile before you go sneaking out. Wait for the cocoa to work."

Martha couldn't believe it. Aunt Hannah went upstairs, and sure enough, in less than half an hour, she heard the unmistakable sound of Uncle God, snoring.

She headed out into the night, slipping quietly between the shadows splashed like black ink on the road under a bright moon. She did not see that there was someone waiting for her, leaning patiently against the side of the barn; someone who, after a prudent interval, drew himself upright and then followed.

*   *   *

The next day, the harbour police found a body, washed up on the shore of the Island. A crowd gathered, and the word spread.

"Jesus, Godfrey, Eldon's body's been found in the harbour."

"Can't be."

"Yep. I told you it was a fool idea, sending him after her. Trying to scare her into coming back. He must have messed it up."

"But—how did he end up…he outweighed her. He was…"

"You should have done it yourself. Now she's gone for ever—with my egg money, too."

"It's not the end of the world, Hannah. After a while, I'll make an offer for Horton's farm again—no way he can manage on his own, now. Maybe it's for the best."

"And Martha? Your daughter? You're just going to let her go—just like that?"

"That girl always took after her mother, not me. I knew you'd never make a go of bringing her up right. That's why God made you barren, woman. We should have let Emma live, and packed the brat off with her, too. But no, I had to

46

listen to you and your carrying on, and risked my neck to please you."

"And didn't I risk my neck, too? Towing my own sister behind the boat like a piece of driftwood? Who left her for the police to find? You think I didn't risk everything, too?"

The argument lasted for another five years, until Hannah, worn out, put something into Godfrey's cocoa to make him sleep forever, then blew her brains out in the barn.

Martha sold the farm to the Hortons, for a song.

H. Mel Malton's Down in the Dumps *was shortlisted for an Arthur Ellis First Novel Award. Her crime stories have appeared in the Ladies' Killing Circle's* Menopause is Murder *and* Fit to Die. *She lives in Muskoka, Ontario, with two dogs, Karma and Ego, and writes freelance to pay for kibble and smokes.*

Fish or Cut Bait

Pat Wilson and Kris Wood

"'Blood is thicker'n water', she sez. 'You have to take care of your own,' she sez. 'He's comin' no matter what,' she sez. 'Be on the Zinck bus tomorra,' she sez. 'He can start with you right away.'"

Willard spit over the side of the boat and wiped his mouth on his greasy sleeve. "Goddam it, I shoulda just paid the goddam interest at the bank steada takin' the money from her. Iffen I hadn't been so desperate at the time, what with me old boat burnin' to the waterline and no insurance and all, I woulda never taken her money. Shoulda paid her back, too, but I figures 'blood is thicker'n water' works both ways. Now she wants the money back, and I sure as hell ain't got it, so she says the boat is as good as hers. Not even like I bought a new boat with the money. This old tub ain't worth what she wants back from me. Got me by the short and curlies, she has." He spat again. "Gotta take that good-for-nothin' lay-about Dwayne just 'cause he's in some kind of trouble. As if he'd be any use on the boat. Wouldn't know a lobster iffen it came up and bit him in the ass." With practiced ease, he brought the boat about and slowed the engine until it lay beside the yellow and white buoy. "Don't know why I'm tellin' you all this, Tank. You ain't got the brains God gave a cod."

He watched Tank shamble across the deck, his huge bulk causing the boat to list with his weight. Dark coarse hair spilled out from under the old knitted cap he wore. His yellow rubber overalls were stained and slimed with the offal of several years' worth of lobster fishing. His enormous rubber boots, turned over at the top and cracked in a dozen places, trod the deck as if in a complicated dance, the steps of which only Tank knew. A gaff hung from his massive fist. As the boat swung by, Tank reached out and hooked the buoy, hauling it up and over the pulley at the end of the boom arm. Willard had to admit that Tank might not be playing with a full deck, but he was the best boathand anyone could want, that is, if you didn't expect sparkling conversation or anything beyond the grinding routine of lobstering.

The first season, he'd wondered if he'd made a mistake taking Tank on as a favour. The boy's mother, Nina, had always been good to Willard, but then, Nina was good to most of the lusty young fellows in the harbour in those days. He might even have married her, but at the time he couldn't be certain, and he didn't want to be the laughing-stock of the harbour if he was wrong. However, as Tank grew older, Willard would look at the boy and wonder. Aside from his obvious disabilities in the brain department, Willard saw a familiarity in the way he cocked his head and a look in his eyes.

Unlike other deck hands Willard had taken on, Tank didn't mind the trip to the east arm each morning at four, walking the two miles from his Ma's house in the harbour in order to get to Willard's isolated wharf. Unlike the others who'd shipped with Willard, Tank didn't complain about the general state of The *Mary J*, the ramshackle equipment or the paucity of creature comforts on board. He didn't carp about Willard's miserly ways, argue with him about wages or expect Willard to help him pull in the traps. Tank even helped haul the *Mary J* up the slipway onto blocks at the end of the twelve-week fishing season. While Willard repaired the more complicated netting of the old wooden lobster traps, Tank scraped, caulked and painted the aging twenty-six foot hull of the Cape Islander.

Having lived alone in his small house on the point for most of his sixty-five years and preferring the solitary life, Willard thought that having Tank on the boat was almost as good as being on the boat by himself. No chit-chat, no small talk, no jokes, no gossip, and most of all, no personal revelations or discussions. By the end of the eighth week of that first season, Tank had the routine ground into the grist of his very small mental mill. Now, fifteen seasons later, they worked as a single entity: Willard operating the boat, Tank hauling the traps. Best of all, Tank worked without complaint for the few dollars Willard tossed him at the end of each week.

Now, Tank hauled in the wooden trap, pulled the buoy rope over the pulley as if the trap weighed seven pounds and not seventy, then released three good-sized lobsters, putting rubber bands on their big claws and throwing them into the hold, tossed back two smaller ones, removed the old bait, rummaged in the bait box for a chunk of fish which he spiked in the trap, then swung the heavy trap back into the water, all with an economy of motion that Willard loved to watch. Seconds later, they were on their way to the next buoy. Only a hundred or so left to go.

"She expects me to pay that miserable little weasel," Willard grumbled on. "Like a regular deck hand. Oh hell, I don't even pay you like a regular deck hand, and you can do the work. That no-good bum wouldn't last an hour. Prob'ly get seasick."

"Seasick." Tank picked up on the words and laughed like a

seven year old, his mental age. "Tank don't get seasick." His high-pitched voice matched his laugh, an incongruous sound, coming as it did from such a massive chest. He made mock gagging noises, leaning over the side and pretending to throw up. He giggled. "Seasick," he said again.

As the *Mary J* moved from buoy to buoy, Willard wondered what kind of trouble his nephew was in this time. Dwayne must be all of thirty-five, thirty-six by now, he thought. As far as Willard knew, the lad had never worked a full job in his life. Sat around on his ass all day, letting his mother and his four older sisters wait on him hand and foot. Foolish Alice, spoiling him rotten from the day he was born. "My Dwaynie is delicate," Alice told everyone. Once he had hit school age, the real trouble had started, and Alice found more excuses to explain his behaviour. "His teachers don't understand him. He's just too smart for them. He gets bored, so he gets in trouble. The other children are jealous of him." Then, when he couldn't stick to a job, she told people, "He hasn't found himself yet. His boss doesn't like him. The work doesn't suit him." Over the years, the excuses piled up higher than Willard's stack of traps on his wharf in the off-season. Like so many others, Dwayne had tried "going down the road". First to Calgary, but without success. He'd gone to Toronto then to Montreal. Even Moncton hadn't worked out. Each time, Dwayne had slunk back home in the middle of the night and lain low for several months.

Although Willard had never heard the exact reason for Dwayne's comings and goings, he had his suspicions. Now, it looked like Halifax was too hot for him, and Willard's boat was going to be Dwayne's latest hide-out. "God knows what kinds of fellas is goin' to be lookin' for him," Willard told Tank as they nosed the *Mary J* into the wharf and began to unload the crates of lobster. "Iffen that dang fool's gotten hisself into trouble in Halifax, won't take no genius to figure out where he is and follow him down here."

When Dwayne arrived, instead of slinking off the bus like a weasel on the run, he swaggered down the steps like he'd just won the lottery. Willard saw a hundred-and-ten-pound skinny, smart-mouthed, bantam rooster with thinning hair in the beginnings of a bad combover, a worm of a moustache crawling across his upper lip and several pornographic tattoos decorating his scrawny biceps, completing the picture of a small-time hood. Willard could only hope that Dwayne would hate the job and, in a couple of days, head back for the bright lights of the city.

Dwayne, against all odds, "took" to life on the water. That is, he took to the idea of being captain, not deck hand. He did no work, leaving the physical labour to Tank. He lurked in the wheelhouse, watching every move Willard made and peppering him with questions. At first, Willard wondered if the boy just might have the makings of a lobsterman in him, despite all appearances. The first time he let Dwayne take the wheel, it looked like maybe blood was thicker than water after all.

However, after a few days, Dwayne began to talk. Non-stop. He brimmed with ideas for the *Mary J*. Worse, he began calling the *Mary J* "my" boat. He wanted to paint it up, a nice bright yellow that would stand out; he wanted to re-name it, something catchy like "Adventure Queen"; he wanted to run charter tours for the tourists.

"Tourism, that's where the real money is," he told Willard. "Fishing is dying out. Dead. Gone. Kaput. Over. Fished it to death. That's what you old fellows did. Fished it to death. And the government'll give you money for tourism. Big money. Clean money. They'll even buy back your lobster license. I can use the money from that to fix up this old tub. Get some slick advertising going. Whale watching. Tuna. Whatever."

Willard watched Tank go from his usual carefree self to a silent shadow on the boat. It didn't help to tell Dwayne to stop, since Dwayne never listened to anyone. "What the hell, Uncle Willard. The dummy doesn't understand two words out of three. Anyways, we won't be needing him. Put a lump like him in the boat, and it'd scare the tourists away."

Willard tried to protest, but Dwayne took great delight in reminding him that Willard might be the captain, but Alice now as good as owned the *Mary J*, unless, of course, Willard could come up with the do-re-mi to pay her back. Which all meant that Dwayne ran the show, not Willard. And Dwayne would say who stayed and who went.

Next morning, Dwayne began measuring up the boat for the refit he planned. "Gotta have seats," he said. "Life vests. Snacks. Good money in snacks. Maybe some souvenirs—you know, things with "Adventure Queen" on them. Hats, T-shirts. And we'll need some lobster stuff—pillows and the like. After all, tourists'll go for the idea that they're on what used to be a working lobster boat."

Willard didn't miss the finality of Dwayne's last sentence. He gritted his few remaining teeth in anger. It wouldn't do any good to argue with Dwayne or curse him out as he longed to do. Dwayne ignored everything except his grand plan. Willard knew the only way to get Dwayne off his boat and out of his life was to come up with Alice's money. For a week, his brain worked in endless circles, trying to think of what he could do. He knew selling his house wouldn't solve the problem. Even if he could find a buyer, he'd be lucky to get thirty thousand for a shack at the end of a dirt road. Besides, if he lost his place, he'd lose his wharf. There'd be nowhere for his boat. Besides, he needed the boat to keep on fishing. Even if he gave Alice every cent he made this season, it still wouldn't come close to clearing up the debt.

He worried the problem over and over during his sleepless nights, listening to Dwayne snoring on the couch in the front room. No matter how he looked at it, he couldn't see a way out. Short of throwing Dwayne over the side, and God knows, he was tempted to do just that, Willard knew he was stuck.

Now, he swore under his breath and swung the boat through the thick morning fog to the next buoy. Tank got into position at the rail, gaff ready for the buoy line.

"Hey, lard ass! Move out of the way." Dwayne strutted out of the cabin. "I need to get some measurements here." He tried to elbow Tank away from the gunwale. He might as well have been trying to move a block of granite.

"Tank's gotta get the line," Tank protested, planting his feet on the deck.

"Geez, Uncle Willard. Talk about thick! How can you stand being out here all day with this dummy?" Dwayne pushed against Tank again. "Move, you idiot."

Tank ignored him. He hooked the buoy and hauled up the heavy trap, dripping with seaweed and water. Tank stepped sideways and swung the boom with the trap dangling on its end across the deck as he always did. It caught Dwayne on the side of his head. Dwayne toppled over, hitting the far gunwale as he went.

Blood poured out of a large gash on his head and mixed with the sea water already sloshing in the scuppers.

"Holy shit!" Willard shut down the engine and stumbled out of the house. "What the hell you done, boy?" He dropped on his knees beside Dwayne, pressing a shaking hand into Dwayne's neck, even putting his ear on the boy's skinny chest, praying for signs of life.

He thought of trying mouth-to-mouth, but even a fool could see it wouldn't do any good. The copious flow of blood from Dwayne's gashed skull had stopped. His cooling flesh and the angle of his neck told Willard that nothing could be done.

Willard looked up at Tank. "What have you done, boy?" he repeated, his voice shaky.

"Got the trap up, okay. Four big 'uns, too." Tank continued with his routine, banding the lobsters and throwing them into the hold. He rebaited the trap and swung it back over the water. "All done," he said.

"Lord Jumpin' Jesus! Don't you know you killed the bastard? Now what're we going to do?" Willard felt a cold chill crawl across his shoulders. Alice would call in his debt and sell the *Mary J* to the first bidder when she found out her Dwaynie had died on his boat. Poor Tank would end up in some institution for loonies and retards. Worst of all, a full police investigation would pretty much take up the rest of the lobster season. He wouldn't put it past them to impound the damn boat, too. All because of some stupid accident.

"Tank throw him in the water?" Tank suggested. He bent down as if to pick up the body.

"No, no! Don't do that! Body'll wash up on Shoal Beach in a day or two. Everything washes up there from around here. Some nosy fool's bound to find him. And then what? There'll be questions. We gotta get rid of him so's nobody will find him." Willard sat down on a bait box and contemplated their situation. "We gotta get rid of the body," he repeated. "Then, tomorra, I'll just report him gone missing to the RCMP. With his record, and the way his mother was goin' on about his troubles afore she sent him here, they'll figure either he got scared and ran off again, or his friends from Halifax caught up with him and did him in. Won't never suspect us."

"Tank gotta do the traps." Tank shuffled from foot to foot, uncomfortable with this break in their routine. "Tank gotta get some bait. Tank need 'nother box." He eyed the box under Willard.

Willard felt the glimmering of an idea.

"Ya don't need no new box, Tank. We got plenty of good bait right here." He nudged the limp form of Dwayne, hoping that Tank would catch on. "Good fresh bait," he said, nudging Dwayne again.

Willard fetched the axe he kept ready in case the pulley ever jammed. He handed it to Tank.

Tank grinned. "Okey-dokey," he said.

Willard turned his back on Tank and started up the engines. He decided he wouldn't look around again until they finished the last trap. For the next few hours, he closed his ears to the intermittent "thunk thunk" of Tank's axe.

"Keep those scuppers washed out," he hollered over his shoulder. "And sluice off the deck. Don't want you fallin' down or nothing."

Once they were snubbed into the wharf, he helped Tank give the boat a good cleaning. When the water flowing out of the scuppers no longer ran pink, Willard threw his arm around Tank's broad shoulders.

"Ya done a good job, boy. No need to mention this to anyone, you hear."

"Tank ain't gonna say nothing. Tank is smart."

"Tomorra I'll report him missing, and that'll be the end of it." Willard watched as Tank hauled the filled lobster crates onto the slippery planks of the wharf. "It was just an accident, Tank. Not your fault. Coulda happened to anyone. Don't want no police nosing around, right, Tank?"

Tank grinned and mimed a smack on the side of his head. "Bop! Dwayne gone! Bop! Bop!" He smacked his head again, grinning even wider. "Tank's got a secret," he giggled.

Willard's mouth dropped open. He stared at Tank in disbelief. "Judas Priest, boy! Don't go talkin' like that. It was an accident, pure and simple. You don't want to say nothin' about it, ever again, you hear me?"

"Okey-dokey," said Tank.

"You'll be all right, boy. Just do like I tell you. After all…" Willard hesitated. "Son," he said deliberately, "blood's thicker'n water."

Pat Wilson and Kris Wood *have been friends for over thirty years. They are both authors in their own right, but together have co-authored several short stories for mystery collections by the Ladies Killing Circle and written two full-length books on Maritime subjects, as well as numerous other humorous pieces.*

ALONE WITH THE DEAD AT KAKABEKA FALLS

Jason S. Ridler

Dedicated to Gladstone and George Ridler

"**Lord, what a face.** You bashed him into a monster!"

"God no, Duggin! Looked like a train-wreck when he walked into Max's last night. Drank two pints of rye like it was water but had no coin, so they tossed him. Still on the street when they closed up, so Max woke me, and I dragged him here. Thought he might be a stray from your farm."

Rick stayed as still as a corpse on the jail floor, hands rammed in his pockets. All he had left was sown into the secret pocket in his trousers, hidden from prying hands. He tapped it. The sharp points of the cross were still there against the stitches. *Phew,* he thought through the razor haze of the hangover, *I still have a chance.*

"No one's escaped yet, Jack. Nah, he's a 'bo. Moving like rats across the rails now. How much does he owe?"

Where am I? Rick wondered. Fort William? Yeah, barely out of Manitoba and still hundreds of miles from Ottawa. He shouldn't have jumped from the train, but he was desperate. He'd been awake for two days when he hit this stop, shaking, stash long dead. Thankfully, the rye had worked. He'd slept like the dead through the night. Dreamless.

"Duggin, you gonna take him or what?"

"Oh, I'll take him, maybe charge admission. Hey! Sunshine!"

Rick opened his one good eye.

A bald man in a grey uniform smiled at him with brown teeth. "Time for work, handsome."

Rick retched over the side of the bouncing truck. Of the ten other men lying on the flatbed, only the coloured one looked at him.

"You okay, son?" said the coloured man, thin as a reed, old but well cultivated, wild grey hair giving him a strange authority.

"Could be worse," Rick coughed, wiping his mouth.

"Really?"

"Yup," Rick said, dryly. "Could have crapped myself."

The coloured man laughed, but Rick wasn't joking.

"Today, you'll dig holes and knock in posts for a wire fence," Duggin hollered. He looked at Rick. "With a new arrival, I'll repeat the rules. You will work a week to pay off your debt, then get the hell out of Fort William, don't care how. You are free to run, but not even a coon run faster than a bullet from Jericho's Ross. How far'd *your* boy get, Bishop?"

"Gates of Heaven," said the old coloured man, curtly.

Rick stood very still in the awful heat of the morning, mouth dry and pungent as a baked turd, head spinning in the wake of the rye. He focused on the Ross rifle hanging from Jericho's shoulder. After Ypres, Rick had dumped his Ross and snatched a Lee Enfield from a dead Tommy as soon as he was able. A Ross was only good for sniping, not in the trenches; jammed if you looked at it funny. The kid holding it didn't look old enough to shave, yet there were a dozen notches on the stock.

Rick thought of the war. He wouldn't stay the night.

He dug alone, planning his escape. "Seems we got something in common," Bishop said, carrying a handful of posts to Rick's holes, uninvited.

Rick stomped in his shovel. "Yeah? What's that?"

"People afraid of us. Scared of how we look."

"Why ain't you scared of me?"

"Because ugly ain't evil."

"Really?"

"Ugly is just ugly. Evil can come in any package, pretty or otherwise. Same goes for virtue. You got a problem with negroes?"

Rick shook his head, sweat dropping like rain. "Only ones I ever met were in France, American blacks. Good in a fight, and they bleed as red as anyone."

"Spoken like a true Christian soldier."

Rick snorted. "You talk like a preacher."

"Job came with the name." He smiled and Rick, despite the pain, smiled back.

"How'd a holy man end up here?"

Bishop rammed in a post, and they worked on another hole, counting their paces. "I'm a wandering preacher, dying breed of holy man, spreading the word while moving my feet. I was born running up the Underground Railroad, and I ain't stopped since. Me and Georgie were heading to the west when Georgie mistook a farmer's apple tree for God's charity. Almost got us a hide full of buckshot. Quoting verse kept us from trouble and got us time on the farm instead. When Georgie ran," Bishop said, shakily, "I got his week."

"Coon!" Jericho yelled from twenty yards away, rifle in hand. "Quit chirping and get digging!"

At lunch, Rick's ration of lard and toast sat uneaten on his lap. Bishop gave him his cup of water. "Back at the bunker, we got a cot and a government blanket, and the men ain't so bad."

Rick drained the cup. "Thanks. Look, Bishop, I ain't sticking here."

60

"You'll be out by Friday. Hell, not like you robbed a bank."

"Can't wait that long. I gotta cut out to Ottawa." His lips trembled.

"Son, there's nothing wrong with working off debt."

"I ain't afraid of work. And I never meant to shirk nobody, but—"

"Hooch got you bad, huh?"

He blinked. "No. Well, yes. You won't believe me."

Bishop sighed. "Son, I believe in a god who gives a woman a baby without dropping his trousers. I believe in saints that slay dragons. And I believe that we can all get to heaven if we take the time to learn from a good book. That book says I got to believe in you."

No padre had ever spoken like that. Rick nodded.

"I got awful nightmares. They're killing me. Slowly. Every night. Because of this," he pointed to his mangled face. "But I can't remember how this *happened*. It's like a locked closet in my mind. I remember training for a trench raid, how to kill a man close up. I can see us crossing through no-man's land, but that's it. Everything goes white, then dark, then all I see is this nurse above me, apron all red. Said the stretcher-bearers ripped my face from the barbed wire and got me on the next ship to England with enough morphine to choke a horse. But I don't remember squat.

"Got home to Edmonton. Had a wife. Good mill job. Government cheque for my medical. Then the Legion headed to the armistice anniversary in France. Said they'd pay my way. Delia didn't want me to go. But I went. Didn't think I'd get another chance. Maybe I'd remember once I hit the soil.

"Walking those fields again, though." He gripped his shaking hands. "When I slept, that locked closet opened up. But no memories came out. Just this *thing*."

The hot pit in Rick's stomach clawed up his throat. He choked back the memory of the eyeless Krauts charging out of the darkness, *plunging into his dead eye.*

"Liquor was the only thing that drowned the nightmares, so I'd get tight, every night, pass out cold. Delia left, but I didn't care. Only important thing was keeping that closet door closed. But my money ran dry.

"Then a guy at the Legion talked about a new veteran's hospital in Ottawa. Best European doctors. Cured all kinds of things. He gave me the address, and I've been on the rails ever since. Heading for a cure.

"So I gotta go, Bishop. I can stay awake a few days, but I gotta get on a train tonight. That closet door is cracking."

Bishop chewed his crust, looking pensive. "Lotta men be lining up for treatment like that, son."

Rick held his breath, then said, "I got something they don't." He spat. "A Victoria Cross."

He watched Bishop's stunned face. The V.C. had that effect on everyone, except its owners.

"No idea why my C.O. put me down for it, and he earned the wooden cross at Vimy," Rick snorted. "Citation reads that I saved a lot of men in the face of the enemy before getting knocked out on the wire. But all I got is nightmares, no memory. So I'm gonna ram that thing in everyone's face until they kill what's killing me. Maybe then I'll remember." *And I can be free.*

Bishop nodded, but his face was grim. "Duggin won't cut you loose. And escape's near impossible. Four tried. Each a notch on Jericho's stock, including Georgie. But there may be another way."

Dry grass crunched behind Rick.

Rick turned and saw Jericho, rifle in both hands, hustling

toward them. "Nigger, either get to work or start digging your own grave. And take freak show with you."

"Sorry, son," Bishop said, getting up. "Get right on it."

"I ain't no monkey's son!" Jericho kicked Bishop's gut so hard the wind gushed out of him, dropping him to his knees. "That's blasphemy!"

Rick stood up and stared at the youth.

Jericho lazily aimed the rifle at him. "Watch it, freak show."

"Don't touch him," Rick said, cold.

"You talk? Last geek I seen was a snake man travelling with that World of Wonders Caravan, and all he did was bite a head off a chicken."

"My only trick is killing babies with rifles too big for them."

Jericho snickered, but he held the gun more fiercely. A few feet separated them.

"You'll earn a grave that way," Jericho said, face pale.

Rick moved forward very slowly. "Yeah. Yours. Ross rifle only needs two movements to load. But we trained to kill Krauts with a single movement. I remember that." Rick's reflexes tingled. "Sergeant said any idiot can kill at a distance, but it takes a real man to kill with his hands." Rick jabbed forward, and Jericho jerked back—

A sound shot through the air.

"Oww!" Jericho screamed, back on the grass, rifle out of reach, foot caught in a freshly dug hole. "Duggin! Help!"

Rick reached for the rifle, but Bishop stopped him. "They got men out here we can't see! You touch that gun, and we're both dead."

* * *

Rick sat on the floor of the cell they called "solitaire," too scared to be hungry. *Never should have listened to Bishop,* he thought, *should have taken a chance with a rifle in hand.*

But hearing that rifle had thinned his defenses. Night came. Terror crept across his skin like a disease while fatigue pulled his lids. *Those dead-socket Krauts are coming.*

A rattle. A snap. A crackle. The sounds pierced Rick's mind. He gripped himself hard enough to burst.

The door opened, then closed, silent as a church mouse.

On the floor was a bottle of clear liquid, a note corking the top. By starlight he read the pencil scratches:

Best can do for now. Another way out tomorrow. Bless you. Bishop.

The next morning, Rick heaved spit and snot over the side of the truck, guts empty, dropping the bottle he'd hid in his pocket.

"Sweet dreams?" Bishop asked.

"Not one," Rick said.

Both laughed while the others stared at them with surly curiosity.

"That moonshine damn near blinded me," Rick said, digging with rubber arms.

"Georgie made it, last of his stash."

"How'd he keep it in here?"

"He didn't. I did. Told 'em it was holy water."

Rick snickered. "You're a cagey bastard, Bishop." He shot Bishop a quick glance but did not stop working. Jericho stood a safe distance away, rifle cocked. "So, what's your plan?"

"A remedy for your mind."

"My remedy is in Ottawa."

"You ain't gonna make it that far, son."

His eye narrowed. "What?"

"You're a fighter, and a hard man, or else war and drink would have killed you, but you ain't hard enough to take three bullets in the back while running a thousand miles. But there's another way. You ever hear of Kakabeka Falls?"

Rick kept digging, trying to ignore Bishop, but the man kept talking. "It flows into the Kaministiquia River, a sacred place to the Ojibway. They had a princess who tricked a bunch of Sioux to follow her down it, and her sacrifice saved them from disaster. Warriors bathed at the bottom of the falls for years to get a drink of her courage. Great remedy for the hooch shakes, too."

"How the hell you know this Indian stuff?"

"Georgie's mother, God bless her, was part Ojibway, and those stories were as close to religion as he got. Kakabeka's where we were headed. Georgie had a problem with nerves, made him fight all the time. Saw things in shadows." He gave Rick a knowing look and rammed in a post. "Hooch was the only thing that eased him, killing him at the same time." *Same as you*, Rick could hear him thinking.

"We could roll off the back of the truck and into the ditch. They won't notice until we're long gone, then hustle to the falls."

"Then what, Bishop? I drop in this drink, get all clean, then?"

"Then you take off, I turn myself in and tell them you headed in the opposite direction." He smiled at Rick. "This farm work suits me fine at my stage. I'll pay off what you and I and Georgie owe and head on out west again. So what do you say?"

"I say it's superstitious bunk." He dug in his pocket and grabbed for the secret pouch.

It was torn. Empty.

He covered his eyes from the sun's glare and stared around the ground. But only one thing glinted in the sunlight on the farm.

"Son of a bitch," Rick spat.

"Careful, son," Bishop said. Rick shrugged off the old man's hand.

He took easy steps. Jericho's rifle stared at him.

"You lost, freak show?"

"Give it back," Rick said, pointing at the medal under Jericho's badge. They stood a few yards apart.

"War heroes don't slave on jail farms. Better stop and drop the shovel." The rifle was trained on his chest.

Rick followed the order and stood his ground. Duggin came over in his truck, the other deputies keeping prisoners at bay. Only Bishop was near.

"What's the trouble?" Duggin said.

"He's got my medal."

"It ain't his," Jericho said. "I found it."

"It's got my name on it. Richard Falcon."

Duggin snapped the medal off of Jericho's chest, examined it, and gave Rick a hard look. "Jesus, is this real?"

He ignored the question. "I need it to get treatment. For this," he pointed at his face.

"Where might this treatment be?" Duggin asked.

"Ottawa."

Duggin stared at the medal like he'd discovered gold in the Klondike. "How did you get it?"

"I don't remember. I got banged up bad in France. I need the treatment to remember."

"Hospital got a name?"

The hazy words of the legionnaire rang in his mind, "When you get to Ottawa, buddy, just ask for —"

66

"The Hospital Grand Vera Copula," Rick said.

Duggin's eyes perked up. "What?"

"The guy said not to stop looking until I found the Grand Vera Copula."

Duggin's belly shook with laughter.

"You got screwed, hero. My Latin ain't great, but I sure as shit done enough Vera Copula."

Rick fidgeted. "What?"

"Hey, Bishop! C'mere."

He strode up beside Rick.

"Tell our hero what Vera Copula means."

Rick stared at the old preacher, eye hungry for relief.

"Tell him!"

"First relations between man and wife."

"Screwing?" Jericho asked. Bishop nodded.

"Looks like you've been screwed, too, soldier," Duggin said.

The world hushed. Rick couldn't remember the face of the man at the Legion, but his message was now clear. He had wanted to send the drunk on a wild goose chase that would kill him, or at least get him out of the Legion.

In that summer sun, Rick's blood froze.

He held still as Duggin and Jericho laughed in greater heaves. When Jericho blinked, he made his first move. The kid never saw it coming and hit the floor like an anvil from heaven, chest heaving. Second move, Rick had the rifle. Third, he had it trained on Duggin. A rifle shot cracked through the air and drove everyone to the ground but Rick.

"Get in front of me, now!" Rick yelled, nerves surging. Duggin did, and shot up his hands. "Tell your snipers to lay down their arms."

Duggin screamed the order.

"We're taking a drive." He nudged the butt of the rifle into his back. He looked back at Bishop. "You coming?"

"Depends on where you're going."

"Kakabeka Falls. You know the way?"

Bishop smiled.

Duggin drove, rifle muzzle in his crotch. Bishop, in the middle, tried to recall the directions. Rick sat on the right, finger on the trigger. The whole cab stank of long dead cigarettes.

"You'll never make it," Duggin said. "My boys will be on you like flies on shit, and then you'll be hurting. And Bishop, you're a dead man."

Bishop smiled. "Made my peace a long time ago, how about you?"

Duggin grunted.

"Rick? You all right?" Bishop said.

"No," he said through clenched teeth. "I've been made a sap, and I had to learn about it from these jackasses. Now I got nowhere to go."

"Except Kakabeka Falls."

"Yeah." But hope was vanishing like his hangover.

*   *   *

They came upon woods, stopped the truck and proceeded on foot, Duggin in the lead. The thick branches shielded them from sunlight as they walked in the shade of day. Distant vehicles rumbled closer.

"Listen," Bishop said, stopping them. "Hear that? Running water." The rushing sound was coming from the left of the woods. Bishop's face went tight. "Oh, no."

Rick realized it too. "We're at the top of the falls. Not the bottom."

Duggin laughed. "Should have got an Indian guide instead of a coon."

Rick cracked his head with the rifle butt. Duggin collapsed and Rick tensed as the medal he'd pushed from his mind snapped from the boss's pocket. It landed face up. The lion emblem held his gaze: then its eyes flared.

Bishop grabbed his head in his tough hands. "Rick, I'm sorry. Georgie's the one that knew the way. I messed up the directions. Hell!"

Rick tore his eyes away from the medal and shook his head. "No. I think you got them right. Maybe Georgie wasn't straight with you."

Bishop scowled. "What you getting at?"

"If he saw no way out, he might think of going over."

"No sir! That's a coward's way to hell!"

"Which is why he told you he was headed to the bottom of the falls, not planning on going over, like an Ojibway princess."

Bishop's hands clenched into mean fists. Rick flinched, preparing to block a blow.

Instead, Bishop closed his eyes. "You're right. Damn." He opened them. "So what do we do now?"

"I won't lie, Bishop. I could use a rest." He stole a glance at the lion: its eyes scrutinized him like a C.O. Rick dropped his guard in fear and wonder.

His jaw flared with pain as Bishop's hand smacked him.

Rick was a breath away from snapping, but Bishop's commanding voice held him in place.

"You will not go out like that," Bishop said. "Even if it is hopeless. Even if it kills you. You're a fighter, Rick. Fight to live."

Rick nodded, nerves burning.

"I want your word, Rick," Bishop said. "Say you'll fight to live."

Rick stared into Bishop's piercing eyes and saw the terrified look of a man who'd lost a son to despair. "Say it!"

The words came out breathless. "I'll fight to live."

Rick felt a hand on his shoulder as a lion roared in his mind.

The crack of a rifle shot killed all noise as the side of Bishop's head exploded across the woods, and the lock on the closet in Rick's mind shattered.

The lion emerged from the medal, its fur copper-red like old blood.

Rick ran for the cover of a tree as shots rang out. He looked back.

Bishop's dead body smothered Duggin, but surrounding them in the forest were his mates, the ones shattered by shell fire, those broken men whose limbs hung in the trees like a macabre Christmas ornament; the sound of grown men screaming for their mothers, or death, cascaded through the air. Then his black memory came alive like a moving picture before two healthy eyes.

A Kraut screams. They're spotted! Machine gun fire devours them. He runs blindly toward the gun nest. The bullets miss him as if he isn't even there. He charges into the hole, firing wild. Five Krauts. He shoots them all, quick and deadly. But one rises. Not dead enough. He guts him with his bayonet, but the Kraut won't die. The blade jams between ribs. He pulls the trigger—click—empty! The Kraut reaches for his face, but Rick is quicker. Now, just like they taught him, his thumbs press into the bastard's eyes, harder, harder. The Kraut gets a shot in, Rick's vision slices, but he grips so tight the skull shakes. They'd killed the platoon, turned friends into scraps of flesh and empty carcasses. He won't let go, he'll stop them, all of them, if that's what it takes. That's why he's here. The Kraut's arm drops. His hands are wet, red claws. Rick jumps into the trench roaring, killing everything with his own two hands. Starshells light up the world like the fires of hell. There's an explosion. He's in the air. He's failed. They're still more of them. The barbed wire closes in to claim him.

He sees the Germans: the sockets of the dead stare at him.

"Come out, freak show! Come out, you coon lover!"

The voice of his enemy snapped him back. He saw Bishop's prone form, and the rage consumed him.

"Jericho! You're a dead man walking, you son of a bitch!"

He ran toward the falls, shots on his heels, nerves eating the fear.

He crouched behind a tree, listening. They trampled though the woods like rhinos. Three men. He threw a rock high in the trees and heard the familiar click of an empty rifle.

He snapped out of the bushes, rifle primed on the three guards, scared lily white, rifles shaking in their hands.

"You'll never get out of here alive," Jericho said.

"Really?" He fired and watched the wet trail form on Jericho's trousers. "I'm a killer, kid. I can see it now. I tried to hide from it, but the dead won't let me forget, because the dead ain't scared of nothing.

"But I'm not going down without a fight. And I ain't gonna let the dead kill me either." The medal lay at Jericho's feet. Behind him the red lion feasted upon eyeless Krauts.

"I'll tell it plain. I'm going to kill you. All of you. For Bishop and his boy and everything you've done wrong."

"You're outnumbered three to one!" one of the guards yelped.

Rick snickered. "I beat worse odds fighting in hell."

"You're crazy!" Jericho said, rifle shaking in his hands.

Rick nodded. "But I'm free." He threw the rifle at the guards then sprinted like a rabid beast. They fired. Rick inhaled the aroma of gunpowder and fear. The lion's roar filled his ears and his sight went red.

It was a blur of blood and bone, savage grunts and desperate yelps, but they could not stop him. They fell like the others against his rage, the sounds of war screaming through his head echoed by a lion's roar.

Then Rick found himself holding Jericho's lifeless skull in his hands. Thumbs jammed hard in the sockets.

Alone with the dead, he made his choice.

*   *   *

Rick watched Bishop's body rush down the river to the falls and hoped the old man was with his son. Duggin was gone, but he couldn't hide. Rick's red hands picked through the human material and retrieved his medal.

The lion's face was dull. *Sleeping,* Rick figured. He held the medal tight as he marched upstream where the current was weak and the tracks were fresh. Across the water was Duggin, running like a scared deer into the woods. Rick dove in. The current pulled, but he fought it. He'd promised he would.

Jason S. Ridler *has dug graves, played bars, and sold his writing to earn his keep. His fiction runs through any genre with bite, including crime, horror, fantasy, SF, and mainstream tales. Now a doctoral student at the Royal Military College of Canada, this Ridler remains Kingston's most eligible bachelor.*

UNDER THE
STAR SPANGLED ROGER

James Powell

The large, famous Canadian eye behind the magnifying glass grew larger still. "Nine hundred and ninety-seven," counted the Prime Minister. "Nine hundred and ninety-eight. Nine hundred and ninety-nine." Looking as tired as the rose in his lapel, he set the aerial photographs of the upper reaches of the Saint Lawrence River down and stared out the window, where a steady cold rain was falling. The damned report had been correct. Yes, one of the Thousand Islands was missing.

Funny the way things come back to haunt you. A few years back at a world-heads-of-state banquet the Prime Minister had, for the umpteenth time, found himself sitting behind a damn pillar. Weary of craning his neck to catch the toasts at the head of the table, he'd mused on ways to get Canada more international clout. That's when he got the Disintegrator Ray idea. Invent one of those babies and watch the world sit up and take notice! Then the States would keep its damn acid rain at home. Then the damn Soviet fishing fleet would steer clear of Canadian waters.

Back in Ottawa, he'd handed the idea over to a minister without portfolio known to have a garage workshop with every power tool from the word go. The subsequent electrical blackouts in the man's neighbourhood encouraged the Prime Minister to believe the details of the Disintegrator Ray were being worked out.

But clearly, the Americans had gotten there first. And of course *they* weren't going to test the weapon out on their own territory. So kiss Canada's Ghost Island goodbye.

The Prime Minister expected to be asked some pesky questions in the House. After all, an island had disappeared. But what could he say? He had to stall. He needed more time, time to come up with an Anti-Disintegrator-Ray Ray or something.

While he brooded over this dilemma, the Prime Minister was massaging his right hand, which sometimes bothered him in wet weather. A certain Mountie had slammed a limousine door on it, the dumb clod. Suddenly a sly glint leaped to the famous eye. Yes, he thought. Yes, that way he could truthfully tell the House the Mounties had the matter of the vanished island under investigation. And suppose the Mountie investigator got disintegrated by the Americans? Well, he could live with that. Yes, indeedy.

As the Prime Minister reached for the phone, the grey day darkened. In that change of light, the portraits of his predecessors in office hanging on the walls in elaborate ormolu frames seemed to look down in disapproval as though, to a man, they found what he was about to do low and paltry.

*　　*　　*

At the foot of Stone Street in downtown Gananoque, Ontario ("Gateway to the Thousand Islands") stands an abandoned wharf with a skull-and-cross-bones warning that it is used at one's own risk. Below, on the same standard, a smaller sign with a smaller skull-and-cross-bones announces "Death's-Head Island Lodge Boat Service."

A large, stocky, red-faced man with trim mustache and suitcase strode out onto the wharf. He was dressed in his "mufti duds", as he scornfully called his civvies. For today he was not Acting Sergeant Maynard Bullock of the Royal Canadian Mounted Police. Today he was Bob Jones, a big butter-and-eggs man from Schenectady, New York. He felt his tie—a loud, stripy affair, Christmas present from that formidable in-law, Mother Fothergill—lent him a real American air. Not that he was far from his uniform. He'd dropped it off for a dry-cleaning at Gananoque Valet Service. After all, Commissioner McNaughton had assured him that if he solved the mystery of the disappearance of Ghost Island, he would surely become a legend in his own time. Which meant reporters. And the press didn't think it was getting its money's worth if you weren't wearing your uniform.

A launch with an awning heaved gently in the swell at the end of the wharf. But a tall, gaunt, long-jawed apparition from another age barred Bullock's way on board, an ancient pirate, whose pouting scar ran from below one eye to the black patch on the other. He wore earrings, had a wicked hook for a right hand, a wooden peg for a left leg and a basket-handled cutlass in his belt. Bullock dropped his suitcase. Before he could step back to get some fighting room, the man's hook found his lapel buttonhole and pulled him forward and up until he stood on tiptoe nose to nose with his captor.

Muttering dark curses, the pirate shoved a passenger roster in Bullock's face. "Be your mark there, or do I gut you like a pilchard?"

"Bob Jones, that be me," blurted Bullock, pointing out his name. The man's one terrible eye bulged and probed the

Mountie's face long and hard. Though Bullock's childhood adventure books had catalogued the many terrors of these freebooters of the sea, none had ever mentioned the horror of pirate breath.

Set free at last, Bullock reached for his suitcase. A cutlass slashed the air just above his knuckles.

"Belay that," growled the pirate. Then he shouted, "Mr. Moon, do a guest of Death's-Head Island Lodge hoist his own duffel?"

A bald sailor with a round, earless head and a crutch hobbled from the boat to grab up the suitcase. "No, sir, Captain Patch, he don't."

Bullock joined the other passenger in the stern and introduced himself. "Bob Jones. Butter and eggs."

"Cleveland Bagshot," the portly man in tweeds and horn rims replied. "I teach geology at S.I.T."

With Captain Patch's salty oaths roaring down on the ancient crew, the launch churned out into the channel. Motorboats darted in and out of the mouth of the Gananoque River. Out farther still, bright sailboats leaned in the wind. Soon the launch entered an armada of islands. Some held small villages, some a cottage or two. Others no more than a rock or a tree. Overhead, the blue sky with its many white clouds seemed a mirror of the river itself.

After a bit of rubbernecking, Bullock asked his travelling companion, "S.I.T?"

"Schenectady Institute of Technology," answered Bagshot. "Where do you hang your hat, Mr. Jones?"

Bullock winced inwardly. Blast! Well, too late to change his story. "Hey, small world. I'm from Schenectady, too."

Bagshot shifted uneasily in his seat. "Nice little town," he ventured.

"You can say that again." Bullock was relieved to see Bagshot nod. By godfrey, that was a close one.

From a small loudspeaker over their heads, a recorded voice said, "Ladies and gentlemen, welcome aboard the Pirate Queen. Allow me to sketch in a bit of the history which we of Death's-Head Island Lodge are dedicated to preserving. I ask you to cast your imaginations back to another time, when all you saw around you was a wilderness of islands thinly populated by civilization's outcasts, who sought only to be left alone. But one day, Canada and the United States tried to assert hegemony over the islands.

"The Thousand Islanders resisted and were declared outlaws. So outlaws they became, pitiless river pirates who raided St. Lawrence shipping and shore settlements. Soon they became a pirate fleet under an elected leader, more president than king. They dreamed of an archipelago republic, a corsair commonwealth that could tax ships instead of plundering them, their flag the Spangled Roger, the grinning skull-and-cross-bones of the pirate ensign studded with a silver star for each island in the republic.

"Under that flag they killed, died and—as many came to learn—avenged their dead. Until the middle of this century, for example, the city of Toronto kept Sunday as a day of municipal mourning, made joyless by law with mandatory hush and curfew to commemorate the bloody pirate raid of 1887.

"And a legend survives that Theodore Roosevelt was so mortified by leaving office without extirpating the river pirates that his ghost still stalks these islands, big stick and all.

"It should be no surprise that during the First World War the Thousand Islanders threw in their lot with the Central Powers, resupplying German submarines in the St. Lawrence, dreaming that with the Kaiser in the White House and

England a German colony, independence would be theirs.

"At the war's end, the victorious armies returned and destroyed the Thousand Islanders. Could cutlasses and cannon withstand machine guns and mustard gas?

"Death's-Head Island Lodge, a faithful reconstruction of the final pirate stronghold, attempts to capture those years when corsairs ruled these islands. It includes the Fresh Water Pirates' Hall of Fame and Scrimshaw City, the world's largest collection of etched bone and ivory art work suitable for family viewing. In addition, there is a nightly re-enactment of the pirates' burning of the Parliament Buildings in Ottawa in 1916, all brought to you by the magic of sound and light."

After a pause the voice began again, "Mesdames et Messieurs..."

Bullock was ignorant of his country's other official language but always listened attentively when it was used in announcements. However, today he was Bob Jones. So when Bagshot asked if he had any ideas on Ghost Island's disappearance, he turned and said, "Hey, you tell me. You're the geologist."

"Most geological thinking about islands centres on the jigsaw theory," explained Bagshot. "Imagine the continents are a giant jigsaw puzzle left unfinished by some higher being. Your islands are the pieces that haven't been fitted into place, your seas and lakes the places where they go."

"So a lake somewhere should have disappeared, too?"

"Beats me," replied Bagshot. He pulled a heavy, three-pronged hook from a paper bag. "I went ashore today to buy this. Maybe I'll know more after I give dragging the bottom a try."

Here the recorded voice switched back into English and said, "Ladies and gentlemen, let us stand for the national anthem of the republic that might have been. Thank you."

A solemn hornpipe began. Bullock might have found it unmountie-like to stand for a pirate anthem, but not Bob Jones. Nor did he bat an eye when Patch marched and muttered to the stern to replace the Canadian flag with the Spangled Roger. The grinning ensign crackled in the wind like a hellish bonfire.

Bullock saw their destination through the trees, a large, stucco, fort-like structure with crenelated walls and square corner towers. For the rest of the trip, he prepared himself for registering by consulting a small piece of paper in the palm of his hand. "Schenectady," he said under his breath. "S-c-h-e-n..."

*　　*　　*

The voice on the launch recording belonged to Elwell Blood, the lodge manager, a mild-mannered, fair-haired young man in striped pants and oxford jacket who showed Bullock to his room personally. "Scratch the sound-and-light show, I'm afraid, Mr. Jones," he said as they started upstairs. "Our mock-up of the Parliament Buildings was set up on Ghost Island, part of our property out behind us toward the American shore. Two weeks ago, island, sound and-light system and all vanished during the night. How, we don't know."

"Well, don't ask me," said Bullock innocently. "I'm just a dumb American tourist."

A shapely green-eyed blonde in a bikini was coming down the stairs. "Miss Pentikov, please meet our newest guest, Mr. Bob Jones," said Blood.

"Call me Marta, Bob," said the woman, giving Bullock an alluring smile and the slowest of winks.

As they continued on their way, Blood said, "She'll be glad

you're here. She and Mr. Bagshot haven't hit it off." Then he added, "Oh, say, I saw the look you gave Captain Patch when he dropped you off at the desk. No trouble, I hope?"

Bullock laughed. "Well, he did threaten to gut me like a pilchard. But I knew that was just for atmosphere."

"Oh, Granddad's gutted a few lubbers in his time," said Blood. "Bootleggers, mostly. During Prohibition. Then the big gangs moved in and scattered the Thousand Islanders to the winds. Granddad went to work for a Bay Street stockbroker in Toronto. Oh, he claimed to like the hack and slash of it. But I remember a sad old man stumping around on the back porch on a Saturday afternoon with a cheese sandwich spindled on his hook and a three-draw telescope up to his good eye staring off in this direction. This was where his heart was.

"The lodge was my dad's idea, a place where the old-timers could work and live out their final years. Before he died, he sent me to hotel school in Switzerland. Granddad and I and the others pooled our money, bought the place and restored it."

"Business seems slow," observed Bullock.

"Three lousy guests," agreed Blood. "But we're still a new concept in vacationing."

*   *   *

From his window, Bullock observed Marta Pentikov out on the river. She was lying on her stomach in a glass-bottomed rowboat peering down into the water through a porthole made with her hands. He changed quickly into his bathing suit, hid his service revolver under a pillow on the bed and came down stairs. On the dock behind the lodge, Patch was applying red paint to the beak of one of the stable of swan pedal-boats. "Be you have another glass-bottomed rowboat?" he asked.

Eying Bullock's midriff bulge, Patch twitched his hook and let the word "pilchard" escape from his muttering. He gestured riverward. "She be using the only one. Out there be where Ghost Island stood before it wasn't." He rolled his eye. "Be you thinking what I be thinking? Be you thinking she be an insurance investigator?"

"Ah, Ghost Island be insured then?"

"Aye, for big bucks," nodded Patch. "But harkee, if ye want a sail the swan, that there next to the end rides like a squid jigger's dory. I be keeping all my boats dry and in sound repair. Why think ye they call me 'Patch'?"

*   *   *

A Mountie would have refused the swan-boat with a scornful laugh. Not Bob Jones. "Just the ticket," he said, clambering aboard. "A little pedal will work up an appetite for dinner." As Bullock pumped away from shore, he heard Patch call out something like "Watch out for Teddy!" Bullock smiled. Roosevelt's ghost must be a doozy to show itself in broad daylight.

Bullock gave the glass-bottomed rowboat a wide berth. He'd float back down for a look-see later after the woman had moved on. He pedalled briskly up river with the wind at his back.

Yes, insurance might just explain everything. He saw himself wrapping up the case and getting back to Ottawa to start on being a legend in his own time. From an island patio on his right, an elderly couple raised their gin and tonics in a friendly salute. Hail the conquering hero. Bullock returned the wave solemnly.

He was pedalling southwestward between two small islands when a glimpse of stately movement made him look back over his shoulder. Above the trees glided the tall afterdecks of an ocean-going bulk cargo ship out in the river channel. It flew the flag of a country unimagined in Bullock's schoolboy geography book. Youthful dreams of a sailor's life came rushing back and stayed with him until the ship slid out of sight.

When Bullock turned face front again, the smile of pleasant recollection still on his lips, he saw disaster rushing up at him. The swan-boat glided full tilt for the gaping doorway of a tumbledown boathouse on an island sprung from nowhere. Abruptly, Bullock was engulfed in darkness.

The pedal-boat thumped to a halt against a landing platform, sending him sprawling out onto the swan's neck. Overhead came a short cry as though someone had been surprised from sleep. An ominous silence followed, one with a cocked ear in it.

Holding his breath, Bullock discovered some rickety steps and tiptoed up to a half-opened door. In a shadowy corner of the room he made out the figure of a large-headed man with a slender body and fat feet. Bullock knocked and stepped inside. "Sorry to crash in," he said with a joke in his voice. Silence. Stepping further into the room, Bullock saw he'd been speaking to an underwater diver's outfit, port-holed steel helmet, rubber suit and weighted boots, hanging down from a rafter.

Something hard jabbed into Bullock's back. A hoarse, wavering voice said, "Turn around easy so I can see what I've got."

When Bullock obeyed, he found a withered old man with a cruel mouth. The codger wore a dark, double-breasted pinstriped suit and a mauve shirt grown too big for his neck. But the machine-gun fit his bony grip perfectly. It was one of those old drum magazine models the Mounties called "cribbage board makers." The man studied Bullock with calm, cold eyes. "I don't like killing strangers. So just who the hell are you?"

"Bob Jones from Schenectady," said Bullock automatically.

The cold eyes grew in amazement, then misted over. With a heartfelt sob, the man collapsed into a nearby chair, the machine gun across his knees and face buried in his liver-spotted hands. When he looked up again, his voice was wet and windy. "Oh, I heard a lot of hooey about the Albany mob moving in and wiping out the Schenectady gang. But I knew you guys would come back some day." He wiped his eyes in the crook of his arm and shook his head. "But, oh boy, sometimes it sure got lonely." He blinked and smiled. "Say, you must be Vito-the-Scumbag Jones's boy."

"You got it," said Bullock. The lie was better than being turned into a cribbage board.

"I bet the Scumbag told you about old Mad Dog Manny Pincus, right? Him and me used to hunt pirates together. For the ears. Yes, sir, back then the Canadian G-men paid a bounty on the ears." He laughed at the memory.

Bullock remembered an old Mountie telling a story around the campfire once, about how he'd worked the door at one of those secret big-wig, powwows to initiate a new Governor General, where the P.M. and all the M.P.s and their ladies came dressed as Indian braves and princesses. The old timer had snuck a peek inside and swore the regalia of the King's representative had included a necklace of tanned human ears with gold earrings in them. Bullock thought of poor, ear-less Mr. Moon.

"Ghost Island, what a sweet set-up," said Mad Dog with a sad shake of the head. "But I don't have to tell you guys that."

"Right," lied Bullock. "So what happened?"

"Don't look at me," shrugged the old man. "I mean, I

moved out and came over here two years ago when the pirates started fixing up the lodge and sniffing around." He gestured at the diving gear. "Oh, I still kept the pipeline in good working order, though it means hiring a local to work the air supply. But I don't have to tell you about the pipeline, right?

"Anyway, you know the drill. Whenever I needed money, I turned on the spigot stateside and sold prime bootleg Canadian rye, mostly to the soldier boys at Camp Tweed." Here Mad Dog jumped up to peer out a shuttered window. "You hear something? That Patch character's swore to pay me and your daddy back for all them ears."

"You were talking about Camp Tweed."

"Right," said Mad Dog, leaving the window. "Well, I must be getting old. Somehow, one night the top sergeant who was my inside man at Tweed managed to follow me back to the spigot. He sucker-punched me. When I came to, the spigot was open with nothing coming out. A big rain and windstorm was moving in. In the lightning I saw a caravan of army tank trucks rolling off down the road. Next morning when I rowed out here, Ghost Island was gone."

Gone where? Bullock decided there was only one way to find out. "I'll be back for you after nightfall," he told Mad Dog. "I'm diving down to poke around." To give the mobster a taste of his own medicine, he added, "I don't have to tell you why, right?"

"There's a lot of the Scumbag in you, kid," said Mad Dog with an old grin.

When Bullock took his place in the swan-boat, the mobster gave him a healthy push off. Waving his weapon, Mad Dog announced, "I'm going to run right out and get me a pirate for old time's sake." Then, as Bullock passed out through the boathouse door, the old man shouted, "Be careful of Teddy!"

Bullock now felt obliged to pedal around the island to lend a covert hand to Patch or whoever it had been, lurching outside the boat-house. He couldn't do much more without blowing his cover. Five minutes later, he rounded the top of the island and started down the other side, moving faster now with the current behind him. He struggled to keep close to the high cliffs of the shore, alert for any sign of Mad Dog's quarry.

The current was flowing faster now. Suddenly the swan-boat shot around an arm of the island, and there it was! Bullock back-pedalled frantically. Those warnings, they hadn't been about a presidential ghost. It wasn't Teddy. It was *the eddy*, a whirling vortex of mad water spanning the forty feet between the island and its nearest neighbour. The swan boat was caught up in it like a fly in a moving web. With maximum effort, Bullock kept to the outer edge. But when his strength finally failed him, he would be drawn into the evil-looking dimple at the eddy's damnable centre.

Just then, he spied Mad Dog on the cliff above him. The old man stood there swaying, hands to his throat. Now the hands dropped to reveal raw flesh torn open as if by a hook. The mobster tried to speak to the sky, but blood came instead of words. Then he pitched into the swirling water. His body circled quickly to the center of the vortex, spun there several times like a propeller and vanished down the dimple with a sucking noise.

Astonishment made Bullock's pedalling falter. The swan-boat sagged down the whirlpool slope. Surely a swan-boat wouldn't get sucked under. Surely it would just spin around and around on the dimple, spin until his blood thickened like the milk in a milk shake, cutting off the supply of oxygen to his brain. This terrible fate squeezed every drop of effort from Bullock's aching body. He pedalled with legs of lead and kneecaps that were balls of fire. But the deadly dimple loomed closer.

Suddenly, a grappling hook and line whizzed past his head. He grabbed the line and made a hitch around the swan's neck. Downriver and beyond the eddy's fatal grasp rode Cleveland Bagshot in another swan-boat. The geologist started pedalling. The rope went taut, and soon Bullock was bobbing free in the water alongside him.

"Thought my number was up," said Bullock with breathless gratitude.

"Schenectady guys have to stick together," said Bagshot.

Handing back the grappling hook, it occurred to Bullock how easily it might tear out a human throat.

As they travelled together back to the lodge, Bullock's eye was drawn to the spot where Ghost Island had been, just as the socket of a pulled tooth attracts the tongue. Bagshot saw him looking and wondered, "Wasn't it Einstein who said, 'We can think objects away, but not the space they occupy'?"

Bullock sidestepped the trap skillfully. If he was too smart, they might suspect he was a Mountie. "What would a dumb cluck like me know about Einstein?"

Bagshot gave him a hard look. "I had my reasons for saving your life, Mr. Jones. I'm curious as hell about what happened to that island. I know where I can put my hands on some diving gear. But I need someone up top to handle the air-pump."

"I sure owe you one," said Bullock. But what he really wanted was a way to get down there under the water himself.

Death's-Head Island loomed ahead. The shapely Marta Pentikov was stepping up out of the glass-bottomed rowboat. Patch watched her without pausing in his task of cleaning something from his hook. Was it dried paint? As the swan-boats approached, Marta turned and winked in Bullock's direction.

He stroked his jaw. The woman was mystery. When he and Bagshot started up the walk to the lodge, it did not surprise Bullock at all that her wet footprints on the pavement looked like question marks.

*   *   *

Bullock changed and came back down into the lobby. Well, at least his Bob Jones cover was working like a charm. Old Otto Duffy, the dramatics coach at the Mountie Academy, once swore Bullock would never get beyond the little teapot, short and stout. Bullock wished the old guy could see him now. Then he turned into the Bucket of Grog cocktail lounge. Bob Jones was the kind who'd have a drink before dinner.

Elwell Blood was behind the bar, dressed in a short white jacket. "What's your pleasure, Mr. Jones?"

"Bob Jones will have a strawberry daiquiri," said Bullock, pulling the name of the drink from somewhere.

"Enjoy your boat trip?" asked the young man.

Deciding Bob Jones was something of a liar and a braggart, Bullock said, "Had to rescue some poor sap who'd got himself caught in the eddy. Say, I heard Ghost Island was insured. I guess the money'll come in handy, business as bad as it is."

Blood gave a sad smile as he put the drink ingredients in the mixer. "It isn't. I just told our people to keep their spirits up. But not to worry. A morticians' convention's booked in for next month, three hundred strong. That should see us through." He delivered Bullock's frothy pink drink. "We'll worry about next year when it gets here."

As Bullock downed his drink, Marta Pentikov arrived dressed for dinner. "Room for me?" she asked in a soft, warm voice.

"The more the merrier." Bullock faked a leer. Bob Jones, he

had decided, drinker of sissy drinks, was also a womanizer. "Barkeep, a drink for the little lady, and hit me again."

Marta laid a soft warm hand on Bullock's wrist and said earnestly, "Bob, I know Schenectady men are real stand-up guys."

Bullock's eyes narrowed. "Who says I'm from Schenectady?"

"I grew up there, and I'd recognize that Schenectady Yacht Club tie anywhere."

By godfrey, does everybody come from Schenectady?

"Bob Jones, do you love your country?"

"I sure do," said Bullock. Little did she know.

"I thought so. We of the Central Intelligence Agency learn to spot things like that." She gave him a soft, warm look. "Bob Jones, your country needs your help." She let Blood set down the drinks and return to the other end of the bar before continuing. "Canada's been working on a Disintegrator Ray in a secret Ottawa installation disguised as a two-car garage. Ghost Island's disappearance must mean they're at the testing stage. My job's to find out for sure. It could cause a drastic change in the world pecking order. Now I can get hold of diving gear. But..."

"If you need somebody to handle the air supply, you'll have to stand in line. Bagshot got to me first."

"But that creep's a Russian spy."

"He saved my life," said Bullock. "I owe him one."

"You certainly do," said Bagshot, coming up behind them on crepe soles. "Mr. Blood, another round, if you please."

Marta stiffened. "Butt out, gulag face. Bob," she insisted, "your country comes first."

"Why don't you team up on the diving job?" Bullock suggested.

"I'm not diving and putting my life in the lovely hands of

this running dog of the capitalists," insisted Bagshot.

"That goes ditto for me in spades," said Marta.

Bullock became a study in innocence. "Hey, what say I do the diving and report back my findings while you two keep an eye on each other topside in the boat?"

By godfrey, if they bought it, he was back in the running for legend in his own time. His only problem was a growing suspicion that Bob Jones couldn't hold his liquor.

*   *   *

Under the water, it was darker than the night above. The weighted boots slid from the last rung of the wire ladder to the river bottom. Oxygen hissed in Bullock's ears. Marta's voice crackled over the intercom. "Can you hear me, Bob?"

"Loud and clear." Bullock switched on the torch tied to his wrist. Moving forward with a dreamy underwater gait, he shone the torch left and right and sent the fishes flashing through the stands of seaweed like startled birds.

In no time, he came upon a large weed-free oblong on the river floor. He calculated it measured about a hundred and fifty feet long and seventy feet across. The long edges were trenches five feet deep and five feet across. Except for the helmet, Bullock would have scratched his head in wonderment.

"Found anything, Bob?" demanded Marta.

"Nothing yet," lied Bullock. Canada must be the first to know what happened to Ghost Island. But what had? Time for a bit of a think.

Bullock found a comfortable rock, sat down and crossed one leg over the other. It was almost as though the island had been unplugged from the river bottom. And equally puzzling was the identity of Mad Dog Manny Pincus's murderer. Patch out for revenge? Or Bagshot or Marta to get the diving gear? Or none of the above? He had too few clues and too many question marks.

But maybe question marks were the answer!

"Come on, Bob," demanded Bagshot over the intercom. "What gives down there?"

"Nothing," insisted Bullock.

Bagshot forgot to turn off the intercom, and Bullock heard him repeat "nothing" in a thoughtful voice. Then the Russian cursed in triumph. "Pentikov, what's left when you disintegrate something?"

"Nothing?" replied Marta.

"Right! And what's the big jerk telling us he found? Nothing! Canada's got a Disintegrator Ray!" Bagshot's next words had a sinister cast. "And my people will be the first to know."

"A gun, Bagshot? That's not nice. We said we'd come unarmed. Not that I go any place without my Schenectady toothpick."

"Ugly thing, that bill-hooked blade," said Bagshot. "If you get to use it."

Bullock heard a metal click, Bagshot's curse, another click, a moan of pain, a loud splash and a woman's soft warm laugh of triumph.

Bullock stood up and came to attention as he always did when about to perform an official act. "Acting Sergeant Maynard Bullock of the Royal Canadian Mounted Police speaking. Miss Marta Pentikov, you are under arrest for murder."

"That was self-defense," she insisted.

"No, I arrest you for the murder of Mr. Mad Dog Manny Pincus," Bullock corrected her. "You slipped overboard from the glass-bottomed rowboat, swam to the island and killed him."

"Prove it."

"If you insist," said Bullock, pacing up and down on the river bottom as if beside a jury box. "Captain Patch keeps his boats tight and dry. But when you walked back to the lodge, you left wet footprints behind you."

There was silence where the hiss of the oxygen had been. Good godfrey. Bullock cleared his throat nervously and urged, "Come along quietly, Miss Pentikov. It'll go easier on you."

"Save your breath, Maynard," said Marta.

The intercom went dead. Bullock's first plan was to take off the weighted boots, bob to the surface like a cork and take the knife away from her. But he couldn't unlace the boots with his gloves on. And to take off the gloves, he'd have to open the little window in his helmet and use his teeth on the leather straps.

The air was too thin for fancy plans. Bullock decided to hoof it for shore, any shore. But with his first step he tripped over the bootleggers' pipeline. He fell magnificently, as a mighty underwater oak might fall. He was gasping for breath and too weak to move. Was this the way it would all end? Bullock imagined good old Mavis, his wife, coming each year in widow's weeds to throw a nice bouquet into the river on this spot.

Suddenly a rasping voice said, "Be you there, Bob Jones? Be you can hear me?"

*   *   *

The oxygen hissing cheerfully again, Bullock broke surface into a night bright with torches. Patch and Elwell Blood waited in the skiff surrounded by swan-boats filled with the Death's-Head Island Lodge staff. Torchlight made all eyes wild and weapons formidable.

"Where's Miss Pentikov?" demanded Bullock as they helped him out of his diving gear.

"When I be boarding the skiff, she came at me like a spitfire with a mean-looking knife," said Patch. "I be'd obliged to gut her like a pilchard."

Blood nodded in confirmation. The lodge manager now wore an earring in every ear and a broad leather belt across the shoulder of his oxford jacket down to the scabbard and cutlass at his waist. "Mr. Jones," he explained, "the morticians' convention people called tonight to cancel. They're having a camp-out at Arlington National Cemetery instead. Of course, that means the end of all we worked for. Well, Granddad always went along with me. And I promised if the lodge failed, I'd follow him and the rest down the pirate trail."

"Tonight we be going to capture the Western tax ship. Be damned if we ain't," declared Patch, bringing much "aying" and weapon-waving from the swan-boats.

Each month, the income taxes withheld from Western Canadian paychecks came eastward to Ottawa in armored ships. The heavy Mountie guard below decks had a well-stocked larder and could outlast the longest siege. Bullock knew the Western tax ship's Sergeant Midlothian, a fine amateur pastry chef whose butter tarts turned coffee breaks and late night snacks into gourmet revels.

"That be why we saved your hide, Bob Jones," said Patch. "Sign on, and it's share and share alike. Otherwise..." He gutted the air.

"I'm with you," said Bullock quickly, figuring to play along for a bit.

"Harkee then, Bob," growled Patch. "One of our mates be working ashore for Gananoque Valet Service. Show him what you stole today, Long John." An old runt of a sailor grinned and passed over Bullock's own uniform in plastic on a clothes hanger. "Mr. Moon be'd the right size," said Patch, "but the hat kept slipping down over his eyes. I judge it'll fit you neat. Your job be to get us inside the tax ship."

"Only if you fill me in on what happened to Ghost Island," insisted Bullock.

"Try submarine pens, for starters," said Blood. "Some Milwaukee Germans shipped the sections up just before the States entered World War I. Our people floated them out here by night and sank them. Then they laid a pipeline to bring diesel fuel from the New York side. The German U-boats used Ghost Island until the Armistice. And it was our people's final hideout until the gangsters drove them off the islands. But as to where's Ghost Island now, search us."

Bullock listened as he dressed. From what he'd learned from Mad Dog, he reckoned the Schenectady gang had stored their illegal whiskey in the fuel storage tanks. When the army boys drained off the last of it, Ghost Island had simply broken loose in rough weather and drifted away. Bullock hitched up his belt and was pleased to find his service revolver in its holster.

"Mr. Moon brought it," said Blood. "Part of his job at the lodge was shining guests' shoes and cleaning any weapons he found under the bed pillows."

Bullock stood up, waved his revolver and announced, "I'm Acting Sergeant Maynard Bullock, and you're all under arrest for conspiracy to commit grand larceny."

The pirates whooped with delight. No knee went unslapped or rib cage unelbowed. Mr. Moon roared so hard he tumbled overboard and had to be fished out. Bullock tried firing into the air to sober things up. The pistol clicked. Puzzled, he looked down the barrel and tried again. Another click.

"Sleeping with a loaded pistol can be dangerous, Bob,"

Blood informed him. "So Mr. Moon always removes the bullets and leaves them at the front desk."

"'Maynard Bullock'—that's rich," wheezed Patch as he started up the outboard. "Bob Jones, I like your style. Welcome aboard. Gibbet Island, here we come!"

*   *   *

Gibbet Island took its name from a giant elm on the shipping channel shore once used for Thousand Islander justice. In this very same tree, Bullock and the pirates took their places with boarding lines tied to a high limb extending out over the water.

The pirates dangled their feet and drank rum straight from bottles. Blood had brought Bullock a thermos of daiquiris made from the last of the lodge strawberries. The Mountie sipped his drink, determined to deliver the pirates into the arms of Sergeant Midlothian's men by some clever ruse.

Patch wiped his mouth on his sleeve. "Hurrah for pirating, Bob Jones," he cried. "Go to bed as late as you please. Leave the vegetables on your plate. See how long you can go without a bath. Aye, once you've tasted cutlass steel between your teeth, you'll never walk easy ashore again."

Bullock poured another drink and thought on that. Merciless Maynard, the Mountie Pirate King, hat brim turned up at three corners, leads an iceboat attack on Ottawa up the frozen Rideau Canal. There he is, cutlass in each hand, reeking of strawberry daiquiris, kicking down RCMP Commissioner McNaughton's door, making the man's jaw drop and the stuffed buffalo head on the wall blink. Then he'd settle the score for promotions passed over, for the dirty ends of the assignment stick, for good old Mavis his wife having to work part-time checkout at Loblaw's supermarket. And when he was done, he'd gut McNaughton like a pilchard.

So savage a daydream startled him. Was this secret burden of resentment really his? Could a Mountie heart have its dark corners too? Bullock put the cap back on the thermos.

The pirates stirred. A ship's running lights approached. "Get ready," growled Patch. Teeth bit down on cutlasses. "Get set." Grips tightened on ropes. "Aw, wait," said Patch when he saw it was only a cattle boat.

But the ten farthest men thought he said "Away!" and off they swung, led by Elwell Blood. They landed on the *Kenya Voyager*'s deck near fifty tall Masai herdsmen dressed in lion skins and leaning on their spears around an oil-drum fire. "Show no quarter, men!" cried Blood halfheartedly. The ship vanished behind some trees before the screams began.

"He be'd a good lad, Elwell. But dainty for a pirate," said Patch and bowed his head in mourning.

"Captain Patch, sir," whispered Mr. Moon at last, announcing the approach of another ship. No mistake this time. She rode low in the water from the weight of her precious cargo.

Patch gauged the vessel's progress carefully. "Now!" he shouted, urging Bullock out into space with the flat of his cutlass. The little party swung down and skimmed the water before heading back upwards to the deck of the ship.

They gathered in a sinister little knot. Pushing Bullock ahead of them, they reached the only way into the tax ship, a small door to the bridge. Bullock hesitated. He still hadn't come up with his clever ruse. But Patch reached past him and pounded on the door.

The captain's scowling, squinting face peered out at Bullock through the bullet proof window. "Who the hell are you, and where did you come from?" the man demanded.

Bullock hesitated again. Patch shouted, "Open up. He be Acting Sergeant Maynard Bullock of the Royal Canadian Mounted Police."

Before these words could work their magic, Bullock shouted, "Don't believe him. I'm only Bob Jones, a big butter-and-egg man from Schenectady, New York."

A smile overwhelmed the face behind the glass. "My own dear mother came from Schenectady." the captain said, unbolting the door.

Patch pushed Bullock through the door. In half a minute, the bridge was in pirate hands. Patch ignored the steel door leading below deck, a door that could only be opened from the other side. Instead, he unfolded a chart and ordered the captain to sail to their secret destination deep in the archipelago, where they would starve out the Mountie guard.

Then Patch limped over with a cutlass in each hand and threw one down at Bullock's feet. "Schenectady, eh, Bob Jones?" he growled. "Aye, I spied a familiar cut to your jib. So you be Vito-the-Scumbag's spawn. I swore to settle with him or any of his blood who crossed my bow." He stepped back and raised his weapon.

Bullock shook his head. "A Mountie doesn't fight the physically handicapped."

"Then die where ye stand!" roared Patch and lunged.

The cutlass thrust made Bullock reconsider. He decided the Mountie code might after all allow him to defend himself, provided he covered his left eye and hopped on his right foot.

Bullock hopped over and snatched up his weapon. A slash pared felt from the brim of his hat. Patch caught the Mountie's roundhouse swing on his blade. They came to close quarters, hilt to hilt. Pirate breath made Bullock's eyes water. Suddenly Patch used his hook to pull Bullock's hat down over his eyes and planted the metal ferrule of his peg leg down hard on the man's foot. Bellowing with pain, the Mountie grabbed up the injured foot and hopped around on the other.

The pirates cheered as if the peg leg blow was an old favorite. Patch mugged and rolled his good eye at the grandstand. Through his pain, Bullock decided it was do or die and hopped aggressively toward his antagonist. But Patch had only to raise a threatening peg leg to stop him dead in his tracks.

As Bullock swallowed indecisively, the Schenectady cuckoo clock on the bridge, a gift from the captain's mother, announced the hour. Simultaneously, the metal door down to the bowels of the ship flew open, and a smiling Sergeant Midlothian appeared with a large tray of hot cocoa and butter tarts. "Hello, Bullock," he remarked. "What're you doing here?"

The swinging door struck Patch squarely in the back, driving him off balance and onto the point of Bullock's cutlass. The old man's curses ended in mid mutter. The weapon dropped from his fingers. His only knee touched the deck, and giving Bullock a one-eyed glance, he pitched forward on his face.

Patch's death so demoralized Mr. Moon and the other pirates they surrendered, a bereft crew that not even cocoa and butter tarts could comfort completely.

Bullock felt something of their pain. For Patch's final glance had said volumes. "I be dying, Maynard Bullock," it had declared. "Yet I be content a Mountie brought me down, a man who took the high road while others of us chose the low." And it said, "So furl the Spangled Roger forever and play the last slow hornpipe. Farewell to the last of the unfettered buccaneers who never gave up a seat on the streetcar to nobody unless he pleased." Then it said, "No, don't mourn for old Patch. He died with his boot on. Just march straight and tall, a legend in your own time, the Mountie who solved the mystery of Ghost Island."

So spoke Patch's final glance. And Bullock was visibly moved. At least, he was seen to refuse a third butter tart.

*   *   *

The very next morning, the *Pavel Chichikov*, a factory ship serving the Russian fishing fleet off the coast of Newfoundland, vanished without a trace. A dying sailor found clinging to a folding chair claimed they struck an uncharted island and claimed to have witnessed a rare night mirage, a fiery pirate attack on the Parliament Buildings in Ottawa. Moscow and Washington dismissed this last bit as the ravings of a dying man. But clearly the Canadian Disintegrator Ray was far enough along that it could destroy a target at sea. So the Russian fishing fleet withdrew to international waters, and the United States put the acid rain problem on a front burner and abolished the tariff on Canadian cheddar cheese.

Back in Ottawa, Commissioner McNaughton and the others explained to Bullock why geopolitical considerations demanded that the true story of the disappearance of Ghost Island never be told. He was not to become a legend in his own time after all.

Bullock returned to guarding the flowerbeds on Parliament Hill. Yet sometimes, during that magic hour right after lunch when Mountie daydreams come, he would become Maynard the Merciless again, prowling the halls of officialdom, all cutlass, reek and snarl, and kicking in whatever door he damn well pleased.

James Powell's *first short story appeared in* Ellery Queen *in 1967. Since then, his body of work has been acknowledged by the Crime Writers of Canada with their Derrick Murdoch Award. We are honoured to reprint a story featuring his well known character, Acting Sergeant Maynard Bullock, of the RCMP. Mr. Powell will receive the 2006 Grant Allen Award from the Scene of the Crime Festival.*

High Seas

Vicki Cameron

They say the war is over.

I don't think it is, just because Hitler is beaten.

I think there's war still smouldering under a soft surface. Like the skin on my stomach, stretched smoothly over a roiling mass of child. Like my *bon voyage* to a new home, to be reunited with a husband I hardly know, and all my friends and relatives left behind on the dock, waving cheery white hankies while my mum wrings her hands. Like the water in the English Channel, frilly and blue on the surface, ready to lurch up at any moment and wrench a girl's stomach inside out. Uniformly choppy waves hiding all manner of death and destruction below. We are probably steaming above a torpedoed troop ship right now, full of skeletons and lost hopes.

"Feeling a little better today, are we?" The steward tucked the ship's-issue grey travelling rug under my feet. "Like I told you, sit in the fresh air and don't look at the waves, stare in the distance. You'll be right as rain once we're clear of the Channel. By tea time, you'll be fit for the dining room. Mark my words." He smiled and went on his way, weaving through the deck chairs, delivering hope to the legions of seasick passengers clustered amidships, according to his instructions, staring at the horizon, waiting for the angry English Channel to give way to the reputedly placid North Atlantic.

I cuddled into the cushions. The steward said twenty-four hours, and the vomiting would all be behind me. He said don't go to the dining room until you are certain you can stay there. Mum said don't go running across the ocean for a man unless you are certain you can stay there.

I don't think this war is over.

*　　*　　*

The dining room overwhelmed me with its vastness. White tablecloths, white walls, white-jacketed waiters bearing immense silver trays piled high with all manner of foods I hadn't seen for the six war years. Young women laughed and talked at every table. There was scarcely a man in sight, and only a few couples.

A waiter asked me my last name and directed me to my assigned seat at the table for surname F. Only one other person sat at my table, a tall slender girl with a bobbed hairstyle, a pink cardigan and a print cotton frock with a plunging lace-trimmed neckline.

"Hello, I'm Shirley Foster," she said. Her voice was crisp, like a person accustomed to being obeyed. Not like me and the other girls working in the munitions factory, doing as we were told and no questions asked. "They said I should sit here. I haven't eaten yet. I've been sick."

"So have I." I tucked a stray strand of hair into a hairpin and thought how much easier it would have been to be sick with short hair. "This is my first meal since we sailed."

A small oval silver locket hiding in the lace of her neckline swung into view when she pushed up the wire frame of her glasses and inspected me. "What's your name?"

"Phyllis." I found my hand straying to the high neckline of my navy wool frock to fend off her scrutiny.

The waiter placed a plate of roast beef and mashed potatoes in front of each of us. The gravy trickled down the white mound, made a delta through the peas, and curled to a stop at the lip of the white plate. I felt like running back to my cramped cabin.

"Oh look, Lucy, our tablemates have arrived." A plump dark-haired girl in a full-skirted maroon wool frock bustled to our table in a cloud of flowery cologne, trailing a wan red-headed child in a green plaid pinafore. The child regarded us with huge sad green eyes, then turned her attention to her black oxfords.

"I'm Alice Foster, lovely to see you've finally arrived to share our table, this is my daughter Lucy," the newcomer babbled as she arranged her daughter in a chair and flounced into her own seat. "Been seasick, have you? I've been just fine. Nary a shaky moment. One of my ancestors must have been a seafarer, I took to the water so well. Our Lucy has been a good little soldier, just like her dad. Neat as a button and twice as pretty, aren't you, Lucy?"

The little girl just blinked and stared across the table at me with those heartbreaking eyes.

"We're off to Canada," Alice said. "My William said we were to come right smartly when the war finished. Mind you, my family wasn't too keen on me running halfway around the world after some Canadian soldier, but I said he's my husband, and Lucy's father, and it's going to be just fine. My mum said she'd never see her grandchildren again, but I said, William says Canada is full of prosperity, we'll be able to nip back and forth any time we want."

I tried to imagine volunteering to take this voyage a second time as the ship dipped and swayed. Right or wrong, I'd made my decision, and I'd never see my mum again. I glanced at Shirley and wondered what I would find when we arrived.

"So, are you off to meet your soldier husbands, too?" Alice didn't pause to hear our answers. "There were ever so many weddings in our town when the Canadians came to stay. They were stationed for six weeks, and ours was the first wedding. We didn't have much, a bit of sponge cake from the neighbour who hadn't used up her sugar ration, and a few folk gathered in the front room. The chaplain from William's regiment officiated, Chaplain Alf Schouten, a nice young man he was, good friend of my William. Always together. William had a weekend pass, so we nipped down to Wales for a little romance. And here's Lucy come of it." Alice waved her hands around as she talked, sending billows of cologne across my plate. "My William was shipped out to the front the following week. I've not seen him since, and Lucy going on four, but he writes the most wonderful letters. *My dearest darling Alice,* he starts, *I miss you like fresh flowers miss water.* Or, *I miss you like the night sky misses the sun.* He has such a way with words, my William." She patted a silver locket dangling around her neck. "Here's our dinner, then, and it's roast beef. Eat up, little Lucy."

I wanted to cry, but I hadn't the energy. Alice tucked in with gusto. Shirley jabbed at the peas. I tried the mashed potatoes. They slid down my throat like medicine. Lucy poked at her plate with her fork.

"So, who are your fellows? What's your name?"

"I'm Shirley Foster." Shirley's eyes bored through Alice like the quality inspector examining the day's work.

"Didn't I just know they'd seated us alphabetically? Didn't I say that, Lucy? I did. Did you meet a Canadian, too? Or are you running off to meet one of those Yanks?"

"Bill is Canadian," Shirley said. "I met him in the hospital. He'd been injured by shrapnel and spent a couple of weeks in my care. The chaplain married us the day he was discharged. He was shipped home the following week. I'm determined to join him in Canada." She glared at Alice. "Determined."

A vision of a convalescent ward wandered through my mind, a row of cots, a handsome wounded soldier wheedling his way into the heart of a steely-eyed nursing sister in white starch.

"And how about you?" Alice asked between mouthfuls.

"I'm Phyllis. Phyllis…Foyers. I met my…John…on holiday at Blackpool." What more could I say? The silence at the table suggested I needed to continue. "There was a group of soldiers at the train station, just in from somewhere, on a three-day pass."

We'd barely left the platform before he was chatting me up. Reflecting on it, I could see how gullible I'd been to his charm. My friend Evelyn from the factory who went with me said I shouldn't take him seriously, just have a bit of fun.

Alice leaned forward and nodded. "And?"

"We got married the next day. It was the war, and everyone rushing to grasp a little bit of happiness. My mum was furious." At least he married me. Evelyn was not so lucky. She's confined at home, with her mum going on about having a fallen woman in the house.

Alice rapped the tablecloth as if mine was the correct answer to a mystery question. "Didn't I say the same thing to my mum, once it was evident Lucy was on the way? Rushing for some happiness. Four long years, and our waiting is over, isn't it, Lucy-love? We're on our way to meet William. I hope he got our letter telling him when we'll be landing. We didn't receive his answer, but I know he was sent home. He'll just have to get himself to Halifax Harbour to fetch us." She unclasped her locket and flipped it open. "Here's my William. This is my wedding present from him." She passed the locket to me.

I fingered the polished silver oval while I gazed at the tiny likeness of a cheerful young man. Even though it was a black and white photo, I could tell he had red hair. I passed the locket to Shirley. My stomach clenched and unclenched. The aroma of hot potatoes drifted up from my plate and cloyed at the back of my throat.

Shirley clutched the open locket with such ferocity, I thought she might break the hinge. She bit her lower lip and gazed at little Lucy as she passed Alice's locket back. I watched the gravy trickle and pool on my plate.

"Not quite up to eating the full meal?" Alice asked. "Never you mind. We'll soon have you right. Waiter? Waiter! Yes, hello, bring this lady some toast, will you please? She's a little off her stride."

A hand whisked the plate of roast beef away from my place, and moments later returned with a plate of toast, butter and strawberry jam. I would have been grateful to Alice if I could have found a scrap of human decency inside me.

Instead, I spread a little butter and jam on the corner of the toast, while Lucy watched me with jealous eyes.

*   *   *

The morning seas were calmer, but I remained amidships, selecting a deck chair with a good view of a lifeboat, so I wasn't tempted to watch the sea sparkle and pitch. The brisk breeze worked its way through the threads of the travelling rug and spread salty dampness on my skin. The deck was silent with an undercurrent of sighing wind through the steel. I felt as lost as a wedding ring dropped in the sea.

"Oh, there you are!" Alice's voice sliced though my troubled thoughts, and her cologne wrapped me in a warm stink. "We knew we'd find you here, with the other seasick people. Are you feeling better today? I thought you might be. I said to Shirley, I fancy a little activity, a game of something on the foredeck. I said, we'll find Phyllis, she won't want to run and jump, and Lucy can sit with her. Can't you, Lucy?" She thrust Lucy at me with one hand and dropped two storybooks on my lap with the other. Lucy flopped onto the chair beside me and cuddled under my arm. Alice scurried away along the deck.

"Hello, Lucy," I said, reminding myself that none of this was her fault. "Shall I read about Mrs. Tiggy-winkle?"

"Yes, please." Her voice was thin, like the rest of her, and I wondered if she'd felt the effects of the sea.

"Your mummy says you weren't seasick."

She shook her head.

"But you don't feel very well, do you?"

She shook her head again.

"It's funny, isn't it, how something ordinary like water can make you feel so funny inside. The steward says we'll be fine now we're in the open ocean. We should pretend it isn't there. Let's see if we can visit some hedgehog friends instead." I began reading, and partway through realized I was stroking her wonderful red hair. Perhaps my condition brought out the mothering in me, but I felt I ought to love this child, and soothe her upset stomach somehow.

We both nodded off, and when we woke, people were drifting toward the dining room. I took Lucy by the hand and went in search of Alice and Shirley. We found them playing a rowdy game with a ball, where the players pushed each other for possession, and snatched at the ball carrier if she neared the goal.

Although it looked rough, most of the girls playing were barefoot and laughing. I marvelled that someone didn't fall overboard.

*   *   *

That evening someone suggested a singalong in the main lounge. A couple of girls played the piano quite well, and everyone knew the popular songs. I pulled up a chair close to the piano and kept my hanky handy. I didn't consider myself sentimental, but something about crossing an ocean to an unknown new country with one frock, one nightie and a spare pair of knickers sent tears down my cheeks. Especially when the pianist played "We'll Meet Again".

Before long, some of the girls asked for a jitterbug, and Alice took to the dance floor like a hollow maroon whirlwind. Shirley joined her under duress, but I could see a flicker of enjoyment behind her starched façade, a blush in her cheeks that wasn't just the reflection of her cardigan. My mood lifted. Perhaps it wasn't quite the end of the world. I danced a few numbers with Lucy, until my feet throbbed. She curled up beside me in the big chair and was fast asleep when Alice took a break and whisked her away.

*   *   *

I was the first one at our table for breakfast, and grateful for the solitude. The waiter offered eggs any style with rashers of bacon and sausage. Feeling guilty, after years of scrimping, I asked for a plain boiled egg and toast.

When I finished, I noticed I'd dripped a little egg yolk on my frock. I'd only the one, like all the other girls, and it wouldn't do to arrive in the new land stained on the outside as well as the inside. I hurried to the loo to clean up the spot. The lurching of the ship made me work quickly, and I was soon up on the main deck with a book from the ship's library.

Halfway into Chapter One, Lucy arrived in her little plaid pinafore. She didn't speak, just paused, stared at me solemnly with her baleful green eyes and marched away. She seemed to be on some kind of inspection tour, as she stopped at the foot of each deck chair and studied the occupant. Half an hour later, she was at the foot of my chair again. She stared at me and my book and burst out crying.

"Lucy, what's wrong?" I put the book down and motioned for her to sit beside me.

"My mummy's gone." She didn't move from her position. "I looked at every chair on the deck. I didn't find her."

"Did you lose her after breakfast?"

"I tried to find her at the table. The man brought me an egg. She didn't come." Her shoulders shuddered. "I lost my mummy."

I gathered her into my arms while she sobbed. "We'll find mummy, don't worry. We'll go look together, shall we? We'll see if she's in your cabin, or in the loo. Or maybe the dining room, she might be late for breakfast. I think lots of girls were up late last night. Not like you and me, who went to bed on time." I took her hand and manoeuvered down below deck, where the cheaper cabins huddled, six berths to a room, and if you owned a suitcase you could store it under the lower bunk.

Lucy and Alice's cabin was a few doors away from mine. The cabin was empty. The other girls were long gone, to the deck chairs or the games. "Which bunk is yours?"

She pointed and wiped her nose on her hand. Lucy's bed was all rumpled. Alice's bed lay smooth.

"Does your mummy always tell you to make your bed in the morning?"

Lucy nodded, looking sheepish, and pulled the blankets up to the pillow in a child's version of a made bed.

"Mummy does a good job on her bed. It looks very tidy. Does she always make it this tidy?"

Lucy seemed unable to make a judgment. Perhaps she thought I would criticize her efforts, or her mum's efforts. It looked to me like a bed that hadn't been slept in since the steward changed the sheets.

"Never mind, we can see she's not here. Let's go look in the loo."

We went to the closest ladies' lavatory and peaked under the stalls for Alice's shoes. We didn't find them.

Out in the passageway, I stopped a steward with an armload of towels. "We're looking for a lady who wasn't at breakfast and isn't in her cabin. We think she's lost. Can you help?"

He nodded. "She might be in the baths. Down to the lower deck and turn right at the base of the steps."

We followed his instructions and found a big door guarded by a matron in a white uniform. "We're looking for Alice Foster. Has she come down for a bath?"

"Wait here. I'll check." She glared at us as if we were going to burst into the bath area and stare at the naked girls in tubs if we weren't suitably restrained. I took Lucy's hand and backed up into a neutral corner.

The matron failed to find Alice for us.

*　　*　　*

"And you say she's missing?" the captain asked, pushing papers away to clear a spot on his desk.

"Yes, sir, and we've searched everywhere for the last three hours. Here's her passport, it was in her handbag." I put on the bravest face I could muster, while inside I repressed shuddering thoughts.

He flipped the passport open and looked at her photo. "Is this her daughter?"

"Yes. I'm taking care of her for now. I'm her…aunt," I lied, taking Lucy's hand. Poor lost child, adrift on the ocean like me.

"Good for you. Safe hands. Leave it with me, then."

I tried to console Lucy as we made our way to the dining room for lunch. Shirley was nearly finished her meal, dawdling over a bowl of rice pudding with raisins, her arms covered in goose bumps. She looked a little peaked, like someone had passed a bottle around the dance floor a few too many times.

I ordered something soothing for Lucy and tackled my own plate of chicken with little enthusiasm and many demands from my unborn child. "You look chilly, Shirley. You ought to put on your cardigan."

"I'm fine." She rubbed her upper arms.

"My mummy's lost," Lucy said.

"Alice is missing," I said. "The captain said he'd get the crew to look for her."

"Not too many places to hide on a ship," Shirley said. "Maybe she's found one of the waiters to her liking. They have separate quarters, you know."

"Shirley! How outrageous to suggest such a thing!"

She shrugged. "It happens. After six years of war and all the lads away in France. I shouldn't worry. She'll show up in a day or two."

"We dock in a day or two."

"Exactly. She'll be running down the gangplank at the last minute."

*   *   *

We were five days into the voyage, and I felt well enough to look that ocean in the eye. All I could see, in any direction, was the deep blue of wavy water. I had moved into Alice's berth, to be with Lucy, and the passage was not so tossed at night.

Alice was still missing. The captain and crew looked uneasy, and some avoided my eyes. Lucy was coming around, not crying herself to sleep every night, and not clinging to my skirt all day.

I couldn't believe Alice was cavorting somewhere below decks. There were few places to hide on the ship, despite its size. Every nook and cranny was accounted for and utilized.

Lucy and I sat in our usual deckchair, I reading and she colouring. Shirley walked past, chatting with one of the other girls, shivering in her print cotton frock with a travelling rug wrapped around her shoulders. The wind off the North Atlantic is cold and carries a salt spray to dampen your heart as well as your clothes. I wondered how cold the water was. Probably just above freezing, if the air temperature was an indication. I was glad I had chosen a wool frock for the crossing.

As Shirley neared the bend in the deck, I stood up. "You stay here, Lucy. I'll be back in a few minutes. Just off to the loo."

I followed Shirley as she took the stairs down to her cabin. I lurked around a corner until she left again, still wrapped in her travelling rug. When I heard her footsteps vanish up the stairs, I nipped into her cabin. There were the usual six bunks, a couple of large handbags and two small suitcases. I decided to be brazen. In two minutes, I had ascertained that the pink cardigan was gone.

I went straight to the captain.

We sat in a row in the captain's office, Lucy, Shirley and me.

"So, you've an idea where the missing Alice is, have you?" the captain asked.

"Yes, sir." I steeled myself to be clear and factual. "I know you've conducted an exhaustive search, and I gather that means if a person is missing on a ship, and can't be found on the ship, she must have gone overboard."

The captain sighed. "That's the prevailing wisdom, sad to say. We've got railings and warnings and ledges, yet still it happens."

"Some people fall overboard when they've had too much to drink at a party," Shirley said.

"A lively woman like Alice wouldn't go overboard easily. A person would have to wrestle with her. A person might even find Alice had a grip on her cardigan, and pulled it with her when she fell." I looked at Shirley, wrapped in her travelling rug. "Shirley's pink cardigan is missing. It's been missing since the day Alice disappeared. We girls don't have many belongings. Shirley only had the one cardigan. Now it's gone."

Shirley shrugged. "It blew away. We took off our shoes and stockings for a ball game and I took off my cardigan, too. It was caught in a gust of wind and flew into the sea."

"That also happens frequently." The captain nodded and looked back at me. "I find your accusations impertinent and groundless, young lady. I put your impudence down to your delicate condition."

*   *   *

The more I thought about it, the more I knew I was right. Shirley had had her cardigan at the party. The following morning, there had been no deck games as most of the girls were feeling queasy.

There were only a few spots on the decks where a woman could toss another woman over and have her hit the water and not a lower deck or a lifeboat.

Lucy and I went for a walk. It was difficult, being that close to the railing. If I looked down, the dark cold of the ocean lunged at me against the black of the ship's hull. So far below. Far enough to regret having married in haste and run off into the unknown. Far enough to grieve for your only child, about to be an orphan, as you felt your body smack the water and plunge down, down, down, into blackness. Down with the skeletons on the troop ships and the torpedoed submarines.

I studied the railing closely as we strolled along like a mother and child taking the air. Eventually I found it, clinging to a rough joint between railing and post.

A tuft of pink and maroon woollen threads tangled together.

The voice behind me startled me. "I suppose you think that's proof."

"Yes, I do. The captain will believe me now."

"Not if he doesn't see it. It's your word against mine. And we know you're not thinking straight, in your delicate condition."

Shirley snatched for the fluff. I blocked her hand. She seized me by the shoulders and lifted. She was amazingly strong, and I felt my feet swing off the deck. My stifled inner war broke out. I grabbed her hair and yanked hard. I scrabbled with her, fighting for my baby's life, fighting to stay out of the dreaded ocean, which lapped below with cold welcoming lips.

I fought with strength I didn't know I had, drawn from a well of disillusionment. If I survived this enemy, I could survive anything.

It's amazing how many people come running when a small child in a plaid pinafore starts screaming.

*   *   *

The captain glowered at Shirley. "Why would you do such a thing, young lady? You were on your way to meet your husband in your new home. You had everything to live for. Why would you jeopardize your own happiness?"

Shirley glared at him. "I did nothing. She's making this all up."

"I'll tell you why, Captain," I said. "Shirley is going to meet her husband Bill Foster, a Canadian soldier. She is determined to meet him. Nothing will stop her. Alice was going to meet her husband, William Foster, also a Canadian soldier. Alice had a locket with William's photo in it, which she showed us one night in the dining room. Shirley is wearing an identical locket, although she has never shown us the photo inside. It's a photo of her husband. Show it to Lucy, Shirley."

"No." Shirley cupped her hand over the locket. "This is a wedding present from my husband. It's no concern of yours."

The captain leaned forward, slapped her hand away and yanked the locket from the chain. He opened it, looked at the photo and passed it across the desk. "Lucy, who is that person in the locket?"

Lucy stared. "That's my daddy. Mummy says that's my daddy."

*   *   *

The sixth day we saw land. A great cheer went up from all the girls, and we glued our eyes to the horizon, watching the faint blue line grow greener and taller. We could barely drag ourselves away for meals. *Land ho.* A more delightful pair of words never passed my ears. Far happier than "I do".

Halifax Harbour was calm and crowded with ships. We docked smoothly at Pier 21, although it took endless hours, it seemed, to secure everything and lower the gangplank. We poured off the ship, a great wave of excited girls.

My husband was not at the pier to meet me.

Not that I expected he would be, after what I had learned on the voyage.

The other passengers boarded the train to Toronto, or found their husbands and dashed away to roast beef dinners and "Welcome to Your New Home" decorated cakes.

Lucy and I were left.

Me, Phyllis Foyers Foster, with the child of William John Foster churning inside me, and another child of the same William clutching my hand. That's my legacy of three days in Blackpool with a glib red-haired soldier with heartbreaking green eyes. He gave me an oval locket with his picture in it when he left. He said it was my wedding present. I have never taken it off since, although the neckline of my frock hides it from public view.

I wrote to him, in care of his regiment. He wrote back, *My dearest darling Phyllis, I miss you like hot fudge misses ice cream, but I'm posted to Gibraltar.* He said he looked forward to seeing me after his tour of duty, if he could get back to England. When the war ended, I wrote to say I was coming to Canada. I gave him all the details of the ship's crossing. He didn't write back.

How many women were tricked by William Foster and his friend "Chaplain" Alf Schouten? Alice and Shirley believed them. I did too, when Chaplain Schouten stood over our clasped hands and recited the Service for the Solemnization of Matrimony. If I had stopped at the S table in the dining room, I might have met some women married to Alf Schouten, the wedding officiated by "Chaplain" Foster.

How simple it had been to trick me. I was afraid of dying in a bombing without having lived life to the fullest. I loathed the dullness of my life, every day at the munitions factory and mum serving bread and butter for tea. William was a handsome charmer holding a promise for an exciting future, his scam founded on my fear of becoming an unwed mother. One bogus wedding later, that's exactly what I was.

I asked the dock steward where I could go for assistance. He pointed me toward a church. Lucy and I began plodding through the streets, guided by the church spire looming closer at every corner.

They say the war is over.

I think my war has just begun.

Vicki Cameron *is the author of* Clue Mysteries, More Clue Mysteries *and* That Kind of Money, *a young adult novel nominated for an Edgar and an Arthur Ellis. Her stories appear in the Ladies' Killing Circle anthology series and* Storyteller *magazine. She based this story on her memories of sailing for Canada on the* HMS Georgic, *and losing her mother en route. Mum had gone to take a bath.*

BOW TIDE

Jayne Barnard

Five wireless webcams? Check. Ten miniature motion sensors? Check. Portable floodlights? Check. Lacey McCrae ticked off the last item on her list and closed her day-timer. Nothing was left to do before her Friday afternoon appointment but eat lunch and pat herself on the back for being safely divorced.

The two thirty appointment, a new client named Nicolette Crane, hadn't actually said she was recently unmarried. But she had admitted she was "now living alone", and wanted a full security installation this very day. The risks posed by ex-spouses were real enough for Lacey to lay mental odds on a recent separation. Any woman who waived a discussion of costs had to really believe she needed protection. Backup camera batteries? She made a mental note to pick up spares on the way out of town.

She flicked on the noon news and sat down with a bowl of leftover salmon salad. The lead story was the ongoing controversy over the Bow Ridge golf course expansion. The developer, a short man with tall ambitions, was being hustled past a thicket of picket signs outside City Hall. Although dressed for a TV appearance, he would clearly not be stopping to deliver the patented sound bite about surfing the rising tide of growth in Calgary.

Lacey was about to change the channel when the scene shifted to Edworthy Park, the ten-klick turnaround on her regular running route. The popular green-space straddled the Bow River approximately midway between downtown Calgary and the Bow Ridge Golf Course. Sunlight glittered on the water and on a police helicopter that hovered perilously close to the high cement footbridge. Was there a floater? Or someone in trouble on the river?   She crossed her fingers that the rescuee was still alive.

Lacey hated floaters. She still dreamed about those she had seen during her years with the RCMP: white waxy torsos, missing digits and nibbled-away faces, eternally being fished out from the murky Fraser River. Whenever she saw dark water, she imagined them beneath the surface, their lifeless fingers waiting to seize unwary swimmers. But how did a grown woman explain that irrational fear to her Swimming-for-the-Scared-Stupid classmates?

Back on the news, a body in a wetsuit dropped from the chopper, plummeting thirty feet or more into the current. The diver splashed down, was swept under the bridge and, as the watchers and the camera anxiously rushed to the downstream rail, surfaced again with a thumbs-up. A police rescue boat cruised upstream to collect the diver, and the chopper swung away. The camera followed it, panning over a field full of lounging police officers and scattered dive equipment. Not a rescue, then. A training exercise or demonstration. Lacey relaxed enough to scrape the spoon around the bowl one last time.

The scene jumped into the field, where a female reporter was almost licking her microphone as she gazed up at a well-muscled man in a navy blue T-shirt. Lacey couldn't fault her for that reaction. She'd had much the same impulse on being introduced to those chiselled cheeks at last week's swimming lesson.

"I'm here with Tyler Marshall, dive master," the woman cooed. "He's supervising the river rescue training. Mr. Marshall, how dangerous is what we just saw?"

"Very," said Tyler, meeting the camera's eye with a solemn blue gaze. "A sudden shift in the wind could drop a diver over a gravel bank instead of into the channel, knocking him out or even breaking his neck. But he can't let the risk stop him if there's a boater in trouble. The Bow River is notoriously unforgiving of mistakes. Between the low water temperature and the strong current, it's deceptively dangerous."

He smiled then, and the same twinkle appeared in his eye that had led Lacey to accept his invitation for post-class coffee. "Nobody gets badly hurt rafting inside city limits on the Elbow River. Although they sometimes fall off their air mattresses and hit a rock while reaching for their beer string. Some folks just don't get the connection between booze and boating accidents."

"But falling off your raft on the Bow could kill you?"

The twinkle vanished. "Too easily. At least once a month, a body turns up in that alder swamp below Prince's Island. Rafters, wear a life jacket on the Bow River. Please. The twenty minutes it can take a rescue boat to arrive is too long for most people in water this cold. It's worth dropping from the chopper if we can save a life, but we'd rather not have to take that risk."

Tyler Marshall was training police dive teams? He hadn't mentioned that when he was coaxing her to go rafting with him. Surely she would be safe with a man the Calgary Police Service trusted. She would phone him tonight and tell him she had decided to chance it after all.

As she watched the camera follow Tyler back to the helicopter for another jump, she changed her mind about phoning. Edworthy Park was almost on the route she would take to the Crane house. She could stop by and tell him in person.

* * *

When Lacey reached the park, the place was packed with spectators. The noon news had taken effect. All parking lots were full, and cars were lined up on both sides of the narrow gravel road. She turned around with difficulty and finally inched her car into a space a block away. She made her way back along the river path, winding through rollerbladers and jogging moms until she reached the yellow tape that surrounded the helicopter field. Tyler was here somewhere, in the throng of physically fit men in blue police T-shirts. How could she find one set of powerful shoulders in this mass of masculine muscle?

She walked along the least crowded side of the field and finally recognized Tyler just inside the yellow tape. Half-hidden by a clump of bushes, he was talking to a short man in an expensive suit.

Lacey wasn't about to interrupt them. She waited on the far side of the bushes, watching the bustle as the helicopter loaded up for another pass over the river. If Tyler talked too long, she would have to leave, and phone him tonight instead. She wasn't listening, but the wind blew a couple of scraps her way, enough to tell her Tyler was talking about dropping into the river from a height. Just once, she heard a full sentence, "She'll be floating in the Bow as soon as the old man's gone." But then the helicopter's blades began to move, the conversation ended, and Tyler strode away.

Lacey ducked under the tape and hurried after him. If she

didn't catch up, it would be a wasted detour. "Tyler! Tyler Marshall?"

A cop wearing a bright neoprene dive suit snared him and pointed towards Lacey. Tyler turned. The next minute, he was hurrying back, a huge grin filling the space between them. "Lacey! This is great!"

"I saw you on TV, thought I'd stop by and say hi."

"I'm glad you did. Does this mean you'll come rafting?"

"If you still want me to."

"You bet. What about tomorrow? I could pick you up in the morning and float you back down the river as far as the zoo."

"Great! I live right across from the zoo."

"I know." Tyler's eyes got brighter. "I looked you up in the phone book. If you didn't call me, I was going to call you."

Lacey smiled. This was what a girl liked to hear. "So, tomorrow?"

"Sure. Ten a.m.?"

That was barely settled when the helicopter's roar took on a new intensity. "Got to go," Tyler shouted. "See you in the morning."

Lacey backed away and watched the giant insect lift off. But she couldn't make herself stay to see the jump. The river creeped her out with its cold, impersonal power, that could suck a person down and keep her down until she was nothing more than a lump of white, waxy fat waiting to be washed aground. But she was going rafting tomorrow, on this river. *And the only reason,* she reminded herself, is *because Tyler knows the Bow well enough to train police divers. He won't let anything happen to me.*

*   *   *

121

A short time later, she turned off the Trans-Canada onto a well-gravelled road that ran along between barbed wire fences. The western edge of the city dropped behind a gentle rise. Trees filled the spaces between fence posts, first aspen and poplar, then darker firs. A springtime meadow appeared, alive with breeze-tossed blossoms. White rail fences lined the road. One track veered right, towards a large wooden barn. Another swung left to a small, shabby bungalow and a third led beyond a screen of lilac bushes.

Lacey passed the lilac hedge and pulled up in front of a modern log monster of a house, with the obligatory cathedral windows for scenic viewing. Not another house was in sight, and it seemed impossible that the western edge of Calgary was less than half a mile away. No wonder Nicolette Crane felt nervous, living in this isolated spot. No neighbours would come running if she yelled for help.

A woman stood on the veranda. Lacey put her age at around forty, based on the lines revealed by harsh afternoon light. Her thin face was topped by pale, fine hair. Her lips lifted in what was meant to be a smile, but it did not reach faded blue eyes. The hand she held out was tanned and trembling. "Ms McCrae?"

"Mrs. Crane." Lacey shook the hand, shifted her bag of tricks and offered the pale woman her business card. "I'm a bit early, I'm afraid."

"It's Ms Crane," said the woman. "Call me Nicolette. Will you come in, or would you rather talk on the porch?"

Lacey glanced at the well-padded deck chairs. An ashtray on one wide chair arm gave off a curl of smoke. "Out here is fine."

Nicolette Crane pointed to a chair, picked up her cigarette and got straight to business. "You wired the cameras and alarms at my tennis club. Can you do that here?"

"Overt and hidden video surveillance, motion sensor alarms both silent and loud. Is that what you want?"

"On all my doors and windows. And I want it done right away. I won't spend another night out here without some protection."

Lacey gave Nicolette Crane a discreet once-over. Stress showed in the fine lines around the eyes, in the rigidity of her shoulders, in a faint tremour of the hands. A paler line on the third finger suggested a recent breakup. Score one for that mental bet.

Nicolette lit another cigarette from the stub of the last. "Someone prowls around here at night. If I tell you who I suspect, and I'm wrong, can I be charged with slander?"

Yup. Domestic. That careful checking of possible penalties was a sure sign of a manipulator, if not an overt abuser, in her life. "Expressing concerns privately to another person is not slander. There has to be demonstrated damage to the person you name."

Nicolette chewed on her lip. "It's a businessman," she said. "My ex-husband."

"How long have you been divorced?"

Nicolette's fingers rubbed the line where a wedding ring had been. "It's been final about six weeks," she said. "It was okay, as divorces go. Then, just last week, I started feeling like I wasn't alone, if you know what I mean. At first I thought maybe there was a bear, or coyotes. But I found boot prints by the barn one morning. I don't know for sure my ex-husband is behind it, but I can't think of anyone else who'd bother. I called the RCMP three times last week, but they've never found anyone by the time they got here. They're starting to think I'm a nutcase."

The next obvious question. "Did you tell them you have an ex-husband?"

The faded eyes flitted away. "I couldn't do that. He's well known in this city. He gives to the right charities, goes to the right parties. Who'd believe he was petty enough to terrorize me? He goes around telling people how depressed I am, as if I'm pining for the old skunk. I'm not. I'm just standing up to him for once."

"Is he trying to get a better property settlement?" Big-time businessmen could turn brutal where money was concerned.

"No. He's okay with that. What he wants is this place, my grandfather's land. He wants to build a luxury development past Bow Ridge, with a bridge across the ravine for people to drive their golf carts down to the club. He even has a name picked out. 'Bow Bluffs.' He doesn't even own it, and he already has the plans drawn up."

"It's your grandfather's property, you said. How can he pressure you for it?"

"I'm going to inherit," said Nicolette. "Any day now. My grandfather's in a coma, not expected to recover. He knew the city would expand, though. When he sold the land for Bow Ridge to the city, he got his lawyers to write in a buffer clause. I forget the legal term, but it means the city can't develop right up to the new boundary. They have to leave the west face of that last ravine undeveloped, the one between my house and Bow Ridge. My grandfather wants that strip protected as a wildlife corridor down to the river. I have his power of attorney, so I could overturn the clause. But I won't. No matter what Derek pulls."

"Derek's your ex-husband?"

Nicolette nodded. "Sometimes I think he only married me for that land. In the divorce, he wanted to swap me my house here for a luxury condo overlooking Prince's Island. But the house is really Granddad's; he built it for me to live in when I got married. So that didn't fly. And then he tried to sneak a clause about 'future inheritances' past my lawyer. When I inherit, the pressure's going to increase. Unless I can force him to leave me alone."

"Like with photographs of him sneaking around your place at night. Evidence that could be used to lay stalking charges."

Nicolette nodded again. "Not that I would. But I need something against him."

Another obvious question, but Lacey was willing to bet nobody had asked it. "Who gets the land if something happens to you?"

"I made a will the day the divorce came through. I left all my real estate to my nearest surviving Crane relation. And I sent a copy to Derek."

"And you've never felt physically threatened by your ex-husband?" Statistics Canada had recently announced that twenty-eight per cent of homicides involved a current or ex-partner. Any cop with more than a year's experience could have ball-parked that number for them. A history of domestic violence was one of the indicators of spousal murder, recent separation another. Lacey could have told StatsCan that, too.

"Never." Nicolette shook her head. Then she sucked on her cigarette like she was facing a firing squad, leaving Lacey to guess the answer was politic rather than an absolute truth. Abuse was part of the equation, but so was denial.

Lacey leaned down for her bag. "So you primarily need evidence of harassment. I can rig up motion-sensors and lights on the entrances to the property and the house, along with surveillance cameras that will send regular pictures back to a central computer. Do you want noise alarms and a hot-link to the RCMP dispatch?"

Nicolette shook her head. "I want to catch him in the act, and have proof, not to get the police involved. Lights and cameras will be fine."

Lacey wished Nicolette didn't sound so positive. All cops had seen that denial in at-risk women. Despite piles of evidence to the contrary, they could not believe a man who had once said he loved them might kill them. *Photographs won't do you any good if you're dead,* she wanted to say. *Don't become part of this year's twenty-eight per cent.* She gently tried to urge the police link, but she soon sensed Nicolette wasn't listening. Well, maybe she would change her mind with the photos in her hands.

Lacey stood up. "I'll need to look over the property, so I can place sensors. Is that road the only way in?"

"One and only way, by car. Everything else is fenced off. You have to go up past the barn to get into the fields along the highway."

Lacey took a good long look at the layout. "So anyone driving in would have to come past those posts where the rail fences begin? I can set up battery sensors there."

"There's power to the posts," said Nicolette. "You'll find grounded outlets on the back sides. And there are floodlights along the trees. The main switch is in my garage, but I never turn them on. I like to see the stars."

Lacey nodded. "I ought to be able to patch the sensors into the floodlight circuit. If anyone passes between those posts, the lights will come on. The down side is that large animals, deer and such, will also trigger them."

"The deer prefer the ravine. A creek runs from the highway down to the river. It's shady and cool, and I guess they feel safer down there."

"Could a person follow the ravine up to your house?"

"It's steep. Rocky at the bottom. Impossible in the dark. You can see for yourself." Nicolette led the way around the veranda. The trees had been cleared away behind the house. The opened view included a lake, distant hills, and, away to the northwest, snow-dusted mountains. It was a vista so spectacular that Lacey gasped.

"It's beautiful!"

A genuine smile swept across Nicolette's thin face. "It is, isn't it? I spent my summers here as a child. But I never appreciated it until I did four years at university in Toronto. All that concrete and glass gave me a cramp in my soul, and I swore I'd never live in a city again. The architect placed this house so you can't quite see the power station towers down there. We're right above Bearspaw Dam."

"Impossible," said Lacey. "We might be miles from the city."

Nicolette led the way to a rustic deck that leaned out over a drop-off. Lacey looked down and found herself clutching the railing. It was a long, long way down, with a rocky shore and the aqua ribbon of the Bow River at the bottom. Twin towers of galvanized steel poked their noses above the miniature trees, marking the Bearspaw Dam in the midst of what would look, from the river's edge, like deep wilderness.

Nicolette pointed to her right, where a wooden staircase wound away down the bluff. "That leads to a little dock where my rowboat is kept. There's a bit of an inlet off the Bow. Upstream is the dam, downstream there's a good gravel bank below the golf course. In the old days, my cousin and I played over there all summer while our moms caught up on the family gossip. They grew up here, and they were convinced nothing could hurt us. We'd swim or row around on the river, cook hot dogs over campfires, stuff like that. He was always stealing my marshmallows. I used to beat him up until he got bigger than me. But he was never as tough as he thought he was. Good times."

She sighed. "Now it's all citified. Even the river path is paved on this shore, for the roller-bladers."

Lacey could sympathize with the wistfulness for unspoiled nature, but she was here to work. "What stops your ex-husband from coming along by boat and climbing the stairs into your yard?"

"There's a locked gate part-way up," Nicolette said. "And it's quite a hike to the top. Derek hasn't walked up anything steeper than a sand trap in twenty years. And he'd rather fall in a pit of rattlesnakes than set foot in a small boat. He can't swim a stroke, and he's utterly paranoid about drowning. He wouldn't even try that way."

"I'll cover it anyway," said Lacey. "But I'll wire the sensors on the road first. Isn't it nice to have daylight at suppertime again?"

"Supper? Oh, it's getting late, isn't it? It'll be dark soon." Nicolette frowned, fumbling for her cigarettes.

Lacey recognized the mood change. The woman had been relaxing throughout the tour, but now she was afraid again. "Nicolette, stop second-guessing yourself. A woman's instinct for danger can keep her alive, if she listens to it. When those lights come on, you call the cops. It's their job to deal with creeps in the night."

*   *   *

Nicolette Crane was still alive at ten o'clock the next morning. She called Lacey's cell phone and proclaimed, "It worked!"

Lacey leaned against the front of her condo building. "The

lights came on? Did you see anyone? Did you call the Mounties?"

"I was so scared, I called them right away. The Mountie is still here. He wants to know how to access the surveillance pictures. I don't want to drag you out here on a Saturday, but could you explain it to him over the phone?"

"Certainly. Do you remember how to reset the computer? You don't want to be unprotected tonight."

"I'm sure I remember, but I won't need to. If Derek's face is on that tape, they'll charge him today. It was one thing to only *think* he was spying on me, but it's another to *know*. He won't dare show up again with charges hanging over him."

Lacey didn't have the heart to tell the excited women that even restraining orders didn't always stop an enraged ex-husband. But she could drop a hint in this cop's ear while she had him on the phone. If she said she was ex-Force herself and that her spidey-sense was tingling, he'd make any further midnight calls from Nicolette Crane a priority.

*   *   *

Tyler Marshall arrived in a beat-up pickup truck just as Lacey flipped her phone shut. She climbed in beside him, smiling wide to disguise her sudden attack of nerves. The inflatable boat in the back looked too small for even a single person. This was a terrible idea. Maybe Tyler would settle for coffee.

"Boat, personal flotation device, and me," said Tyler, apparently reading her thoughts. "Three lines of defense between you and the river. You'll never be safer."

Lacey swallowed. "You're right. But can we stay in the shallows for a bit?"

"Sure," said Tyler, and talked about their day's course as he drove: from Bearspaw Dam through the old town of Bowness, past Edworthy Park and Prince's Island, under Centre Street Bridge and the old train trestle to the portage across from the Zoo. From there, it would be a short stroll up to Lacey's condo complex.

Eventually, he swung the truck into a gravel parking lot. "We'll walk from here."

Lacey nodded. She picked up her end of the too-small-for-her-nerves inflatable boat when instructed and followed Tyler toward the Bearspaw launch point.

With every step, the city retreated. Traffic noise faded into the murmur of water and whisper of trees. Car exhaust and hot grease odours lost to spicy willow and fresh green alder. And no people anywhere. When they reached the dam, the place felt as isolated as she had imagined yesterday, when she had looked down from Nicolette Crane's deck. She took a huge breath of the sweet, moist air. "This is great!"

She had another qualm when, zipped and strapped into a flotation vest, she was crawling into this boat no bigger than a single bed. But she made it, and sat clutching the sides while Tyler crawled in behind her.

"All set?"

Lacey nodded, although she wanted nothing more than to scramble back to shore. When Tyler pushed off, she stared at the rippling water, daring it to turn dark and deep. But he kept them in the shallows, and soon she got used to the motion. She even felt safe enough to look around. The north shore was low, with scrubby bushes and wiry grass. The south shore was all immense treed bluff. She craned her neck, trying to spot Nicolette's cliff-side staircase.

"It's super, isn't it?" said Tyler. "I spent my summers on this river. My grandfather's house is on that bluff. It'll be mine soon."

His grandfather? Then Tyler must be related to Nicolette. Lacey was about to exclaim at the coincidence when it struck her that Nicolette too thought she'd inherit. Which one was doomed to disappointment?

Better not to open that can of worms with a man she hardly knew.

She wriggled around so she could see Tyler. He sat smiling, looking up, trailing a plastic paddle as a rudder. "I'll sell the fields and pasture to a developer, and I'll drink my coffee looking down on this every day."

But what about the wildlife corridor? Lacey couldn't ask that without revealing a lot of knowledge about his family. And something had picked at her, when he mentioned selling. That short man in the bushes. He had been at City Hall. "The developer. That's who you were talking to yesterday. At Edworthy Park?"

Tyler's eyes fixed on her. "How'd you know he's a developer?"

"He's on TV a lot, giving corny speeches about riding the tide of growth."

Tyler kept staring, his face hard.

What was wrong about being seen with a land developer? Unless...was it that *particular* developer? "Was that guy Nicolette's husband?"

Now he looked really mad. "What do you know about my cousin?"

"I guessed you were cousins when you said it was your grandfather's house." But that was not all Lacey guessed. If Tyler was Nicolette's cousin, was he her nearest living relative? Could he inherit that land from her?

She tried to keep the monstrous new suspicion from showing on her face. Surely Tyler, who was so nice about her fear of water, wouldn't hurt his own cousin?

What had he said to Nicolette's husband? Something about dropping from a height into the river, and "she'll be floating down the Bow once the old man is gone."

Lacey's eyes traced the long upward line of the bluff. Somewhere up there was Nicolette's cliff-side deck. Nobody who fell from there could survive, whether they hit shore or water. Tyler, with his powerful shoulders, could easily lift his thin, delicate cousin over the railing. No. She had to be imagining things.

The boat swung fast around. She clutched the side again and looked at Tyler.

He had drawn in his paddle and laid it on the floor, leaving the raft to twirl on the deep, dark water of the main channel. His expression sent her spidey-senses into overdrive. And she was trapped in this tiny boat with him. If she bailed out now, would she make it back to shallow water? Or would she become a floater, drifting, turning to a white, waxy lump?

"Foolish woman, going without a life jacket," said Tyler, shifting his weight to his knees. "You panicked. I tried to save you. But don't worry about floating long. I'll call in the divers once you're beyond help."

He lunged.

Backed over the side, her hair trailing in the blue water, Lacey fought. She clawed his hands when he tried to undo her life-vest, kneed his ribs as he pushed down on her shoulders, but she couldn't push him off. The cold river lapped at her head. It touched her ears. It stroked her forehead. It swallowed her eyes. It crawled up her nose and kissed her mouth, ready to swallow her.

But it didn't. The pressure vanished.

The boat's air-filled rim pushed her head up. She wiped the water from her face. Tyler lay across the stern, eyes closed, blood oozing from a gash across his cheek.

Above him stood Nicolette Crane, balancing in a rowboat like an avenging Neptune, with a stubby wooden paddle for her trident.

"Can you make it over here, Lacey?" she asked, eyes firmly on her cousin.

Lacey crept into the wooden boat. When she was shivering in the stern seat, Nicolette pushed the raft away. They watched it go twirling down the river, with Tyler motionless in its stern.

"Thanks," Lacey said. "How'd you know to come?"

"It was him on the computer, sneaking up the ravine stairs. I came outside to think and saw you both down there. I know Tyler's temper. If he figured out you wired my place, he'd flip out on you. So I told the cop to call the river rescue then came down. I told you he wasn't so tough."

"Tough enough for me." Lacey sat up straighter. "I saw him with your ex-husband. When he said he'd inherit the land and sell it, things clicked."

"I didn't tell Tyler about my will, but Derek must have." Nicolette raised her voice, calling over the stutter of an approaching helicopter. "I'll make a new will on Monday, leaving everything to the Wildlife Fund."

The chopper hovered. Divers dropped, swam to the raft and steered it towards the golf course, where a paramedic unit tore across greens to reach the shore.

Nicolette started rowing. "It serves Derek right, getting his precious golf course chewed up. And I hope they can prove he conspired with Tyler. No more surfing the tide of development. A trial will finish him."

Lacey sighed. "Your ex might not know much about water, but Tyler does. He, of all people, should have known there's no tide on the Bow River."

Jayne Barnard *lives in the angle of the Bow and Elbow Rivers. Her fiction has been short-listed in* Storyteller, *long-listed in the* Toronto Star, *won and placed in Calgary competitions, and has appeared in miscellaneous magazines. She has fallen out of at least two rafts but denies beer was ever involved.*

LAKE WHISPER

Steven Price

I got the news when I slipped into the general store to pick up my mail. The fossil leaning on the counter hadn't heard me come in, and neither had the spinster who ran the place. The first words I caught were "Earl Henderson", enough to jam anyone's heart into their mouth. Despite the sudden chokehold on my throat and a second invisible hand squeezing my bladder, I was able to step quietly into the aisle with the junk food and fresh bait to listen better. I just didn't want to hear my name next.

"Yep, this is bad for all of us," old Roy McCann said, "but it's especially bad for Reggie Finn."

Shit. And piss on Roy for snickering. Being linked to Earl Henderson isn't funny for any reason, but especially not this. Damn it all.

Before I get too far along, I ought to make it clear I don't give a damn about the locals flapping their gums about me. Truth of the matter is I'm one of the more interesting souls around this neck of the woods. But even my recent bad luck and other hijinks had been knocked off the front page by the saga of Earl, and the disappearance of his wife Wendy and brother Joel. In a town like Lake Whisper, there isn't much to talk about, except fishing, and hardcore gossip beats that ten times out of ten.

So, you couldn't blame them for beating the story to death. It was a pretty good one, after all. Earl was the local heavyweight champ when it came to brawling and drinking. He'd been banned from hockey leagues, bars and fair grounds for a radius that stretched miles. But even champs push their luck sooner or later. Earl had made that mistake the night he beat the crap out of a cop who'd snared him in a speed trap. The reinforcements had caught up with Earl at his home and settled the score. When the cops were finished messing him up, they added a charge of "assault: police" for good measure, which must have hurt even more than the heavy boots caving in his ribs. In the end, Earl got ten months behind bars, and Lake Whisper got some badly needed peace. Too bad all good things come to an end. We all knew that somewhere in that caveman brain of Earl's, he must have figured the town was laughing at him. Once he was out, he would rip Lake Whisper apart until he got his revenge, and maybe some answers too. The locals were smart to begin hiding the breakables. Like their teeth.

"Suppose we ought to let Reggie know?" Roy asked.

"Sure we oughta, if only for poor old Mrs. Henderson," Claire Munson replied through lips that were cracked from constantly running her tongue over them, either swiping at the last trace of salt from the peanuts she compulsively ate or just to keep the words flowing easier. "Poor old soul. Imagine being happy to have that piece of work come back. The wrong son ran off."

"Ain't that the truth. What time did you say his bus got inta Peterborough?"

"'Round noon. Should be back here by two, three at the latest."

"Then you won't be seeing me after one. Nice knowing ya." He wheezed his way into a laugh.

I stepped into the open at that point, a bag of BBQ chips innocently held in my grip. My legs had finally stopped shaking, and I wanted them to know I was there before my name came up again.

Claire saw me first. Even through the solid mask of make-up she wore, I saw her face redden. Roy turned as if on cue and let his jaw drop a centimetre, purely out of shame. He was the worst gossip in the county, but he didn't like the other men to know it.

"Uh, hi, Reggie," they both finally managed in unison.

I decided to play it cool. After all, I was known as a cool customer around town. Handsome Reggie Finn. Never got in trouble, got angry, or got caught. It had been that way all my life. You get into your forties, and it becomes harder to live up to, but I had no intention of giving up now.

"Hey, Roy, hey Claire." I set the chips on the counter and pointed at the smokes over her shoulder. I'd been buying my darts here for twenty-five years. She didn't have to ask what brand. She put a carton of Players on the counter, then went to get my mail.

I gave Roy a sly sideways glance. He was picking at a hangnail and wishing to hell he were somewhere else. The silence was eating him alive.

"Haven't seen ya for awhile, Reggie. How come you didn't open the camp this year?"

I was amazed he had the nerve to mention the camp, let alone ask why it wasn't open. Pretty daring for a liver spot like Roy McCann, but I guess he was counting on my play-it-cool rep.

I didn't say anything for a minute, just to see the crease on his forehead get deeper. When it threatened to crack his skull, I said, "My back was acting up all winter, so nothing was ready for the season. I'll get her done for next year, though."

"Uh-huh," Roy mouthed, happy to see Claire return, even if she were wrapped in a cloud of cheap Avon perfume. The pause I'd given him before answering had done the trick. He didn't really want to talk about the bad publicity the camp had had last year.

"Looks like mostly bills, Reggie. There's one here for Donny. Haven't seen that boy in an age."

"I saw him the other week. I'll take the letter on down to him next time I get that way."

"Don't know how ya can stand Toronto. There was another murder there last night, ya know." Claire managed to sound almost concerned.

"Ah, he'll be okay," Roy chimed in. "It's mostly the ni-, uh, negroes shooting each other for drugs and such, ain't that right, Reggie?"

"I really wouldn't know, Roy." I scooped up my things while Claire added the smokes and chips to my tab.

Christ! A conversation with Roy, and the pending return of Earl Henderson, all in one morning. I slit open the Players carton with my jackknife and fumbled a dart into my mouth before I even started the pick-up.

*　　*　　*

There was no reason for Earl to be pissed with me, I tried to tell myself. Sure, I'd been poking his wife since about ten minutes after they'd locked him up, but nobody knew it for sure. It was just another whisper off the Lake. On the other hand, the whole town knew Wendy had run off with Joel. That those two were together was as big a surprise to me as anyone. Bigger even.

But there was no reason for people to avoid Big Finn

Fishing Camp either. It wasn't my fault some pansy city boy from Ottawa had taken one of my seventeen-footers out an hour before a big storm whipped through the region. Everyone knows I'd never let a customer do that, especially with one of my best outboards. Whisper is a big lake; dangerous, deep and treacherous. Even I don't go out if the weather is shaky. The OPP found my boat (minus the outboard, of course) capsized and drifting miles from the camp. They never found the corpse, though. Stupid bastard. I figure he'll show up sooner or later. So will my customers, but only after a year or so of lying low.

I sat in the pick-up truck for a long time thinking about it, lighting a new smoke from the butt of the one before. There were a couple of reasons I guessed Earl might come after me. Maybe he'd do it just in case the rumour was true, or maybe he'd figure he could beat the truth about his brother and slut wife outta me. Then I remembered who I was talking about, and that "maybe" was a stupid word where Earl and violence were concerned. He'd bust my skull just for the hell of it. I dropped another butt onto the pile rising from the gravel driveway. I could run, but everything I had was tied into this place. Besides, I'd grown up with the Henderson boys, and running was something I didn't do. I grabbed the mail and went into the lodge.

I set the envelopes down on the table by the front door. The bills I could take care of later. When a dead guest is found at your resort, your cash flow takes a major hit. You have to be pretty canny about where your next dollar is coming from. Luckily, I had a few investments, one of which would pay a dividend next week. Besides, you learn to live cheap when you have to. I catch plenty of fish, and I've got a freezer full of critters I've hunted, sometimes even in season. Between the investments and my savings, I was okay for at least another year.

The letter was different. I knew without even checking the postmark that it was from Donny's sister in P.E.I. Big Finn was the last mailing address she had for him, and even though she barely got any replies, she didn't know when to give up. From what Donny had told me, his upbringing had been shitty to say the least. His father was one of those religious zealots who'd taken the spare-the-rod philosophy seriously. Donny's mother had been too weak to do anything about it, and something of a juice-head to boot. His sister had been old enough to make a break for it years before. Bad break for Donny.

I had heard all about it when he and I worked in Toronto. I was doing the same thing Donny was, getting away from my old man, not that he was abusive or nothing. I just didn't like him. I didn't like the food he ate, the way he smelled or the movies he watched. I didn't like his friends, of which there were precious few, his values, even fewer, and I especially didn't like the way he ran the fishing camp. Gossiping and ogling the bored wives of the fishing junkies up from the cities. He made me sick, so much so that I had to move away before I ended up killing him. Toronto was the furthest point I could afford a bus ticket to. I didn't have a plan until I got there and found out I hated everything about being in a city. The only break I caught was Donny being one of the other tenants in the rooming house I was staying in. He got me a job at the parts factory he worked at and showed me where the cheapest beer could be found. I decided not long after that the best I could do was work for a year, save like hell, then head west. See the mountains and the ocean, then find a quiet place to settle down. Someplace I could fish and hunt.

About seven months later, life turned really sweet. My aunt

tracked me down with news that my old man's heart had finally quit. Suddenly I had a small inheritance and zero reason to sweat it out for minimum wage any more. I was packed and back in the camp within forty-eight hours. The timing was perfect, with the season ready to open and everything. Donny even managed to join me after a couple of months. He'd injured himself on the job, but not as much as anyone thought, including the quack at the walk-in clinic. The company had put him on long-term disability, then he came to work for me under the table. Everything was beautiful, until that bloody wimp from Ottawa got himself killed.

*   *   *

It wasn't much past dark when Earl showed up.

I had cleared away the dinner dishes (fresh bass, baked beans and toast) and was watching TV with the lights off when I heard truck tires on the gravel driveway. I got up off the sofa and chanced a peek through the curtains. Headlights danced against the pine trees as the vehicle made its way up the rutted track. It came into view a moment later, and I knew I was right. A red Chevy pick-up truck with a white cab. It was the same truck the Toronto cops had found and returned to Joel Henderson's mother after he and Wendy had vanished. It actually belonged to Earl, which never ceased to make folks laugh when they thought about it.

I could tell Earl wasn't laughing, though. He didn't bother shutting off the engine or headlights, and when he walked through the twin beams, there was no mistaking him. He was a big bastard, tall, heavyset and full of misery. The moon-glow caught his blond hair and the varnish on the baseball bat he carried in his hands.

I tried to control my breathing as I watched him walk up the path then step onto the verandah. The old planks groaned under his weight. I'd been meaning to pull the worst of them up and paint the rest but had never gotten around to it.

Earl stopped at the screen door. I couldn't see him any more because I was hiding behind the open front door, but I could smell the beer on his breath. Then the screen door opened on its rusty hinges, and he entered the lodge. He stopped dead in his tracks when he saw the television, or rather the porno tape playing on it. It took a minute for him to grapple with the fact the woman performing on it was his Wendy. No need to tell you who the grinning fool enjoying her attention was.

I had a baseball bat too, but mine was aluminum, because I found the wooden type break when you need them the most. It took two steps to close within striking range, and Earl really should have heard me, because the tarp under the threadbare old carpet made quite a rustling. But ol' Earl's attention was fixed on his naked wife. It was nice she was the last thing he ever saw, though I'm guessing on that point. The first blow only dropped him to his knees; it took another two whacks before he was face down on the carpet. I think he was still alive, so maybe his own blood was his last conscious vision.

I didn't waste time thinking about it just then. The job was getting sloppy, and it still wasn't done. Sweat was pouring down my face by the time I was finished, but I managed to roll him up in the carpet and the tarp. His body flinched, or so I thought, and I panicked a little. I brought the bat down again and again, until the dark stain spread through the carpet and beaded on the thick vinyl tarp. But not a drop spread to my hardwood floor, I noticed with considerable relief.

I lost the grin after I turned on the lights. There was a spray from the arc of the bat going right back to the front door. I walked beside the red droplets carefully, counting them until I got to fifty. There were a few more on the wall, and across the table where I'd left the mail. The letter from Donny's sister was absorbing the blood through the envelope, saturating it to the point where the return address was no longer legible. Didn't matter. I had committed it to memory over the months.

I stood with my hands on my hips, surveying the damage. It might have been better to ambush him outside, I s'posed, but this had been a perfect set-up. I just hadn't counted on him being so hard to kill. Joel had gone down after one swing, but he was the runt of the litter, after all. Live and learn.

I spent the next two hours cleaning up the lodge. I left the homemade tape on while I went about my business. There were hours worth of footage on it. Wendy was like that. I paused every now and then while I was cleaning up to watch her, wondering if Earl could see this little scene wherever he was: his wife satisfying another man, the same man who busily cleaned up the blood and brains from around his own shrink-wrapped body. The thought made me smile, but it also reminded me to get back to work. Still, it was tough to tear my eyes off Wendy. I hadn't watched the tape since she'd vanished, and I'd forgotten how beautiful she'd been.

I was sweating hard by the time I was happy with the interior of the lodge. There had been some blood spray forward too, of course, but mostly on the back of the couch, which I'd been planning on getting rid of anyway. Maybe now I'd just haul it out to the workshop in the garage and reupholster it.

I looked at my watch. Well past midnight. This late in the year meant the lake would be quiet. My end of it was well clear of the cabins near the channel that fed into Lake Whisper proper. Down that way was a sandy beach, vacation properties, the marina and all the rest of the trappings of a summer town. Up here, there was only one other road that lead to the water, and a fallen tree had blocked that last winter.

I dragged Earl out through the front door, then around the side of the lodge and down to the boathouse, where the rest of my supplies were. Once inside, I flicked on the light. The first thing I did was unroll Earl. His blond hair was black with congealing blood, and the smell of it quickly attracted what flies still survived on this late Indian summer night. I didn't bother trying to wave them away; there was still too much work to be done. I started by winding a length of chain around Earl's legs, then securing it with a padlock. That left an extra three feet, which I fastened to a cinderblock already in the bow of my rowboat. Then I used a safety knife to cut off the excess tarp. I figured I only needed enough to wrap around him twice. That had done well enough for the others. Before I closed the tarp, I put both of the baseball bats in with him, then finished by mummifying him with a roll of duct tape from head to toe.

It was one o'clock by the time I pushed off from the boathouse. Obviously, one of my motor boats would have done the journey much faster, but it's true about sound travelling on the water. No point in setting tongues to wagging with stories of boats without running lights out on the lake the same night Earl Henderson went searching for his missing wife and brother. A smile creased my lips. He'd find them soon enough.

*   *   *

I went fishing the next day, even though I was dog-tired. It had taken two hours to drive to Toronto in Earl's truck, and another hour to find a suitable place to dump it. Just like before, I'd taken my motorbike with me in the cargo bed. One of these days I'll have to make that trip in a season other than fall or spring.

The Toronto cops would find the truck eventually, and when they did there would be more questions to answer. In fact, I expected a visit from the police any time now. Earl would never have told anyone he was coming to kill me, but people would have guessed. Good thing I'm as clever as I am handsome.

I cast my line out hard, and a few seconds later there was a satisfying plunk fifty feet from the boat. This was my secret fishing spot, the place I didn't even bring the tourists I liked. It was deep here, and the bottom was weedy, but still, on a sunny, crisp day like this, you could see a long way down. If I tried hard enough, I could probably even see the Henderson boys, and that slut Wendy. It had been the biggest shock of my life when I'd found out she was cheating on me with Joel. I got the news one night when I paid her a surprise visit. She and Earl had lived in a rented farmhouse on fallow ground. The house was exposed to the highway, so I'd always parked on a concession road and cut across the fields. While Earl was in prison, he'd loaned his brother the Chevy pick-up truck, so when I saw it parked out front I knew straight away what it meant. I ambushed Joel with my tire iron when he left an hour later. His blood was still warm on my face while I strangled the little whore with my bare hands. Christ, that had been a busy night, driving back and forth.

Right close to the Hendersons was the little queer from Ottawa and my missing outboard. He was the one who'd taught me about wooden bats breaking. I'd caught him while he slept, and for a moment I'd actually hesitated; until I thought again about the way he'd leered at me, and the comments he'd made. I'm not sure how many blows he took before the bat snapped, but my arms had felt like lead when it was over. Getting rid of the blood-soaked mattress wasn't as tough as I thought it would be. I'd let it dry, then dragged it outside the next night and burned it. Once the coils had cooled down enough to touch, I'd pulled it into the part of the woods that had long been a Finn family garbage dump.

Donny was a few yards away from the others. I wouldn't have felt right about putting him beside the queer, and I sure as hell couldn't have left him with white trash like the Hendersons. I still felt bad about Donny. He'd been a big help to me, both in Toronto and at the lodge, even if he was a drunk. Matter of fact, he'd been on a hell of a bender the night the homo had died. But I still think Donny knew what I'd done. He started making noises about going back to the city, and I couldn't have that. Besides, he had that disability money rolling in every month. An investment like that is hard to find.

The late September sun was losing its strength, and a cool wind whispered across the lake, scuffing the water into small waves. But the fish were starting to bite, so I decided to stay a little longer. If the OPP were waiting on the dock, it would look better if I had a fresh catch.

Steven Price *is a Toronto-based author. His work has previously appeared in magazines, anthologies and on the internet. His stories tend to be dark and edgy, whether it's a tale of crime and espionage, or literary fiction. Price is currently working on a non-genre novel.*

UNDERCURRENTS

Bev Panasky

Leaves whispered around my feet as my dog, Bailey, and I wandered along the shore of Embury Island. Overhead, Canada geese formed Vs, heading south. They were the smart ones. At the top of Norman's Cliff, I stood looking out at the perfect fall day. When I was eight, my cousin Norman had slid down the steep slope and hadn't been found for hours. He'd ended up with a broken arm and the honour of having the landform named after him. It offered one of the best views on the island.

We headed back toward the cottage. Running ahead, Bailey barrelled to the end of the dock, forcing a fat black crow into flight. I snuggled into Dad's old plaid coat and turned my face toward the sun. September had put the boots to summer, and the air blowing down from the Cambrian Shield hinted at darker, colder times to come.

Fall in northern Manitoba is a riot of colour. I flopped onto the dock, crossed my legs and drank in the scene. My gaze turned to the water of the bay, smooth like glass, sunlight bouncing off it in every direction, but every now and then a dark shadow moved under the surface. Paul, my husband, was like that—bright and golden on the surface but with dark shapes lurking beneath. I'd put up with his name-calling and taunts for three years, but then the words had turned to slaps. After the last time, I'd told him that if he ever raised a hand to me again, I'd kill him. Two days ago, standing over him, holding a butcher knife like a dagger, I'd come close.

Instead, I'd grabbed Bailey and my purse and left Winnipeg behind. We'd spent the first restless night in a dingy motel on the outskirts of Flin Flon. Running away and running home at the same time.

Though my sister and her kids came up to the island regularly, I hadn't been back in years. The cottage, thirsty for a coat of paint, listed slightly to the east, having given up after years of resisting heavy winds. It was perfect. And it was the only place I could think of where Paul wouldn't find me.

I stared across the bay at the early fall colours, his final words ringing in my head. "You can't get away from me. I'll find you. Then you'll wish you'd killed me when you had the chance."

The sound of an outboard motor undulated across the bay, bringing me out of my gloomy thoughts as a small fishing boat with two people on board rounded the point.

I waved, and the boat veered toward my dock. The driver cut the engine and tossed me a line as they drifted in. I looped it around one of the mooring posts.

"I'll be darned," a voice from the boat said. "If it's not Lizzie Wolanski."

The man's voice was familiar, but his face wasn't.

"It's me, Adam Durant," he said.

I tried to hide my surprise. I remembered Adam as a tall, slim, dark-haired boy who'd once told me that I looked like I'd been beaten with an ugly stick. I took satisfaction in the portly, balding man smiling up at me.

"Adam! It's good to see you."

We spent a few minutes catching up. Or, I should say, he caught me up, since I couldn't shoehorn a word in. Finally, he turned to his passenger.

"Lizzie, this is my fiancée, Marie."

A slender hand appeared from the sleeve of an oversized taupe sweater. Her fierce grip startled me.

Adam read the surprise on my face. "Marie is a competitive swimmer. She does a couple kilometres every day when we're up here."

"Not in this weather?" I asked.

Marie smiled. "It's deceiving really. At this time of year, the water is warmer than the air. It's what causes the morning mist."

I shivered. "You wouldn't catch me in the water this late in the year."

"Lizzie always did take the easier route," Adam said.

My teeth snapped together, a flush running up my face.

Marie smiled. "We'd better get going."

Adam started the motor. "Be careful, there have been some break-ins at cottages on the island," he said.

"It's okay, I've got Bailey." I pointed at my half-grown beagle.

"That little thing? Not much more than bear bait if you ask me," Adam said.

I snorted.

"Hey," he said, "since we're the only people on the island this late in the year, why don't you come over for dinner one of these nights? We could shoot the breeze, as they say."

"I'd like that," I said.

He looked at Marie, then at me and shrugged. "Hell, why don't you come over tonight?"

Marie stared at the side of his face, eyes hard like little stones. I wanted no part of that. "I don't know about tonight."

"Why not?" he asked. "What else are you going to do?"

Marie bared her teeth in something that resembled a smile. "We'd be happy to have you."

Hell, it was better than being alone. "Well, all right. Can I bring anything?"

* * *

After dinner, we sat bundled up on the screened-in porch, staring at the darkness and talking. Conversation drifted to the summers we'd spent on the lake.

"I remember you and that Fobert kid used to go skinny-dipping all the time," Adam said.

I took a sip of wine. "Denny Fobert." I laughed. "That was a long time ago. You wouldn't catch me baring it all now."

"I don't know." Adam smiled. "I'm sure you'd look fine."

Marie stood, her chair scraping on the wood floor. "I'm going to start the dishes," she said through tight lips.

"I'll help," I said.

Marie's smile was more of a grimace than anything. "No, you stay here and talk."

The door closed behind her. Lost in thought about long ago summers, I missed part of what Adam said.

"...she gets jealous."

I smiled. "Then maybe you shouldn't flirt with other women when she's around."

"I wasn't flirting!"

I raised my eyebrows. "Yeah, right."

"Anyway, you're married," he said, indicating my ring.

"Yeah, I am." Though for how much longer remained to be seen.

"So, you going to tell me about him?"

I took a sip before responding. "Not a lot to tell. He's an architect. We live in Winnipeg. Unfortunately, he couldn't get the time off to come up here." It had been too many years since I'd last seen Adam to feel comfortable telling him more.

Adam shrugged. "His loss."

"Yep." I sighed. "It's getting late. Bailey and I should go home."

I called in a "goodbye" to Marie, then Adam and I walked down the long staircase to the dock. Though I hadn't been to the lake in a number of years, there are some skills you never forget, and running an outboard is one. Bailey hopped into the front of my fourteen-foot aluminum boat while I perched on the back bench.

Adam untied the tether and pushed the boat away from the dock. With one pull of the starter cord, the engine roared to life. I looked back. Marie stood, backlit, in the porch window. With a wave, I swung the bow toward home.

The night wind was crisp with the scent of water. As we scudded homeward along the six miles of shoreline, I tried to remember the long ago owners of the cottages we passed. There were the Saundersons, the Belofskys, the Andersons and the Leons. As I approached the Dubois' cottage, I noticed lights moving around the perimeter. I squinted inland. As I watched, the lights moved away from the cottage and toward the shoreline. A motor roared to life.

Heart thumping, I cranked the throttle and booted it for home. At the dock, I tied up quickly and scrambled up the slope to the cottage, throwing the dead-bolt behind me. It must have been the burglars Adam had mentioned. *What if they know who I am?* The cottage felt empty and cold. I pulled all the curtains, wanting to light a fire or a lamp but afraid to draw any attention.

I pulled out my cell phone, unsure of what number to call, since I doubted the cottages had 911 service. Anyway, what good would calling do? The prowlers were long gone. I looked at the illuminated dial of my watch. Nine thirty. "Kinda late anyway, isn't it, Bailey? We should just go to bed."

Bailey wagged his tale in agreement.

*   *   *

I lay in the dark thinking about promises, broken and kept, as sleep swam just out of my reach. We'd tried marriage counselling—Paul had walked out of the second session, saying it was a waste of time. I had considered getting his best friend to talk to him, but I was afraid that it might be seen as the ultimate betrayal. After what felt like hours, fitful sleep rescued me.

Morning dawned wet and grey. "Well, Bailey, I guess the burglars didn't get us, huh?"

He whined in response and pawed at the door. I let him out, but he was back in a flash, smart enough not to stay out in the rain. He curled up by the wood stove while I spent the morning with a mug of hot chocolate, reading and listening to CBC Radio.

As lunch time approached, thoughts of Paul and the future kept distracting me. The rain stopped, and the sun pried at the clouds while I paced the width of the cabin, unwilling to think about Paul, unable not to. I had to do something, had to get out of the cabin.

I grabbed my cell phone, dug a scrap of paper out of my jeans pocket and tapped in a number.

Twenty minutes later, I stood on the Dubois dock, watching Adam pull his boat up.

We walked around the building looking for signs of a break-in.

"You must have scared them away," Adam said.

"They weren't the only scared ones."

Adam took my chin in his hand and looked into my eyes. "You should have called. I could have come over, made sure everything was secure."

Reading things that may or may not have been there, I said, "Adam, I'm married and you're engaged. What do you think you're doing?"

He pursed his lips and looked away. "Nothing."

"Are you and Marie okay? She seems kind of—intense."

He laughed. "You could say that. Look, I'm sorry if I came across wrong. I just meant as a friend, you know?"

I watched the colour creep up his face. "I know."

* * *

After dinner, I poured a glass of wine and settled in front of the wood stove. I'd brought in a full load of wood, and the fire roared merrily. Outside, the wind picked up, whistling past the eaves as loneliness descended on me. I dialed my sister Sharon's number, bracing myself for another round of listen-to-my-horrid-life.

"So, where are you?" she asked after running out of complaints.

"At the cottage."

"That's what I figured. It's what I told Paul when he called."

My mouth went dry. "What?"

"That's what I told Paul. It's where you always go to sulk."

"You didn't tell him how to get here, did you?"

"Of course I did. You can't hide from your problems." She laughed. "It's hard to believe your perfect life has problems. Perfect little Lizzie."

She started to say something else, but I pushed the END button. I shivered, my skin coated in a light film of sweat. *He knows where I am.* He must have told Sharon some sad story to get her to give him directions. I had to leave. I stood at the window staring at the inky night—too windy and too dark to cross to the mainland.

The warmth of the fire seeped into me, but any feeling of safety I'd gained in the last two days was gone. I nursed the wine, wondering what to do.

Bailey woke. His ears pricked up, and he leapt to his feet.

"What's wrong, big guy?" I whispered.

He ran to one of the side windows, barking. The bark deepened to a growl as he stood stiff-legged, the hair along his spine standing straight up.

He's here. I stumbled to my feet and blew out the oil lamp. Pressed against the wall, blinded by the darkness, I couldn't see through the window from my angle. After a last couple of barks, Bailey quieted down and went back to his spot.

I spent the rest of the night in the chair by the fire, wrapped in a comforter.

*　　*　　*

Dawn arrived with a crack of thunder, the bruised sky threatening rain. Bailey whimpered to go out and, although I didn't feel safe opening the door, I had no choice. As he snorted through the leaf litter, I went around to the window he'd been barking at the night before. There, in the mud, was a set of footprints. My heart pounded as I bent to study them.

The imprints were large, much bigger than my own feet. *He's been here.* I stared into the trees. All was quiet.

"Bailey. Bailey, come on," I called, my voice quivering.

No response.

I circled the cabin, calling for Bailey. I didn't see any more footprints, and I didn't see Bailey. *Why did I let him out of my sight?* I stood on the cottage steps, tears in my eyes, as I called and called.

I took three deep breaths, trying to regain some control. *He's probably fine, he's a beagle, he's likely off chasing a squirrel or something.*

From the warmth of the cabin, I watched as the storm built, whipping the lake into whitecaps and blowing leaves off the trees. Clouds swirled overhead. No sign of Bailey.

I fumbled my cell phone out of my purse as I paced, debating who to call. Adam and Marie were closest, they seemed the obvious choice.

I punched in their number and listened to it ring. Finally, a voice penetrated the static.

"Marie? It's Liz, is Adam there?"

"I can't hear you. Who is this?"

"Marie, it's me, Liz," I shouted into the phone.

"Sorry, the connection's really bad. I can't hear you," she said and hung up.

All alone, fear played with me. Every sound made me jump, the wind in the eaves made my hair stand on end. I had to get to Adam's place, even if it meant leaving Bailey behind. I prayed he'd be okay.

Grabbing a life jacket, I stepped out onto the porch. The wind snatched the words from my mouth as I called Bailey one last time. There was no response.

I ran down the hill toward the dock, but halfway there

turned around and went back to the woodpile. I picked up the hatchet, hefting it in my hand, its weight a comfort.

*   *   *

The storm raged around me, spitting rain in my face as the wind bludgeoned me. Water ran inside my too-big slicker, soaking my jeans. It took almost twenty minutes to reach Adam's. I was surprised not to see his boat bobbing alongside the dock. Tying up quickly, I ran up the long flight of stairs, clattered across the porch and banged on the cottage door.

"Adam? Marie? Anyone home?"

Only the shrieking wind responded.

I tried the door. The knob turned, and I stumbled inside. "Hello?" I called. Nothing.

I deposited my slicker on a peg by the door and walked through the main room, stopping in front of the kitchen window. A sound caught my attention.

Buzzing, a bloated housefly bounced against the kitchen windowpane, reanimated by the warmth of the cottage. It battered itself against the pane of glass, trying to make good its escape.

Boards creaking under my feet, I crossed the small eat-in kitchen, wondering where they could be. As I walked past, the bedroom door groaned and swung open a few inches. The sound of buzzing flies reached my ears. I turned back and pushed the door wider.

The room was dark. My hand floundered along the wall, feeling for the light switch. Finally, halfway into the room, I found it. With a flick, the room lit up in the garish light of an exposed bulb.

"Oh, God!" I cried.

Adam lay on the bed, one side of his face pulverized. The sickening smell of fresh ground meat filled the air. I stood gasping, unable to think. His single remaining blue eye looked at me in surprise. Flies crawled over his face, humming.

My stomach rolled, and I turned away. My head pounded, threatening to explode as I slumped against the wood-panelled wall.

There was a rustling sound. I looked toward the door.

Marie stood in the doorway, dressed in rubber boots and a yellow rain slicker that was much too big for her.

"What happened?" I asked, my voice cracking. "Who did this?"

"Must have been the burglar," she smiled.

The hair prickled on the back of my neck. "The burglar?"

She shrugged. "Unless you did it."

"Me? Are you crazy?"

Her face contorted. Baring her teeth she said, "Crazy? Don't you dare call me crazy!"

I couldn't look away from her face.

"What are you doing here, anyway?" she asked.

I backed up until I was pressed against a small dresser. "There was someone prowling around my cottage." Tears welled up in my eyes. "Then Bailey disappeared."

She took two steps forward, leaving muddy prints behind. I stared at her boots. They seemed way too big for her small frame. She smiled when she saw me looking.

"They're Adam's. I don't have any, so I cram socks in the toes of these."

Nausea threatened to overwhelm me. It had never been Paul.

"Why?" I asked. "Adam loved you. Why would you do this to him?"

She snorted. "Oh, don't worry, there are worse ways to die. A handful of sleeping pills made sure he didn't feel a thing. You, on the other hand, aren't going to be so lucky."

"I've never done anything to you."

Her hard eyes glittered. "Haven't you?"

I shook my head.

She advanced toward me. "Do you think I'm stupid? Do you think I was born yesterday?" She pulled her right hand from behind her back. A boning knife glinted.

I wedged myself between the dresser and the side of the bed, trying not to look at Adam. *It's okay. Calm her down. Don't panic.* "I have no idea what you're talking about," I said in as placid a voice as I could muster.

"'I have no idea what you're talking about,'" she repeated in a singsong voice. 'I have no idea what you're talking about.'"

Cornered, there was only one way to get by her, and that involved climbing over Adam. I couldn't bear it.

"Why did you call him to meet you yesterday?"

"It was about the break-in at the Dubois cottage."

"Yeah, right."

"It was, honest to God."

"Do you think I'm an idiot? I saw the way you looked at him. You want him. You want to take him away from me." She looked me up and down. "You came over here to seduce him and make him leave me." She waved her arm toward the bed. "Well, there he is. He's all yours."

"No. You're wrong," I said, my breath coming in short, sharp gasps.

She tightened her grip on the knife. "Oh, I don't think so." She lunged forward.

Leaping sideways, I landed on the bed. On Adam. I rolled

over him and pushed myself off the other side. The palm of my left hand slipped in something that felt like cold oatmeal. *Don't think about it. Don't think about it.*

I bolted toward the door, hoping to reach it before Marie could get turned around. The flash of a blade coming toward me sent me diving to the floor. Sprawling half in, half out of the bedroom, I glanced up, as Marie attempted to pry the knife out from the doorjamb, where she'd rammed it.

She screamed in rage.

I leapt up, shot across the cabin, through the door and down the slope toward the stairs.

The cottage door banged open as I started down the stairs. Just before I reached the landing, midway down, something whizzed past my head. I looked back to see Marie at the top with an armful of firewood. At least there was no sign of the knife.

I turned away, concentrating on keeping my footing on the worn, wet wood.

Halfway down the last flight, something hard and heavy hit me between the shoulder blades. I stumbled, balanced for a moment, my arms pin-wheeling before somersaulting down the remaining stairs.

Lying face up on the dock, vision blurred by the rain, I watched Marie descend, smiling at me.

It felt as though I'd hit every step on the way down—twice. My chest throbbed and, with every breath, I pictured ragged rib-ends poking at my innards.

Marie smiled as she picked up a chunk of firewood from the stairs. "This is the perfect weapon. You beat someone to death, then you just burn it."

I felt her step onto the dock.

"You'll never get away with this," I said, the breath rasping in my throat.

"Of course I will. Convenient about these cottage break-ins. I'll just say that I went over to your place to check on you, not knowing you'd come here. The burglars must have struck during that time. Then I came home to a scene of carnage."

Time to make a deal. "You could let me go. I wouldn't say anything. I'd go along with whatever story you want."

She laughed. "First you think I'm crazy. Now I'm stupid too?"

I sighed. *So this is how it ends.*

She raised the piece of wood over her head like a club. "Now, if you'll just lie still, I'll make this as quick and painless as possible."

I thought of Paul, of all the times I'd taken the insults, the shoves and finally the slaps. *Lie still, my ass!* I rolled out of the way as the club descended.

On hands and knees, I scurried toward the end of the dock. One of my boat's tie ropes had let go, and it bobbed at the end of its remaining line. I grabbed the rope and pulled it toward me.

"Damn you!" Marie shouted as the log skittered across the dock and dropped into the water.

I untied the boat and got a hand onto the gunnel.

She hit me like a linebacker and we tumbled into the boat. There was a sharp CRACK as the back of my head hit one of the seats. Images doubled and tripled. She grabbed me by the throat, and the sight of three Maries strangling me was almost enough to make me give up.

The boat rocked under us. She pinned me in the dirty, cold rainwater. My hands flailed, brushing something smooth and hard. Fingers wrapping around it, I swung with all my strength.

The flat side of the hatchet hit Marie in the head. Not enough to disable her, but enough to make her lose her grip. Air squealed through my battered throat.

I pulled myself up against the back bench. Marie touched the gash on her head. "I'm bleeding!" Her white-rimmed gaze locked on me.

She launched herself forward, her extended hands like claws. Exhausted, I brought the hatchet up, resting its base on my chest.

Her eyes widened in surprise as she drove herself into it.

Marie pulled herself off the blade. "Look what you've done," she said, feeling at the gash in her chest as her voice bubbled, blood frothing on her lips. Marie staggered with the rocking of the boat. Backing away from me, her legs caught the front bench seat. I threw my weight against the side of the boat, tipping it. With a splash, she tumbled over.

Sobbing, I dropped the blood-soaked hatchet.

Marie thrashed, then slipped under the water. Being a champion swimmer didn't save her.

I thought about my cell phone, safely in the cabin, in the pocket of my slicker. I couldn't face going back there. Instead, despite the storm, I pointed the boat toward the mainland, knowing there was an emergency phone at the boat-launch.

In the parking lot, cold and wet and holding my aching chest, I dialed the operator.

* * *

The paramedics had me bundled up and in the back of the ambulance by the time the police showed up. As we pulled out of the islanders' parking lot, I saw them turn my boat back toward the island.

A young doctor in the Emergency room at the Flin Flon General Hospital held the police off long enough to wrap my broken rib and patch up my other injuries.

Then a tall bloodhound of a man with piercing blue eyes introduced himself as Detective Bauer. "I hear it's a hell of a mess out there," he said. "You're lucky to be alive."

I nodded.

"You feel up to giving a statement?" he asked.

"Sure," I croaked.

"Just so you know, my guys went by your place and found your dog. He'd slid down the embankment just west of the cottage. He's wet and cold but okay."

Tears welled up in my eyes. "Of course, Norman's Cliff."

He pulled a notepad out of his coat pocket then paused. "Before we start," he said, "is there anyone you want me to call?"

I thought for a minute then managed to smile. "You know what? I'm okay on my own."

Bev Panasky *spent many childhood summers splashing around at her family's cottage in Northern Ontario. Now based in Ottawa, Bev is a member of Capital Crime Writers, CrimeStarters and the local chapter of Sisters in Crime. "Undercurrents" is Bev's third published short story.*

BOOM TIME AT BUFFALO POUND

Violette Malan

That's his hut, the one furthest out from the others, at the end of the ice road."

I squinted to where Barb was pointing. The ice fog, still hanging in the air when we'd left her place, had faded away as the sun rose, and now I could see right down the length of the lake.

I could also see the fishing huts we'd come to look at. "There's a road out on the ice?"

"Sure. Some people even have mailboxes."

Barb had stopped her car in the middle of the causeway that carried Highway 301 over the lake in Buffalo Pound Provincial Park. The land dropped off sharply to the water on my left, but on my right were rolling hills dotted with scrubby pine trees. We'd driven twenty minutes out of Moose Jaw, not for privacy, but to see where the man who wanted to ruin her life spent his free time. The more I knew about him, the better.

"Ice fishing in Saskatchewan," I said, shaking my head. I'm from Ontario. We tend to believe that—barring an ocean or two—we've got all the water there is in Canada. "Who would have thought?"

Barb thumped the railing with her mittened right hand, and we turned back to her old Volvo. Even though she'd left it running, as everyone does in Saskatchewan in the cold part of the winter, I still had to yank hard on the passenger door to get it open. I was glad to get out of the wind and back into the warm car.

"I don't know, Lillian," Barb was saying. "Maybe you can't help me. Maybe I should just try again to speak to Stefan myself. If I could get him to understand, I could clear this all up."

I shivered, even though the heat was on full blast. I looked out into the landscape. It wasn't any colder than Stefan Janobev.

"You planning to tell him what he wants to know?" I said, pulling the seat belt around my double layer of coats. "'Cause I think that's all the explanation he's going to understand." And Barb knew that already. She hadn't asked me to come out here to hold her hand. I wasn't the only criminal she'd ever met, but I was the only one she could trust.

Barb pulled off her mittens to reveal her leather driving gloves. "You know," she said, blowing on her fingers, "being a reporter isn't what I'd imagined it would be—oh, I didn't think it was going to be like a movie, but I never thought it would turn out as…well, as ordinary as it did."

My head jerked up in surprise. I'd heard her say this kind of thing before, but then her tone had always been cynical. Now I heard a kind of wistful longing, as if, even though she denied it, she'd really wanted the life she'd seen in the movies.

"It doesn't sound very ordinary just at the moment," I said.

I wriggled my toes in my boots and shoved my hands deeper into the pockets of my leather coat. When it's minus forty outside, with the wind off the lake making it minus sixty, it's hard to feel warm, no matter how many layers of sweaters you have on.

"You know what I mean," she said, turning toward me as much as the combination of her thick winter coat and the steering wheel would allow. "Sure, I saw myself valiantly refusing to reveal my sources, but I thought I'd be in a courtroom. Even then, selling out your sources to the cops is one thing, selling them to the mob..."

"Especially when your sources *are* the mob," I said.

"It was going to be the feature that made my career," was the way Barb had put it yesterday as we sat around her kitchen table in Moose Jaw's west end. Trading on the popularity of TV shows like *The Sopranos*, and *Growing Up Gotti*, Barb had prepared a series of articles on the home life of Canada's criminal elite—not calling them that of course, and with everything completely anonymous. She reasoned, correctly it turned out, that regardless of how they paid the mortgage, everyone with a fancy designer home wants to see it laid out in a photo spread in the Sunday magazine.

"But there were a couple of things I hadn't counted on," she'd said. "First my editor takes a job in Vancouver, and the new one kills my story. While I'm looking around for another market, Stefan 'the Hammer' Janobev figures out that my research would be pretty useful to him."

"What we need," I'd said, tapping the side of my tea cup with my fingertips, "is the cops."

Barb had looked up with the first natural smile I'd seen since she'd met me in the airport in Regina. "Buy me some ice skates," she'd said. "Hell has frozen over."

Barb had every right to do her drama queen imitation. People in my family don't go to the police for help. My name is Lillian Caine, and I make my living persuading people who have too much money for their spiritual health to give some of it to me. In other words, I'm a con artist. Which explains why

Barb had called me. She was a university friend of my sister's, and when she'd wanted to break into journalism, she'd come out to Saskatchewan, where it's easier to get picked up as a stringer for the big papers then in Toronto or Montreal. I knew she hadn't found the newspaper business to be all she'd hoped for, but I don't think either of us had expected it to get dangerous.

I blinked back into the present as Barb leaned on the horn for a farmer pulling out in front of us without either stopping or checking the road.

"Tell me again why you don't go to the cops," I said. I know why *I* don't, but Barb's a straight citizen.

Barb shrugged, negotiating the bend in the road that constitutes highway landscaping out here on the prairie. "It's not what you think," she said. "They're honest and competent—and I'm not stupid, present circumstances to the contrary. I went to the police right away, and at first they were really excited. They've been trying to find something incriminating on Janobev for ages. I offered to wear a wire and everything." She glanced at me to see how I would take this.

"And so?"

"And so it turns out Stefan the Hammer isn't stupid either. Wearing a wire does no good if the person you're trying to incriminate won't meet with you. He says he'll see me when he sees me and that he'll decide when. The police can't assign me someone forever—"

"So you called me," I said, nodding.

"They're not even really threatening to kill me. That I *could* go to the cops with. But they can make it impossible for me to work. First, they'll want the information I've already got—you know the kind of thing I mean, who owns what, where it is and how much it's worth, household routines, personal habits. Once they've used everything they can, they'll send me after information I haven't got. Next thing you know, I'm an official mob researcher. Today Saskatchewan, tomorrow the world. I'd quit the whole business if I thought I could get away."

"What would you do if you couldn't be a reporter?" I said, turning to watch her profile. A couple of times growing up I'd thought about not going into the family business—anyone with a family business does, I guess—especially when my older sister had announced that she was going to graduate school, but when push came to shove, this is what I was good at.

"My cousin in Ireland wants me to 'come home', as he puts it, and help him run the family business," Barb said.

Small world, I thought. "What is it?"

Barb grinned without taking her eyes from the road. We were in Moose Jaw now, and negotiating the intersections, where month-old snow had frozen into hard ruts, was tricky "He owns a small chain of community newspapers. I'd be the managing editor."

"Going over to the enemy, eh?" We both laughed. We needed to. "Why don't you just go then?"

"Someone followed me to the airport yesterday," she said. "Maybe to stop me going somewhere, maybe not. You think I should bet my life on it?"

Barb pulled into her driveway and turned the engine off. The sudden silence made the cold seem colder.

"You can do what the cops can't do," Barb said finally. She picked up her mittens and looked at them without pulling them on over her gloves. "You can trick the bad guys into forgetting about me. You can con them into letting me go."

I knew where she was coming from, I just wasn't sure I could take her where she needed to go. A few months ago, I'd had a problem similar to the one Barb was facing right now.

The son-in-law of the local crime boss had felt he had a grievance against me and had tried to kill me. My mother had come up with a solution that had turned the tables on him.

I shook my head. "I've got no contacts here, no connections. It would be hard to pull the same kind of game…" I fell silent, and it's a mark of Barb's intelligence that she kept quiet herself and let me think. My mother had tricked the son-in-law into exposing his dangerous ambitions to his far more dangerous father-in-law. She could do that because however we might prefer not to think so, we're part of the criminal underworld. Barb wasn't. Going to the people Stefan was trying to infiltrate would only put Barb in someone else's criminal hands. So there was no bigger bad guy I could con into disposing of Stefan for us. Cops both provincial and federal were itching to get their hands on him…but they needed something concrete to act on.

Concrete. Cement overshoes. Ice fishing.

"You're smiling," Barb said, "you've thought of something."

*   *   *

"It's like this," I said to Barb once we were back in her kitchen, and she'd handed me a steaming mug of tea. "You said yourself the police are dying for an excuse to investigate the guy, so that's what we'll give them."

"But he won't meet with me—" Barb stopped as I held up my hand.

"Not an excuse involving you," I said, as she lowered herself into a chair across the kitchen table from me, "an excuse that has nothing to do with you." As a reward for my brilliance, I ripped open the pack of chocolate chip cookies I'd been ignoring. "And Buffalo Pound's perfect for what I've got in mind. Think about it, what besides criminal activity brings out the cops?"

Barb shrugged. "Fires? Accidents?"

I nodded. "Sure. Police on the scene because someone's gone through the ice."

"It's far too cold this time of year for that kind of accident," Barb said, biting her lower lip. "The ice is much too thick."

"Bad ice isn't the only way to fall into the lake. In fact, almost any other way is better, from the point of view of attracting police attention. Go amuse yourself for a bit," I told her. "Leave me alone with my phone."

Like any other business, running a successful con is part *what* you know, and part *who* you know. I had an idea, but I needed to talk to some experts. I called my friend Dingo back in Ontario, and after some personal chit-chat, he gave me the name of someone who owed him a favour.

"Oh, sure," Jim said when I got him on the phone. I could tell he was interested from how his quiet voice resonated. Right there on the phone, he came up with three ingenious methods of achieving my goal, but they struck me as a little *too* ingenious.

"It has to look rigged," I said, "but like he or one of his guys might have rigged it. Not as though he called in an EOD guy to set it up for him."

"Oh, you want something *easy.*" I could hear him drumming his fingers. "Takes the fun out of it, but okay, if that's what you want." He thought a few more minutes. "There's not a lot to work with in an ice hut," he said, his voice getting even softer. "Hole in the ice. Auger. Hole in the ice." His tone sharpened, and I pictured him sitting up straight. "I've got it. Who's doing the set up for you?"

"I was hoping you would," I admitted.

"Well now, aren't you lucky I'm free?"

I had a feeling Dingo had told him to be free, but I wasn't going to look a gift horse in the mouth. I'd worry about what I owed Dingo later. Jim and I batted it around, shaking the bugs out of it before we were both satisfied with his idea. I took note of his last few instructions and hung up the phone.

"Say Barb," I said, tracking her down in her home office. "Can we rent one of those ice huts?"

*   *   *

I was pleased when I saw that most of Jim's luggage looked like lovingly packed sports equipment. In February, no one looks twice at a hockey bag or a case for cross-country skis. We were still in the airport parking lot when my cell phone rang.

"Now's our chance," I said to Jim as I hung up and checked my watch. "We could go straight out there, if you thought we could be finished by two o'clock."

"The sooner the faster," he said, a big grin lighting up his face.

The ice road was well sanded, and we had no trouble reaching Stefan Janobev's ice fishing hut.

"There's the one we rented," I said, as we drove past it on the way to Stefan's.

"Hmm. Couldn't get one closer?"

"Not without having to answer too many questions," I said. Jim's frown lasted until we reached Stefan's hut.

"How much time do you think you'll need?" I said, as I slowed carefully to a stop. "Should I wait in the other hut?"

"Oh, no," Jim said, "you're coming with me."

"I am?"

"Think about it," he said. "If I'm caught out here by myself, what's my explanation going to be? If I'm caught out here with you, well, I'm obviously just some guy looking for a place to score."

"Only a guy would believe that," I said.

"Only a guy needs to."

I shook my head in admiration. "You've got the makings of a fine con man," I told him.

"I'll put that on my resumé."

The hut seemed even colder and more isolated than it had looked from the causeway. I felt delicate walking on the ice, even though I knew that since it was thick enough to hold up the car, it could hold me up without difficulty. The door to the hut was unlocked, and we were only seconds getting Jim's equipment inside. We couldn't risk starting the wood stove, but our body heat was enough to warm the place to the point where we could take our coats off.

Jim eyed the interior, rubbing his hands together and frowning.

I've seen apartments smaller than Stefan the Hammer's ice fishing hut. And more poorly furnished too. Besides the big old Fisher wood stove, there was the kind of worn but still serviceable furniture you see in cottages, a love seat with worn upholstery, two mismatched end tables, no real floor, but plenty of old rugs, some with their fake oriental pattern still visible, were layered around a metre-wide space in the centre, where the exposed ice was rough from being bored and re-frozen.

Jim squatted, frowning. Suddenly he sat back on his heels, eyes focused, alert. "Let's move the couch," he said. "Pull back those bits of rug under it."

We tore the last rug a bit getting it off the ice, but the love seat would cover it again once we moved it back.

"Okay, now for the auger," Jim said. "We'll have to make more than one hole."

Jim showed me how to use the auger—the ice was so thick we had to put an extension on it—and as I drilled three holes close enough together to make one big one, Jim pulled bits of equipment out of another bag, made minute adjustments with a pair of needle-nosed pliers and taped the bits together with what looked like a whole roll of insulating tape. Finally, he pulled a wet suit and two air tanks out of his big blue pack.

"You mind turning your back?" he said with a big grin.

I shuddered. "You can't be going into that water. Maybe we should rethink." It was so much colder than it had seemed when we'd talked about it on the phone.

"I won't be more than ten minutes," he said, pulling the hood tight around his face, adjusting the opening for the face mask and breather with a lot of care. "In fact, I can't be more than ten minutes, even with the insulated suit on. That's the real reason you're here, to pull me out if anything goes wrong. Here—" he attached one end of his safety line to the leg of the wood stove and fastened the other to a ring on his weight belt. "I've given myself enough line to reach the other hut, but first I'll attach the device."

I knew he'd said device because he figured the word "bomb" would scare me. It wasn't the bomb that worried me though, but the idea that he was going into that water—and that I had to save him if something went wrong.

"Stop worrying," he said, holding his mask inches from his face. "Nothing's going to go wrong." I helped him strap the smaller tank to his back and watched as he let the other one, "device" attached, into the water. He looped a large coil of line to his belt, gave me a thumb's up, and lowered himself into the hole.

Well, okay, nothing did go wrong, that's why you hire experts. But by the time Jim came back up, with only one tank, it felt like ten hours, not ten minutes. His face was red from the cold, even though he hadn't been exposed to the water.

"You must be freezing," I said, helping him pull off the wetsuit and drag on his clothes.

"No, I'm not, that's the problem. Lucky thing I didn't need the whole ten minutes, or I wouldn't feel anything ever again. There's a couple of hand warmers in my bag, can you get them?"

Between the warmers and chafing his hands, it still took longer than I liked for Jim to feel that his fingers were up to the needed level of dexterity. I kept looking at my watch as he pulled on his coat and boots and started fixing another little gizmo to the bottom of the wood stove.

"Look, see this bit?" he said when I asked him about it, flicking a part that looked broken. "What's in the water—the real device—will sink to the bottom. This thing's to make it look like some amateur put the detonator too close to the wood stove and set the explosive off prematurely, though it won't be much of a bang. That's what you wanted, isn't it?"

"Right now, I want us to get out of here before Stefan the Hammer finds us." I looked at my watch again, zipped the blue pack shut and put on my coat.

"Timing is everything in your business too, eh?"

I took a moment at the door to check out the interior of the hut. Everything was back in place, matching the picture my brain had taken when we'd come in. The wet spots on the rug didn't show, and the love seat covered up the extra large hole, which had already begun freezing solid again.

"It's got to be done in the next twenty-four hours, thirty-six maximum, or I can't guarantee it'll work," Jim said as he stowed his gear back in the car. I resisted looking at my watch yet again.

"The devices are supposed to work in much colder temperatures, but this government issue stuff is notoriously under specs."

"You're telling me Canadians can't make bombs that will explode in the cold?" I pulled the door shut on the rental car and strapped myself in, not waiting for Jim to do the same before putting the car in gear.

"Sure, but it's easier to steal from the Americans."

* * *

There comes a time in every con game when you have to talk to the mark. Most people think of "con" as short for "confidence", as in what you abuse; it's also short for "convince", as in what you need to do. This is the part I do best, but this time it wasn't me who had to do it.

I waited until the next morning to broach the subject. Barb would work better on a night's sleep.

"You've got to get them to meet you at the lake," I said. "And soon enough that the device will still be working."

Barb balked at first, but in a few minutes I had her on the phone. Convincing is what I do best.

"Yeah, hi, is this Daniel? Dani, it's Barbara," she said, making a face. I knew how she hated to be called Barbara. "I'd like to speak with him. No, I mean if he still wants to talk to... Yeah, that's what I mean... Great, great. Can I make a suggestion? No, I thought out on Buffalo Pound... Precisely *because* you never do business out there, no one will think anything of it... right, right. I'll be waiting for your call..." Barb looked up at me, the corners of her mouth turned down. "That's my cousin from out east... sure, I'll tell her." She put down the phone and looked at me. "They've been watching me, like I thought," she said. "Dani

174

thinks you're cute." I checked my watch, hoping Barb wouldn't see my hands shaking. You don't want people like one of Stefan the Hammer's boys noticing you.

"Be ready," I said. "They'll know the place is clean, they were just out there themselves, but they won't want to give you time to set anything up with the police." I looked at my watch. We were closing in on the twenty-four hour mark, but well within the thirty-six. Luck would just have to be with us. I picked up my coat and slipped my phone into the pocket. "I'll call Jim on the way."

It took me about thirty minutes to get far enough out on the 301 causeway to see the ice hut through my binoculars. In a way, it was a good thing that Stefan's guys knew me, they wouldn't mistake me for a cop on lookout. If the bad guys weren't out here already, they would be soon, watching that Barb came alone.

I was very glad when I picked out Barb's car moving slowly along the ice road. She parked it in the turn around just before the road extended out to Stefan's hut and got out. Just as we'd counted on, she'd been given instructions to approach the hut on foot.

As Barb got closer, a mental countdown started going in my head. Any second now the device should blow. Any second. Barb should be close enough to look good, but far enough away not to be in any real danger, far enough away that anyone could see she had nothing to do with it. Any second. I lowered the binoculars and stamped my feet. What was taking so long?

A figure came from around the hut, and I lifted the binoculars to my eyes again just in time to focus on the unmistakable silhouette of a policeman in his winter uniform. I sucked in a lung full of bitingly cold air. The cop was waving

Barb away. Barb kept going, the movement of her arms showing me that she was trying to get the cop to come to her, away from the bomb she knew was in the hut. "Back away, Barb," I whispered. "Come on, get out of there."

The cop seemed to hear something and turned back to the hut. Barb stopped and put her hands up to her mouth—

A flash of light, followed a split second later by a BOOM! and the hut disappeared in clouds of dark smoke. Not much of an explosion, Jim had said. Well, that sure looked like much to me. I almost bit through my lip until I saw Barb. She was down on the ice but got up while I was watching. Other people had come barrelling out of a couple of the other huts, just in time to see Stefan Janobev's hut settle on a slant half way through the thick ice into the freezing water. A couple more people came out of the huts closest to the damaged one, pulling on coats as they came, one wearing a toque with a jaunty red pompom. I could see that quite a few of them had their cell phones out, but had any of them seen the cop?

Stomach sinking just a little, I pulled out my own phone and dialed 911.

*　　*　　*

My suitcase was packed and in the rental car when Barb finally got home. She was tight-lipped and steely-eyed.

"I've managed to keep you out of it so far," she said, "but they're bound to question me again."

"Why would you need to mention me?" I said.

"Lillian, a cop died out there! They're still looking for the body."

"And they'll be looking extra hard at Stefan and his boys, now, won't they?"

"Lillian." Barb's voice was a steel thread. "Somebody *died.*"

"Nah, nobody died." Jim came out of the bathroom towelling his still wet hair. We'd come here straight from Buffalo Pound, and he'd needed a hot shower. There were still red patches on his cheeks where he'd gotten a little too cold.

"There was no cop," I said, giving Barb a hug. "Just a uniform that's ended up at the bottom of the lake with the walleye. But thanks to your eyewitness account, the police think there was a cop. They'll be looking for the body for quite a while."

Barb looked from Jim to me and back again. "But how did you...?"

"I followed a cable under the water to the hut we rented," Jim said.

"I drilled the holes for him in the other hut before I went back to the causeway," I said.

"But it's too cold..."

"That's what anyone would think," I agreed. "By the time the police figure that out—if they ever do—you'll be in Ireland."

Barb looked at me and smiled. I watched the colour come back into her face.

Violette Malan's *published fiction includes mystery, romance, fantasy and erotica. Violette was co-winner of the first Bloody Words Bony Pete. Her mystery fiction is included in the noir anthology* Crime Spree, *and the Ladies' Killing Circle's* Fit to Die *and* Bone Dance. *She is co-founder of the annual Wolfe Island Scene of the Crime Festival.*

Don't Make Waves

Pat Withrow

No one talks to me, which is just one of the great blessings of my life. Mostly they don't talk to me because I used to be the police around here. That was back when an accused's falling downstairs twice at the police station was regarded as remedial. For both the criminal and the police officer. I know I felt better after these incidents. And the taxpayers used to know it kept the tax burden lower. Cheaper than jail.

When you're a policeman, people don't talk to you because you know about things like Snoogy's illegal (and rigged) curling bonspiel pool, and what goes on at the motel down the road when it isn't tourist season (and how much it costs) and what happened to the good Reverend's daughter when she went up to Halifax with the hockey team (and how often). Because you know those things, everybody suspects you know the truth about them too. About most of them I do, even if I don't have sufficient evidence.

And nobody talked a lot to Truly Ryan either. They couldn't. It was the accent.

Truly had been a Florida sheriff. Not in beach-and-mouse ears Florida, but in cows-and-piney-woods Florida. Think Jack Daniels and grits and people who hunt the backwoods wild hogs with assault rifles. Truly had a fog of a peckerwood accent.

Every summer when he came back up here with his trailer to escape Florida's heavy, sweaty summers, it would take me four-five days to begin to understand him again, even when he wasn't chewing tobacco. Gordon at the bar said he wished Truly was close-captioned or had a simultaneous translator, because otherwise it took eighteen minutes to get his drink order. That wasn't true, because Gord knew that Truly always had the same thing: Jack and water ("Jug un walda.").

Gord at the bar had also complained about Truly's bringing his dog into the bar, until Truly told him it was okay. When Truly said a situation was okay, people tended to believe they'd agree with him. I gave Gord a bit of a way out when I explained Truly needed the dog: the dog was an aid to the aged. That was actually true: the dog had been trained to fetch the remote control for Truly's television. Blessing in our later years. Truly said he'd strongly urge the puppy shelters to include the feature: "Fluffy can search down and fetch the dumb remote."

Truly'd been saying and doing some odd things lately. Old men watch each other.

He had bought cans of Planter's mixed nuts from every truck stop on his way up to Nova Scotia. He'd labelled them and done a forensic examination of how many of what kind of nuts were in each can. He'd then mailed the evidence to the Planter's company complaining that the number of cashews, or pecans or macadamias or some other dumb nuts was out of proportion to the large number of peanuts.

Planter's sent him a gift pack of nuts. But I don't think he was raising the whole fuss because he wanted nuts. I think it was because he was going nuts.

Also, I thought Truly was unhappy that summer. Sometimes he embraces unhappiness, but that could be because he is actually happy and worries that God is setting him up for something.

Truly's complicated.

When we were at Gord's, I'd always order a rum and Coke, Truly would get the usual, then Truly and I would sit there and not talk to each other for a while. Maybe after three we'd talk, but he found the process difficult too because I, to his mind, had an accent.

I speak fluent Lunenburg County, although I lost it when I went to university and learned enough to be a Bachelor of Arts and also learned enough to know that being a Bachelor of Arts wasn't much. I got the accent back after joining the police here, and I made myself fully understood to three generations of local miscreants before retirement.

*   *   *

The body showed up on Hertle Beach. Everybody knew that it was Walter Gallagher, even though he wasn't wearing any of the country squire clothes that very much impressed the local widowhood. Walter was completely unhaberdashed. Nude. That was a condition I'd always suspected a lot of the local widowhood had seen him in. The two officers who found him recognized him by the little goatee he devotedly trimmed. Some of the other bits were a little chewed up, but the fish and the gulls had left the goatee.

The state of the body meant local seafood sales would be down for the next few weeks.

I got the phone call about it at Gord's.

I sometimes get these phone calls, even though nobody wants to talk to me. I get them exactly because I don't talk to anyone. I also get them because I am no longer formally attached to the force. So when there's a difficult situation, the force can maintain its distance and therefore its reputation.

Walter Gallagher was evidently a difficult situation. I was invited to view the body, and I invited Truly to see what the coroner had done, although I indicated he could leave his dog somewhere else. He said, "Taught the dog not to eat off the table," and pulled on the dog's leash. "It's okay."

*　　*　　*

To me, Walter Gallagher hadn't been much in life, and he was certainly less in death. There'd been an air about him that made some people believe that he'd rode to the hounds or that he was a confidant of cabinet members or done something that involved wearing a lot of tweed. When he'd arrived in our town seven years before, he'd left his previous life carefully unexplained. Just as carefully, he'd insert vague hints: "The French can be superb yachtsmen, but their behaviour at sea can be dreadful"; "Bush's funding? Never adequately accounted for. To the public"; "You can still get an good pair of hand-lasted shoes if you know where." He carried around a copy of *The Economist*. It was usually three months old.

Looking at the body on the stainless steel table told me just about nothing: thin, white, seventy-year-old dead male, six feet tall, 156 pounds. Thinner than I would have thought. No marks. No bruises. Truly looked for a few minutes and shrugged slightly. The dog was nervous. We turned to the recently-hired, young, pretty Doctor Blevin, who'd done the examination of the body. Who said: "This kind of thing is fairly common. Go out on a boat. Drink too much. Go on deck nude for a pee. Wave comes. You fall off. You drown. He tested about .24 alcohol." Dr. Blevin was right: this kind of accident is common. Any coroner or insurance agent in proximity to a body of water will tell you those who go down to the sea in recreational watercraft are likely to have recreational beverages with them.

So I nodded.

But then Truly asked the question. I had to translate it for the doctor: "Who goes for a pee with a condom on?" She peered at the appendage in question. I could understand how she might have decided to overlook it

"Always tell a lot about a man from his dick," Truly said. I didn't translate. I just said we'd call her back later when she wasn't so rushed and had had a larger opportunity to explore the nuances of the problem. Give them a way out when they need it. Inexperienced, young, probably not too happy handling the messy remains of a corpse of an older man and therefore too anxious to jump to the usual conclusion.

But then, somebody else had heard her too-fast results earlier than I had. That somebody also thought something was wrong with the usual conclusion, or I wouldn't have got the phone call. And somebody thought the whole thing had a potential for embarrassing some important people, or I wouldn't have got the phone call from the person I got it from.

*   *   *

"Fell off the boat? That'd mean there had to be a boat. So where's the boat?" Truly nodded: he could have been actually looking for the boat in his glass of Jack. The dog was curled around the bottom of his barstool. Truly thoughtfully dropped a peanut from the bowl on the bar to the floor. The dog just as thoughtfully ate it.

"We appear to be short a woman too. The condom." Truly

nodded some more.

"We're looking for a woman and a boat," he said.

"Great analysis."

"My specialty." Actually, I thought Truly's specialty had likely been cleaning out barrooms, which requires a certain amount of analysis, but a lot more efficient violence. I hadn't been good at it. In those years, I tended to lose patience, which had led to inefficiency. I had later gained patience, because you have to. Not a great deal, though. "Woman and a boat," I said.

"We'll go look in his house."

"The woman and the boat are in his house?"

"No. But we don't know what else to do."

I phoned the man who had phoned me and made arrangements. We'd go look at Walter's house.

*   *   *

Where Walter had lived wasn't a house, only part of one. It was an apartment in one of the big old timber homes that lined the street overlooking the harbour. They'd been built back when the captains of the fishing schooners in the cod fleet used to have a lot of children. The view from their porches was postcard stuff, rustic and calm. However, the mortgage you'd have to take on to buy one now was frightening. This was retirement country, full of people who'd cashed in their city house and paid a local in town too much for a pile of damp cuteness.

The apartment was like the man: neat, natty, tidy, tweedy. A lot of brass. Some hunting prints. It looked like an ad for single malt scotch or an investment broker. Any moment now, somebody was going to come out of the kitchen and ask me how I liked my dumb latte.

That kind of place.

Truly was doing what most women and some smart cops did when they first walked into the living quarters of a stranger—checking out the medicine cabinet. He carefully nudged each of the items with the eraser end of a pencil, shifting his tobacco from one cheek to another, then he slowly closed the mirrored door and came back into the living room with his head tilted.

"Watch golf? On television?"

It is a measure of something in my life that although I didn't play it, I did watch it, and so I nodded.

"Used to be Buick that sponsored it, or Shell gasoline." He shifted the tobacco. It wasn't a big baseball player-sized wad, just a little thing he could worry at. "Now it's erectile dysfunction medications. Viagra. Cialis."

"The ones that tell you if you have an erection for longer than four hours you should see your doctor?"

"Wouldn't be going to see my doctor about that. I'd be smuggling that rascal over to see Mrs. Hoskins who used to work over at the library." He considered the possibilities for some long seconds.

I interrupted: "So we have some sort of confirmation that there was a woman involved."

"How do you buy your condoms?"

"Don't remember. Last time I did that was when most people were going to Halifax or at least another town to do that kind of shopping. It was before sex was officially allowed around here."

"Walter bought them in the same quantities a hooker at a logger's convention would. Giant-sized pack. Not the condoms: the pack. Giant-sized."

"Thrifty."

"Strike you he was tight with a dollar?"

"Not too."

"My own analysis would be that there was more than one woman involved."

* * *

We walked back to Gord's, following Truly's brown and white hound. The dog walked oddly if you looked at it from the back. It made you think of the way two guys walked in a horse costume. You've seen two guys in a horse costume. They don't get quite coordinated, and the gait is inelegant. Imagine the two guys drunk. That was Truly's dog.

This whole thing was inelegant and uncoordinated and not quite fitting together, and I said that to Truly when Gord had brought the drinks and the dog had curled itself around the bottom of Truly's bar stool again.

"No, I think it's starting to fit together," Truly said. "We've got a dead drunk with erectile dysfunction, found naked except for a condom." I think Gord understood part of what Truly was saying, because he started to stare. Truly stared back. Gord went to the other end of the bar. Truly gave good stare. I think they teach it to police in Florida. He scooted his stool a little closer to me and said, "So I believe what we're looking for is a group of sixty-year-old women with access to a boat and liquor."

"Oh," I said. "You mean the yacht club. On the island."

"That what I mean?"

"Yes, I guess."

"Well, we should get ourselves over there. I'm thinking we have some bad news for the ladies."

*   *   *

The ladies weren't at the yacht club. Truly asked me to ask the waitress there the two simple questions that got us to where they were: "Mr. Walter Gallagher go out on a boat with some folks yesterday?" and "Know where they live?" The questions were easy, but the answer came a little hard because, as I've mentioned, people don't like talking to me, even the sunny, slender student summer help that was serving that afternoon. She did talk, though: I'd helped her uncle once. And I guess she saw I was looking stupid and worried and she wanted to help.

We found them at the second house where we rang the doorbell.

There are a number of things which make a police officer nervous about a person of interest. Three of them are fame, political power and wealth. We had all of them in the dim living room we entered. The drapes were half shut, and the three ladies' glasses were half empty.

On our drive from the yacht club, Truly had told me what had to be said to them, and when we got there, I said it quickly. Didn't even sit down, because I knew we weren't staying: "They found Walter Gallagher this morning, drunk with a condom on. He was naked."

They didn't look up.

"We asked ourselves this: what was a seventy-one-year-old guy doing with a condom on? I mean, we know what he was doing, but why was he doing it with a condom on? Because who he was doing it with was likely to be of his own age and not likely to get pregnant from doing it. So the condom wasn't to prevent conception, it was to prevent disease. Then we thought that the good ladies of that age in this town weren't likely to have STDS, because...I mean, you just don't think of that in conjunction with the good ladies of this town. And so we thought that it might be that the guy was the person who was trying to stop the disease from transmitting. But in Florida you see, they've found this problem.

"This problem is…in retirement communities, there are more women than men. Some of the retirement communities in Florida have seven women to every man. Which didn't used to be more than an occasional problem, because men in retirement communities aren't like the boys in, say, high school. Things aren't functioning the same. In the retirement communities, the men used to sit around watching golf and the women used to tat potholders or something.

"Any of you watch golf?"

Slight nods.

"Those advertisements about erectile dysfunction drugs? Man aged seventy-one. Surrounded by a lot of surplus ladies. Starts taking erectile dysfunction drugs. Ladies stop tatting potholders because they're suddenly otherwise occupied. Which leads to a problem."

Some slight nods.

"Problem's this. Because everybody's of an age, no one is using any protection. Result is this: HIV is growing twice as fast in people over fifty than it is in people under forty. Women over sixty are at the greatest risk."

At that, Truly walked to the front door and opened it. I followed him out and heard the screen slam behind.

*　　*　　*

In the car on the way back, I asked Truly, "You think they knew about the HIV thing?"

Truly nodded.

"You think they got it from him?"

"Don't know. Don't want to. I believe they know what to do, and they'll do the right things."

"You think they got him on board, got him drunk, showed him a good time and then rolled him off the stern?"

"Could have happened that way. On the other hand, I lean towards believing it was a heart attack. Erectile dysfunction is a red flag for heart disease. Bad circulation causes limp dick. Also they warn you about drinking with those pills, because that can trigger an angina attack in some people. The risk ratchets up when you add in strenuous activity. Which sex is, if memory serves. Times three women…"

"Heart attack. Yes."

We could agree on that.

I think we could arrange general agreement on that. There was no good thing to come of not agreeing on that. I'd phone the man who phoned me and tell him that there was nothing to worry about; heart attack, nothing for the police, and he'd be happier.

We went back to Gord's with the dog and sat there not talking. Sometimes I don't want to listen to people every bit as much as people don't want to talk to me. For example, I didn't want to hear how Truly knew about all this: the facts and the figures and the contra-indications. He probably read about it in the *Readers' Digest*. I think we could agree on that.

Pat Withrow *is pretty retired and divides his time between Sarasota, Florida and Port Hope, Ontario. He's ghost-written books, and written books under his own name. He's also written songs, television shows, product labels, matchbook covers, magazine articles, political speeches and bus stop information panels. This is his first short story.*

THE VENGEFUL SPIRIT OF LAKE NEPEAKEA

Tanya Huff

This story is offered by the editors as an homage to
Conan Doyle's The Hound of the Baskervilles

"Camping?"

"Why sound so amazed?" Dragging the old turquoise cooler behind her, Vicki Nelson, once one of Toronto's finest and currently the city's most successful paranormal investigator, backed out of Mike Celluci's crawl space.

"Why? Maybe because you've never been camping in your life. Maybe because your idea of roughing it is a hotel without room service. Maybe..." He moved just far enough for Vicki to get by, then followed her out into the rec room. "...because you're a ..."

"A?" Setting the cooler down beside two sleeping bags and a pair of ancient swim fins, she turned to face him. "A *what*, Mike?" Grey eyes silvered.

"Stop it."

Grinning, she turned her attention back to the cooler. "Besides, I won't be on vacation, I'll be working. You'll be the one enjoying the great outdoors."

"Vicki, my idea of the great outdoors is going to the Skydome for a Jays game."

"No one's forcing you to come." Setting the lid to one side, she curled her nose at the smell coming out of the cooler's depths. "When was the last time you used this thing?"

"Police picnic, 1992. Why?"

She turned it up on its end. The desiccated body of a mouse rolled out, bounced twice and came to rest with its sightless little eyes staring up at Celluci. "I think you need to buy a new cooler."

"I think I need a better explanation than 'I've got a great way for you to use up your long weekend,'" he sighed, kicking the tiny corpse under the rec room couch.

* * *

"So this developer from Toronto, Stuart Gordon, bought an old lodge on the shores of Lake Nepeakea, and he wants to build a rustic, timeshare resort so junior executives can relax in the woods. Unfortunately, one of the surveyors disappeared, and local opinion seems to be that he's pissed off the lake's protective spirit..."

"The what?"

Vicki pulled out to pass a transport and deftly reinserted the van back into her own lane before replying. "The protective spirit. You know, the sort of thing that rises out of the lake to vanquish evil." A quick glance toward the passenger seat brought her brows in. "Mike, are you all right? You're going to leave permanent finger marks in the dashboard."

He shook his head. A truckload of logs coming down from Northern Ontario had missed them by inches. Feet at the very most. *All right, maybe metres, but not very many of them.* When they'd left the city, just after sunset, it had seemed logical that Vicki, with her better night sight, should drive. He was regretting that logic now but, realizing he didn't have a hope in hell of gaining control of the vehicle, he tried to force himself to relax. "The speed limit isn't just a good idea," he growled through clenched teeth, "it's the law."

She grinned, her teeth very white in the darkness. "You didn't used to be this nervous."

"I didn't used to have cause." His fingers wouldn't release their grip, so he left them where they were. "So this missing surveyor, what did he..."

"She."

"...she do to piss off the protective spirit?"

"Nothing much. She was just working for Stuart Gordon."

"The same Stuart Gordon you're working for."

"The very one."

Right. Celluci stared out at the trees and tried not to think about how fast they were passing. *Vicki Nelson against the protective spirit of Lake Nepeakea. That's one for pay-for-view...*

* * *

"This is the place."

"No. In order for this to be 'the place', there'd have to be something here. It has to be 'a place' before it can be 'the place'."

"I hate to admit it," Vicki muttered, leaning forward and peering over the arc of the steering wheel, "but you've got a point." They'd gone through the village of Dulvie, turned right at the ruined barn and followed the faded signs to "The Lodge". The road, if the rutted lanes of the last few kilometres could be called a road, had ended, as per the directions she'd received, in a small gravel parking lot—or more specifically, in a hard packed rectangular area that could now be called a parking lot, because she'd stopped her van on it. "He said you could see the lodge from here."

Celluci snorted. "Maybe *you* can."

"No. I can't. All I can see are trees." At least, she assumed they were trees, the high contrast between the area her headlights covered and the total darkness beyond made it difficult to tell for sure. Silently, calling herself several kinds of fool, she switched off the lights. The shadows separated into half a dozen large evergreens, and the silhouette of a roof steeply angled to shed snow.

Since it seemed they'd arrived, Vicki shut off the engine. After a heartbeat's silence, the night exploded into a cacophony of discordant noise. Hands over sensitive ears, she sank back into the seat. "What the hell is that?"

"Horny frogs."

"How do you know?" she demanded.

He gave her a superior smile. "PBS."

"Oh." They sat there for a moment, listening to the frogs. "The creatures of the night," Vicki sighed, "what music they make." Snorting derisively, she got out of the van. "Somehow, I expected the middle of nowhere to be a lot quieter."

Stuart Gordon had sent Vicki the key to the lodge's back door, and once she switched on the main breaker, they found themselves in a modern, stainless steel kitchen that wouldn't have looked out of place in any small, trendy restaurant back in Toronto. The sudden hum of the refrigerator turning on momentarily drowned out the frogs, and both Vicki and Celluci relaxed.

"So now what?" he asked.

"Now we unpack your food from the cooler, we find you a room, and we make the most of the short time we have until dawn."

"And when does Mr. Gordon arrive?"

"Tomorrow evening. Don't worry, I'll be up."

"And I'm supposed to do what, tomorrow in the daytime?"

"I'll leave my notes out. I'm sure something'll occur to you."

"I thought I was on vacation?"

"Then do what you usually do on vacation."

"Your foot work." He folded his arms. "And on my last vacation—which was also your idea—I almost lost a kidney."

Closing the refrigerator door, Vicki crossed the room between one heartbeat and the next. Leaning into him, their bodies touching between ankle and chest, she smiled into his eyes and pushed the long curl of hair back off his forehead. "Don't worry, I'll protect you from the spirit of the lake. I have no intention of sharing you with another legendary being."

"Legendary?" He couldn't stop a smile. "Think highly of yourself, don't you?"

*　　*　　*

"Are you sure you'll be safe in the van?"

"Stop fussing. You know I'll be fine." Pulling her jeans up over her hips, she stared out the window and shook her head. "There's a whole lot of nothing out there."

From the bed, Celluci could see a patch of stars and the top of one of the evergreens. "True enough."

"And I really don't like it."

"Then why are we here?"

"Stuart Gordon just kept talking. I don't even remember saying yes, but the next thing I knew, I'd agreed to do the job."

"He pressured *you?*" Celluci's emphasis on the final pronoun made it quite clear that he hadn't believed such a thing was possible.

"Not pressured, no. Convinced with extreme prejudice."

"He sounds like a prince."

"Yeah? Well, so was Machiavelli." Dressed, she leaned over

the bed and kissed him lightly. "Want to hear something romantic? When the day claims me, yours will be the only life I'll be able to feel."

"Romantic?" His breathing quickened as she licked at the tiny puncture wounds on his wrist. "I feel like a box luuu...ouch! All right. It's romantic."

*   *   *

Although she'd tried to keep her voice light when she'd mentioned it to Celluci, Vicki really *didn't* like the great outdoors. Maybe it was because she understood the wilderness of glass and concrete and needed the anonymity of three million lives packed tightly around hers. Standing by the van, she swept her gaze from the first hints of dawn to the last lingering shadows of night and couldn't help feeling excluded, that there was something beyond what she could see that she wasn't a part of. She doubted Stuart Gordon's junior executives would feel a part of it either and wondered why anyone would want to build a resort in the midst of such otherness.

The frogs had stopped trying to get laid, and the silence seemed to be waiting for something.

Waiting...

Vicki glanced toward Lake Nepeakea. It lay like a silver mirror down at the bottom of a rocky slope. Not a ripple broke the surface. Barely a mile away, a perfect reflection brought the opposite shore closer still.

Waiting...

Whipper-will!

Vicki winced at the sudden, piercing sound and got into the van. After locking both outer and inner doors, she stripped quickly—if she were found during the day, nakedness would be the least of her problems—laid down between the high, padded sides of the narrow bed and waited for the dawn. The bird call, repeated with Chinese water torture frequency, cut its way through special seals and interior walls.

"Man, that's annoying," she muttered, linking her fingers over her stomach. "I wonder if Celluci can sleep through..."

*   *   *

As soon as he heard the van door close, Celluci fell into a dreamless sleep that lasted until just past noon. When he woke, he stared up at the inside of the roof and wondered where he was. The rough lumber looked like it'd been coated in creosote in the far distant past.

"No insulation, hate to be here in the winter..."

Then he remembered where *here* was and came fully awake.

Vicki had dragged him out to a wilderness lodge, north of Georgian Bay, to hunt for the local and apparently homicidal protective lake spirit.

A few moments later, his sleeping bag neatly rolled on the end of the old iron bed, he was in the kitchen, making a pot of coffee. That kind of a realization upon waking needed caffeine.

On the counter next to the coffee maker, right where he'd be certain to find it first thing, he found a file labelled "Lake Nepeakea" in Vicki's unmistakable handwriting. The first few pages of glossy card stock had been clearly sent by Stuart Gordon along with the key. An artist's conception of the timeshare resort, they showed a large L-shaped building where the lodge now stood and three dozen "cottages" scattered through the woods, front doors linked by broad gravel paths. Apparently, the guests would commute out to their personal chalets by golf cart.

"Which they can also use on..." Celluci turned the page and shook his head in disbelief. "...the nine hole golf course." Clearly, a large part of Mr. Gordon's building plan involved bulldozers. And right after the bulldozers would come the cappuccino. He shuddered.

The next few pages were clipped together and turned out to be photocopies of newspaper articles covering the disappearance of the surveyor. She'd been working with her partner in the late evening, trying to finish up a particularly marshy bit of shore destined to be filled in and paved over for tennis courts, when, according to her partner, she'd stepped back into the mud, announced something had moved under her foot, lost her balance, fell, screamed and disappeared. The OPP, aided by local volunteers, had set up an extensive search, but she hadn't been found. Since the area was usually avoided because of the sink holes, sink holes a distraught Stuart Gordon swore he knew nothing about—" Probably distraught about having to move his tennis courts," Celluci muttered— the official verdict allowed that she'd probably stepped in one and been sucked under the mud.

The headline on the next page declared "DEVELOPER ANGERS SPIRIT", and in slightly smaller type, "Surveyor Pays the Price". The picture showed an elderly woman with long grey braids and a hawklike profile staring enigmatically out over the water. First impressions suggested a First Nations elder. After actually reading the text, however, Celluci discovered that Mary Joseph had moved out to Dulvie from Toronto in 1995 and had become, in the years since, the self-proclaimed keeper of local myth. According to Ms Joseph, although there had been many sightings over the years, there had been only two other occasions when the spirit of the lake had felt threatened enough to kill. "It protects the lake," she was quoted as saying, "from those who would disturb its peace."

"Two weeks ago," Celluci noted, checking the date. "Tragic, but hardly a reason for Stuart Gordon to go to the effort of convincing Vicki to leave the city."

The final photocopy included a close-up of a car door that looked like it had been splashed with acid. "SPIRIT ATTACKS DEVELOPER'S VEHICLE". During the night of May 13th, the protector of Lake Nepeakea had crawled up into the parking lot of the lodge and secreted something corrosive and distinctly fishy against Stuart Gordon's brand new Isuzu trooper. *A trail of dead bracken, a little over a foot wide and smelling strongly of rotting fish, lead back to the lake.* Mary Joseph seemed convinced it was a manifestation of the spirit, the local police were looking for anyone who might have information about the vandalism, and Stuart Gordon announced he was bringing in a special investigator from Toronto to settle it once and for all.

It was entirely probable that the surveyor had stepped into a mud hole, and that local vandals were using the legends of the spirit against an unpopular developer. Entirely probable. But living with Vicki had forced Mike Celluci to deal with half a dozen improbable things every morning before breakfast, so, mug in hand, he headed outside to investigate the crime scene.

Because of the screen of evergreens (although given their size barricade was probably the more descriptive word) the parking lot couldn't be seen from the lodge. Considering the impenetrable appearance of the overlapping branches, Celluci was willing to bet that not even light would get through. The spirit could have done anything it wanted to, up to and including changing the oil, in perfect secrecy.

Brushing one or two small insects away from his face, Celluci found the path they'd used the night before and followed it. By the time he reached the van, the one or two insects had become twenty-nine or thirty, and he felt the first bite on the back of his neck. When he slapped the spot, his fingers came away dotted with blood.

"Vicki's not going to be happy about that," he grinned, wiping it off on his jeans. By the second and third bites, he'd stopped grinning. By the fourth and fifth, he really didn't give a damn what Vicki thought. By the time he'd stopped counting, he was running for the lake, hoping that the breeze he could see stirring its surface would be enough to blow the little bastards away.

The faint but unmistakable scent of rotting fish rose from the dead bracken crushed under his pounding feet, and he realized that he was using the path made by the manifestation. It was about two feet wide and led down an uncomfortably steep slope from the parking lot to the lake. But not exactly all the way to the lake. The path ended about three feet above the water on a granite ledge.

Swearing, mostly at Vicki, Celluci threw himself backwards, somehow managing to save both his coffee and himself from taking an unexpected swim. The following cloud of insects effortlessly matched the move. A quick glance through the bugs showed the ledge tapering off to the right. He bounded down it to the water's edge and found himself standing on a small, man-made beach staring at a floating dock that stretched out maybe fifteen feet into the lake. Proximity to the water *had* seemed to discourage the swarm, so he headed for the dock, hoping that the breeze would be stronger fifteen feet out.

It was. Flicking a few bodies out of his coffee, Celluci took a long, grateful drink and turned to look back up at the lodge. Studying the path he'd taken, he was amazed he hadn't broken an ankle and had to admit a certain appreciation for who or what had created it. A greying staircase made of split logs offered a more conventional way to the water and the tiny patch of gritty sand, held in place by a stone wall. Stuart Gordon's plans included a much larger beach and had replaced the old wooden dock with three concrete piers.

"One for papa bear, one for mama bear, and one for baby bear," Celluci mused, shuffling around on the gently rocking platform until he faced the water. Not so far away, the far shore was an unbroken wall of trees. He didn't know if there *were* bears in this part of the province, but there were certainly bathroom facilities for any number of them. Letting the breeze push his hair back off his face, he took another swallow of rapidly cooling coffee and listened to the silence. It was unnerving.

The sudden roar of a motor boat came as a welcome relief. Watching it bounce its way up the lake, he considered how far the sound carried and made a mental note to close the window should Vicki spend any significant portion of the night with him.

The moment distance allowed, the boat's driver waved over the edge of the cracked windshield and, in a great, banked turn that sprayed a huge fantail of water out behind him, headed toward the exact spot where Celluci stood. Celluci's fingers tightened around the handle of the mug, but he held his ground. Still turning, the driver cut his engines and drifted the last few meters to the dock. As empty bleach bottles slowly crumpled under the gentle impact, he jumped out and tied off his bow line.

"Frank Patton," he said, straightening from the cleat and holding out a callused hand. "You must be the guy that developer's brought in from the city to capture the spirit of the lake."

"Detective Sergeant Mike Celluci." His own age or a little younger, Frank Patton had a working man's grip that was just a little too forceful. Celluci returned pressure for pressure.

"And I'm just spending a long weekend in the woods."

Patton's dark brows drew down. "But I thought..."

"You thought I was some weirdo psychic you could impress by crushing his fingers." The other man looked down at their joined hands and had the grace to flush. As he released his hold, so did Celluci. He'd played this game too often to lose at it. "I suggest, if you get the chance to meet the actual investigator, you don't come on quite so strong. She's liable to feed you your preconceptions."

"She's..."

"Asleep right now. We got in late, and she's likely to be up...investigating tonight."

"Yeah. Right." Flexing his fingers, Patton stared down at the toes of his workboots. "It's just, you know, we heard that, well..." Sucking in a deep breath, he looked up and grinned. "Oh hell, talk about getting off on the wrong foot. Can I get you a beer, Detective?"

Celluci glanced over at the styrofoam cooler in the back of the boat and was tempted for a moment. As sweat rolled painfully into the bug bites on the back of his neck, he remembered just how good a cold beer could taste. "No, thanks," he sighed with a disgusted glare into his mug. "I've, uh, still got coffee."

To his surprise, Patton nodded and asked, "How long've you been dry? My brother-in-law gets that exact same look when some damn fool offers him a drink on a hot almost summer afternoon," he explained as Celluci stared at him in astonishment. "Goes to AA meetings in Bigwood twice a week."

Remembering all the bottles he'd climbed into during those long months, when Vicki had been gone, Celluci shrugged. "About two years now—give or take."

"I got generic cola..."

He dumped the dregs of cold, bug-infested coffee into the

lake. The Ministry of Natural Resources could kiss his ass. "Love one," he said.

*   *   *

"So essentially, everyone in town and everyone who owns property around the lake and everyone in a hundred kilometre radius has reason to want Stuart Gordon gone."

"Essentially," Celluci agreed, tossing a gnawed chicken bone aside and pulling another piece out of the bucket. He'd waited to eat until Vicki got up, maintaining the illusion that it was a ritual they continued to share. "According to Frank Patton, he hasn't endeared himself to his new neighbours. This place used to belong to an Anne Kellough, who...what?"

Vicki frowned and leaned toward him. "You're covered in bites."

"Tell me about it." The reminder brought his hand up to scratch at the back of his neck. "You know what Nepeakea means? It's an old Indian word that translates as 'I'm fucking sick of being eaten alive by blackflies; let's get the hell out of here.'"

"Those old Indians could get a lot of mileage out of a word."

Celluci snorted. "Tell me about it."

"Anne Kellough?"

"What, not even one 'poor sweet baby'?"

Stretching out her leg under the table, she ran her foot up the inseam of his jeans. "Poor sweet baby."

"That'd be a lot more effective if you weren't wearing hiking boots." Her laugh was one of the things that hadn't changed when she had. Her smile was too white and too sharp, and it made too many new promises, but her laugh remained fully human. He waited until she finished, chewing, swallowing, congratulating himself for evoking it, then said,

"Anne Kellough ran this place as sort of a therapy camp. Last summer, after ignoring her for thirteen years, the Ministry of Health people came down on her kitchen. Renovations cost more than she thought, the bank foreclosed, and Stuart Gordon bought it twenty minutes later."

"That explains why she wants him gone—what about everyone else?"

"Lifestyle."

"They think he's gay?"

"Not his, theirs. The people who live out here, down in the village and around the lake—while not adverse to taking the occasional tourist for everything they can get—like the quiet, they like the solitude and, God help them, they even like the woods. The boys who run the hunting and fishing camp at the west end of the lake..."

"Boys?"

"I'm quoting here. The boys," he repeated, with emphasis, "say Gordon's development will kill the fish and scare off the game. He nearly got his ass kicked by one of them, Pete Wegler, down at the local gas station, then got tossed out on said ass by the owner when he called the place quaint."

"In the sort of tone that adds, and a Starbucks would be a big improvement?" When Celluci raised a brow, she shrugged. "I've spoken to him, it's not that much of an extrapolation."

"Yeah, exactly that sort of tone. Frank also told me that people with kids are concerned about the increase in traffic right through the center of the village."

"Afraid they'll start losing children and pets under expensive sport utes?"

"That, and they're worried about an increase in taxes to maintain the road with all the extra traffic." Pushing away from the table, he started closing plastic containers and carrying them to the fridge. "Apparently, Stuart Gordon, ever so diplomatically, told one of the village women that this was no place to raise kids."

"What happened?"

"Frank says they got them apart before it went much beyond name calling."

Wondering how far "much beyond name calling" went, Vicki watched Mike clean up the remains of his meal. "Are you sure he's pissed off more than just these few people? Even if this was already a resort, and he didn't have to rezone, local council must've agreed to his building permit."

"Yeah, and local opinion would feed local council to the spirit right alongside Mr. Gordon. Rumour has it they've been bought off."

Tipping her chair back against the wall, she smiled up at him. "Can I assume from your busy day that you've come down on the mud hole/vandals side of the argument?"

"It does seem the most likely." He turned and scratched at the back of his neck again. When his fingertips came away damp, he heard her quick intake of breath. When he looked up, she was crossing the kitchen. Cool fingers wrapped around the side of his face.

"You didn't shave."

It took him a moment to find his voice. "I'm on vacation."

Her breath lapped against him, then her tongue.

The lines between likely and unlikely blurred.

Then the sound of an approaching engine jerked him out of her embrace.

Vicki licked her lips and sighed. "Six cylinder, sport utility, four wheel drive, all the extras, black with gold trim."

Celluci tucked his shirt back in. "Stuart Gordon told you what he drives."

"Unless you think I can tell all that from the sound of the engine."

"Not likely."

*   *   *

"A detective sergeant? I'm impressed." Pale hands in the pockets of his tweed blazer, Stuart Gordon leaned conspiratorially in toward Celluci, too many teeth showing in too broad a grin. "I don't suppose you could fix a few parking tickets."

"No."

Thin lips pursed in exaggerated reaction to the blunt monosyllable. "Then what do you *do,* Detective Sergeant?"

"Violent crimes."

Thinking that sounded a little too much like a suggestion, Vicki intervened. "Detective Celluci has agreed to assist me this weekend. Between us, we'll be able to keep a twenty-four hour watch."

"Twenty-four hours?" The developer's brows drew in. "I'm not paying more for that."

"I'm not asking you to."

"Good." Stepping up onto the raised hearth as though it were a stage, he smiled with all the sincerity of a television infomercial. "Then I'm glad to have you aboard Detective, Mike—can I call you Mike?" He continued without waiting for an answer. "Call me Stuart. Together we'll make this a safe place for the weary masses able to pay a premium price for a premium week in the woods." A heartbeat later, his smile grew strained. "Don't you two have detecting to do?"

*   *   *

"Call me Stuart?" Shaking his head, Celluci followed Vicki's dark on dark silhouette out to the parking lot. "Why is he here?"

"He's bait."

"Bait? The man's a certified asshole, sure, but we are not using him to attract an angry lake spirit."

She turned and walked backward so she could study his face. Sometimes he forgot how well she could see in the dark and forgot to mask his expressions. "Mike, you don't believe that call-me-Stuart has actually pissed off some kind of vengeful spirit protecting Lake Nepeakea?"

"You're the one who said bait..."

"Because we're not going to catch the person, or persons, who threw acid on his car unless we catch them in the act. He understands that."

"Oh. Right."

Feeling the bulk of the van behind her, she stopped. "You didn't answer my question."

He sighed and folded his arms, wishing he could see her as well as she could see him. "Vicki, in the last four years I have been attacked by demons, mummies, zombies, werewolves..."

"That wasn't an attack, that was a misunderstanding."

"He went for my throat, I count it as an attack. I've offered my blood to the bastard son of Henry VIII, and I've spent two years watching you hide from the day. There isn't anything much I don't believe in any more."

"But..."

"I believe in you," he interrupted, "and from there, it's not that big a step to just about anywhere. Are you going to speak with Mary Joseph tonight?" His tone suggested the discussion was over.

"No, I was going to check means and opportunity on that list of names you gave me." She glanced down toward the lake then up at him, not entirely certain what she was looking for in either instance. "Are you going to be all right out here on your own?"

"Why the hell wouldn't I be?"

"No reason." She kissed him, got into the van, and leaned out the open window to add, "Try and remember, Sigmund, that sometimes a cigar is just a cigar."

* * *

Celluci watched Vicki drive away then turned on his flashlight and played the beam over the side of Stuart's car. Although it would have been more helpful to have seen the damage, he had to admit that the body shop had done a good job. And to give the man credit, however reluctantly, developing a wilderness property did provide more of an excuse than most of his kind had for the four wheel drive.

Making his way over to an outcropping of rock, where he could see both the parking lot and the lake but not be seen, Celluci sat down and turned off his light. According to Frank Patton, the blackflies only fed during the day, and the water was still too cold for mosquitos. He wasn't entirely convinced, but, since nothing had bitten him so far, the information seemed accurate. "I wonder if Stuart knows his little paradise is crawling with bloodsuckers." Right thumb stroking the puncture wound on his left wrist, he turned toward the lodge.

His eyes widened.

Behind the evergreens, the lodge blazed with light. Inside lights. Outside lights. Every light in the place. The harsh yellow white illumination washed out the stars up above and threw everything below into such sharp relief that even the lush, spring growth seemed manufactured. The shadows under the distant trees were now solid, impenetrable sheets of darkness.

"Well, at least Ontario Hydro's glad he's here." Shaking his head in disbelief, Celluci returned to his surveillance.

Too far away for the light to reach it, the lake threw up shimmering reflections of the stars and lapped gently against the shore.

*   *   *

Finally back on the paved road, Vicki unclenched her teeth and followed the southern edge of the lake toward the village. With nothing between the passenger side of the van and the water but a whitewashed guardrail and a few tumbled rocks, it was easy enough to look out the window and pretend she was driving on the lake itself. When the shoulder widened into a small parking area and a boat ramp, she pulled over and shut off the van.

The water moved inside its narrow channel like liquid darkness, opaque and mysterious. The part of the night that belonged to her ended at the water's edge.

"Not the way it's supposed to work," she muttered, getting out of the van and walking down the boat ramp. Up close, she could see through four or five inches of liquid to a stony bottom and the broken shells of fresh water clams but beyond that, it was hard not to believe she couldn't just walk across to the other side.

The ubiquitous spring chorus of frogs suddenly fell silent, drawing Vicki's attention around to a marshy cove off to her right. The silence was so complete, she thought she could hear a half a hundred tiny amphibian hearts beating. One. Two...

"Hey, there."

She'd spun around and taken a step out into the lake before

her brain caught up with her reaction. The feel of cold water filling her hiking boots brought her back to herself, and she damped the hunter in her eyes before the man in the canoe had time to realize his danger.

Paddle in the water, holding the canoe in place, he nodded down at Vicki's feet. "You don't want to be doing that."

"Doing what?"

"Wading at night. You're going to want to see where you're going. Old Nepeakea drops off fast." He jerked his head back toward the silvered darkness. "Even the ministry boys couldn't tell you how deep she is in the middle. She's got so much loose mud on the bottom, it kept throwing back their sonar readings."

"Then what are you doing here?"

"Well, I'm not wading, that's for sure."

"Or answering my question," Vicki muttered, stepping back out on the shore. Wet feet making her less than happy, she half hoped for another smartass comment.

"I often canoe at night. I like the quiet." He grinned in at her, clearly believing he was too far away and there was too little light for her to see the appraisal that went with it. "You must be that investigator from Toronto. I saw your van when I was up at the lodge today."

"You must be Frank Patton. You've changed your boat."

"Can't be quiet in a fifty horsepower Evinrude, can I? You going in to see Mary Joseph?"

"No. I was going in to see Anne Kellough."

"Second house past the stop sign on the right. Little yellow bungalow with a carport." He slid backward so quietly, even Vicki wouldn't have known he was moving had she not been watching him. He handled the big aluminum canoe with practiced ease. "I'd offer you a lift, but I'm sure you're in a hurry."

Vicki smiled. "Thanks, anyway." Her eyes silvered. "Maybe another time."

She was still smiling as she got into the van. Out on the lake, Frank Patton splashed about trying to retrieve the canoe paddle that had dropped from nerveless fingers.

*   *   *

"Frankly, I hate the little bastard, but there's no law against that." Anne Kellough pulled her sweater tighter and leaned back against the porch railing. "He's the one who set the health department on me, you know."

"I didn't."

"Oh, yeah. He came up here about three months before it happened, looking for land, and he wanted mine. I wouldn't sell it to him, so he figured out a way to take it." Anger quickened her breathing and flared her nostrils. "He as much as told me, after it was all over, with that big shit-eating grin and his, 'Rough, luck, Ms Kellough, too bad the banks can't be more forgiving.' The patronizing asshole." Eyes narrowed, she glared at Vicki. "And you know what really pisses me off? I used to rent the lodge out to people who needed a little silence in their lives; you know, so they could maybe hear what was going on inside their heads. If Stuart Gordon has his way, there won't *be* any silence, and the place'll be awash in brand names and expensive dental work."

"If Stuart Gordon has his way?" Vicki repeated, brows rising.

"Well, it's not built yet, is it?"

"He has all the paperwork filed; what's going to stop him?"

The other woman picked at a flake of paint, her whole attention focused on lifting it from the railing. Just when

Vicki felt she'd have to ask again, Anne looked up and out toward the dark waters of the lake. "That's the question, isn't it," she said softly, brushing her hair back off her face.

The lake seemed no different to Vicki than it ever had. About to suggest that the question acquire an answer, she suddenly frowned. "What happened to your hand? That looks like an acid burn."

"It is." Anne turned her arm so that the burn was more clearly visible to them both. "Thanks to Stuart fucking Gordon, I couldn't afford to take my car in to the garage, and I had to change the battery myself. I thought I was being careful..." She shrugged.

*   *   *

"A new battery, eh? Afraid I can't help you, miss." Ken, owner of Ken's Garage and Auto Body, pressed one knee against the side of the van and leaned, letting it take his weight as he filled the tank. "But if you're not in a hurry, I can go into Bigwood tomorrow and get you one." Before Vicki could speak, he went on. "No wait, tomorrow's Sunday, place'll be closed. Closed Monday too, seeing as how it's Victoria Day." He shrugged and smiled. "I'll be open, but that won't get you a battery."

"It doesn't have to be a new one. I just want to make sure that when I turn her off on the way home, I can get her started again." Leaning back against the closed driver's side door, she gestured into the work bay, where a small pile of old batteries had been more or less stacked against the back wall. "What about one of them?"

Ken turned, peered, and shook his head. "Damn, but you've got good eyes, miss. It's dark as bloody pitch in there."

"Thank you."

"'None of them batteries will do you any good though, 'cause I drained them all a couple of days ago. They're just too dangerous, eh? You know, if kids get poking around?" He glanced over at the gas pump and carefully squirted the total up to an even thirty-two dollars. "You're that investigator working up at the lodge, aren't you?" he asked as he pushed the bills she handed him into a greasy pocket and counted out three loonies in change. "Trying to lay the spirit?"

"Trying to catch whoever vandalized Stuart Gordon's car."

"He, uh, get that fixed then?"

"Good as new." Vicki opened the van door and paused, one foot up on the running board. "I take it he didn't get it fixed here?"

"Here?" The slightly worried expression on Ken's broad face vanished, to be replaced by a curled lip and narrowed eyes. "My gas isn't good enough for that pissant. He's planning to put his own tanks in if he gets that goddamned yuppie resort built."

"If?"

Much as Anne Kellough had, he glanced toward the lake. "If."

About to swing up into the van, two five-gallon glass jars sitting outside the office caught her eye. The lids were off, and it looked very much as though they were airing out. "I haven't seen jars like that in years," she said, pointing. "I don't suppose you want to sell them?"

Ken turned to follow her finger. "Can't. They belong to my cousin. I just borrowed them, eh? Her kids were supposed to come and get them but, hey, you know kids."

According to call-me-Stuart, the village was no place to raise kids.

Glass jars would be handy for transporting acid mixed with fish bits.

And where would they have gotten the fish, she wondered, pulling carefully out of the gas station. *Maybe from one of the boys who runs the hunting and fishing camp.*

*   *   *

Pete Wegler stood in the door of his trailer, a slightly confused look on his face. "Do I know you?"

Vicki smiled. "Not yet. Aren't you going to invite me in?"

*   *   *

Ten to twelve. The lights were still on at the lodge. Celluci stood, stretched and wondered how much longer Vicki was going to be. *Surely everyone in Dulvie's asleep by now.*

Maybe she stopped for a bite to eat.

The second thought followed the first too quickly for him to prevent, it so he ignored it instead. Turning his back on the lodge, he sat down and stared out at the lake. Water looked almost secretive at night, he decided as his eyes readjusted to the darkness.

In his business, secretive meant guilty.

"And if Stuart Gordon has gotten a protective spirit pissed off enough to kill, what then?" he wondered aloud, glancing down at his watch.

Midnight.

Which meant absolutely nothing to that ever-expanding catalogue of things that went bump in the night. Experience had taught him that the so-called supernatural was just about as likely to attack at two in the afternoon as at midnight, but he couldn't not react to the knowledge that he was as far from the dubious safety of daylight as he was able to get.

Even the night seemed affected.

Waiting...

A breeze blew in off the lake, and the hair lifted on both his arms.

Waiting for *something* to happen.

About fifteen feet from shore, a fish broke through the surface of the water like Alice going the wrong way through the Looking Glass. It leapt up, up, and was suddenly grabbed by the end of a glistening grey tube as big around as his biceps. Teeth, or claws or something back inside the tube's opening sank into the fish, and together they finished the arch of the leap. A hump, the same glistening grey, slid up and back into the water, followed by what could only have been the propelling beat of a flat tail. From teeth to tail, the whole thing had to be at least nine feet long.

"Jesus H. Christ." He took a deep breath and added, "On crutches."

*　　*　　*

"I'm telling you, Vicki, I saw the spirit of the lake manifest."

"You saw something eat a fish." Vicki stared out at the water but saw only the reflection of a thousand stars. "You probably saw a bigger fish eat a fish. A long, narrow pike leaping up after a nice fat bass."

About to deny he'd seen any such thing, Celluci suddenly frowned. "How do you know so much about fish?"

"I had a little talk with Pete Wegler tonight. He provided the fish for the acid bath, provided by Ken the garageman, in glass jars provided by Ken's cousin, Kathy Boomhower—the mother who went much beyond name calling with our boy Stuart. Anne Kellough did the deed—she's convinced Gordon called in the Health Department to get his hands on the property—having been transported quietly to the site in Frank Patton's canoe." She grinned. "I feel like Hercule Poirot on the Orient Express."

"Yeah? Well, I'm feeling a lot more Stephen King than Agatha Christie."

Sobering, Vicki laid her hand on the barricade of his crossed arms and studied his face. "You're really freaked by this, aren't you?"

"I don't know exactly what I saw, but I didn't see a fish get eaten by another fish."

The muscles under her hand were rigid, and he was staring past her, out at the lake. "Mike, what is it?"

"I told you, Vicki. I don't know exactly what I saw." In spite of everything, he still liked his world defined. Reluctantly transferring his gaze to the pale oval of her upturned face, he sighed. "How much, if any, of this do you want me to tell Mr. Gordon tomorrow?"

"How about none? I'll tell him myself after sunset."

"Fine. It's late, I'm turning in. I assume you'll be staking out the parking lot for the rest of the night."

"What for? I guarantee the vengeful spirits won't be back." Her voice suggested that in a direct, one-on-one confrontation, a vengeful spirit wouldn't stand a chance. Celluci remembered the thing that rose up out of the lake and wasn't so sure.

"That doesn't matter, you promised twenty-four hour protection."

"Yeah, but..." His expression told her that if she wasn't going to stay, he would. "Fine, I'll watch the car. Happy?"

"That you're doing what you said you were going to do? Ecstatic." Celluci unfolded his arms, pulled her close enough to kiss the frown lines between her brows and headed for the lodge. *She had a little talk with Pete Wegler, my ass.* He knew Vicki had to feed off others, but he didn't have to like it.

*   *   *

Should never have mentioned Pete Wegler. She settled down on the rock still warm from Celluci's body heat and tried unsuccessfully to penetrate the darkness of the lake. When something rustled in the underbrush bordering the parking lot, she hissed without turning her head. The rustling moved away with considerably more speed than it had used to arrive. The secrets of the lake continued to elude her.

"This isn't mysterious, it's irritating."

*   *   *

As Celluci wandered around the lodge, turning off lights, he could hear Stuart snoring through the door of one of the two main floor bedrooms. In the few hours he'd been outside, the other man had managed to leave a trail of debris from one end of the place to the other. On top of that, he'd used up the last of the toilet paper on the roll and hadn't replaced it, he'd put the almost empty coffee pot back onto the coffeemaker with the machine still on so that the dregs had baked onto the glass, and he'd eaten a piece of Celluci's chicken, tossing the gnawed bone back into the bucket. Celluci didn't mind him eating the piece of chicken, but the last thing he wanted was Stuart Gordon's spit over the rest of the bird.

Dropping the bone into the garbage, he noticed a crumpled piece of paper and fished it out. Apparently the resort was destined to grow beyond its current boundaries. Destined to grow all the way around the lake, devouring Dulvie as it went.

"Which would put Stuart Gordon's spit all over the rest of the area."

* * *

Bored with watching the lake and frightening off the local wildlife, Vicki pressed her nose against the window of the sports ute and clicked her tongue at the dashboard full of electronic displays, willing to bet that call-me-Stuart didn't have the slightest idea of what most of them meant.

"Probably has a trouble light if his air freshener needs...hello."

Tucked under the passenger seat was the unmistakable edge of a laptop.

"And how much to you want to bet this thing'll scream bloody blue murder if I try and jimmy the door..." Turning toward the now dark lodge, she listened to the sound of two heartbeats. To the slow, regular sound that told her both men were deeply asleep.

* * *

Stuart slept on his back with one hand flung over his head and a slight smile on his thin face. Vicki watched the pulse beat in his throat for a moment. She'd been assured that, if necessary, she could feed off lower life forms—pigeons, rats, developers—but she was just as glad she'd taken the edge off the Hunger down in the village. Scooping up his car keys, she went out of the room as silently as she'd come in.

* * *

Celluci woke to a decent voice belting out a Beatles tune and came downstairs just as Stuart came out of the bathroom, finger combing damp hair.

"Good morning, Mike. Can I assume no vengeful spirits of Lake Nepeakea trashed my car in the night?"

"You can."

"Good. Good. Oh, by the way..." his smile could have sold attitude to Americans, "...I've used all the hot water."

*   *   *

"I guess it's true what they say about so many of our boys in blue."

"And what's that?" Celluci growled, fortified by two cups of coffee made only slightly bitter by the burned carafe.

"Well, you know, Mike." Grinning broadly, the developer mimed, tipping a bottle to his lips. "I mean, if you can drink that vile brew, you've certainly got a drinking problem." Laughing at his own joke, he headed for the door.

To begin with, they're not your boys in blue and then, you can just fucking well drop dead. You try dealing with the world we deal with for a while, asshole, it'll chew you up and spit you out. But although his fist closed around his mug tightly enough for it to creak, all he said was, "Where are you going?"

"Didn't I tell you? I've got to see a lawyer in Bigwood today. Yes, I know what you're going to say, Mike; it's Sunday. But since this is the last time I'll be out here for a few weeks, the local legal beagle can see me when I'm available. Just a few loose ends about that nasty business with the surveyor." He paused with his hand on the door, voice and manner stripped of all pretensions. "I told them to be sure and finish that part of the shoreline before they quit for the day—I know I'm not,

217

but I feel responsible for that poor woman's death, and I only wish there was something I could do to make up for it. You can't make up for someone dying though, can you, Mike?"

Celluci growled something non-committal. Right at the moment, the last thing he wanted was to think of Stuart Gordon as a decent human being.

"I might not be back until after dark, but hey, that's when the spirit's likely to appear, so you won't need me until then. Right, Mike?" Turning toward the screen where the blackflies had settled, waiting for their breakfast to emerge, he shook his head. "The first thing I'm going to do when all this is settled is drain every stream these little bloodsuckers breed in."

*   *   *

The water levels in the swamp had dropped in the two weeks since the death of the surveyor. Drenched in the bug spray he'd found under the sink, Celluci followed the path made by the searchers, treading carefully on the higher hummocks, no matter how solid the ground looked. When he reached the remains of the police tape, he squatted and peered down into the water. He didn't expect to find anything, but after Stuart's confession, he felt he had to come.

About two inches deep, it was surprisingly clear.

"No reason for it to be muddy now, there's nothing stirring it..."

Something metallic glinted in the mud.

Gripping the marsh grass on his hummock with one hand, he reached out with the other and managed to get thumb and forefinger around the protruding piece of...

"Stainless steel measuring tape?"

It was probably a remnant of the dead surveyor's equipment.

One end of the six-inch piece had been cleanly broken, but the other end, the end that had been down in the mud, looked as though it had been dissolved.

When Anne Kellough had thrown the acid on Stuart's car, they'd been imitating the spirit of Lake Nepeakea.

Celluci inhaled deeply and spit a mouthful of suicidal black flies out into the swamp. "I think it's time to talk to Mary Joseph."

*   *   *

"Can't you feel it?"

Enjoying the first decent cup of coffee he'd had in days, Celluci walked to the edge of the porch and stared out at the lake. Unlike most of Dulvie, separated from the water by the road, Mary Joseph's house was right on the shore. "I can feel *something,*" he admitted.

"You can feel the spirit of the lake, angered by this man from the city. Another cookie?"

"No, thank you." He'd had one, and it was without question the worst cookie he'd ever eaten. "Tell me about the spirit of the lake, Ms Joseph. Have you seen it?"

"Oh yes. Well, not exactly it, but I've seen the wake of its passing." She gestured out toward the water but, at the moment, the lake was perfectly calm. "Most water has a protective spirit, you know. Wells and springs, lakes and rivers, it's why we throw coins into fountains, so that the spirits will exchange them for luck. Kelpies, selkies, mermaids, Jenny Greenteeth, Peg Powler, the Fideal...all water spirits."

"And one of them, is that what's out there?" Somehow he couldn't reconcile mermaids to that toothed trunk snaking out of the water.

"Oh, no, our water spirit is a new world water spirit. The Cree called it a mantouche—surely you recognize the similarity to the word Manitou or Great Spirit? Only the deepest lakes with the best fishing had them. They protected the lakes and the area around the lakes and, in return..."

"Were revered?"

"Well, no actually. They were left strictly alone."

"You told the paper that the spirit had manifested twice before?"

"Twice that we know of," she corrected. "The first recorded manifestation occurred in 1762 and was included in the notes on native spirituality that one of the exploring Jesuits sent back to France."

Product of a Catholic school education, Celluci wasn't entirely certain the involvement of the Jesuits added credibility. "What happened?"

"It was spring. A pair of white trappers had been at the lake all winter, slaughtering the animals around it. Animals under the lake's protection. According to the surviving trapper, his partner was coming out of the highwater marshes, just after sunset, when his canoe suddenly upended and he disappeared. When the remaining man retrieved the canoe, he found that bits had been burned away without flame, and it carried the mark of all the dead they'd stolen from the lake."

"The mark of the dead?"

"The record says it stank, Detective. Like offal." About to eat another cookie, she paused. "You do know what offal is?"

"Yes, ma'am. Did the survivor see anything?"

"Well, he said he saw what he thought was a giant snake, except that it had two stubby wings at the upper end. And you know what that is."

...a glistening, grey tube as big around as his biceps. "No."

"A wyvern. One of the ancient dragons."

"There's a dragon in the lake."

"No, of course not. The spirit of the lake can take many forms. When it's angry, those who are facing its anger see a great and terrifying beast. To the trapper, who no doubt had northern European roots, it appeared as a wyvern. The natives would have probably seen a giant serpent. There are many so-called serpent mounds around deep lakes."

"But it couldn't just *be* a giant serpent?"

"Detective Celluci, don't you think that if there was a giant serpent living in this lake that someone would have gotten a good look at it by now? Besides, after the second death, the lake was searched extensively with modern equipment—and once or twice since then as well—and nothing has ever been found. That trapper was killed by the spirit of the lake, and so was Thomas Stebbing."

"Thomas Stebbing?"

"The recorded death in 1937. I have newspaper clippings..."

In the spring of 1937, four young men from the University of Toronto had come to Lake Nepeakea on a wilderness vacation. Out canoeing with a friend at dusk, Thomas Stebbing saw what he thought was a burned log on the shore, and they paddled in to investigate. As his friend watched in horror, the log "attacked" Stebbing, left him burned and dead and "undulated into the lake" on a trail of dead vegetation.

The investigation turned up nothing at all, and the eyewitness account of a "kind of big worm thing" was summarily dismissed. The final, official verdict was that the victim had indeed disturbed a partially burnt log and, as it rolled over him, was burned by the embers and died. The log then rolled into the lake, burning a path as it rolled, and sank. The stench was dismissed as the smell of roasting flesh and the insistence by the friend that the burns were acid burns was completely ignored—in spite of the fact he was a chemistry student and should therefore know what he was talking about.

"The spirit of the *lake* came up on *land,* Ms Joseph?"

She nodded, apparently unconcerned with the contradiction. "There were a lot of fires being lit around the lake that year. Between the wars, this area got popular for a while, and fires were the easiest way to clear land for summer homes. The spirit of the lake couldn't allow that, hence its appearance as a burned log."

"And Thomas Stebbing had done what to disturb its peace?"

"Nothing specifically. I think the poor boy was just in the wrong place at the wrong time. It is a vengeful spirit, you understand."

Only a few short years earlier, he'd have understood that Mary Joseph was a total nutcase. But that was before he'd willingly thrown himself into the darkness that lurked behind a pair of silvered eyes. He sighed and stood. The afternoon had nearly ended. It wouldn't be long now until sunset.

"Thank you for your help, Ms Joseph. I...what?"

She was staring at him, nodding. "You've seen it, haven't you? You have that look."

"I've seen something," he admitted reluctantly and turned toward the water. "I've seen a lot of thi..."

A pair of jet skis roared around the point and drowned him out. As they passed the house, blanketing it in noise, one of the adolescent operators waved a cheery hello.

Never a vengeful lake spirit around when you really need one, he thought.

* * *

"He knew about the sinkholes in the marsh, and he sent those surveyors out anyway." Vicki tossed a pebble off the end of the dock and watched it disappear into the liquid darkness.

"You're sure?"

"The information was all there on his lap top, and the file was dated back in March. Now, although evidence that I just happened to have found in his computer will be inadmissible in court, I can go to the Department of Lands and Forests and get the dates he requested the geological surveys."

Celluci shook his head. "You're not going to be able to get him charged with anything. Sure, he should've told them, but they were both professionals, and they should've been more careful." He thought of the crocodile tears Stuart had cried that morning over the death, and his hands formed fists by his side. Being an irresponsible asshole was one thing, being a manipulative, irresponsible asshole was on another level entirely. "It's an ethical failure," he growled, "not a legal one."

"Maybe I should take care of him myself then." The second pebble hit the water with considerably more force.

"He's your client, Vicki. You're supposed to be working for him, not against him."

She snorted. "So I'll wait until his cheque clears."

"He's planning on acquiring the rest of the land around the lake." Pulling the paper he'd retrieved from the garbage out of his pocket, Celluci handed it over.

"The rest of the land around the lake isn't for sale."

"Neither was this lodge, until he decided he wanted it."

Crushing the paper in one hand, Vicki's eyes silvered. "There's got to be something we can... Shit!" Tossing the paper aside, she grabbed Celluci's arm, dragging him with her as the end of the dock bucked up into the air and leapt back one section. "What the fuck was that?" she demanded as they turned to watch the place they'd just been standing rock violently back and forth. The paper she'd dropped into the water was nowhere to be seen.

"Wave from a passing boat?"

"There hasn't been a boat past here in hours."

"Sometimes these long narrow lakes build up a standing wave. It's called a seiche."

"A seiche?" When he nodded, she rolled her eyes. "I've got to start watching more PBS. In the meantime..."

The sound of an approaching car drew their attention up to the lodge in time to see Stuart slowly and carefully pull into the parking lot, barely disturbing the gravel.

"Are you going to tell him who vandalized his car?" Celluci asked as they started up the hill."

"Who? Probably not. I can't prove it, after all, but I will tell him it wasn't some vengeful spirit and it definitely won't happen again." At least not if Pete Wegler had anything to say about it. The spirit of the lake might be hypothetical, but she wasn't.

* * *

"A group of villagers, Vicki? You're sure?"

"Positive."

"They actually thought I'd believe it was an angry spirit manifesting all over the side of my vehicle?"

"Apparently." Actually, they hadn't cared if he believed it or not. They were all just so angry, they needed to do something and since the spirit was handy...she offered none of that to call-me-Stuart.

"I want their names, Vicki." His tone made it an ultimatum.

Vicki had never responded well to ultimatums. Celluci watched her masks begin to fall and wondered just how far his dislike of the developer would let her go. He could stop her with a word. He just wondered if he'd say it. Or when.

To his surprise, she regained control. "Check the census lists then. You haven't exactly endeared yourself to your neighbours."

For a moment, it seemed that Stuart realized how close he'd just come to seeing the definition of his own mortality, but then he smiled and said, "You're right, Vicki, I haven't endeared myself to my neighbours. And do you know what; I'm going to do something about that. Tomorrow's Victoria Day, I'll invite them all to a big picnic supper with great food and fireworks out over the lake. We'll kiss and make up."

"It's Sunday evening, and tomorrow's a holiday. Where are you going to find food and fireworks?"

"Not a problem, Mike. I'll e-mail my caterers in Toronto. I'm sure they can be here by tomorrow afternoon. I'll pay through the nose, but hey, developing a good relationship with the locals is worth it. You two will stay, of course."

Vicki's lips drew back off her teeth, but Celluci answered for them both. "Of course."

*   *   *

"He's up to something," he explained later, "and I want to know what that is."

"He's going to confront the villagers with what he knows, see who reacts and make their lives a living hell. He'll find a way to make them the first part of his expansion."

"You're probably right."

"I'm always right." Head pillowed on his shoulder, she stirred his chest hair with one finger. "He's an unethical, immoral, unscrupulous little asshole."

"You missed annoying, irritating and just generally unlikeable."

"I could convince him he was a combination of Mother Theresa and Lady Di. I could rip his mind out, use it for unnatural purposes, and stuff it back into his skull in any shape I damn well choose, but I can't."

Once you start down the dark side, forever will it dominate your destiny? But he didn't say it aloud, because he didn't want to know how far down the dark side she'd been. He was grateful that she'd drawn any personal boundaries at all, that she'd chosen to remain someone who couldn't use terror for the sake of terror. "So what are we going to do about him?"

"I can't think of a damned thing. You?"

Suddenly he smiled. "Could you convince him that *you* were the spirit of the lake, and that he'd better haul his ass back to Toronto, unless he wants it dissolved off?"

She was off the bed in one fluid movement. "I knew there was a reason I dragged you out here this weekend." She turned on one bare heel, then turned again and was suddenly back in the bed. "But I think I'll wait until tomorrow night. He hasn't paid me yet."

*   *   *

"Morning, Mike. Where's Vicki?"

"Sleeping."

"Well, since you're up, why don't you help out by carrying the barbecue down to the beach. I may be willing to make amends, but I'm not sure they are, and since they've already damaged my car, I'd just as soon keep them away from anything valuable. Particularly when in combination with propane and open flames."

*　　*　　*

"Isn't Vicki joining us for lunch, Mike?"

"She says she isn't hungry. She went for a walk in the woods."

"Must be how she keeps her girlish figure. I've got to hand it to you, Mike, there aren't many men your age who could hold on to such a woman. I mean, she's really got that independent thing going, doesn't she?" He accepted a tuna sandwich with effusive thanks, took a bite and winced. "Not light mayo?"

"No."

"Never mind, Mike. I'm sure you meant well. Now, then, as it's just the two of us, have you ever considered investing in a timeshare..."

*　　*　　*

Mike Celluci had never been so glad to see anyone as he was to see a van full of bleary-eyed and stiff caterers arrive at four that afternoon. As Vicki had discovered during that initial phone call, Stuart Gordon was not a man who took no for an answer. He might have accepted "Fuck off and die!" followed by a fast exit, but since Vicki expected to wake up on the shores of Lake Nepeakea, Celluci held his tongue. Besides, it would be a little difficult for her to chase the developer away if they were halfway back to Toronto.

*　　*　　*

Sunset.

Vicki could feel maybe two dozen lives around her when she woke and she lay there for a moment, revelling in them.

The last two evenings, she'd had to fight the urge to climb into the driver's seat and speed toward civilization.

"Fast food."

She snickered, dressed and stepped out into the parking lot.

Celluci was down on the beach, talking to Frank Patton. She made her way over to them, the crowd opening to let her pass without really being aware she was there at all. Both men nodded as she approached, and Patton gestured toward the barbecue.

"Burger?"

"No, thanks, I'm not hungry." She glanced around. "No one seems to have brought their kids."

"No one wants to expose their kids to Stuart Gordon."

"Afraid they'll catch something," Celluci added.

"Mike here says you've solved your case, and you're just waiting for Mr. Congeniality over there to pay you."

Wondering what Mike had been up to, Vicki nodded.

"He also says you didn't mention any names. Thank you." He sighed. "We didn't really expect the spirit of the lake thing to work, but..."

Vicki raised both hands. "Hey, you never know. He could be suppressing."

"Yeah, right. The only thing that clown suppresses is everyone around him. If you'll excuse me, I'd better go rescue Anne before she rips out his tongue and strangles him with it."

"I'm surprised she came," Vicki admitted.

"She thinks he's up to something, and she wants to know what it is."

"Don't we all," Celluci murmured as Patton walked away.

The combined smell of cooked meat and fresh blood making her a little lightheaded, Vicki started Mike moving toward the floating dock. "Have I missed anything?"

"No, I think you're just in time."

As Frank Patton approached, Stuart broke off the conversation he'd been having with Anne Kellough—or more precisely, Vicki amended, *at* Anne Kellough—and walked out to the end of the dock, where a number of large rockets had been set up.

"He's got a permit for the damned things," Celluci muttered. "The son of a bitch knows how to cover his ass."

"But not his id." Vicki's fingers curved cool around Mike's forearm. "He'll get his, don't worry."

The first rocket went up, exploding red over the lake, the colours muted against the evening grey of sky and water. The developer turned toward the shore and raised both hands above his head. "Now that I've got your attention, there's a few things I'd like to share with you all before the festivities continue. First of all, I've decided not to press charges concerning the damage to my vehicle, although I'm aware that..."

The dock began to rock. Behind him, one of the rockets fell into the water.

"Mr. Gordon." The voice was Mary Joseph's. "Get to shore, now."

Pointing a finger toward her, he shook his head. "Oh no, old woman, I'm Stuart Gordon..."

No "call-me-Stuart" tonight, Celluci noted.

"...and you don't tell me what to do, I tell..."

Arms windmilling, he stepped back, once, twice and hit the water. Arms and legs stretched out, he looked as though he was sitting on something just below the surface. "I have had enough of this," he began...

...and disappeared.

Vicki reached the end of the dock in time to see the pale

oval of his face engulfed by dark water. To her astonishment, he seemed to have gotten his cell phone out of his pocket, and all she could think of was that old movie cut line, *Who you gonna call?*

One heartbeat, two. She thought about going in after him. The fingertips on her reaching hand were actually damp when Celluci grabbed her shoulder and pulled her back. She wouldn't have done it, but it was nice that he thought she would.

Back on the shore, two dozen identical wide-eyed stares were locked on the flat, black surface of the lake, too astounded by what had happened to their mutual enemy, Vicki realized, to notice how fast she'd made it to the end of the dock.

Mary Joseph broke the silence first. "Thus acts the vengeful spirit of Lake Nepeakea," she declared. Then as heads began to nod, she added dryly, "Can't say I didn't warn him."

Mike looked over at Vicki, who shrugged.

"Works for me," she said.

Tanya Huff *lives and writes in rural Ontario with her partner, six and a half cats, and an unintentional chihuahua. She has written twenty novels ranging from heroic fantasy to military science fiction as well as produced enough short fiction for three collections. Her latest book is* Smoke and Mirrors, *published July 2005 by DAW Books Inc.*

CURRENT EVENT

Mavis Andrews

It was noon on Monday, and I was downtown waiting for a bus. The sidewalks were packed with end-of-season tourists on the stroll and office workers speeding through errands so they'd have time for lunch.

The No. 2 Oak Bay pulled up, and this kid got off, maybe ten years old at a stretch, pushing a little girl in a stroller. She was about two and had a death grip on a stuffed panda. I'd seen them just the day before down at the Chinese Cemetery, around the corner from my place on Harling Point. I remembered because a storm had started blowing that afternoon and left a fresh load of driftwood on the little beach.

I was watching them, expecting to see their mother step off the bus, when the kid wheeled the stroller down the street, and the bus pulled away from the curb. I might have taken time to think it was odd, an unsupervised kid taking a baby downtown, but just then my bus came.

The afternoon passed like such afternoons do, and at about four thirty I staggered back to the office in time for a coffee with my sister.

As my business card says, I am a duly licensed private investigator. In my single days, I was hot stuff, working out of a Vancouver high-rise and doing contract investigations for some of the big firms back East. Post-divorce, I'm in Victoria, licking my wounds and doing a bit of missing persons and surveillance work, but mostly credit checks and document service. When I had come slinking back into town, my sister had let me use a little back office in her business centre. "Until a paying client comes along," she'd said.

We played catch-up for a few minutes over coffee, then I knuckled down in front of my borrowed computer, fired up those handy-dandy programs available only to P.I.s and ran a few checks, thereby earning my bread and butter.

I caught the last bus, made it home by ten, and capped the day with a grilled cheese sandwich washed down with a glass of $8.95 Okanagan chardonnay.

The next morning I was up early enough for a brisk stroll to the Chinese Cemetery. I like to wander over there in the mornings, unless the weather's dirty. Sometimes on the weekend I sit on the beach, just gazing out at the Straits. Back in the early years, the town fathers were reportedly delighted to pass off this supposedly worthless chunk of low-lying land to the Chinese community, who, for their part, were equally delighted because it had all the favourable feng shui aspects they could want for their dearly departeds. For years it had been pretty much deserted, except for occasional picnickers, but the Chinese Benevolent Association had reclaimed it, spiffed it up with informative plaques, and now it's a regular stop for tourist buses.

One was parked on the roadway, its contents disgorged throughout the cemetery, most of them snapping pictures of their companions in front of the big stone altar. It was too busy for peaceful browsing, so I headed back and amused myself until the city bus came in trying to juggle my woeful income and outsized expense figures.

That day was much like the previous, except that Mr. Lucchio, my landlord, called me in for a late dinner. He's got a way of cooking—lots of garlic and olive oil—that makes me forget how I'd prefer to be on my own. He settled me at his kitchen table with a glass of red wine and started wielding his knife, all the while watching his countertop television. I wasn't paying much attention, until he started waving his knife at the screen. "See that? See what happens to women on their own?"

Some poor schmuck out fishing at the crack of dawn had spotted the body of a woman on Brotchie Ledge over by the breakwater. No identifying marks, no obvious signs of foul play, and no I.D.

"Wouldn't happen if she'd had a man," Mr. Lucchio muttered.

I shrugged. "When there's a body, it's usually either drugs or domestic."

He snorted, but he had a healthy respect for my P.I. license, probably more than it deserved. I might be a female in need of a man, but I was also a Person Who Knows Things.

It was all over the paper Wednesday morning: a Jane Doe aged thirty-something had drowned, as evidenced by water in her lungs. Forensics had not come up with any indication of foul play, but she had a pretty high blood alcohol count. The police artist had put together a sketch in the hope of someone stepping forward to identify her.

Over the next week, reporters were hard-pressed for information. The pathologist determined she'd been in the water about thirty hours; the water temperature ensured she would have died within twenty minutes. Reporters speculated she was a transient who'd fallen off the breakwater or a boater gone overboard somewhere out in the Straits.

I frowned as I read that, remembering something maybe ten years ago about a guy who had survived eight hours at sea after falling off a B.C. Ferry. There was a big hullabaloo, people claiming it was a publicity stunt, because no one could have survived that long, but in fact his salvation had been the warm summer current flowing from the Fraser River.

Jane Doe gradually moved to the near obscurity of a few paragraphs, mostly filler, near the back of the paper, but the thought of currents kept niggling at my mind. I'd once drowned my sorrows on a handy beach and fallen asleep in the sunshine. What if I'd been washed out to sea?

Thanks to a few old contacts, work was trickling in, but nothing fully occupied my mind. The upshot of it was a call to Environment Canada. "Who can I talk to about currents and tides?" I asked, and the next day I was out in Sidney meeting a guy named Mike at the Institute of Ocean Sciences.

I asked him, "If a person fell asleep on a beach around here and was washed out to sea, where would they end up?"

"The water's not exactly friendly," said Mike. "They'd wake up fast enough."

"What if they didn't?"

"Well, mostly they'd get swept out on the flood tide." He led me through a maze of chart-covered hallways to a big chart of a drift test done some ten years ago, using buoys with underwater sails. "There's a strong clockwise current along here. If the person gets caught in that, they could be dumped onto land at a few spots."

"Such as?"

"Chinese Cemetery, Ten Mile Point or Brotchie Ledge," he said.

"Like Jane Doe?"

"Exactly like her."

I hadn't seen a word of this in the papers. "Do the police know this?"

"Yes."

My mind was whirling.

"So for Jane Doe to end up on Brotchie Ledge, she would have to have come from one of the other spots?

"Have to? No, but there's a strong possibility."

The clockwise current was clear as day, as long as you had a scientist at your elbow to interpret the tracks of buoys, looking like giant fallen mushrooms. A buoy—or body—caught by the flood tide would drift eastward from Brotchie Ledge to Harling Point. The next flood tide would likely send it out through a couple of channels off Ten Mile Point where, caught in the tide again, it'd circle westward through the faster current off Haro Strait. The body might lollygag around Constance Bank, if fishermen didn't spot it, until the next flood tide swirled it around the bank, then west and north again to Brotchie Ledge. On the map, the whole cycle took thirty-two hours.

"The body was found on Tuesday morning, which means she could have left the Victoria shoreline late Sunday night during the storm—"

He shook his head. "She might have landed overnight; also, she could have bobbed in the surf awhile."

We headed to his office and cross-referenced the tide tables with the atlas of currents. As we flipped the pages, the blue arrows indicating currents changed from thin to thick, looking frantic and powerful in their clustered thickness. Probabilities crystallized. I quickly did the math, taking into account lollygagging, bobbing and middle of the night landings. "If she reached Brotchie Ledge in the wee hours, she probably left Constance Bank just before the fishing boats arrived Monday morning."

He nodded. "If so, unless she entered the current from a

boat, she likely would have left Ten Mile Point sometime late Sunday night."

Ten Mile Point is a ritzy area with lots of wooded properties and fences going down to the high tide line to ensure limited beach access to the unworthy. I had a flash of a society matron shooing poor Jane off her multi-million dollar shorefront and into the current with a boat hook.

"If she didn't come from the Ten Mile Point area," Mike was saying, "she probably would have drifted up the channel there during evening, which means she could have drifted out Sunday afternoon from a point of land like the Chinese Cemetery."

The bus back to the city took a long, meandering route through the Saanich Peninsula, which gave me time to think, but the cogs didn't really start turning until a woman got on with her two kids just as we were coming into town. She perched on one of the sideways benches, hauled the little one out of her stroller and handed him to the older child, who'd slumped onto the window seat. The boy was maybe ten, clearly unimpressed at being saddled with a toddler.

That put me in mind of the boy I'd seen wheeling his little sister off the bus a few weeks back, and something clicked. I'd seen them the very day Jane Doe had likely ended up in the water. What if she was their mother, swept out to sea?

What if the kid was taking care of his sister because his mom wasn't around any more?

It was so far-fetched, I was almost ashamed of myself. After all, a woman can't get swept out to sea with her kids right there, not without them raising an alarm, and the kid couldn't be looking after his little sister without the authorities being involved. Besides, school had started, and people would notice if he wasn't going. No, there had to be another answer.

Still, the police seemed to have no leads, and I kept thinking about the kids. I'd only seen them in two places: once getting off the No. 2 bus, and one Sunday at the Chinese Cemetery. I wasn't going to lurk at the bus stop, but it wouldn't be hard to hang out at the cemetery. After all, the criminal always returns to the scene of the crime, as the saying goes. Not that this could possibly be a crime, but I couldn't help but wonder at the coincidence.

The next Sunday, I took a thermos of coffee, a bag of almonds and the *New York Times* crossword puzzle and headed for my stakeout. Happily, the mellow September weather held, but no luck. I tried again the following Sunday, and this time I hit paydirt, because around noon, along came the kid, pushing the stroller. He let his sister play with the rounded beach rocks and hauled out a squished sandwich when she got fussy. Mostly he didn't say a word, just watched her as if he was afraid a wave would carry her off.

After a while, I strolled over to crouch down near the baby. "Hi, there, what's your name?" I said in that inane tone adults adopt for toddlers. I gave him a glance, and he mumbled something that might have been "Ginny."

"They're quite a handful at this stage," I said with a sympathetic smile. "You babysitting?"

"Yeah," he mumbled, busying himself with the diaper bag.

"Where's your mom? She sick today?"

"C'mon, Ginny, we gotta go." He hauled up the little girl, ignoring her protests, and battled her into the stroller.

I skedaddled it for the bus stop, not wanting him to worry that I might be following. He strolled up a few minutes later; I busied myself with the puzzle.

Readying a baby to get off a bus involves a few predictable moves, so I was able to be at the door before him. He hiked down the street, and I dawdled behind, taking time to deke out of sight and slip a T-shirt on over my tank top and tuck my hair into a hat. I completed the disguise by adding a sway to my hips, and after one cursory backwards glance, I could see the kid relax.

They lived in a shabby four-storey building with blotchy white stucco and aluminum-frame windows. With the ease of long practice, he manoeuvered the stroller up the steps and out of sight through a controlled entrance that had a double row of yellowed buttons and beside each a strip of paper with a name neatly typed.

I crossed the street and watched for a while in case he'd appear at one of the windows, the way it happens so handily in the movies, but no such luck. The names were my best shot.

Back home, I looked up the names I'd jotted down. A few were new listings, and I blew five bucks on directory assistance, but eventually I had all but a couple, and I started dialing.

"Good afternoon! My name is Bobbi-Sue," I said to one after another, "and I'm calling on behalf of Evergreen Charities. Is Mrs. (fill in name) at home?" If Mrs. Whoever answered, I'd ask a few survey questions and cross off the name.

Three-quarters of the way through the list, I heard a familiar voice on the line. I added a little nasal tone and went through my spiel, asking for Mona Christie. There was a hesitation, then he said, "She's sleeping."

"What'd be a good time to catch her?"

Another hesitation. "She won't want to talk to you."

"Well, I'll just try again sometime, shall I?" I was the epitome of a thick-skinned telephone solicitor.

Apartment 403 it was. Early Monday morning found me cooling my heels on the front steps until the paperboy arrived. I gave what I hoped was an apologetic smile. "I forgot my keys, and I didn't want to wake anyone up."

He took pity on me, and I was in.

On the fourth floor, I kept the stairwell door ajar; 403 was two doors away. A few times I had to pretend to be tying my shoes when someone came along, but mostly it was just a matter of waiting. At seven thirty, the door to 403 opened, and out came the kid, pushing the stroller with one hand and hanging onto the bouncing toddler with the other. Leaving the door ajar, he walked halfway along the hall and knocked on a door, and as he stepped in I heard him say something about "mom" and "sleeping". Well, if mom really was in the apartment, I'd have to think fast, because no sooner had he disappeared, than I hightailed it through his door. I chose the hall closet for a hiding place on the grounds that it was too nice a day for coats.

A moment later, he was back. I heard the sound of gargling and the flushing of a toilet, then he padded past and out the door. He didn't say goodbye.

Carefully, I inched the door open and crept out. The place was worn and cheap, but it was tidy, a standard two-bedroom apartment with beige carpeting and tacky veneer cupboards in the alley kitchen. The living room looked like it'd been furnished from the Salvation Army; a collection of empties was stacked in a corner.

I checked the bathroom (empty), then turned towards the bedrooms. The first was immaculate, a single bed topped by a neatly-rolled sleeping bag, and a crib filled with toys.

With this much tidiness, Mom had to be around, but I crept to the next door, hardly breathing, and edged it open. A tornado had surely been through the room. Clothes hung from every surface; the double bed was a mess of lumps and bumps, but no sleeping mom.

I eased forward, thinking I was mistaken but no, the room was empty of all but the signs of a wild, disordered life. A cashmere sweater with security tag intact occupied the chair in front of the dressing table. On the tabletop was an array of costume jewellery and makeup, all covered with a film of face powder.

I picked my way through strewn laundry, shoes and bags and started opening drawers, and when I was done I prowled through the front room. On the end table were two photos; in one the woman, looking not too dissimilar from the police sketch, smiled into the camera. The other showed her at a younger age with her arms around a beefy guy; someone had given him a beard and glasses in blue ballpoint. There were no pictures of the kids.

A desk sat in what was meant to be the dining alcove. Its centre drawer revealed rows of pens and pencils lined up with mechanical preciseness, flanked by scissors and a box of sharpened crayons. The top side drawer held a stack of bills and papers for me to rifle through, arranged in alphabetical order. A rent receipt had been issued just days before; the phone bill was paid up. A bank statement showed that Mona Christie's monthly stipend had been duly deposited the day after Jane Doe's retrieval, on Welfare Wednesday, and several withdrawals made since.

It appeared that Mona was still in the land of the living, a fact that should have sent me creeping shame-faced from the apartment, instead of which I returned the papers to their drawer and headed for the kitchen. Her purse was in a drawer by the kitchen sink, wallet in place, complete with photo I.D. and bank card. I stared at them for a good five minutes before turning my attention to the garbage can. It had been recently emptied; nothing in it but a soiled diaper tied up in a plastic bag and a few empty packets of Swanson's frozen dinner. The recycling box was more helpful: a tidy pile of flyers and what appeared to be draft pages of the kid's homework, presumably rejected on account of excess erasures and cross-outs, with the name "Brian Christie" written in the upper corner in a neat cursive hand.

Near the bottom of the pile I found a page with the name "Mona Christie" written over and over, each version morphing ever so slightly, from ungainly writing to, finally, a signature like the one on Mona's I.D.

It was too early to draw conclusions. I had a few facts to check out first, and I started with the building manager, transforming myself, as I knocked on his door, into a doe-eyed visitor.

"Gee, can you help me? I'm looking for Mona, Mona Christie? We're supposed to have lunch, and she's not answering."

"Sorry," he said and would have closed the door, except my foot was in the way.

"Have you seen her around?"

A woman appeared at his shoulder. "What is it, Albert?"

"This one wants to know have I seen Mona."

The woman eyed me suspiciously. "Who's asking?"

"I'm Jeanine," I said brightly, sticking out my hand. She took it reluctantly. "I'm Mona's cousin on her mother's side."

"We don't know nuthin' about any cousin," grumbled Albert.

His wife removed her hand from my friendly grasp. "Truth is, we don't see much of Mona nowadays—"

"She's a wild one," inserted Albert, "all them goings on and cops here pretty near every week, it's enough to make a man—" I never did find out what, because his wife shut him up with an elbow to the gut.

"It must be hard, her being on her own and all."

Albert snorted; his wife nodded vigorously. "That's it exactly. We all got our burdens to bear, but that boy of hers—"

"Brian," I said, "is he a burden?"

"Heavens, no, just the opposite. Mona's more blessed than she deserves. Lord only knows what'd come of that baby if it wasn't for him."

I nodded. "When's the last time you saw Mona?"

"Let's see…she paid her rent, a day late, but when's the last time?" Albert had already retreated. Without so much as turning around, she repeated the question at a higher volume, and a muffled rumble emanated from the depths of the apartment. "A month or so?" she repeated. "Come to think of it, I suppose it has been that long, not that it's surprising, with the hours she keeps and all."

I found the babysitting neighbour at the park with little Ginny and another toddler, busily wielding shovel and bucket in the sandbox. "That one's mine," she said, nodding at Ginny's companion. "I don't really do babysitting, just a favour to Mona…well, to Brian, really. He's such a good kid, and what he puts up with! I thought Mona'd never settle down, but now that she's got this here night job, things are nice and quiet over there."

I nodded knowingly. "It's been about a month, now, hasn't it?"

The neighbour frowned thoughtfully. "I suppose, though Brian looked after his sister until he started back to school; 'course that's nothing new." She looked me up and down. "If you ask me, he's too old for his years, what with taking care of Mona all this time and now the baby, too. It'll be good for the boy to have a relative around."

I left her gazing at the toddlers and headed for the bus. At the office, I listened to my voicemail, then ran a few checks on Mona. What came up wouldn't win her any Mother of the Year awards in my book: a smattering of petty theft, a few charges of prostitution, a couple of drunk and disorderlies.

About then, my sister came along with a couple of cups of coffee. I told her what I'd been up to. "It's far-fetched, I know, but I have to check."

She wasn't impressed with me prowling uninvited through someone's apartment, but she just said, "What are you going to do if it turns out she's really missing?"

"Call the cops?"

"Maybe he doesn't know what happened to her."

"What's not to know?"

She frowned. "And what about the powder on the dressing table? Not many people use loose powder these days."

I got back to 403 before school was out and used the time to poke around some more. First thing was the powder, which wasn't powder at all but a fine layer of dust. About a month's worth.

I'd left the apartment door ajar so I'd hear Brian, in case the babysitter scared him off. After an hour or so, I heard murmuring voices and stepped into the hall.

Brian's glare said he recognized me, but he didn't say a word until we were in the apartment with the door closed behind us. Then he turned on me. "You've been saying you're my mother's cousin. It's not true."

"Could be."

"She doesn't have any." He followed little Ginny into the front room.

"Are you sure?"

"Not a single one. What are you doing here?"

"Any other relatives?"

"What's it to you?"

I sighed and perched on the easy chair. "What it is to me, Brian, is that I'm the one who's figured out where your mommy is."

His face went pale, and he sat down fast, like his knees had given out. "I don't know what you're talking about."

"Sure you do. I've heard how responsible you are, how she'd be in even rougher shape if not for you." I nodded towards the toddler playing happily with a bunch of coloured beads. "I know you've been taking care of her, taking care of the whole place, paying the bills—you've got your mom's signature down pretty good." I held up his practice sheet.

His face was tight and mulish. "I haven't done nuthin'."

"Haven't you?" I just sat there, letting the question hang in the air between us. Ginny toddled over to him with an armload of beads, and he started snapping them together. Finally, I said, "She's a cute kid."

His throat worked.

"Must be tough with your mom gone missing this past month."

That got him. "She hasn't just been missing for a month. She's been missing for a long time before that."

"Before what? The day you pushed her in? Walked away?"

"I didn't touch her!" he screamed, eyes bright with unshed tears. Ginny started to cry. He stroked her head and said brokenly, "It's okay, baby."

"Is she hungry?"

"Prob'ly. I usually fix her something after school."

"Maybe I can help," I said. He fixed me with a glare, and I shook my head. "I'm not the enemy, Brian. There's something really wrong here, and don't you even think I'm going to walk away before we've sorted it out."

He was shaking too much to be any good in the kitchen, so I set him to playing with his sister and whipped up a frittata. She swallowed it down, but he and I mostly picked at ours, then he took her off for a bath while I cleaned up. I heard him carry her into bed, heard him singing a lullaby. After a while I went in. He was slumped over the crib with his hand resting on her back. She was sound asleep.

I drew him back to the couch. Up close, I could see the shadows under his eyes. A good kid, everybody said.

"Tell me about that day."

"I didn't do nuthin'!"

"I know. Tell me about it…you all went down to the Chinese Cemetery for a picnic…"

"It was a stupid day for a picnic," he said. "It was supposed to storm, but she didn't care. Ginny was cutting a tooth, and she put sherry in her bottle. I wouldn't let her drink it, and we had a fight, her saying she's the parent and what the hell do I know. So I couldn't do nuthin' but take off. But I didn't go so far I couldn't see the stroller, and when the wind came up, I went back. They were both asleep at the edge of the water, and the tide was coming in."

His voice broke, and he took a minute to recover himself. "I tried to wake her up, but the sherry bottle was empty, and I couldn't. So I put Ginny in the stroller and caught the bus."

"You left her to the incoming tide."

He jumped up, screaming at me. "I didn't know that! She might've woken up, somebody might've found her." He slumped down and sat hunched over, his shoulders heaving, and I realized in that moment that he was just a kid. A kid who'd been faced with a choice, and at ten years of age a kid doesn't know what he's got, he's just learning what a choice is.

I sat in silence for a while, thinking while he cried it out.

After a time I gave him a glass of water and got a damp cloth from the bathroom so he could wash his face. He'd been taking care of his little sister all her life; he'd made the only choice he could. And no wonder he hadn't reported Mona as missing. The authorities would swoop in, and Ginny would be lost to him; heck, if Mona had lived, sooner or later the authorities would have taken Ginny anyway.

That day on the beach, he wouldn't have been thinking of consequences, of how to cope. He'd been doing it all anyway; but, boy, it must be easier without her.

He squared his shoulders and faced me, braving the unknown. "What are you gonna do now?"

"I've got to call someone. I can't just let it go," I said, watching his knuckles go white as he clutched at the fabric of his pants. "Do you have a dollar?"

He went still, then hauled a toonie out of his pocket and handed it to me.

I wrote out a receipt. "I'm a private investigator," I said, "and you've now given me a retainer so I'll find your mom. I bet she's been away on benders before, hasn't she?"

He nodded.

"And I bet you were too busy to worry a lot, what with Ginny and going back to school, so that you didn't notice how much time had gone…" I hesitated. "You know she's dead, don't you?"

"I figured."

I nodded, looking at the ink-bearded man in the photo, knowing that'd be Brian's dad, probably long gone, but surely a private investigator on retainer could track him down.

"We're going to call the cops now, Brian," I said, and held him when he turned a white face to me. "You're not alone any more. After all, I'm your mother's cousin, aren't I?"

He dared a wobbly something that was almost a smile, and I picked up the phone to call the cops. I'd tell them there were a couple of kids I needed to take care of; after all, besides Mr. Lucchio's cooking, I didn't have anything to keep me home nights, and there was no way this ten-year-old survivor was going to lose the most important person in his world, not if I could help it.

Mavis Andrews *lives in a 1912 character house near the parkland waterfront of Victoria, British Columbia. A former editor of* Focus on Women *magazine, Mavis is a freelance editor and writing coach who shares her space with a feisty tortoiseshell cat, a gentle-giant Jellico cat and a mortadella-shaped dachshund.*

A Lifetime Burning
in a Moment

Rick Mofina

John Devlin knew the boys who lived in the clapboard houses by the railroad tracks not only liked beating him up, but needed to beat him up.

He was the only part of their lives they could defeat, because he didn't dare hit them. Not like their fathers, who were always reeking of beer and cigarettes, or bruised mothers drowning in guilt.

"We can do whatever we want to you." The biggest boy with the broken tooth would punch Devlin's face and stomach, always failing to make him cry. "Nobody's ever going to stop us."

It was understandable then that years later, colleagues at his firm would tell you that Dev, the quiet son of a widowed math teacher, listened more than he talked, as if conversation were a form of confrontation, something he had averted since the dark days of his boyhood by the railroad tracks.

As an actuary, Devlin took comfort in the parameters, calculations and sums of an orderly world where everything added up. But whenever life required him to deal with mundane matters, he felt out of place. Like today, with Blake, his little boy, waiting with him in the checkout line at the auto parts store.

The air smelled of rubber, echoed with compressors and the clank of steel tools dropped in the repair bays. This was a domain of grease-stained knuckles, rolled shirt sleeves and tattooed arms; of two-day growths, ballcaps and T-shirts emblazoned with skulls, flames and creeds on living, dying.

Devlin had come to buy a pea-sized bulb for his Ford's dome light.

In line ahead of them, a boy, a stranger slightly taller than Blake, turned and eyeballed Blake from head to toe. The boy's face oozed contempt before he drove his fist into Blake's shoulder. Blake tensed, then retaliated with a punch just as the bigger boy's father turned to see it. The man fired glances at Blake and Devlin, then drew himself to his full height. He had a scar on his chin and a toothpick in the corner of his mouth.

"What the hell're you doin?"

Alarm rang in Devlin's ears.

"Nothing," he said. "I mean, it was a mistake. Blake, apologize."

"But *Dad?*" Blake's face reddened.

"We're sorry. Blake, say you're sorry."

"But *he* started it."

"Did not!" the bigger boy said.

"Liar!" Blake said.

"All right. Okay," Devlin laughed nervously. "Just a little harmless horseplay. We're terribly sorry."

At that, the other man's height appeared to increase as he assessed Devlin. The stranger shifted his toothpick, sucked air through his teeth, then reduced Devlin to a waste of his time and turned away.

In the car, Devlin smarted from the incident but tried to conceal it as he struggled to replace the tiny bulb in the parking lot. He exaggerated his concentration, giving significance to an insignificant task. His sweating fingers lost their grip, and he lost the bulb under his seat.

"Can we just go, Dad?" Blake asked.

Driving home, Devlin found his son's face in the rear view mirror and the sting of shame for having let him down.

"You have to understand something, son."

Blake watched strip malls roll by.

"Non-violence is the best way to handle these situations."

Blake said nothing.

"It's just wise to back off. Because you never know how these things are going to go. You just never—"

"It's all right, Dad."

And with those words and with his tone, Devlin's nine-year-old boy had passed judgement on him. Devlin was guilty of a monumental failing. He had been tested and shown to be a father incapable of defending his son.

At dinner that evening, Blake didn't reveal to his mother and his older sister what had happened. Neither did Devlin. It was not mentioned in the morning when they packed their Ford before setting off for their family vacation at the lake in eastern New Brunswick.

But it was all Devlin could think about.

It weighed on him as they drove through the rolling hills and low rugged highlands that straddled the border with Maine. They dropped the windows and cracked the sunroof. Elise, his wife, was barefoot, wearing shorts, a summer top and sunglasses. Her hair flowed in the breezes. Annie, their daughter, was listening to CDs and snapping through *Wired* magazine. Blake took in the countryside, blinking thoughtfully at the forests.

Watching him, it dawned on Devlin that Blake's reaction to the kid in the store was heroic. That in a split second he'd made a clear, morally justified choice to defend himself.

Something Devlin had lacked the courage to do. But Blake was a boy, hardly mature enough to fathom the consequences, or appreciate the ramifications of a conflict. At least, that's how Devlin tried to rationalize it as the miles passed.

They navigated the route to their rented cabin from the crudely sketched map the manager had faxed. After they got off the highway, Elise identified the landmarks. "There's the red-roofed barn, turn left there." They drove along a ribbon of pavement that wound through rolling fields and pastures creased by streams with railroad tie bridges.

It wasn't long before it narrowed into a twisting, hilly dirt road, darkened by the thick cool sweet-smelling forests of cedar, pine, hemlock, butternut, maple, tamarack and birch. Under a quilt of light and shadow, the trees hid sudden peaks and valleys that hugged small cliff edges. It was beautiful, Devlin thought, loving the winding, undulating road. Annie and Blake were awed, as if they were penetrating a lost world. True to the map, after some forty-five minutes, they arrived at a hamlet made up of a few buildings clustered around a sleepy four-corner stop with a blinking yellow light.

The Crossroads, the hand-painted sign read.

It had a small mall with a restaurant, a postal outlet, a one-pump gas station, and Pride's General Store with a fat drowsy dog nearly asleep on its front porch.

"Pride's. That's where we pick up the key to our cabin," Elise said.

"Place looks like a ghost town." Devlin parked.

The planks of the porch creaked, and the dog raised its eyebrows to greet them as they entered. Elise bought a few groceries and snacks while Devlin showed the teenage clerk his driver's license. She produced a small envelope from the till. It contained a single bronze key with the number 7 carved into it.

Back in the car, as they started off on the final portion of their trip, Elise tilted an open bag of potato chips to Devlin, then pointed to the restaurant. "It looks nice. Let's go there for dinner after we settle in at the cabin."

"Sounds good."

The last stretch lasted some twenty minutes along a treacherous pathway that seemed even more primeval than the road they'd already travelled. Leafy branches slapped and scraped the Ford as gravel popcorned against the undercarriage. Soon the lake made its first appearance on the left, flashing between the trees in patches of brilliant blue.

It seemed so near.

"This is so cool." Annie slid off her headset. "It's like the loneliest place in the world. Like we travelled back in time or landed on a strange planet or something. I love it. It's so cool."

Blake wondered about native legends and lost trapper ghost stories.

"Oh, turn here." Elise pointed to a broken birch which suggested the letter T. "This is it."

Devlin stopped and dust clouds enveloped them as he inched off the road onto an earthen path curtained with a tangle of tall shrubs that swallowed their car. Through the stands of trees they glimpsed the lake and their cabin.

It was built with hand-hewn pine and had a wide deck with Adirondack chairs. There was a hammock tied between a pair of tall cedars. The cabin's lake front wall was a floor-to-ceiling window with French doors. Inside, hardwood floors gleamed to the fieldstone fireplace.

The main floor had a large living room/dining area. The kitchen had a small fridge, freezer and stove, which were state-of-the-art energy-efficient, powered by batteries and solar panels on an exposed hillside. The sink had a pump to draw clean well water. There was a small hot water reservoir. There was a master bedroom downstairs and two large, spacious bedroom areas in the loft, which Blake and Annie found immediately.

There was one sink in the small bathroom, but that was it. Beyond that, there was no indoor plumbing. No toilet. No tub or shower. There was a small outhouse at the rear. The lake was where people bathed. No phone, no electricity. No computers, no internet, no faxes. Neighbors were rare in those parts. "It's just you, the lake and the woods." Elise smiled after she'd finished reading the manager's note.

Energized, they unpacked, changed, then waded into the water of their private beach to swim off the sweat and dust of the drive. Curious, Devlin walked through waist-high water to inspect the gleaming boat tied to the dock. It came with the cabin.

"Think you can drive it?" Elise smiled.

"You bet, let's go for a ride."

They all climbed into the aluminum craft. The twenty-five-horsepower outboard came to life with a bubbling rumble that churned a creamy white wake as Devlin eased it ahead before opening up the throttle. The motor whined, raising the bow as he adjusted the tiller, centering its point squarely on the middle of the lake. Warm breezes brushed their faces.

It felt good.

A baptism of sorts, Devlin thought, warmed by the absence of others.

Bedrock as old as time formed the distant peaks that guarded the lake. They jutted from rolling forests laced with clear water streams and meadows jewelled with red trilliums, orange daylilies, blue flags and bunchberries. The lake was known as God's secret sanctuary, according to the history Devlin had read. For years, it had been all but forgotten, hidden in a remote reach of Canada's border with New England. Other than an abandoned Jesuit outpost, no lasting settlements had ever been recorded here. Much of the territory had remained unexplored well into the late 1800s. The demanding terrain had repelled lumber companies.

In 1893, a Halifax shipping tycoon had bought a four hundred-acre section surrounding the lake. He died without ever having set foot on it. His acquisition was ignored by his estate, except for the sale of a few lakeside tracts to satisfy an obscure turn-of-the-century property requirement. Situated on a peninsula, the parcels were separated by several acres of dense forest and accessed by narrow bush roads. It resembled skeletal fingers shaping a claw, the final extension of some unfortunate who had reached the lake to die.

"See." Devlin pointed his fork at the map on the paper placemats in the restaurant, where later that day, he continued telling his family about the region's history over dinner.

"Like a skeleton's hand," Blake agreed. "Mom, where's our map, so we can see where our cabin is and where we drove in the boat?"

"In the car on the front dash. We'll check later, sweetie."

Devlin and his wife had club sandwiches. The kids had cheeseburgers. They were the only customers. After dessert of homemade apple pie and ice cream, they strolled outside for some window shopping at the adjacent craft shop which had just closed for the day.

"This place is a dead zone," Annie said after oohing and ahhing with her mother over a bracelet in the shop window. As they turned to leave, Devlin saw a man walking away quickly from the side of their Ford to a pickup truck in a far corner of the empty lot.

He thought nothing of it until his family approached their

doors and Devlin saw the beer bottle wedged between the right rear tire and the ground.

He stared.

It had been placed strategically so it would shatter and shred their tire when they drove off. Now why would someone do something like that? Devlin glanced around for an answer, glimpsing the man nearing the pickup. He heard the man's snickering, echoing with the chuckling of a second man waiting behind the wheel of the truck.

For a few heated seconds, Devlin didn't move. The sight of the bottle hit him. The laughter hit him. Like blows to his stomach, his head, his dignity, they pounded him back through time, past the humiliation in the auto shop, back through his life to the railyard beatings. He pulled the bottle out and began walking to the truck without realizing he was heading that way until Elise begged him to come back.

Devlin kept walking.

It might've been because all his life he'd failed to stand up for himself. Had always bit back on his anger. It might've been because he'd failed to stand up for Blake. It might've been the pressure pent-up from years of never standing up to anyone. But deep in his gut, Devlin felt the quaking of an explosion. *You just don't pull a stunt like this, laugh and walk away. No, sir. There has to be an accounting.* And by God, he'd eaten too much crap in his life, not to be entitled to a little respect. Indignation hammered in his chest as he neared the truck.

The engine started.

The battered truck lumbered triumphantly toward the lot's exit, ticking and creaking. As it moved slowly away, the two men looked at Devlin. He stared into the darkened cab, then glanced at his family, feeling their fear pulling him back to the safety of doing nothing. Of letting it go. But he couldn't let it go.

Something was burning with such intensity it consumed him.

A sudden yelp of laughter triggered his final decision.

Devlin trotted after the pickup. Planting himself alone in the lot, he pulled out his weapons. A pen and notebook. Defiantly ignoring the fact the two men were watching him in their mirrors, he scrawled down their plate.

Good. He had their number. That's all he needed, he thought, turning to join his family in their car.

"John, what's wrong with you?" his wife asked. "Running after those two guys. That was so foolish."

"Excuse me," Blake said.

"Yeah, Dad!" Annie said. "It was so embarrassing!"

"Excuse me," Blake said.

"Why didn't you just let it go?" his wife said.

"Excuse me," Blake said. "But I think those guys are coming over here."

The truck had veered from its course and was approaching them. Devlin's Adam's apple lifted, then dropped. He hadn't expected this.

"Please just stay in the car," his wife said. "Calm down and don't make this any worse. Kids, put your windows up."

Devlin pressed the button automatically, locking all four doors. The truck ticked and creaked as it eased beside him, stopping when the driver's door drew up across from Devlin's, leaving about six feet between them. The driver's window was down. Devlin lowered his.

Halfway.

One muscular arm tattooed with a spider's web was draped over the truck's wheel, the other rested on the door frame. The old pickup had a beat-up fibreglass cap over the bed and a crumpled front fender, as if it had rammed something. The driver took his time dragging on his cigarette and spewing a smoke stream to the sky before turning to Devlin.

"Is there a problem, mister?"

Devlin figured the man to be his age. He was wearing dark glasses, a filthy ballcap and looked as though he hadn't shaved for several days.

"Your friend seems to have misplaced his beer bottle under my tire. I think he wanted to give me a flat."

"Give you a flat?" The man's face soured. He turned to his passenger, who appeared mystified. The driver turned back to Devlin. "I think you're mistaken."

"Mistaken?" Devlin made a point of surveying the empty lot. "You're right. Obviously, with no one else here, it couldn't have been you."

The air tightened, as if a gun had been cocked.

"John, please!" his wife whispered.

"John?" The man had heard. "That your name?"

The driver said something to his passenger, and they laughed. Devlin couldn't make out what he'd had said about his name as Elise squeezed his knee. He glanced at the frightened faces of his children in the mirror. Elise was now squeezing so hard it hurt.

"I'm sorry," Devlin said. "It was a bad joke. You're right. I'm mistaken. It must've rolled under there. I'm sorry I chased you. I was wrong. Please forget it."

"Did you call me *a bad joke,* John?"

Devlin saw his reflection in the driver's dark glasses. Tiny. Small, shrinking away, as he always did.

"No. Forgive me. I made a bad joke. I was wrong to accuse you of anything. Totally out of line. I apologize."

The driver's face hardened as he and his passenger scanned

Devlin, his family and their car for a long, cold moment. Then the driver studied his cigarette butt. Before he flicked it away, he half-grinned and nodded.

"No harm done, John."

The truck's motor ticked as it rolled away, then vanished down the road.

Elise wanted them to wait. So they did. For a long moment, Devlin sat motionless behind the wheel. Then he cursed under his breath, turned the Ford's ignition and started back to their cabin along the serpentine dirt road.

No one spoke.

The ping of gravel punctuated the silence, decompressing the tension as each of them withdrew into their thoughts. Devlin soon took comfort in the soft strains of music leaking from Annie's headset as she listened to a CD. Blake looked toward the lake while Elise glanced in her passenger side mirror.

"Oh, God, they're following us!"

Devlin's skin prickled when he saw the pick-up's grill and damaged front fender half-concealed like a phantom in the dust behind them.

"Hang on!"

He accelerated, and the Ford roared along the narrow route, bobbing on its sudden hills and valleys, sunlight flashing through the thick woods, branches slapping the car as stones boiled against its undercarriage.

"Daddee!" Annie gripped her armrest.

Blake was numb with fear.

"Oh, God, John," his wife said.

"We just need to buy some distance." Devlin's ears pounded with each curve he rounded. "There it is." He braked, the car slid, creating thick, choking dust clouds as he turned into the underbrush of their entrance. The Ford bounced. He tucked it neatly into a leafy canopy and shut off the motor.

No one moved.

For several desperate moments, they heard nothing but their breathing, which halted when the pick-up approached, crunching gravel, then the ticking engine. Under her breath Elise prayed for the two strangers to *please just go away*. Seconds later, the truck rolled through their fading dust curtain, leaving another in its wake.

Devlin allowed a full minute to pass before he turned to Elise.

"Well, that was an adventure," he smiled weakly. "All right back there?"

"Just fine, Dad," Annie groaned.

Elise shook her head, muttering something about brainless men.

"I think that's the end of it," Devlin said. "I think it's over."

That night they built a fire by the beach, huddled together, toasted marshmallows and watched the constellations wheel by as Devlin assured Blake and Annie that everything was fine. Later, after the children had gone to bed, Devlin and Elise lay awake and considered telling the police about what had happened. But Devlin hesitated.

"When you think about it, it was really nothing."

"John, what if those men come to our cabin?"

"El, those idiots were drinking, probably passing through town and decided to have fun at our expense."

"I hope you're right."

"Sure I'm right. They're probably passed out, or a hundred miles away by now."

That's what Devlin wanted to believe as he stared into the darkness, listening to every sound in the night until finally he was taken by sleep. It was accompanied by a dream that Elise was shaking him and wouldn't stop until he— "John, wake up. There's something outside!"

"Wha—what?"

At that moment, there was a wooden snap near their window. Oh, Christ, Devlin thought, swallowing hard. Then all went quiet.

"I'm scared, John, do something!"

Quickly and quietly Devlin pulled on his jeans, found the new flashlight he'd bought especially for the trip and crept to the deck for the axe he used for the fire. He padded around the cabin in the pitch black in time to hear a rustling in the bush near the bedroom window. His flashlight beam captured the furry fat behind and striped tail of a raccoon vanishing into the forest.

When he told Elise, they had to stifle their laughter.

"This is just too silly," she said before falling soundly to sleep.

The next morning was glorious.

Devlin spent much of it reading *Crime and Punishment* in the hammock. Elise and Annie collected wildflowers in front of the cabin while Blake fished off the dock. For lunch, they cooked hot dogs over an open fire near the beach. That afternoon, when Devlin went to the car for his copy of *Ulysses*, he noticed the Ford was leaning at an odd angle. Then he discovered why. The right rear tire was flat.

The same tire that those jerks had targetted.

And there was another problem, but before Devlin could figure a way to deal with it, Elise was standing behind him, hands thrust to her face.

"It was them," she said. "Those two assholes did it in the night." Elise never swore. She turned to look at Blake and Annie on the dock. "I want to go home."

Devlin tried to calm her by pointing to a rusted nail.

"It wasn't them. Look, this is why the tire's flat," he told her. "We simply ran over a nail. The bad news is we don't have a spare. No jack, nothing. We pulled it all out to pack more stuff in the trunk. It was dumb."

"My God, John, what are we going to do?"

Devlin had an idea and told her. They all climbed into their boat. The outboard rumbled as they cut across the water under a darkening sky. Taking stock of the forested hills and the vast lake, Devlin felt imprisoned and vulnerable but kept his thoughts to himself.

They had no other option.

It was a long time before they reached the Crossroads and the gas station, where Devlin asked the attendant to send someone out to fix his tire.

"That's going to take a couple of days. Jed's got the truck, and he went to the city. His wife's having a baby. Besides, he's going to have to pick you up a new tire, too. We don't have much stock here. I'd say, day after tomorrow is the soonest."

Devlin saw worry creep into Elise's face.

"Is there anyone else, or a spare, anything?"

The attendant shook his head. Devlin squeezed her hand.

"We'll be fine."

They returned to their cabin and finished their vacation without a single incident. Not even a chipmunk to startle them in the night. Relief came two days later when Jed, a twenty-something under-the-hood type with a nice smile, arrived to fix their tire. It was perfect timing. While he worked, the Devlins packed. When he finished, Jed showed off pictures of his baby daughter.

"She's brand new," he beamed as Elise cooed. "We named her Ivy. She's the good news that we need in the county, especially after what happened a few days back at the north end of the lake."

Elise and Devlin looked at each other then stared at Jed.

"What're you talking about?"

"That's right, you wouldn't know—being out here all isolated and stranded with your tire situation." Jed went to the cab of his truck, came back and handed Devlin a newspaper, *The County Beacon.* The main story on the front page was headlined: "TRIPLE MURDER: RETIRED DOCTOR, WIFE, GRANDSON, SLAIN AT CABIN."

Devlin and Elise read how police suspected the killers had followed the doctor and his family to their remote lake property in what one source called a gruesome multiple homicide. "In all my years, I've never seen anything like this."

Devlin's heart leapt when he read the next paragraphs. Investigators were seeking the public's help locating a vehicle seen in the area at the time. "A dark, older model pickup truck with a damaged front fender, and a light coloured cap over the bed. Two male occupants were seen inside."

When they finished packing, John Devlin and his family drove for three hours to the RCMP subdivision. Sergeant Lew Segretti of the Major Crimes Section was one of the Mounties investigating the killings. He took careful notes. Another officer brought coffee, juice and doughnuts for the kids.

"Your encounter with the men in the pickup, your description of the tattoo and the licence plate number could be critical leads. We'll keep you posted," Segretti told Devlin.

They returned to the city and the routine of their quiet lives, trying and failing to put the incident behind them. Devlin scrutinized the newspapers and TV reports, but the story faded. Weeks passed, a month, then three, until one weekend afternoon, when Devlin got a call at home during the first quarter of the football game.

"Mr. John Devlin? Lew Segretti, RCMP Major Crimes. You provided us with information on the Cushing family murders at the lake?"

"Yes, Sergeant."

"Mr. Devlin, there's been a break in the case, and it stems from your report. It led us to two suspects, Aaron Sikes and Daniel Johnson. Both dead now."

"Dead?"

"They tried shooting it out with the ERT team in a trailer in the foothills near Pincher Creek."

Devlin's pulse quickened.

"Mr. Devlin, we couldn't tell you at the time, but your thorough description was the linchpin. It helped us identify them. Sikes and Johnson were a murder team. We've connected them to the three homicides here and four more in Ontario. We've been working with police across Canada, tracking these men, until they led us to K-Division."

"I'm sorry?"

"Alberta."

"Alberta. I see. And you're certain both are dead?" Devlin sat up.

"One hundred per cent. Johnson died at the scene. Sikes died in Lethbridge a few hours later."

"In hospital?"

"Yes, but before Sikes died, sir, he spoke to one of our members, who took a declaration, a taped final statement. I think you'd better sit down. I have a transcript, and he mentions your encounter."

Devlin cast about the room. His wife was in the doorway, holding a dish towel. Devlin swallowed.

"I"ll just summarize it, but Sikes told the Corporal that he and Johnson had selected you and your family."

"Selected? Selected for what?"

Segretti hesitated. "To kill you." The hairs on the back of Devlin's neck stood up as the Mountie continued. "But you'd spotted the bottle, confronted them, and somehow threw them off their game. That's why they pursued the older couple, Doctor Cushing, which is horrible, and our sympathies go to the Cushing family. But the point is, your action saved not only the lives of your family, but of seven more people."

"I don't understand?"

"Mr. Devlin, these men were psychopaths. They were not very sophisticated, not clever the way the movies make out. But they were extremely dangerous. They had targetted another family in Alberta, a single mother who lived with her six kids on a rural property in an isolated area near the Rockies around Pincher Creek and Cardston. They were about to move on her and her children when we locked on to them, because of what you did. You stopped them. We just wanted you to know that, sir."

Segretti ended the call, but Devlin sat dumbfounded with the phone in his hand, for the longest time.

"John, was that the RCMP?"

"Yes, they got the guys. They're dead. It's over."

"Did they tell you everything?"

Devlin nodded, and his mind reeled, racing at the speed of memory back through the stand off at the Crossroads, back through his humiliation at the auto parts store, back to his youth and the beatings he'd taken from other boys at the railyard.

The boys who'd said he would never stop them.

Rick Mofina's *suspense novel,* Blood of Others, *won the 2003 Arthur Ellis Award for Best Novel. Mofina is a former journalist who has reported from the Persian Gulf, Africa and the Caribbean. His true-crime articles have appeared in the* New York Times, Reader's Digest *and* Penthouse. *Visit him at www.rickmofina.com*

TIT FOR TAT

Victoria Maffini

I was kicking it into high gear when I saw *them* coming at me. Glistening and straining against bonds of pink spandex triangles, they mesmerized me with rhythmic bouncing. I thought I saw a sherpa plotting his way over the rose tattoo when I fell in the ditch.

"Are you, like, okay?" A very tanned face asked from above the swaying bosoms.

"Must have lost my balance." I heaved myself out of the ditch, my body covered in grass stains, prickly stuff and stagnant green summer slime.

"You dropped your walky dealy." She extended her hand with my pedometer and a whopper of a diamond ring. "I'm Star."

Star and Maurice had purchased a "cottage" in our lovely western Quebec community of Val des Monts. Most people would consider an eight thousand square foot, timber frame home with two acres of pristine gardens and swimming pool to be a mansion, not a little getaway in the Gatineau hills. It made my sweet country home look like a roach motel.

"Maurice will be so pleased that there are people like, you know, *his age,* on the lake. It was totally awesome to meet you." Star flounced off with her streaked blonde hair streaming behind her. Her short white skirt glowing against the deep brown of her half-exposed buttocks left me slack-jawed.

I've been told I don't look my age. I work out, watch what I eat and wear sunscreen religiously. Not to toot my own horn, but I look mighty fine for fifty-five. Star's taut skin was a depressing dose of motivation. I was determined to finish my daily six-kilometre walk but was limping from the after effects of ditch diving. Theo was busy transplanting daylilies when I returned. Theo was my twenty-five-year old, perpetually-shirtless gardener, whose services I had received as a divorce gift from my best friend, Dana. He was, as she had promised, god-like.

"Gwen!" Theo rushed over, wiping his filthy hands on ripped Levis. "What happened?" He inspected the scrapes on my unshaved knees. Concern rippled through his tensed, chiselled jaw. I shifted, trying to remove my hairy legs from his clutches.

"It was a cleavage-related accident." Theo's blue eyes travelled from my broken skin to my chest, his brows contorted in confusion. I quickly changed the subject.

"Listen, we have new neighbours, they bought the Hill House. I'm sure they will need work done with all that property. You should go introduce yourself. I could give you a recommendation if you like." It was an empty gesture. Theo's work was amazing, and his knowledge of plants intimidating, even to a retired florist like myself. A flip of his wild black hair, and lack of shirt, usually got his foot in the door.

*   *   *

Within a week, all of Lac St. Antoine was buzzing with gossip of the new arrivals.

"I mean, Jesus Christ, who the hell swims topless in front of a group of teenage boys?" Dana was feigning outrage. She was perched on my kitchen table in the lotus position. Her grey braids provided an interpretive dance for the story. "The Martins said their grandson wants to spend the whole summer with them now." I knew she was secretly happy to have the focus of scandal be someone else for a change. Dana's "special" tomato plants and subsequent "special" brownies had not gone over well at the last picnic. "Nobody has even met this Maurice." Truth be told though, several of us had nearly been mowed down by his BMW. He was all driving gloves, sunglasses and flowing silver hair. I was taking an early morning power walk when he buzzed me and flicked a lit cigarette onto the road.

The doorbell chimed. It was Gordon, formally of Gwen-and-Gordon.

"I thought I smelled something," Dana snarled. There was no love lost between her and my ex.

"Funny, all I can smell is self-righteous old hippie." He bravely turned his back on Dana. "Just here for a swim. I'll stay out of your way." He squeezed my shoulder and left. The back of his T-shirt said "Porn Star". He actually smelled very nice. It reminded me of how much I missed him and us.

When we'd divorced, I got the house and some money; it had been one of the most pleasant break-ups our attorneys had been part of. We didn't fight; there were no threats or property damage, no name-calling. Gordon came to me one day and said, "Gwennie, I think I've fallen out of love with you." He wanted another chance at romance before it was too late. I watched as our twenty-seven-year marriage was divided up like a pizza, and our life as Gordon and Gwen ended. I cried daily in the beginning. Eventually, I decided it was all a big mistake, and one day we'd be together again. This was just a pause in our relationship; sooner or later, everything would be back the way it should be. That was three years ago. I'd never let Dana in on my denial; hating Gordon had become her favorite sport.

*   *   *

The St. Jean Baptiste BBQ was an event on the lake. The beach was decked out with flags and paper lanterns, and my neighbours ate and played under a perfect sky. Star's arrival sent a ripple of gasps through the ladies of the crowd. Stomachs on their husbands were noticeably sucked in. The Martins' grandson was first to bring Star lemonade. "Nice bathing suit." His newly pubescent voice cracked. Her blue nail polish matched the sequence of three well placed, but ill-equipped fleur-de-lys.

"Could you put a little vodka in this for me, sweetie?" She rolled the ice in her glass seductively at the stunned boy.

Even though she didn't seem to mind, I felt uncomfortable leaving Star to be gawked at and went to chat.

"Thank you so much for sending Theo over. I'm looking forward to letting him play in my garden." She winked in a less than subtle manner. I wouldn't say I felt jealous, but I was keenly aware of what Star had to offer that I did not. I had no desire for a relationship with Theo, but I also had no desire for Star to have a relationship with Theo. If he had been there, I might have peed in a circle around him.

Luckily, Star had set her sights on someone else. Unfortunately, it was Gordon. She sidled up to him as he seared steaks and flipped burgers. I began knocking back my piña coladas, watching my ex-husband being "accidentally" jostled from his barbequing by two underdressed beach balls.

"What the hell is he doing here, anyway?" Dana emerged from the woods with a puff of smoke, seeking munchies. "He doesn't even live here any more."

"We're all still friends, Dana. He divorced me, not the Association." I said it, but I was more inclined to agree with Dana at that moment. Star was giggling and prancing all around Gordon. If I wasn't mistaken, he was staring into her eyes with an expression I'd never seen before. Maybe this was the second chance he'd been looking for.

Territorial and a tad drunk, I weaved over to the BBQ. "Gordon, I'd like my steak rare, please." He jumped at the sound of my voice, then fixed his gaze at the ground in guilt. "So, Star..." My voice rose two octaves, mimicking the Martin's grandson. "Where's Maurice? We're all dying to meet him."

"It's like, all about work with Maurice." She leaned into me. "It wouldn't surprise me if he's got a new girlfriend on the side." A sneer melted across her lips. "But, what's good for the goose is good for the goosettes, right, Gordo?" And with that, she pinched him, eliciting a squeak I was also unfamiliar with. "Gordon promised to take me sightseeing this week, didn't you, Gordo. We're going to hike up the falls, take a ride on the steam train and go see the internal flame on Parliament Hill."

Gordon chuckled in discomfort. He'd never been one to flaunt his girlfriends in front of me. This was doubly awkward, because it looked like his new squeeze was also the wife of my new neighbour. I was surprised he was so open about this affair. I abandoned the idea of dinner and headed back to my pitcher of piña coladas to sulk and ponder the "internal flame".

*   *   *

The next weekend, Maurice introduced himself to the Martins by floating up to their dock wearing his driving gloves and sunglasses. Of course, this neighbourly moment was marred by his being dead. Danny, their grandson, decided that dead-guy-in-the-lake far outweighed any giant booby sightings and went home that afternoon. When they fished Maurice out, he still clutched a crumpled photo of Star draped over Gordon at the local *dépanneur*.

"That cocky bastard. Everyone knows that's *your dépanneur.*" Dana as usual was fixated on the evils of Gordon. "I've always known he was a cold-blooded killer."

"We don't know that!" I could not believe someone I was married to would be capable of murder. "Besides, for years you claimed Gordon was a yellow bellied self-pleasuring weasel, who was afraid to take a crap in the dark."

"I still stand by that."

The police interviewed me early. They asked about Star and Maurice, but mostly they asked about Gordon. Was he jealous? Did he have rage issues? Did I know anything about his relationship with Madame Star Renard? Did he ever discuss drowning Maurice?

Dana came in the back door as the cops went out the front. She prided herself on never cooperating with the fuzz. "They're going to arrest him, especially since Star says he made inappropriate advances towards her. He said if he couldn't have her, no man could." Things were not looking good for Gordon. Meanwhile, my moral compass had lost its bearings. Had Gordon ever loved *me* enough to take someone's life? I thought not. I felt shame over this sick envy.

*   *   *

For two days, we listened to the wailing of the widow Star Renard. It carried across the lake like a loon's haunting song. The Association called an emergency meeting on the third night. The group email called it a "candle-lighting ceremony in memory of our new neighbour", but I knew it was going to be an all-night gossip session. I replied that I'd be unable to attend because of an imaginary walking injury. Dana would fill me in later. Star also declined the offer, because it was too soon, and she felt strange having a service before they released the body. She graciously thanked us for our "support and like, stuff." A pang of guilt slithered through me. I'd been hoping she would attend so she wouldn't cry all night in her mansion.

I decided to drop her a note and flowers. Theo was pruning the hedges by the pool when I reached the top of the nearly vertical driveway. I thought I saw him straighten with pride at the sight of the bouquet of flowers he'd grown.

"That's really sweet of you, Gwen." Theo met me at the garage door. He patted my shoulder, then let his hand slide to the small of my back, where it stayed long enough for my whole head to turn bright red. "I think Madame Renard is very lonely. She's asked me to come all week, and after I fix the hole she burned in the lawn, there's nothing left to do." We walked to the charred circle. "She needs a girlfriend at a time like this."

Star answered the door sporting a black chiffon robe with marabou trim. It did nothing to hide *her* marabou trim, or disappointed look when she saw me. Theo turned quickly; as a gentleman, he would not want to ogle a grieving woman. "I've got to find that wheelbarrow. It's like it just disappeared."

I presented the posies and note to Star sheepishly, seeing the kitchen was packed to the rafters with three hundred dollar flower arrangements. "I'm just down the street if you need me."

"Thank you, Gwen. It means so much." She shut the door in my face. I couldn't say I blamed her for not wanting to hang out with the ex-wife of Maurice's suspected killer.

Theo offered to escort me home. He needed to borrow a

wheelbarrow. "How are you holding up? I mean with your ex being arrested for murder."

"I can't seem to wrap my head around it." We paused to admire the bird's eye view of the lake. "You know. Do you really think he's capable, Theo?"

Theo turned to me, serious and sad. "I can't believe he would make the mistake of leaving you." I caught a glimpse of something shiny and red in the lake and was straining for a better look when he kissed me. He crushed me against him and dipped me. How ridiculous did we look? Like a raisin and a grape, I imagined. And Theo's face was smooth and his mouth soft, nothing like Gordon's stubble and scratchy mustache. It just seemed wrong.

Dizzy with lack of oxygen, and being dangled practically upside down from the cliff-like driveway, I couldn't be sure if I saw Star watching us from her deck. Perhaps the swirling black spot was a sign of stroke, not chiffon blowing in the wind.

*   *   *

Star Renard was at my door with two bottles of very nice Château Margaux. She had on a normal sized shirt and sweatpants. She looked tired. "I'm sorry I wasn't up for a visit earlier."

"No need to apologize. You must be exhausted." I showed her into my cozy home, and she plunked herself onto my white slip-covered sofa.

"With everyone else at this meeting, I thought we could have a few drinks and chill out a bit. Being at my house only reminds me of poor Maurice." Her eyes looked to the floor, but her expression was blank. "We were only married for three months, you know."

I opened the first bottle of wine and pulled out some

crystal glasses. Star was talking about how she and Maurice had found the Hill House. We took turns filling each other's glasses. The more we drank, the more comfortable I got. Soon, I felt like I was floating on air, and Star became a distant jersey-clad spot on the other end of the couch.

"How are you feeling, Gwen?" Star was standing over me, removing the wineglass from my hand. "You look a bit out of it." Her tone was icy and sarcastic. From her waistband, she produced my condolence note.

"What's that?" is what I meant, but instead I said, "Whaaaazzzzits?"

"Why, it's your little note." Star snapped on a latex glove. She laid the note on the table beside the wine and a pile of prescription pills. Funny, I didn't remember us breaking out the Oxicotin. I felt gravity pushing me into the couch. Useless, I watched Star wipe down all of the surfaces she'd touched and wash her glass, returning it to the cabinet. In my fairly happy and sluggish state, I still didn't know where this was headed.

"It's like, so sad. A desperate divorced old lady, committing suicide over the disgrace her ex-husband brought to the neighbourhood." Star smirked.

I was becoming worried about the turn in our evening of bonding. I remembered my note and struggled to focus on it as it lay beside the Margaux. She'd ripped the part off the top that said "Dear Star, You know if you need to talk my door is always open." Now my note said, "I can't tell you how sorry I am. I hope you can find comfort in your memories. Love, Gwen."

"Like, *as if* Theo is interested in an old prune like you!" Star was over me again. "Why should I have to compete with you?" She pulled the top of my shirt open and looked inside. "You're all...saggy!" With that she rolled me off the couch onto my favorite summer blanket. I knew it should have hurt, but

I was way beyond pain. I was fighting just to stay conscious.

"Stupid Maurice and his private investigator. Like I'm gonna give him a friggin' divorce! We signed a pre-nup. I'd get squat. I mean, everyone knows that the young hot wife gets to *do* the gardener while her workaholic old fart of a husband is at the office! Everyone knows that!" She spit in my face. "And I didn't even *get* any action from Theo. He turned me down for *you!* Even Gordo, that moron, said he felt like he was cheating on *Gwennie!*" She gave me a kick to the ribs. "By the way, thanks for the wheelbarrow. I saw you spot mine in the lake. Although I don't know how you could have noticed much with Theo's tongue down your throat!"

She grumbled something that I didn't catch, because my face was now wrapped in waffle-woven cotton. Luckily, I was pleasantly distracted by the idea that Gordon might still have feelings for me.

*　　*　　*

The ride to the lake was rather bumpy, and I rolled out of my wheelbarrow a couple of times. My legs and arms were heavy and floppy and didn't respond to my brain's requests for them to move. I could feel the wet sand on my feet as Star propped me up.

"I think it's time to go to sleep." Star spun me from my cocoon. I landed on my back in the shallow water with a splash. "Crap!" She grabbed at my limp arms, trying to put me face down. There was water in my eyes, and I was choking on lake, but I saw a dark figure lunge at us. Then another figure, swearing and swinging and smelling of pot, flew through the night. For a brief moment, I was peacefully sinking below the waterline and not terribly concerned.

"Take that, you silicone slut!" A tie-dyed blur was pummelling Star.

"Gwen! Can you hear me?" Theo came into focus. The cold water had worked to sober me. He lowered his open lips to mine.

"I don't need mouth to mouth."

Theo smiled, "I know." And he leaned in again.

*　　*　　*

Star Renard was arrested for the murder of Maurice Renard and attempted murder of myself. Star explained to the police that she had never met anyone "as like, hot as herself" and had fallen in love with Theo the minute she'd laid eyes on him. She'd also never been rejected before, much less for a fifty-five year old divorcée in a B-cup. Star hadn't really wanted to *kill* me, she just wanted Theo all to herself.

Maurice had hired a PI to follow his lovely wife and had caught her half naked, flirting shamelessly with half the men in the Outaouais. He confronted her with a stack of incriminating photos, so Star had walloped him with the frozen shepherd's pie he'd requested for supper. The idea to frame Gordon had come to her in a rare moment of inspiration. She'd waded through the pile of pictures, chosen one where her breasts were clearly resting on Gordon's arm and stuffed it into her dead husband's clenched fist. After a bonfire of Kodak moments, she'd rolled him down the driveway in her red wheelbarrow of death, straight into the lake. Star had simply spoon-fed Gordon's imaginary advances to the police and *voilà,* motive.

"And who wouldn't believe it, a gorgeous over-inflated bimbo being pursued by a Viagra-filled old pervert?" was Dana's take on it.

I picked up the pervert at the Hull jail. I brought him back to what used to be *our* house and told him about the new developments in my relationship with Theo.

"So, there's been some kissing."

"Kissing," Gordon repeated. He did nothing to hide his unhappiness. His body slumped. "I guess I have no right to feel jealous."

"No, none at all." I hadn't mentioned that I'd told Theo I was flattered but not interested in dating someone thirty years younger than me.

I still felt married to Gordon. I was still in love with him. It didn't take long for us to start dating again. I guess a brush with a life sentence gives you a fresh perspective on things. Gordon told me months later that he'd looked into Star's eyes at the St. Jean Baptiste BBQ, and all he'd seen was a silly old man reflected back at him. In *my* eyes he saw the second chance he knew he would never be worthy of, but, if I would allow it, he would spend the rest of time trying to make it up to me. I let him move back into the spare room that week.

Theo still looks after the garden. Dana had paid him in advance for two years. "That should keep your stain of a husband on his toes." Indeed it would.

Victoria Maffini *is an artist, photographer, writer and co-owner of Hellina Handbag Designs. She lives in Val des Monts, Quebec. Her love for mysteries blossomed with years working at Prime Crime Books. Victoria's first story, "Down in the Plumps" appeared in The Ladies Killing Circle anthology* Fit to Die *(RendezVous Press).*

EGYPTIAN QUEEN

Joanna C. Szasz

Peter held the newspaper ad up to the light coming from the street lamp. Gabrielle Maisonville, the HELP WANTED ad said, but it didn't mention how intriguing she looked. Black hair pulled back in a ponytail and a smile that could blow out a transformer, Ms Maisonville clutched a bistro chair under each arm and wrangled them through the coffee shop door. "Moulin Bleu" flashed in gold print as the door swung shut behind her.

Peter looked at his watch. Seven fifty p.m. He had ten minutes to plead for an interview. He grabbed his accordion case and walked across the main street of Shale, dodging mud puddles and weaving between cars. He pushed the door open, and a bell clanged. The woman looked up as she wiped a table. "I close in ten minutes."

"Gabrielle Maisonville?"

She picked up a dirty plate. "Who's asking?"

"Peter Holmes." Peter put down his accordion case and held out his hand. "I'm here for the job interview."

The woman blew aside a curl. "The interview was four hours ago."

Peter slipped his outstretched hand into his blue jeans pocket. "There was a ten-car pile up on the Malahat—a fatal accident. I've been stuck in traffic for the last five hours."

"A horrible tragedy, Mr. Holmes." Gabrielle stepped around him and walked behind the counter to the open dishwasher. "But there are such things as cell phones."

"I called! Left a message with Joel? Noel?"

Gabrielle closed the dishwasher and straightened. Joel hadn't given her any message. She placed her hands on her hips and eyed Peter Holmes. Tall, with a Rasputin air about him, his jeans clung to his thighs, and his T-shirt had the Canadian flag on it. She glanced at the unusual suitcase at his feet. "What's in the suitcase? A bomb?"

"No, an accordion."

"That's worse than a bomb."

Peter frowned.

"Sorry. Are you a musician, Mr. Holmes?"

"No. I'm a writer. The accordion was my father's."

Gabi crossed her arms and leaned against the counter. "Really?"

"Yes."

She looked at the floor and swept her foot over the tiles. "My mother was a writer." She glanced at Peter. "She could spin a damn good story, make you believe you were looking over Niagara Falls when you were only sitting on a splintering wood deck. Can you spin a good story, Mr. Holmes?"

Peter straightened. "I've had a few short mysteries published."

Gabi glanced at the digital clock on the stove. 7:55. The coffee shop could stay open a little longer. "Grab a seat, Mr. Holmes."

He smiled. "The name's Peter."

"There are two Pepsis in that display case, and a day-old pastrami sandwich if you want it."

Peter placed his accordion case against the wall, retrieved the Pepsis and the sandwich and placed them on the table. He pulled up a chair, twisted the cap off one bottle and placed it before Gabrielle.

Gabrielle took a cigarette pack out of her shirt pocket. At least he had manners. After a few attempts with a lighter, she lit a cigarette. She tilted her head, blowing smoke away from Peter. "Don't tell management."

He smiled as he twisted the cap off his own bottle and sucked back a mouthful of the drink. He ripped open the plastic wrap on the sandwich. "Is this my interview, Ms Maisonville?" He took a bite.

"Gabrielle, or Gabi. I'm going to tell you a story, Peter. If you still want the job after you've heard it, then you can start tomorrow."

He swallowed and picked up his pop bottle. "And if your story sucks?"

"Then you're driving back to wherever you came from." Gabi settled in her chair, crossed her legs and began telling the story of her father and his Egyptian Queen…

*   *   *

The coffee shop had been busier than usual, many of the regulars stopping for a coffee during their mid-afternoon shopping. Gabi was swirling milk into a cup, forming a rosetta in a latte when her father walked in. Shoulders back, chest out, at seventy-five Frank Maisonville still looked good in a golf shirt and plaid slacks.

Gabi passed the latte to her customer and looked at her father.

"Gabrielle, you haven't lost your touch."

"Father." Gabi untied her apron and stepped around the counter. She gestured to a large brass fixture shaped like an inverted daffodil. "Our new Italian espresso machine."

Twenty-thousand dollars apiece, and Gabi now had two. "Beautiful, Gabrielle. Your mother would be proud."

"Joel," Gabi called, "two double espressos? We'll be outside." Gabrielle hooked her arm into her father's and led him through the open French doors and out onto an unfinished patio. "What do you think?" She walked into the middle and turned around. "The carpenter assures me it will be finished by my birthday. And look—" she skipped over to the railing, "—at the view!"

Frank walked over to Gabrielle. Across from them, two mountains, dressed in evergreens untouched by civilization, guarded the entrance into the waters known as Finlayson Arm. *Mon Dieu,* Gabrielle," Frank said, weaving slightly. He held onto the rail.

"Careful father, it's a long drop, and the carpenter still needs to reinforce the railing."

"Beautiful."

"I've been wanting to show you this for a long time, but you've been so preoccupied with—*her.*"

Frank stared at the blue water dotted with sailboats. "Cleo will love it."

Gabrielle's smile froze. "Cleo. What does she have to do with it?"

"Come. Joel has brought us our espressos." Her father led her to a small wrought iron table.

Joel smiled and pulled out Frank's chair.

Gabrielle sat across from her father. She picked up her tiny cup. "What does Cleo have to do with this?"

Frank nodded at Joel. "I'll miss him when he leaves."

Gabi brought the espresso to her lips. "Father, why is Cleo going to love the patio?"

He sighed. "Gabrielle. Why can't you two get along?"

Gabrielle's stomach churned. "She's twenty-three and was an employee until she hooked up with you. How could you love someone as honest as mother and then be with—her?"

"She loves me."

"Your money."

A breeze lifted a napkin from the table, and Gabrielle caught it. "So why is Cleo going to love the patio?"

Her father smiled. "She has brilliant ideas."

"For what?"

"Hell-loooo. Darling, I'm here."

Gabi groaned. She heard the click of Cleo's heels. Distinct. Mincing. Then smelled her perfume, Passion.

"Hello, darling. The manicurist at the spa took forever. Hello, Gabi. I've bought you something." Dressed in a long white wool coat and knee-high boots, Cleo flicked her black ringlets over her shoulder, then pulled a tiny box out of a white Chanel bag. "It's anti-aging cream," she whispered as she slid the box toward Gabi. "Great for those lines around the eyes and nose. Now, look at this," Cleo said. Her voice raised an octave as she sauntered over to the railing. "This is magnificent." Cleo gripped the railing and leaned over.

Gabrielle told herself to breathe. She should warn her ex-employee. It would be such a tragedy if she fell.

"Cleo, dear," Frank said, "be careful." He shuffled over. "It needs reinforcing, right, Gabi?"

"Uhunh," she said, sipping her espresso.

"I was about to tell Gabrielle about our plans for the coffee shop," Frank said, escorting Cleo back to the table.

Gabrielle choked on her espresso. She thumped her fist against her chest. *Excuse me? What plans?*

Cleo sat beside Frank, linking her arm through his. "We're

turning the coffee shop into a tanning salon and health bar. Isn't that exciting?"

Gabrielle's cup crashed on the saucer. "What?"

"A brilliant idea," Frank said. "People won't have to worry about the, the—" he turned to Cleo, "—what are they called?"

"UV rays."

"Old Ronald Zapotichny had that disease."

"Melanoma," Cleo added.

Gabi's father turned to her. "Do you remember Ronald Zapotichny, Gabi?"

"No father. I've never met Ronald Zapotich—"

"Sure you have. Two years ago at the picnic. You went to school with his son Bobby, or Toby, or was that—"

"Father! It doesn't matter." Gabi turned to Cleo. "You are not—" she jabbed the table, "—turning Moulin Bleu into a tanning salon."

"And health bar," Cleo nodded, sitting back as Joel placed a Serpent latte in front of her.

"No!"

"Gabrielle—" her father patted her hand, "—I know you have memories of your mother here, but you need to move on."

No, Cleo needs to move on.

Gabi clenched the edge of the table, her fingers slipping over the mosaic design. "This coffee shop is mine. That's what Mother wanted. That's why she left it to me in her will."

Frank and Cleo exchanged glances.

Gabi's heart pounded. "What?"

"You see, Gabi, there's a problem with the will."

"What?"

"A handwritten notation that your mother never initialed."

"What?"

"So actually, dear…" Her father looked her in the eye.

"The new will is invalid, and the coffee shop is *mine.*"

Gabrielle felt sick. Her mother—taken away. Her shop—taken away. Her memories—taken away. She fumbled with her cigarette pack. The lighter shook in her hand. She finally lit a cigarette and inhaled.

"Gabi, honey—" Cleo slurped her latte, "—let's not fight. We'll have the health bar out here, and in that corner you can still serve your little coffees."

"Espressos," Gabrielle said, teeth clenched. She dropped back in her chair and took another long drag. She had pictured black iron tables with tourists looking over the water at the mountains, enjoying an iced latte or a frappuccino. Not fake and bake Barbie dolls fussing over tanlines. She should throw herself over the rail and put an end to her misery. She looked at her father. "What about the regulars?"

"We'll have new ones," Cleo chirped. "But honey," Cleo waggled her finger at Gabi's cigarette, "that nasty habit will have to go."

Gabi glared, then forced her attention on her father. *"Father.* The *regulars.* The people who stayed with us even after Mom died."

"Gabrielle, those people will not bring your mother back."

No, but they could share her stories. Gabi looked at the espresso cup on the table. She and her mother had chosen those cups one Saturday afternoon—black china with a collage of white lettering, now blurred by her tears.

Gabi cleared her throat. She took one final drag of her cigarette. She would not let that bitch see her cry. "Excuse me." She pushed back her chair, butting the cigarette out. "I've got a coffee shop to run."

*　*　*

Now, sitting across from Peter, the emotion still got to her. Gabi swiped her hands across her cheeks and downed the rest of her Pepsi, wishing she had a little Captain Morgan to spike her soft drink. "So." She looked at Peter, an empty pop bottle and a crumpled sandwich wrapper in front of him "If you're interested, I have a job for you clearing tables and whipping up lattes. My father and Cleo are planning their wedding, and I can't guarantee how long you'll be employed. A month. Maybe two." She lit another cigarette. "Still interested?"

"That's it?" Peter said. "You're giving up?"

"There's not a hell of a lot I can do."

Peter stood. "If this was your mother's story, she'd think of something."

Gabi swallowed. "My mother isn't here to write this story. And if she was, I wouldn't have this *problem.*"

Peter picked up his accordion case. A smile tweaked the corners of his lips. "I'll see you tomorrow, Gabrielle. And I'll write the ending to your tragic tale."

*   *   *

Two weeks later, on time as usual, Peter stepped into the coffee shop, lugging his accordion case. He heard the scattered notes of a violin in the lulls of conversation and smelled the decadent aroma of pastry and glazed sugar.

Gabi, her back to him, pulled a sheet of croissants out of the oven. Peter stepped behind the counter just as she turned.

"Good morning, Peter. You're still lugging that thing around?"

Lately, his accordion had taken on the personality of an albatross. "I didn't want to leave it at the Crazy 8 Hotel."

"Can you play it?"

"Hell no, but my father could. He was a cop. Toronto Police.

Killed on duty. I should throw the thing into Finlayson Arm."

"No!"

"What the hell am I going to do with it, Gabi? I can't play it."

The bell above the door clanged. "Hell-loooo. I'm here."

"Crap," Gabi whispered, jamming her oven-mitted hands against her hips.

"I heard that, Gabrielle Maisonville. I'll put the accordion in the back." Peter squeezed past.

Gabi stepped up to the counter.

Cleo stood in her white wool coat and black boots.

"Good morn—"

"Stop the legal action, Gabi. It's killing your father."

Gabi stared. "I thought you were."

"Don't start with me, Gabrielle." Cleo flicked her ringlets over her shoulder. "This place is mine. You know it. I know it. Soon a judge will know it."

"Really? I thought it was Father's."

"Contesting the will won't get it back!"

"Not according to my lawyer."

Cleo's face flushed. She popped her hip to the side. "You can call up your mother's ghost, Gabi, it won't make a goddamn difference. I'll still get this place. If you don't want to be road kill, get off the road."

Gabi popped her hip to the side. "If you're scared of a fight, get out of the ring."

Cleo's eyes widened. "Where's Peter?"

"He's *busy.*"

"I want a Serpent! And I want *him* serving *me.*" Cleo clicked over to a table.

Gabi clenched her fists. She'd kill her. Wrap her fingers around her neck and squeeze. Or, better yet, grab her ringlets and shake her like she used to shake her rag dolls.

Peter reappeared, tying his apron. "Gabi, you okay? You look like you could kill someone."

"Her Highness wants a Serpent latte, prepared and served by you."

Peter slid the grounds-packed filter into the slot and pressed the "double long shot" button on the espresso machine. "Why did you ever hire her?"

"I was desperate. Little did I know she'd make a play for my father."

"He's lonely, Gabi." Peter poured milk into a stainless steel pitcher.

"Why couldn't he have found someone his own age?"

Peter slipped the pitcher under the nozzle. "It doesn't matter if you're seventeen or seventy—" He cranked the knob, frothing the milk. The hissing drowned out any sound. He removed the pitcher and swiped the nozzle with a damp cloth. "—men are suckers for a pretty face." He tilted the cup with one hand and poured the steamed milk into it, going from side-to-side. Slowly, the twisting shape of a serpent emerged.

"Beautiful," Gabi said. "You're a natural when it comes to latte art, Peter."

He smiled.

"So why aren't you gushing over her?"

Peter looked over the display case. Cleo was slathering another coat of pastel pink onto her lips. "I have better taste." His eyes focused on the cup, he walked over and placed it on the table. "Four-fifty, Cleo."

Cleo snapped her compact shut and held up a five-dollar bill. "Keep the change, gorgeous."

Peter took the bill, and Cleo grabbed his hand. "Sit with me."

"I'm working."

"Come on, Peter." She patted the chair next to hers. *"Puhleeze."*

Peter glanced at Gabi. She was placing another sheet of croissants into the oven. "What do you want, Cleo?"

"Moulin Bleu. By week's end, it'll be mine."

"Does Gabi know?"

"God, no." Cleo stroked his hand. "I want you to be the bartender for my after-hours martini bar. I'll show you how to make a caramel green apple martini with lots of sticky caramel."

Peter pulled his hand away. "I work for Gabi."

Cleo snickered. "Yeah, right. Look, gorgeous, forget about Gabi. The girls I'll hire will lovingly hang their g-strings on your taps."

"Not interested, Cleo." He turned.

Cleo held his arm.

"Let go."

She stood. "Think about it, Peter. Hot—" she trailed her finger up his chest "—sticky—" she pressed against him "—caramel. You and I, we'll kick out the Geritol generation and take over this place."

"Cleo—"

"Friday, Peter. I'll be back." Cleo sauntered toward the door.

Peter rubbed the back of his neck. Cleo was going to screw Gabi over.

"The Egyptian Queen didn't like her Serpent?"

Peter flinched.

Gabi stood behind him. "She paid this time," she said.

Peter gazed out the glass door as Cleo strutted across the street. He knew people back east. People who owed him a favour. But he had moved out here to get away from *them*.

"Peter? What's wrong?"

"Nothing." He rubbed Gabi's shoulder. "Nothing I can't take care of."

* * *

Lightning crackled over the mountains as a wall of rain moved across Finlayson Arm. Peter leaned on the patio railing. The dark water below was eerily calm, despite the lightning. Gabi had left early for a meeting with her lawyer, so he would have to close. He had dragged out his father's accordion, intending to toss it over. But he couldn't.

Peter pinched the inner corners of his eyes. It had been his associates who had murdered his father—men Peter had trusted. Cleo reminded him of those people. He had to get rid of her. Killing her would be easy, but his conscience wouldn't let him implicate Gabi that way. He'd buy Cleo off. Every slut had her price.

"Hey, gorgeous."

Peter straightened and turned.

Cleo stood in the doorway, dressed in high-heeled boots and bulky coat. "Planning on serenading me with a little polka?"

"How long have you been standing there?"

Cleo snickered. She clicked over to him, hips swaying. She looked and smelled like a cheap whore. "You're going to accept my offer?" Her hand slid down his shirt to the button of his jeans. "Or are you a hard negotiator?"

He knocked her hand away. "Sit down, Cleo."

"Whatever you say." She positioned herself at the table nearest the railing.

Peter sat to her right, gazing at Finlayson Arm. No sailboats, no fishermen pulling in crab traps.

"What's your answer?"

"Cut the shit, Cleo. You're after the old man's money."

"I have great plans, Peter. But first I need you to get rid of Gabi. Break her precious little heart. The old fart, well, I've been saving myself—" Cleo placed her hand over her chest, "—for our honeymoon. After our first night of sex, he'll be pushing up poppies, just like his veteran buddies. Then it's just you and me."

"I'll give you ten grand to leave Shale."

"But Peter—"

"Cleo, you're a venomous, self-serving bitch. I want you gone."

"You bastard! *You* want the money! That's why you're all over Gabi! You're scared I'll get it instead of you."

"I'm not after Gabi, and I don't need the money." Peter leaned forward. "Take the fucking ten grand and leave."

"Go to hell."

Peter lunged, knocking the table onto its side. His fingers circled Cleo's neck.

She clawed his hands. "Peter."

"Get the hell out of Shale. Tonight."

"You're...chok—"

"Are you going to leave?" Her pulse beat under his thumbs. He squeezed tighter. "Or do I have to kill you?"

"Okay. I'll...I'll...leave."

Peter let go and stepped back.

Cleo gasped. Her hate-filled eyes narrowed. She jumped up and kneed him in the groin. Peter groaned. His knees buckled and he fell.

"You asshole!" She kicked him in the face. He spun back, his head hitting the rail, and fell face down. Black. Spots. Blood...oozing down his face.

"How dare you try to ruin my plans," Cleo shouted.

Peter pushed himself up on one elbow. He heard Gabi.

"Peter? Are you here?"

He had to warn her. He pulled himself to his knees, the railing slanted. "Gab—"

"Look who's arrived. Daddy's little princess." Cleo stepped next to Peter, her boot inches from his hand.

Gabi walked onto the patio. She saw Peter and the blood. She looked at Cleo. "Get out."

"Make me." Cleo stomped on Peter's fingers.

He screamed and slumped.

With both hands, Gabi grabbed the accordion case and swung. It flew over Peter's head, missing Cleo and nearly pulling her over.

"Nice try, Princess."

Gabi swung again, nailing Cleo in the stomach. Cleo stumbled, then toppled over the railing, screaming.

Gabi dropped the case and darted over to the railing. Cleo dangled above the dark water.

"Gabi. Please. I beg you."

"Gabi, no," Peter said, pushing himself up. "You'll both go over."

She hated Cleo, yet… Gabi leaned over and with one hand grabbed Cleo's wrist. With her other hand, she anchored herself to the railing. It groaned under their combined weight.

"Gabi," Cleo pleaded, her hand clutching her arm. "Don't let go."

Gabi stared into Cleo's frantic eyes. Cleo's life was in her hands. For her father's sake, she had to save her.

"Help me," Cleo cried.

Gabi's arm trembled. Blood pounded in her ears, and the rain pelted her face. Her arm felt as if it were being ripped from its socket. Her fingers wet and cold, Cleo's wrist began to slide from her grip.

"Gabi. No."

Gabi's toes lifted from the patio. She couldn't hold her. Cleo would take her over. *"Peter!"* Gabi shouted, looking past Cleo at the dark water. The wooden railing shifted. *"Peter!"*

"Gabi!" Cleo's legs flailed.

Peter struggled to his feet. Then Gabi heard the crack like a tree splitting in half. The railing gave way. Cleo screamed as she plummeted, and Gabi was tackled sideways, knocked back onto the patio—Peter on top of her.

"Peter."

"I'm here, Gabi." His voice spoke in her ear. "I'm here."

Gabi's hands clung to his shoulder blades. She opened her mouth, swallowing gulping breaths.

Peter sat up, pulling her against him. "You're safe, Gabi."

The railing was gone. Only splintered posts remained and a clear view of Finlayson Arm. Gabi dug her heels into the patio, pushing back, but Peter held her in place. "It's okay, Gabi."

She clutched his arm. "Cleo?"

"She's dead. Drowned."

The image of Cleo, eyes wide, mouth open, fingers clawing the air, would be permanently imprinted in Gabi's mind. She had tried to save Cleo. Gabi looked at Peter, the cut along his jaw still bleeding.

"Peter…"

"It's over, Gabi, it's over."

"We have to call—"

"No one can know." He turned her to face him. "Listen to me. They won't believe you didn't do this deliberately. Go home—you were never here."

"But she—"

"She tripped over the accordion and went over. I got these—" Peter gestured at his face, "—trying to save her." He took Gabi by the shoulders and gave her a little shake. "You were never here."

Gabi looked at the mountains and dark water scarred by Cleo's death. Why lie if she had done nothing wrong? But maybe Peter was right. "Okay...I was never here."

Joanna C. Szasz *hated reading until her sister gave her a Bobbsey Twins book—her life changed, and at thirteen Joanna wrote her first mystery. Now, this Vancouver Island writer uses her husband and two teenage daughters for inspiration. Joanna can usually be found sipping a double-shot mocha while huddled over a manuscript.*

RIVER RAGE

Joan Boswell

Jacques' hands shook as he lit a cigarette. The phone's ring brought him back from the dark thoughts threatening to engulf him.

"Jacques, you *know* how sorry we all are about Edmond." Al Carson, superintendent of Johnson Brothers Pulp and Paper Company, spoke as if trying to convince Jacques of his sincerity. "This must have been a *very* bad week for you, you're probably feeling terrible."

Terrible didn't begin to describe Jacques' emotions when he'd watched his twin brother's logging truck being winched out of the Coulonge river, loaded onto a flatbed truck and hauled to the company yard. Sorrow, pain, rage—all these and more—that's how he felt.

"Not great," he mumbled.

"I hope you'll still come to the Company party for the newlyweds next Saturday and take photos for the newsletter."

If he wanted to keep his job, a refusal wasn't an option.

On Saturday evening, he hung his Minolta around his neck, pocketed extra cannisters of 35mm film and set off for the dance at the Company's recreation hall. He felt like hell and knew the smile he'd pasted on his face must seem phony. Hard to imagine he had any tears left, but three months after

Edmond had missed a turn, gone through the river ice and drowned, wrenching sobs continued to ambush his sleep and threaten whenever he thought of his brother. God, how to get through the evening?

Be like Edmond. Their mother said they were as different as two boys could be: Edmond, outgoing, a sunny magnet for friends and family: and Jacques, serious, quiet, thoughtful. Edmond had been the leader, the one who thought up the pranks to irritate the nuns in school, who amused their mother or caught the attention of the girls they admired.

He'd view the evening through his brother's eyes. His breath caught, and he swallowed to push down the lump in his throat.

Inside, he positioned himself near the bar to have a good view of the crowd jamming the hall. Next to him, twenty or thirty men, laughing and joking, bunched three and four deep, waiting for the overworked bartender to sling bottles of Molson, scoop ice into glasses of straight Bols gin, or mix the community's two basic drinks—rye and ginger or rum and coke. Jacques was a Molson man, but Edmond had loved dark rum and coke; he'd give it a try.

The five-piece Yves Lambert orchestra, a group from Val d'Or that travelled the Northern Quebec railway circuit visiting a different town every weekend, had set itself up at the front of the hall. The players, outfitted in red plaid jackets, yellow bow ties, white shirts and dark trousers, sawed and blew with gusto. Edmond's words, he'd called them "the tweety birds", echoed in Jacques' ears.

Plessisville had turned out in force to celebrate the marriage and welcome the bride of one of the young logging engineers. The organizers had borrowed two overstuffed grey plush chairs from a senior engineer's house, wrestled the heavy furniture into a company pick-up and moved it to the recreation building, where they'd plunked the chairs in the middle of the dance floor. The newlyweds, ceremonially installed somewhat like a king and queen reigning over a court, were surrounded by dancers or marooned in isolation when the musicians took a break.

Two years earlier, the community had fêted Edmond and his bride. Jacques had been the photographer that night too. One particularly good photo of the bride gazing up at Edmond took pride of place atop their china cabinet. As he got a good shot of this year's couple, Jacques made a silent wish for them to have better luck.

The groom, a fresh brush cut giving him the appearance of a recently shorn sheep, shouted greetings and traded ribald jokes with friends, colleagues and employees. In contrast, his bride, recently arrived from a small southern Ontario town and unable to speak or understand French, huddled deep in the upholstery, appearing to wish she possessed Houdini's talent for disappearing. Jacques sympathized with her as he clicked the shutter and recorded her misery for posterity. He contrasted the couple with Edmond and his wife, who'd paraded around the room arm-in-arm, stopping to kiss when glasses clinked.

On a card table, separated from the trestle tables destined to hold the mountains of food, a pyramid of brightly wrapped presents covered the surface, providing mute evidence of the community's generosity. Every so often, the bride glanced at the parcels: her wide, startled eyes and half-opened mouth reflected how overwhelmed she felt. Opening the pile would not only keep her and her new husband in the community's spotlight, but would also require responses. Jacques suspected the only appropriate phrase she would remember from her high school French would be *"merci beaucoup."*

At Edmond's party, he and the bride had commented on

everything, making sure they let everyone know how happy they were. Jacques remembered his contribution—"his" and "hers" fishing equipment. "I'll be keeping Edmond much too busy for us to go fishing," she'd said, and the wattage of Edmond's smile had lit up the room. To be fair, she had made his brother happy and been devastated when he'd died, but she'd always had a short attention span—the nuns had called her their *papillon*, their butterfly.

Older women and kids ebbed and flowed in front of and between the rows of folding wooden chairs lined up against the walls. The pretty young things in jewel-bright taffeta and shimmering satin dresses rustled and clustered in the harsh lights near the building's entrance or flitted in and out of the ladies' room. They giggled, tossed their heavily sprayed bouffant hairdos and spied on the young men, handsome and awkward in white shirts and colourful ties tracking to the bar or slipping outside for smokes or pulls from flasks hidden in hip pockets. Jacques sauntered over and snapped more pictures. Had he been Edmond, he would have had something to say to everyone, and each person would have responded as if Edmond had been a royal prince. Again his breath caught—he missed his brother.

Jacques took a break, swigged his rum and coke and fixed his gaze on Edmond's widow, a blonde whose ring-encrusted hands flashed as she gestured and laughed with a circle of admiring men. Jacques didn't think she much resembled a grieving widow. A black dress, particularly one cut as low as hers, didn't exactly define widowhood. And those high-heels, with their rhinestone bows, weren't too mournful either. Even before she'd been widowed, she'd loved sheer black stockings; she said they made any woman's legs look better. Hers didn't need any help.

Shortly past eleven, as if they'd received a signal unheard by others, middle-aged women trekked on Cuban-heeled pumps to the kitchen. They were visible through the kitchen's open hatch. Those who'd planned ahead retrieved folded aprons from their large handbags. Others tucked dishtowels into their waistbands or under the fabric covered belts of their good dresses, crepe or polyester trimmed with lace or sequins. They chatted and laughed as they prepared *le lunch* for the kaleidoscopic groups forming and reforming in the hall.

Jacques moved to watch and take more photos. The women bustled about on their self-appointed tasks. One woman in a navy print dress bent repeatedly to load the oven with *tortières,* traditional meat pies. Other women filled large aluminum kettles, set them to boil on the industrial-sized stove, spooned coffee from gigantic tins, and poured water into the four restaurant size percolators parked on serving carts, ready to be wheeled in when their green lights glowed. Beverages taken care of, the kitchen crew unloaded perishable items from the fridge and deposited them on the over-sized worktable.

Once they had everything ready, the women transferred potato salad from Tupperware containers to serving dishes, mixed dressing with coleslaw and decanted pickles. They overlapped slabs of ham and beef on plates that they garnished with radish roses. Chunks of cheddar cheese impaled on toothpicks, plates of devilled eggs and celery completed the array. Finally, they sliced coconut layer cakes topped with eight minute boiled icing, divided chocolate and vanilla sheet cakes into rectangles, sectioned pies in eighths, and artistically placed squares, cookies and tarts on plates. By now, Edmond would have made at least one sortie through the kitchen, flattering, tasting, teasing; Jacques knew no matter how much he tried to imitate his brother, he'd never manage the casual repartee that had come easily to Edmond.

Between dances, those not employed in the kitchen collected their drinks, wandered outside to the veranda overlooking the Coulonge or clustered near the three sheet-draped tables set aside for the midnight feast. Jacques recorded the scene, although he turned his back on the river.

The orchestra filed in from a smoke break, picked up their instruments, turned pages of music and resumed. What were they playing? "The Tennessee Waltz"—Edmond had loved the song. Never could see it himself; he preferred Gilles Vigneault or Edith Piaf.

The *sorrowing* widow danced with Henri Potvin, the mechanic who serviced the trucks for Johnson Brothers Pulp and Paper. He specialized in the giant log haulers, the kind of truck that had made Edmond's wife a widow.

Before she'd married Edmond, the widow and Henri had dated. Now Henri gripped the widow's behind as if he didn't ever intend to let go. Jacques supposed he couldn't blame him; not with Henri having heart disease in his family. He didn't recall the name, a long fancy one, but it meant that around the age of forty, the Potvin men dropped like flies.

Both Henri and the widow must have had a lot to drink. She was all over him; curving her body to his, caressing him, running her fingers through his thick dark hair. By the look of it, the widow also loved the curly tendrils escaping from Henri's partially unbuttoned shirt. Jacques watched as the fingers of her right hand crept inside the shirt. The village would have something to talk about tomorrow. His stomach turned, and bile filled his mouth. Maybe he'd feel better if he went outside for a smoke.

The spring air revived him. He fumbled for his tobacco pouch, removed one sheet from his package of cigarette paper, deftly spread tobacco, rolled it up, licked the paper and slid the cigarette between his lips. With his back to the wind and his hand shielding the Ronson lighter, he lit up, inhaled deeply and thought about the truck, about the brakes, about Henri and about the life insurance that had made the widow a rich woman. Edmond shouldn't have bragged about how much insurance he'd bought. Jacques ground out the cigarette and stalked inside.

Dancers packed the floor. Their energetic jiving to three successive Buddy Holly numbers liberated waves of perfume, after-shave, sweat, hair spray and the exhalations of smokers and drinkers. Jacques photographed couples and got a particularly good shot of the bride smiling as she spun back and forth. The room itself, as it warmed, smelled of wood, floor polish and years of spilled alcohol. The floor, responding to the impact of hundreds of feet pounding out a rhythm, creaked and groaned.

When the orchestra completed its set and straggled outside for another smoke, the dance area cleared. Even the guests of honour had left the hall. Activity sped up in the kitchen, where a bevy of women scurried about, putting the finishing touches on the late evening lunch. Parted from Henri, Jacques could see the widow loading a metal tray with cutlery, along with salt and pepper shakers. He suspected the widow, who'd never hidden her love of the opposite sex, hadn't volunteered for tasks that might have kept her away from her admirers. She swayed across the deserted dance floor, unloaded the tray and swivelled back to the kitchen. Jacques watched her collect pitchers of cream, glass cylinders of sugar, dishes of mustard, mayonnaise, catsup and pickles along with a stack of paper napkins.

He stopped staring at her—she made him want to cry. Edmond should have been there to tease her, tell her she was gorgeous and make her laugh. How could he ever think he'd be like Edmond—he'd never had a girlfriend, let alone a wife. What a depressing thought. Time for a refill. He plowed his way through the men at the bar and slapped down money for a rum and coke. Henri stood next to him.

"Two rum and coke," Henri said and added, "one for me,

one for your sister-in-law."

"The *grieving* widow."

"Don't be hard on her. She's young and beautiful. You have to use it or lose it," he slurred.

He meant *he* wanted to use it and not lose it.

"She's going to be a while helping get the lunch." Jacques said as he reached over and removed one of the glasses from Henri's hands. "You take one to her. I'll hold yours and grab us a couple of seats. Come and have a drink with me."

Henri lurched, cocked his head to one side and struggled to focus on Jacques. "Good idea. I'll be right back."

Jacques settled in a quiet corner next to the band's empty chairs. He set his camera, beer and the rum and coke on the floor, removed a film canister along with his pouch of Sail tobacco from his pocket and bent over. When he straightened, he watched Henri in the kitchen, snapping a dishtowel at the widow, who giggled as she clutched her brimming glass and half-heartedly moved away.

A few minutes later, Henri zigzagged across the floor and sank down. "Bloody hot in here," he said and downed half his drink in one long gulp. He wrinkled his nose. "Cheap rum— tastes like hell."

The widow continued carrying trays of plates, coffee mugs, platters and bowls of food to the tables. After each trip, she waved to them on her way to the kitchen.

Finally, the women finished and the tables, groaning with food, waited for the attacking hordes. The band launched into the last set before the lunch.

"Hi, Jacques, how are you?" The widow joined the two men.

Jacques was tempted to tell her how terrible he felt, but why do it—she couldn't change—once a butterfly, always a butterfly. "Fine."

"Time for another dance," Henri said parking his glass on a nearby chair before he stepped out and grasped the widow's hand.

"Pennsylvania 6-5000", an old Glen Miller number, blasted through the hall. The French-speaking crowd bellowed the English refrain. Henri stomped his feet, gripped the widow and put her through her paces. When he twirled her around and under his arm, her head flew back and she laughed aloud.

Henri pulled her close. They danced a few steps together. He released her and she whirled away like a thrown yo-yo before she returned to him. Henri's smile disappeared. His eyes widened. He grabbed for his chest, gasped and dropped to the floor.

The widow screamed. The music dwindled as the band, along with everyone else, stood and craned to see what had happened. The newlyweds held hands; they'd never forget their first party. The crowd packed closer and closer until the company nurse pushed through the pack, knelt beside Henri and ordered those pressing forward to back off and give her space.

"Must have been that heart disease," Jacques said to no one in particular as he shoved his cigarette makings and the empty canister well down in his pocket and edged around the mass of onlookers to carry Henri's glass to the sink in the kitchen. He rinsed it thoroughly as he reflected on severed brake lines and the poisonous nature of concentrated nicotine. His rage was gone; the Coulonge had lost its power. Wherever he was, Edmond could rest in peace.

Joan Boswell's *work has appeared in many North American magazines and anthologies. In 2000 she won the $10,000 Toronto Star's short story contest. A member of the Ladies Killing Circle, she co-edited* Fit to Die *and* Bone Dance *and* When Boomers Go Bad. *Her first mystery,* Cut Off His Tale, *was published in 2005 by RendezVous Press.*

DR. SPANKIE'S CAR

Therese Greenwood

A shorter version of this story appeared in the
Kingston Whig Standard, *Summer 2003*

If the water gets any lower, we'll see the top of Dr.
Spankie's car." Father Spratt lifted his cloth cap and scratched his
head as he looked out over the Island's rocky shoreline, bare and
grey and forty feet further out than normal. Too little snow during
the winter had left Lake Ontario smaller and meaner, like
everything else during the Depression. "Lowest water we've had
since the doctor busted through the ice in '23," said the priest,
carefully settling his cap low over his forehead.

Tricky Dicky McDermott was thinking about Dr. Spankie's
car, too, as he brought the priest home from the sick call on
Mrs. LaRush. The wagon ride from the head of the Island took
them all the way along the north shore, and with every foot his
old mare Minnie plodded, Tricky thought about how the first
car on Wolfe Island had gone under ten years before on a wild
January night. Only Dr. Spankie would head out in a storm
like that. Several Island families claimed it had been to deliver
their baby. The roads were done like dinner, and the doc
headed onto the ice, swept clean by a mean wind that started
up in Toronto and whistled like a bullet three hundred miles
down the big lake. But Dr. Spankie hadn't delivered any babies
that night. The black Ford had cracked through the ice and
almost taken the doc down with it, but the big man had heaved

himself through the window just in the nick, then tramped three miles through the snow to the nearest farmhouse. Several Island families claimed he had warmed up by their homestead's woodstove. By the time anyone had looked out the next morning, the lake was dusted over with snow like a prairie field, and there was neither hide nor hair of the doctor's car.

"That old Ford has put more miles on underwater than on land," said Father Spratt. He was pretty cheery, considering he had just given a woman last rites, but Tricky always found Father Spratt a tad cheery for a priest. "People swear they spotted the roof sticking out at the foot of the island," Father said, "or saw a fender down to the head, or a tire in front of the village. Once it even got all the way 'round back to the ridge."

Tricky had a good idea where the old Ford sat. No one knew the winter lake better than him. It was his bread and butter. He had spent years shoving planks over the slushy spots to make toll bridges on the snow road across the ice, charging a nickel to Islanders crossing into town and ten cents to mainlanders coming the other way. He knew all the weak spots and, with the water down and Dr. Spankie in hospital in town breathing out his last, Tricky had been keeping an eye on the most likely location of the old car. Too bad Father Spratt was keeping an eye on Tricky. The priest knew how to keep Island business on the Island, but he was a God man and, Island code or no, a God man had his limits. If the water got any lower and the wrong folks got to Dr. Spankie's car, then Tricky's ten-year wait for low water would have been for nothing.

The horse turned into the laneway by the big stone church, solid on the foundation Tricky's father had hauled loads of rock and sand for, and they rolled past the stained glass windows that were the most expensive things on the Island. Down the back lane into the rectory, the air was heavy with the lilacs that had burst out, and Father Spratt took a deep breath. "Smells like spring," he said.

Tricky helped Father down with the big valise, the one kept by the door with the sick oils in it ready to go, and Father slipped him the usual two bits. Father asked Tricky in for a cup of joe, but time was money, and the priest's coffee was no hell anyway. Tricky hopped back up on the seat, slapped the lines against Minnie's rump and they plodded out the laneway, turning the corner towards the Hitchcock House, which sat smack on the water within spitting distance of the church steps.

The university men were waiting outside the big frame building. Too important to loaf on the veranda, they stood in front with the shovels and picks, which they tossed into the wagon before Minnie came all the way to a stop. Tricky stayed put on the seat and rolled a smoke.

"What's that contraption?" Tricky was all innocence as he nodded at the metal detector the biggest lad was carefully lifting into the wagon bed.

"It tells us what's under the ground, helps us find artefacts and arrowheads," said the professor, a squirt of a fellow, crawling up next to Tricky while his boys piled into the back with the digging gear. The professor must consider Tricky dumb enough to think old arrowheads were made of metal. But Tricky had a pretty good idea what the professor was really looking for, and he let the squirt know it on the drive out the road he had just fetched the priest along.

"Funny you looking for an Indian burial ground up the Bateau Channel." Tricky gave Minnie her head, since she knew the road better than he did. "Most people look at the other end of the Island, up to Brophy's Point."

"That site is exhausted," said the professor, who had a face like a lady's lap dog. "We have some new and promising indications of native settlement along the old Channel land."

"No one has seen an Indian on the Island in a long, long time," Tricky went on, taking a deep breath of smoke and pausing before he dropped his little bomb. "Not since the French left."

"I am aware of that," said the professor, squirming on the seat when Tricky mentioned the Frenchmen.

"Here's a funny thing," said Tricky. "The old-timers tell about a Frenchman who came ashore right around where you are digging."

"You don't say," said the professor and looked out over the lake, fidgeting with the leather book on his lap. Tricky knew he had the squirt then because he had yet to meet a university man who didn't want to hear the old stories, like his listening was doing you some big favour, like he was telling you the stories were important, as if you didn't know. As if Tricky was too thick to figure out that with Dr. Spankie in the hospital, and the doc an important man, warden for the county and an MP and all that, people were looking through his papers and someone in town must have found out the old story about the treasure.

"It was a Frenchman coming across with a sack of gold for LaSalle's camp," Tricky said. "To buy goods and food and pay the men and such. The old-timers say he crossed at Cape Vincent and landed here, burying his gold on the shore and then heading off to find someone to sneak him and his treasure to the fort."

The professor pretended he was reading his big book and not listening to Tricky as they passed the old French castle, burned to the ground a few years back.

"That Frenchman clean disappeared," said Tricky. "Maybe he took off with the gold. Maybe the British got him, or maybe the Indians. Maybe that gold is still sitting out there in the ground."

Tricky waved to the Mac brothers, the whole half-dozen of them picking stones out of the castle field and thumping them onto a stone boat. The Mac brothers straightened up like soldiers and waved back. Not a one put his hand to his back, even though they had been stooping over rocks before the professor crawled out of the feather tick at the Hitchcock House. The Macs were known for their strong backs, and for being tough as nails and wild as bears. Old Sandy Mac had always hoped a hard day's labour would tire his boys out, and when they were young lads, he had them pick stones from that field every Saturday in the spring, sun-up to last light. It was steady work; every winter, the ice and snow stuck frost fingers deep into the island and pulled up a fresh crop of stones to be cleared out before the plow blades got bent. Sandy Mac was ten years under the soil himself now. The Spanish flu had taken him fast, and the boys were men, still picking stone and dumping it along the wood rail fences that divided their smaller and smaller farm lots. Their great-grandfather had been a hard, canny man who had gone from clearing a lone lot with a single axe to owning half of the Island's best farmland. But there was only so much Island to go around, and the Old Mac's ten farming sons had more farming sons and the property had split down and down over the generations, so Sandy Mac's sons were no better off these days than Tricky. They worked together though, and they worked hard. Tricky worked hard, too, but he liked to make more money than some Islanders thought his work worth.

Tricky could still hear the stones dropping onto the stone boat as he touched the lines. Minnie pulled up, and the professor and his boys jumped out. Minnie knew as soon as the professor had handed over the extra two dollars Tricky charged educated men from town, and she started up back towards the village while the professor and his men began turning over rocks and sniffing like dogs with that metal detector. All that education, thought Tricky, and they're picking stones like the Mac brothers. And all for nothing, if he was right about what was in Dr. Spankie's car.

Because Dr. Spankie had been at Sandy Mac's the night his car went through the ice, and Sandy Mac was taking care of his final bit of business, which was a sack that had come up with the stones in the field that year. None of the boys knew what was in it, but their hard-as-nails father had turned white as a ghost at the sight of it, and had taken the sack right back to the house and put it under the bed for safe-keeping. There it sat inside an old feed bag until the flu came. Then Sandy Mac called for Dr. Spankie, an educated man, the sort of man who would know what old French coins were worth and how to keep that money on the Island and how to split it among six sons without those bastards in the government finding out. Tricky figured the coins were still in the car, or the boys wouldn't be picking stone in that poor field. Tonight he intended to find out, when the rest of the Island was at Mosier's dance hall and a man could slip out on the lake and go about his business without the whole north shore watching.

*   *   *

There was only a fingernail moon when Tricky rowed the skiff out and tossed the rusty chain with the broken prop into the water about a mile off the tip of the Flat Rocks picnic spot. It was slow work dragging the bottom when you were rowing, but he didn't want anyone to hear an engine prowling back and forth as he felt around for Dr. Spankie's car. The sound of the band easily covered up his oars, and he could hear Art McKenna's fiddle calling "Bonaparte's Retreat". The music rolled louder out of the dance hall every time the door opened, and the men went out to check the horses and have a sip of rye. Tricky heard the songs change a few times, a reel and a waltz then a reel again. The tune had changed again, to a low sad song, when he caught something not too far below. Sure enough, he leant over the side, and in the light of the muffled lantern he saw the roof of Dr. Spankie's old Ford.

Tricky tugged the prop so it caught hard against the bottom of the car and anchored the skiff, then with special care he tied a rope around his waist. People always seemed surprised that Islanders couldn't swim. An Islander travelled the lake when it was frozen and thawed, in storms and in calm, and took bass and pickerel and muskies out of it to put on the table. Islanders respected the lake for the big thing it was, and they didn't splash around in it like a bathtub the way summer people did. Tricky respected the cold spring water, too, when he stepped over the side of the boat. The freezing lake was like a knife on his calves as he stood on the roof of the old Ford, rusty but still rock-hard. By God, it was a solid old car. Tricky slipped down to his knees and felt under the cold water. He could feel the open window Dr. Spankie had heaved himself out of. Tricky didn't much like the idea of heaving himself inside it, but he was thin, while Dr. Spankie had been quite a size. He took a deep breath and swung himself over the edge of the car and down under the water.

The cold hit his head like a hammer, the chill going all the way to his back teeth. He was blind in the dark night water, too, and gripped the edge of the window tight with his left hand as he felt around inside with the right. He didn't feel anything but what was left of the steering wheel and the slime and muck along the big bench seat, and he had to haul himself back up to the top of the water for another deep breath.

The next time down, he pulled his top half through the window, his stomach hanging over the door, his legs dangling outside. Holding onto the steering column, he pushed himself forward, feeling around in the cold dark with a hand that was going numb. He pulled himself further into the passenger's side, his knees staying just outside, and there he felt it, the right size and shape, spot on where Dr. Spankie had left it ten years before. Tricky grabbed the handle of the doctor's old leather medical bag, slippery and sodden but still in one piece, and wriggled back through the window. The bag moved sluggishly in the cold water, like a catfish coming through mud, and it stuck at the window frame. Tricky was losing his breath, and he pulled hard, tugging with both hands, and when the bag came rushing through, it moved too fast. The handle burst off in his hand and the bag went past him in the blind water, already sinking down towards the bottom.

There was no time for another breath. Tricky loosened the rope and slipped it over his arms then his head, kicking out from the car and hoping like hell he would find a way back up to the top. He waved his arms and thrashed his feet, and if he hadn't been so damn wet and cold, he would have cried for joy when he bumped up against the bag. He wrapped both arms around it, somehow got his feet on the bottom and gave a mighty jump which brought him up to the surface. He could see the dim light of his lantern in the boat a good ten feet away, and he let one arm go free of the bag and started to splash with it, but there was nothing to grab onto, and he felt himself going down again, like the water was air that couldn't hold him up.

This time he couldn't find his feet on the bottom, and he couldn't find the car, couldn't find anything to climb on top of, wasn't even sure which way he was facing. He twisted around in the water, holding the bag with both hands again, panicking when he felt the weed wrap around him, the long, slippery, leech-ridden strings called seaweed, even though this was a lake and not the sea. Tricky had never seen the sea in his life.

Tricky was not a church-going man, but he knew when a prayer was in order. He recalled the rosary his mother had made the family say every night before bed, which they kept saying for five years after she passed on, till their father passed too, and it was funny how you never forgot the words, although when he said Holy Mother, he was thinking of his own mother, not the Virgin Mary. Tricky's lungs were almost gone, like Sandy Mac's had gone—they said he had drowned in the fluid of his own lungs—and the water still seemed freezing but different, too, like a cold wet blanket closing around him and pulling him down. Then Tricky remembered it was still spring, too early and cold for the weeds that the sun brought up from the bottom of the lake. It was not a weed, it was his own rope, and instead of fighting it, he grasped it with his right hand, and hauled himself up and into the boat, somehow still clutching Dr. Spankie's old bag.

He lay there gasping on the bottom of the boat, like the fish he had hauled into it so many times, and it seemed even colder in the night air than in the water. But he reminded himself that he would warm up rowing, that he was not a man for hysterics. He sat himself to the oars and was feeling fine by the time he pulled the boat up on the shore. The Island never looked so good. McKenna's band was playing the "Maple Leaf Rag", Minnie was standing right where he left her, and on the seat of the wagon sat Father Spratt, the one man on the Island who didn't dance any more, putting his black rosary back into his pocket.

"I recall the night Dr. Spankie's car went down as if it was yesterday," said Father, as if they had never stopped their talk on the road. "There are times you need a doctor and times you need a priest. That night Sandy Mac needed a priest and a doctor."

"You have no right to what's in this bag," said Tricky. "I

know the law, and the law says finders, keepers."

"No man has a right to what's in that bag," said Father Spratt in his priest voice, none too cheery now. "Open it up and we'll see."

Tricky didn't like the sound of that. It was a rare bird who put one over on Tricky Dicky McDermott, but if anybody could, it would be this blamed priest. The priest still wasn't smiling when Tricky set the bag down in the wagon bed and used his knife to cut open the clasp at the top. Just like Tricky thought, there were no medicine things inside, no bandages and oils and metal instruments. Just an old feed sack, rotting out and wet. There was no gold inside, just the chalk white bones of a man, a big smashed-in crack in the front of the washed-out skull, like an axe had come down on the forehead.

"That Frenchman has been waiting a long time to lie in a proper churchyard," said Father Spratt, putting the skull back into the bag as if it were a soft and precious metal. "We'll bury him like old Sandy Mac wanted, without putting his family in the professor's history books. We can keep it on the Island, for this old fellow must be part of the Island by now, coming all the way from France with the old island families and staying here all this time."

Then Tricky knew where the gold was, that it had once bought half the Island at a shilling per acre, that it was now inside those hard-working men who hauled the stone out of the soil every year. It was so deep into the Island, even the hardest frost would never bring it up.

Therese Greenwood *grew up on Wolfe Island, the largest of the Thousand Islands, where her family has lived since 1812. The region forms the backdrop for much of her historical crime fiction. She is co-founder of the annual Wolfe Island Scene of the Crime Festival and a two-time nominee for the Arthur Ellis Award for best short story.*

More anthologies published by RendezVous Crime

When Boomers Go Bad

The Ladies' Killing Circle takes a spirited look at baby boomers as they go from young, hairy and hip to old, bald and bad. The children of the sixties are are up to no good in another dastardly anthology of fiction and poetry from this prolific collective of women writers.

1-894917-31-6 / 14.95 CDN, $12.95 U.S

Bone Dance

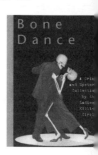

Music may soothe the savage breast, but music provides the background for tales of murder and mayhem in this collection of witty and wicked crime fiction and poetry. Eighteen stories take their inspiration from titles as varied as the upbeat "Wake Up Little Suzie" and the romantic "Summertime". It's a collection you won't want to put down until you've read every one and hummed all the tunes.

ISBN 1-894917-05-7 / $14.95 CDN, $12.95 U.S

Fit to Die

Sport, fitness, games and murder are the main themes of thi collection. From the gym to the golf course to the supposedl peaceful practice of tai chi, murder, rage and revenge refuse t respect the human quest for immortality through fitness an can victimize the most tanned and toned bodies as easily a those of couch potatoes and gourmands.

ISBN 0-929141-87-3 / $14.95 CDN, U.S. $12.95

And check out novels by authors from *Dead in the Water* at rendezvouspress.com:

- The Inspector Green series by Barbara Fradkin
(winner of the Arthur Ellis Award for best novel)
- The Polly Deacon series by H. Mel Malton
- *Cut Off His Tale* by Joan Boswell